Andromeda's War

ANDROMEDA'S WAR

A Novel of the Legion of the Damned®

WILLIAM C. DIETZ

ACE BOOKS, NEW YORK

THE BERKLEY PUBLISHING GROUP
Published by the Penguin Group
Penguin Group (USA) LLC
375 Hudson Street, New York, New York 10014

USA • Canada • UK • Ireland • Australia • New Zealand • India • South Africa • China

penguin.com

A Penguin Random House Company

This book is an original publication of The Berkley Publishing Group.

Copyright © 2014 by William C. Dietz.
Penguin supports copyright. Copyright fuels creativity, encourages diverse voices,
promotes free speech, and creates a vibrant culture. Thank you for buying an authorized
edition of this book and for complying with copyright laws by not reproducing, scanning,
or distributing any part of it in any form without permission. You are supporting writers
and allowing Penguin to continue to publish books for every reader.

Ace Books are published by The Berkley Publishing Group.
ACE and the "A" design are trademarks of Penguin Group (USA) LLC.

Library of Congress Cataloging-in-Publication Data

Dietz, William C.
Andromeda's war : a novel of the Legion of the Damned /
by William C. Dietz. — First edition.
p.   cm.
ISBN 978-0-425-25626-8 (hardcover)
1. Imaginary wars and battles—Fiction.   I. Title.
PS3554.I388A83 2014
813'.54—dc23
2014016849

FIRST EDITION: December 2014

PRINTED IN THE UNITED STATES OF AMERICA

10   9   8   7   6   5   4   3   2   1

Cover illustration © Christian McGrath; background © akiyoko/Shutterstock.
Cover design by Judith Lagerman.
Interior text design by Laura K. Corless.

LEGION OF THE DAMNED is a registered trademark of William C. Dietz.

For my dearest Marjorie

ANDROMEDA'S WAR

CHAPTER: 1

When asked where his officers were, a British NCO replied, "When it comes time to die, they'll be with us."

RICHARD A. GABRIEL and PAUL L. SAVAGE
Crisis in Command: Mismanagement in the Army
Standard year 1978

PLANET ALGERON

Forward Operating Base Vickers sat atop a low mesa located just south of a mountain range called the Towers of Algeron. The FOB was named after a civilian who, according to official dispatches, ". . . Volunteered to fight—and gave her life to protect our legionnaires."

The truth was quite different. Carly Vickers had been working for the Bureau of Missing Persons, which, in spite of the innocent-sounding name, had been created to find and eliminate anyone who might oppose Empress Ophelia. People like Andromeda McKee. The bitch.

Now, as McKee stood on the top deck of the newly reconstructed observation tower and looked out over a snow-dusted plain, her mind was filled with images of the final attack. Thousands upon thousands of Naa warriors had surrounded the mesa, all determined to kill every Human they could lay their hands on. McKee could "see" them coming, and when she closed her eyes, they were still there. "The CO is looking for you, Lieutenant." McKee opened her eyes. "Lieutenant." It sounded strange. But there it was. The Legion had been a place to hide from Ophelia's synths at first. But now it was something more. The fact that she could become a soldier, and a good one, had been a revelation. Recruit, private, corporal, sergeant, and now lieutenant. She'd come a long way.

Most of her superiors thought she deserved the most recent promotion. McKee knew better. She'd been lucky, that's all. Lucky enough to survive as others fell. She turned. Corporal Smith had dark skin, intelligent eyes, and an engaging grin. "I could tell the old man that you went AWOL."

McKee smiled. "Thanks, Smith. Unfortunately there's no place to go. Keep your eyes peeled. I saw a glint of light just to the right of Finger Rock. A scout probably. Shoot the bastard if he gets too close."

The tower had four .50 cal sniper's rifles dedicated to that very purpose. Smith nodded. "Yes, ma'am."

McKee walked over to the stairs and began to make her way down to the ground. Her right calf was still sore where a bullet fired from Vickers's rifle had passed through it. She was lucky though . . . The bone was untouched, and she was alive.

FOB Vickers had undergone an amazing transformation during the last couple of months. Minefields ringed the bottom of the mesa now. Twenty-three autocannons were dug in on top . . . And the gaps between them were protected by heavy machine guns and mortars.

Two companies of legionnaires had been assigned to the mesa, including two platoons of cavalry, one of which belonged to her. McKee returned two salutes as she followed the path that led down into an underground bunker. It was a good deal larger than it had originally been, and that was a good thing.

A sentry snapped to attention as she entered. The ceiling was intentionally high so that Trooper Is could enter, and like the walls, it was made of duracrete slabs hooked together with rails and pins. The floor was covered with pea gravel. McKee's boots made crunching sounds as she approached the front desk. It was a sheet of plywood laid across two upended mortar boxes. A sergeant named Nichols sat behind it. She had a mop of curly red hair and a spray of freckles across her nose. "Hey, Lieutenant . . . The major is looking for you."

"That's what I heard. Is he available?"

"Yes, ma'am. But watch out . . . He's pissed about something."

McKee nodded. "Thanks for the heads-up."

As she made her way past the com section, logistics, and Intel, McKee caught glimpses of the video being provided by half a dozen surveillance drones. The ops center and the CO's "office" came next. If a desk surrounded by makeshift partitions could be dignified as such. McKee paused to knock. "Lieutenant McKee reporting as . . ."

"Cut the crap and come on in," Major Gordon said from the other side of the thin wall.

As McKee entered, she saw that Gordon was stripped to the waist and standing in front of a small wall-mounted mirror. There was white shaving gel on his face, and he was working with a straight razor. "Take a load off McKee . . . We're about to have company—so it's time to make myself presentable."

Gordon was small but muscular, like the bantam-weight boxer he'd once been. His black hair was combed straight back, and for some reason, he had chosen to grow a pencil-thin mustache. McKee sat on an empty cable spool and watched him work. "Company, sir? What kind of company?"

"The *worst* kind," Gordon replied gloomily. "A REMF (rear echelon mother fucker), a civilian, and a combot."

"A what?"

"A combot. Meaning an android equipped to make vids."

McKee felt a rising sense of apprehension. During a recent visit to Earth, she'd been forced to make numerous public appearances, all calculated to benefit the person she hated most . . . Empress Ophelia. No one had recognized her as Lady Catherine Carletto because of the scar that ran from just above her right eye down onto her left cheek. But that didn't mean she was safe. There was no such thing. She cleared her throat. "So, what's up? A training vid?"

"Hell no," Gordon replied, as he wiped the remaining gel off his face. "It's going to be a McKee vid. Yeah, yeah, I know. You don't want to do it. Well, let me tell you something . . . There aren't many people of any rank who have the right to wear the Imperial Order of Merit. And now, having added a Star Cluster to that, you're a big deal on Earth. So the government sent a combot to make a documentary about you. And yes, you have to put up with it. The brass sees you as their number one recruiter."

McKee was about to object when Nichols stepped into the room. "They're here, sir. On pad two."

"We'll be right there," Gordon said as he buttoned his shirt. Then he turned to McKee. "I'm sorry . . . I really am. But there's nothing you can do. Just grit your teeth, let the combot do its thing, and the whole thing will be over before you know it. Come on . . . We wouldn't want to keep our visitors waiting, now would we?"

Apprehension had morphed to fear by that time. And what felt like a rock occupied the pit of McKee's stomach as she followed Gordon up the back ramp and onto the surface. Clusters of floodlights came on as another two-hour-and-forty-two-minute day came to an abrupt end. That was the result of a rotation so fast that it created a bulge at the planet's equator. In fact, some of the higher peaks soared eighty thousand feet up into the sky and dwarfed both Everest on Earth and Olympic Mons on Mars.

A fly-form was sitting on the pad, and like all such aircraft, it was piloted by a cyborg rather than a bio bod. Just one of the many things that made the Legion different from the rest of the armed services. Some of the Legion's borgs were criminals who, having been executed for capital crimes, had chosen life in a brain box over the big nothing. Others were legionnaires who had been wounded so badly that they were left with no choice but to pilot a fly-form, quad, or T-1.

Three figures appeared at the top of the ramp as it was lowered to the ground. The first person to make his way down was a portly colonel dressed in starched camos and wearing a sidearm with ivory grips. Rather than the rough-outs real soldiers wore in the field, he sported mirror-bright barracks boots. A REMF for sure. Gordon and McKee saluted the officer as he arrived on the ground. The response was so crisp, McKee suspected that the gesture had been perfected in front of a mirror. "As you were," the colonel said. "My name is Cavenaugh."

Before Gordon could speak, Cavenaugh turned to introduce his companion. The civilian had shoulder-length black hair, big brown eyes, and olive-colored skin. She was dressed in khakis and desert boots. McKee figured she might weigh a hundred pounds soaking wet. "This is Bindali Jivani," Cavenaugh said. "She's a civilian contractor—and we'll discuss her role shortly."

That was Gordon's opportunity to step forward and introduce McKee. "I've heard about you," Cavenaugh said. "Order of Merit and all that. Well done."

The civilian offered her hand, and McKee shook it. "My friends call me Bindy," Jivani said. "It's a pleasure to meet you."

Jivani was so open, it was impossible not to like her. McKee smiled. "Likewise, ma'am. Welcome to Forward Operating Base Vickers."

"And this is Andy," Cavenaugh said, as the combot arrived. Like most machines that were designed to interact with Humans, Andy was an android. Meaning a robot made to look like a Human being. In this case a thirtysomething male with light brown hair, beige skin, and a perpetual smile. It didn't *need* clothes but wore some anyway. They were made of leatherlike tufskin and were too fashionable for Algeron. "I'm glad to meet you," Andy said brightly. "Please stand closer together. I need a three shot."

That was when McKee realized that one if not both of Andy's "eyes" were cameras. She had no choice but to comply and wondered how long Andy would hang around. A couple of days? A week? Hopefully no more than that.

Gordon led the way back to the bunker, with Cavenaugh at his side. That left McKee to walk with Jivani. Andy followed along behind. "It's very beautiful, isn't it?" the civilian said, as she looked out over the desertlike wasteland. And it *was* beautiful. Or had been. Back before McKee had seen thousands of people die on it.

"Yes," McKee answered. "That's how the whole planet is. Or the parts I've seen anyway. Beautiful but dangerous."

Jivani nodded and said something in a language that McKee knew to be Naa. A Human who spoke Naa! That was rare indeed. Most people relied on computerized translators. "The words you spoke . . . What did they mean?"

"It's an old folk saying. 'The blade that gleams can also cut deep.'"

"So you live here?"

Jivani smiled and shook her head. "No . . . I arrived last week."

McKee wanted to ask more questions, but they were belowground by then. Gordon apologized for the lack of a meeting room as they entered his office. Cavenaugh sat in Gordon's chair. That left the rest of them to perch on cable spools. "So," he said. "Let's get to it . . . I'd like to stay and get a feel for the area—but I promised General Vale that I would join her for dinner at 1800 hours. Annoying, but that's life."

McKee got the feeling that Cavenaugh was anything but annoyed by the obligation and looking forward to dinner. *Any* dinner. But especially one that might help to advance his career.

"Yes, of course," Gordon responded. "It's my understanding that Andy is supposed to make a vid about Lieutenant McKee."

"That's one aspect of the situation," Cavenaugh agreed judiciously. "But not the most important part of what we need to accomplish. I have a mission for Lieutenant McKee. A tricky mission, which, if successful, will help us to fully secure the planet. I trust both of you know who Chief of Chiefs Truthsayer is."

"Yes," McKee answered. Momentarily forgetting to say, "sir." "He's the one who sent warriors north to fight Chief Lifetaker's alliance. They also attacked the village of Doothdown and the legionnaires stationed on this mesa."

"That's correct," Cavenaugh agreed. "And you beat him fair and square."

"No, sir. I wasn't in command."

"Ah, but according to official records, the strategy employed to beat him was *yours*. So you beat him fair and square. And that, according to Ms. Jivani here, means that you are qualified to negotiate with him. A lesser warrior couldn't. Not according to Naa traditions."

"I was given access to some relevant intelligence reports," Jivani said. "The villagers who lived in Doothdown gave you the name Nofear Deathgiver. And it's safe to assume that Truthsayer has heard of you by now."

"Precisely," Cavenaugh said. "So, here are your orders. You will take a mixed force of legionnaires and Naa south, find the chief of chiefs, and give him some gifts. Then you will invite the son of a bitch to come up and negotiate with us."

McKee knew the mission was next to impossible. In order to carry out Cavenaugh's orders, she'd have to enter territory that no legionnaire had visited before—and try to find a Naa who hated slick skins in general and her in particular. A suicide mission for sure. But she couldn't say that. No legionnaire could. So McKee gave voice to the obvious question. "And if Truthsayer says, 'No'?"

Cavenaugh had bushy eyebrows. They rose slightly. "In that case, it will be your duty to shoot him."

McKee wanted to laugh or cry. She wasn't sure which. If she caught up with Truthsayer, and that was a huge *if*, the Naa leader would be surrounded by bodyguards. And were she to so much as lift a finger against Truthsayer, she'd be dead within seconds. A possibility that didn't seem to trouble Cavenaugh at all.

Then McKee realized that the government would score a propaganda coup either way. If she brought Truthsayer to the negotiating table, then so much the better. That's the sort of thing heroes were supposed to do. And if she gave her life in an attempt to kill him, that would suit their purposes equally well. She could imagine the headline. "War hero dies in a valiant attempt to kill rebel leader." With any luck, Andy would have time to upload video of the assassination attempt just before the machine was beaten to death. "I see, sir," McKee said. "I like the first option better."

Both men chuckled, but Jivani frowned. "With all due respect, Colonel . . . That's a bad idea. If the lieutenant assassinates Truthsayer, that could start a war and make negotiations impossible."

Cavenaugh frowned. "We *are* at war because Truthsayer decided to bring all of the southern tribes together under his totem. If we manage to kill him, the savages will turn on each other, and the alliance will disintegrate like wet cardboard. At that point, we can slice and dice the tribes as we see fit. Andy . . . Delete what I said."

"Yes, Colonel," the android said obediently. "Your comment was deleted."

"I object," Jivani said angrily.

"So noted," Cavenaugh replied. "Although Andy will delete that, too." The avuncular manner was gone now. "Listen carefully young lady . . . You were brought here to facilitate negotiations. Not to set policy. So do what you're being paid for—and keep your personal opinions to yourself.

"Enough of that," Cavenaugh said dismissively, as his gaze turned to McKee. "A contingent of Naa troops will arrive soon, and I trust that Major Gordon will provide you with some legionnaires. As for me, well, I have a three-hour flight to endure. Good hunting, Lieutenant. If anyone can complete this mission, you can."

He left, with Gordon in tow. McKee and Jivani looked at each other, and Andy stood. "Please pretend to speak with each other. I need a two shot." The meeting was over.

The next few days were a whirlwind of activity as McKee went about the task of equipping her platoon for what was likely to be a long and arduous journey. Her force included a small headquarters group that consisted of Bindy Jivani, Sergeant Larkin, and the T-1s required to transport them. McKee also had three squads of legionnaires, each of which was made up of four bio bods and four T-1s. That brought the total force up to twenty-nine people. Not counting Andy, who didn't qualify as a person.

It was a deceptively small number since each cyborg could run at fifty miles per hour, could carry a rider while doing so, and was equal to a squad of bio bods. So judged by that standard, the borgs were the functional equivalent of 135 legionnaires.

In addition, Major Gordon had allocated McKee to have three RAVs (Robotic All-Terrain Vehicles). Each unit consisted of two eight-foot-long sections hooked together by an accordion-style joint. Each RAV had four legs, two forward-facing machine guns, and a grenade launcher. Of more importance was their ability to transport up to four thousand pounds of food, ammo, and spare parts. All of which would be critical during the days ahead.

So McKee was with her old friend Larkin, supervising loading, when the general alarm went off. McKee wasn't wearing a helmet but had a radio clipped to her body armor. The Klaxon was still bleating as a private stationed in the observation tower spoke. "We have approximately fifty, that's five-oh, Naa inbound from the northwest at two o'clock."

It wasn't a large force but sufficient to send everyone to their defensive positions. That included McKee and Larkin. Their platoon had secondary responsibility for the so-called ramp on the west side of the mesa. The slide area originally had been the most hotly contested spot during the battle months earlier.

Thanks to frequent drills, the last of McKee's people arrived as she did and took up positions behind the infantry platoon on duty. The scene seemed to leap forward as McKee brought a pair of binos up to her eyes.

The Naa warriors were heavily armed. Even from a distance, she could see that most of them carried Legion-issue weapons scrounged from battlefields or captured in battle. Their heads rose and fell in concert with the huge animals they rode. The dooths were hung with the trappings of war—and galloped along at a good thirty miles per hour. A pace they could maintain for thirty minutes at a time. All for effect? Or as part of an actual attack?

McKee assumed the former, and Jivani arrived to confirm it. "They're northerners," the civilian said, as she studied the Naa through glasses of her own. "See the totem? The one that looks like a spear, with a crosspiece and a pair of animal skulls? That means they take orders from Chief Spearthrow Lifetaker."

McKee hadn't met him but knew Lifetaker was supposed to be an ally. But, during the recent conflict with Truthsayer's army, the northerner had proved himself to be less than entirely trustworthy. In fact, there were rumors that Lifetaker had played a role in Colonel Richard Bodry's death. The upshot was that this particular group was unlikely to attack. "How do you know that stuff?" McKee inquired as she lowered the binoculars. "Especially since you arrived last week."

"I studied the Naa on Earth," Jivani answered. "I have a masters in Naa studies."

"Naa studies? I didn't know such a thing existed."

"I'm the first graduate," Jivani said modestly. "I took the contract so I could come here and work on my doctorate. It's impossible to travel here without some sort of connection to the Legion."

McKee frowned. "If you go south with us, there's an excellent chance that the people you came here to study will kill you."

Jivani nodded soberly. "I'll have to take that chance."

Major Gordon arrived at that point, and the all clear signal was heard. "We made radio contact with them," he explained. "Remember the Naa warriors Cavenaugh promised you? Well, here they are. Come on . . . It's time to introduce ourselves."

Gordon, McKee, and Jivani picked their way down past the defensive positions to the bottom of the slope. The Naa were milling around. A warrior slid down off his dooth. He had variegated white and gray fur. The ears that stuck up from his skull gave him a vaguely feline appearance.

McKee knew that the Naa had four fingers and opposable thumbs just like Humans did. But their feet were wider and lacked toes. This male was about six and a half feet tall and dressed in a vest and trousers. A fully loaded cartridge belt circled his waist, and he had a Legion-issue sniper's rifle slung across his back. As what? An insult? Or simply the best weapon for a sharpshooter to own? Not that both couldn't be true at the same time.

As soon as the Naa's feet touched the ground, he made straight for Gordon. Once they were close enough, he offered the forearm-to-forearm grip employed by warriors of roughly equal status. His standard was stiff but serviceable. "I am Longsee Sureshot. First son to Spearthrow Lifetaker."

McKee swore silently. *Lifetaker's son!* That would make an already-challenging mission that much more difficult. Everyone knew that Lifetaker and Truthsayer hated each other. So if they managed to catch up with the chief of chiefs, Sureshot's presence would be like salt in an open wound. And who was responsible for that? Cavenaugh, of course. Because he was stupid? Or as an insurance policy? Knowing that if she failed to kill Truthsayer, Sureshot would do the job. Yes, that made sense.

"It's a pleasure to meet you," Gordon replied. "I'm Major Gordon, and this is Lieutenant McKee. She will be in command of the expedition."

Sureshot looked at McKee and back again. "The lieutenant is female."

"That's true," Gordon acknowledged. "But it doesn't matter. She will be in command."

Sureshot was about to object when Jivani intervened. "Lieutenant McKee has a Naa name. It is Nofear Deathgiver."

Sureshot's expression changed. He turned to McKee and offered the forearm-to-forearm grip previously shared with Gordon. "I know of the battle for Doothdown. Everyone does. I thank you on behalf of my people."

McKee accepted the grip and thought she saw something other than gratitude in the Naa's gray eyes. Admiration? Yes, but of the sort Human males directed her way. Or had before the disfiguring scar. "You're welcome," McKee said. "But the females of Doothdown fought like true warriors. They are the ones who deserve the credit."

Sureshot stared at her for a moment as if considering a truly novel idea. He knew, as his entire tribe did, that Doothdown's males had been elsewhere, thus opening the village to possibility of an attack. But viewing female Naa as warriors? That was something new. Sureshot nodded. "What you say is true . . . Although none can doubt what you accomplished. We will follow you."

Gordon looked from one to the other. "Good. That's settled then. Let's bring your warriors and animals up onto the mesa. There's plenty of room north of the observation tower."

During the next two days, McKee repeatedly took her combined force down onto the plain, where she put them through every sort of evolution she could think of. And there were plenty of problems. The Naa had radios now, but no notion of radio discipline, and frequently spoke over each other. However, Naa, *all* Naa, put the need for personal glory ahead of unit objectives. That meant they were reluctant to follow orders. Especially slick-skin orders. The fact that the Naa didn't have a formal chain of command made things worse.

Fortunately, Sureshot had trained under the tutelage of his father up north and seen how effective the Legion's methods could be. So in response to McKee's urgings, he divided his force into five subgroups, each led by the equivalent of a noncom. Then he told them to do whatever Lieutenant McKee and Company Sergeant Larkin said. And that was where the problem came in.

McKee's reputation was such that the warriors were willing to submit. But even though Larkin had fought in Doothdown, he wasn't known to them. So it was just a matter of time before he gave an order that one of them didn't like.

When the conflict arose, it was the result of Larkin's ordering a squad of Naa to ride drag. That, it seemed, was the position normally assigned to inexperienced males when the Naa went to war. So to tell any of Sureshot's handpicked veterans to ride at the end of the column constituted an unbearable insult. A problem made clear when their leader, a ruffian named Largemouth Eatbig, refused to fall back and called Larkin a long list of insulting names. The result was a fight, which a couple of T-1s managed to break up.

McKee was riding at the head of the column at the time. Immediately after receiving word of the dustup via radio, she ordered her T-1 to turn around. Sureshot accompanied her. They arrived to find a standoff at the point where the trail dipped into a bowl-like depression. Patches of snow were hiding where the pale yellow sun hadn't been able to find them, and there were lots of hoofprints in the mud.

The adversaries had dismounted and were facing each other from ten paces away. Both had backers, some of whom were fingering their weapons. It was a critical moment. If McKee backed Larkin, which was the obvious thing to do, the Naa would see it as favoritism. And when the chips were down, they might leave the Humans in the lurch.

On the other hand, if McKee couldn't find a way to back her company sergeant, it would have a disastrous effect on Human morale. That left her with a very fine line to walk.

McKee dropped to the ground and made her way over to a point between the combatants, where she paused to look around. "Post some pickets, Sergeant Payton . . . Human *and* Naa. Once they are in place, the rest of the company can gather around."

As Payton went to work, McKee addressed herself to those who were still present. She was wearing a translator, which meant the Naa could understand her. "This company will have to fight during the days ahead. And when it does, there is no way to know what the circumstances will be. We may engage the enemy at a distance—or we may be forced to battle them hand-to-hand."

"So," McKee continued, "Company Sergeant Larkin and Lead Warrior Eatbig are going to put on a demonstration of hand-to-hand-combat techniques. No weapons will be permitted." It was a thin fiction but a necessary one in order to maintain some semblance of military discipline. Cheers went up from both camps, the combatants began to shed weapons, and more people arrived.

McKee had already begun to experience doubts, but it was too late to change her mind. She looked at Larkin, saw him wink, and felt a little better. He understood. But could he deliver? Eatbig was shorter, but thicker, and very confident. Still, Larkin had been raised in the slums of Esparto . . . And spent a good deal of the last year fighting on Orlo II and Algeron. That meant there was reason to hope.

Payton arrived with a large group of Humans and Naa. They flooded in to surround the combatants. "All right," McKee announced, as Larkin and Eatbig stepped forward to face each other. "You can begin the demonstration."

The Human danced, threw a punch, and saw it connect. Eatbig flinched as the legionnaires cheered. But the moment of victory was short-lived.

As Eatbig bored in, Larkin launched a kick. The Naa grabbed the Human's boot and gave it a twist. The legionnaires uttered a common groan as their champion went down.

Larkin hit, rolled to his knees, and was trying to rise when Eatbig kicked him in the side. McKee heard Larkin grunt and saw him fall over. He rolled over onto his knees but was struggling to breathe. "Stand!" someone shouted. "Get up!"

It did no good. Larkin remained where he was, head down, with one knee on the ground. "That didn't take long," Sureshot said, as Eatbig lumbered forward.

"It isn't over," McKee predicted, as Larkin launched himself up off the ground. The top of his head hit the Naa's midriff and Eatbig fell over backwards. Now it was time for the Naa warriors to groan as Larkin straddled Eatbig and went to work with his bony fists. Left right, left right, the blows fell until the Naa gave a mighty heave and threw Larkin off. Then he rolled to his feet and stood with blood running out his nose.

Larkin circled the Naa, looking for an opening, saw one, and sidled forward. That was when Eatbig threw a fistful of dirt at the Human's eyes and went in swinging. Larkin staggered as the blows landed, lost his balance, and fell. Eatbig uttered a Naa war cry and took to the air. But rather than land on top of the noncom, the warrior slammed into solid ground. Mud splattered away from his body.

The opportunity for a devastating follow-up was there—but the legionnaire was still wiping dirt out of his eyes. That gave Eatbig the time he needed to stand and attack his opponent yet again. Strangely, the partisan cheering had given way to silence as the noncoms met face-to-face and began to trade powerful blows. There was no attempt to duck now . . . Just a brutal contest to see which person could take the most punishment. As Larkin took a blow, a mixture of spittle and blood flew from the side of his mouth, and McKee regretted authorizing the fight. But it was too late.

Larkin turned a full circle, launched a kick that connected with Eatbig's jaw, and sent his adversary flying. There was a thud as the warrior hit the ground and lay staring at the sky. Larkin staggered, found his balance, and paused to wipe the blood off his lips. "Damn . . . That bastard can take a punch."

It wasn't planned, at least McKee didn't think so, but the comment struck just the right note. There was laughter followed by applause from Humans and Naa alike. And it grew stronger as Larkin went forward to give his opponent a hand. McKee was happy to seize the opportunity. "Well, done! I think all of us learned something today . . . When the enemy has the upper hand, throw dirt in his eyes."

All of them laughed. McKee waited for it to die down. "Now listen, and listen good. The drag position is extremely important because the enemy may attack us from behind. So if a noncom assigns you to the rear guard, you will obey. And remember this . . . *Everyone*, Human and Naa alike, will rotate through that position, and *everyone* will walk point. Now mount up. We have work to do."

"You were lucky," Sureshot said, as they returned to their mounts. "It could have gone the other way."

"The outcome was never in doubt," McKee lied.

Sureshot laughed as he walked away.

The company was assembled on the flat area in front of the ramp. McKee could feel the weight of Major Gordon's gaze and knew he was up on the mesa watching through binoculars. Almost an entire day had passed since the fight between Larkin and Eatbig. The sun was little more than a yellow smear in a gray sky—and snowflakes were twirling down as McKee gave the order. "Move out!"

Three can-shaped drones went first. As they sped away, the machines spread out to cover a mile-wide swath of ground with their sensors. A party of three Naa scouts went next. Sureshot was one of them, and McKee knew they would see and understand things that her legionnaires wouldn't. It was *their* planet, and they had a visceral connection to it.

Next came McKee on a T-1 named Sam Vella and Jivani on a cyborg named Dor Cory. Each bipedal Trooper I was eight feet tall and weighed half a ton. They were equipped with three-fingered pincer hands, or interchangeable shovel hands, and could run at speeds up to thirty-five miles per hour. Each cyborg was armed with a Storm .50 caliber machine gun and underbarrel grenade launcher. And the RAVs were carrying the launchers and rockets required to equip four of the T-1s should that become necessary.

Andy was traveling on its own. McKee had hoped that the robot would be unable to keep up and quickly learned that it could. Not only that, but the combot was fast enough to dash ahead in order to capture shots of the column coming straight at the camera or passing by it.

Such jaunts were dangerous, but McKee never complained. It was her fervent hope that Andy would step on a mine, fall into a deep ravine, or run afoul of a Naa war party. Any of which would allow her to write the robot off.

Most of the column consisted of alternating squads of legionnaires and Naa. They were followed by the RAVs, four construction droids that McKee had wheedled out of the FOB's supply officer, and a rear guard presently under Larkin's command. Under normal circumstances it would have been regarded as a substantial force—but the company was nothing compared to the tens of thousands of warriors that Truthsayer could send against it.

McKee's thoughts were interrupted by a voice in her helmet. "Charlie-Six to Alpha-One. Good hunting, over." McKee tried to come up with something snappy to say, failed, and clicked her mike twice by way of an acknowledgment.

Thanks to satellite imagery, the Legion knew where all of the villages in the southern hemisphere were, which meant McKee knew, too. And that would have been valuable intelligence if she had orders to attack one of them. But McKee wasn't looking for a settlement . . . She was looking for a single individual. And Truthsayer could be anywhere. That's why the Legion's Intel people had agreed to provide her with a guide. A southerner named Longtalk Storytell, who, according to her orders, ". . . Will join the expedition at a point south of FOB Vickers."

That didn't mean much since it didn't say where they would meet. And if Storytell failed to show, she was to ". . . Proceed according to your best judgment." Which meant that all the responsibility for whatever happened would rest with her.

Despite the rather uncertain arrangements where Storytell was concerned, McKee felt better and better as the mesa dwindled behind them and eventually disappeared. Because here was what any junior officer worth his or her salt desired, even if it was fraught with danger. And that was an independent command.

So McKee took pleasure in the cold, crisp air as she sent Vella up and down the column. She made a point out of falling in step with legionnaires to chat. And thanks to the translator she was wearing, McKee could do the same thing with Sureshot's warriors.

The purpose of the exercise was to learn their names, gauge personalities, and listen. The latter was very important because having come up through the ranks, McKee knew that while some enlisted personnel were full of shit, others had good ideas. Things they were willing to share with officers who would listen.

Meanwhile, noncoms were being tested; squads were being rotated through every possible position so that the weak links could be identified. It was a process McKee would have enjoyed if it hadn't been for the omnipresent Andy. But she had learned to ignore the machine's incessant requests for tight shots, additional takes, and sound bites. As a result, Andy was more like an annoying insect than a serious problem.

After three two-hour-and-forty-two-minute days had come and gone, McKee called a halt. Then she gave orders for Larkin to throw up a marching camp not unlike those used by the Romans. It consisted of a ditch backed by a dirt rampart. And that, as it turned out, was *not* something the Naa were accustomed to, a fact that became abundantly clear when Sureshot came to see her. "Sergeant Larkin ordered my warriors to dig a ditch," the Naa said, "and warriors do *not* dig ditches. When it is time to rest, they seek high ground that offers both cover and forage for their dooths."

"High ground of the sort you describe is not always available," McKee countered. "But, even if it were, I would dig a ditch around it. We are in enemy territory, and the southerners might throw a thousand warriors at us. Should that happen, you will be glad of every advantage that you have, including a well-dug ditch and rampart. Fortunately for all of us, the T-1s and the construction droids will do half the work. But when it comes to preparing defenses, it's important that *everyone* lend a hand. Here's a shovel."

Sureshot looked her in the eye as he accepted the shovel. It was difficult to know what he was thinking, but McKee thought she saw annoyance mixed with something else. Something that had more to do with males and females than war. But she already had someone. Or hoped she did. His name was John Avery. *Major* John Avery, and she had served with him on Orlo II. What was he doing now? she wondered. And what would he think of the promotion? They could see each other legally now that both of them were officers. *If* they lived long enough to do so. "Come on," she said. "Let's show the troops how it's done."

So the perimeter ditch was dug, and rations were distributed, much to the amusement of the troops—who took the opportunity to sample each other's food. Then it was time for the legionnaires to return to work. Each bio bod was responsible for performing maintenance on their T-1, with the exception of Jivani, that is, who didn't have the necessary training. She was trying to learn however . . . And had taken to wearing a sidearm.

The Naa had similar responsibilities. Their dooths had to be fed, groomed, and treated for various maladies. All of which consumed a couple of hours. Once their chores were completed, it was time to stand guard or sack out—depending on where each individual fell on the watch list. That, at least, wasn't subject to controversy since the Naa had strict traditions where sentry duty was concerned.

The eight-hour rest period passed without incident, and although the process of breaking camp went more slowly than McKee would have preferred, the column was under way by 0830. The second day was much like the first insofar as the weather was concerned—with cloudy skies and the occasional snow flurry.

But the landscape had begun to change. The previously flat plain had begun to break up into clusters of low-lying hills, gullies, and islands of rock. That made the terrain more interesting to look at but dangerous as well since there were plenty of places for enemies to hide.

So McKee added two T-1s and their bio bods to the party of Naa scouts, knowing that the cyborgs could "sense" things that the locals couldn't. Examples included heat and electronic signals. But in spite of the scouting party's best efforts, it was a drone that made first contact.

All of McKee's bio bods were cross-trained in at least two disciplines, and Corporal Dara Boyer was the company's lead com tech. Which meant that in addition to maintaining her

T-1, the legionnaire had to keep the company's drones up and running, too. Her voice flooded McKee's helmet. "Alpha-Four-One to Alpha-One. Over."

"This is One . . . Go. Over."

"Drone 2 has a contact on channel seven. Over."

"Roger that," McKee said, as she brought channel seven up on her HUD (Heads Up Display). The video was projected on the inside surface of McKee's visor and gave her a drone's eye view of a middle-aged Naa. He had a scarf wrapped around his head, was wearing a dooth-leather jacket, and was seated with his back against a slab of gray rock. If the drone was a surprise to him, he gave no sign of it. His command of standard was excellent. "It's about time you people showed up," he said. "My name is Longtalk Storytell. I was going to stay hidden until you arrived, but the bastards spotted me. Now I'm pinned down and running out of ammo."

"This is Alpha-One," McKee replied. "What can you tell me about the surrounding area?"

There was a pop as someone fired a distant rifle, and McKee saw rock chips fly as the slug glanced off a rock. Storytell smiled grimly. "Humans like to say that a picture is worth a thousand words . . . So tell your drone to make the picture larger but to stay low. Your machine makes a nice target."

McKee gave the necessary order, and the drone obeyed. As it zoomed out and floated sideways, she was able to peer through a gap between the rocks. A heavily rutted road led up into the gap that separated two hills. The fortification sat atop the elevation to the right. It boasted a crooked flagpole from which a brightly colored pennant drooped. "That's Graveyard Pass," Storytell said. "Assuming it's in the picture. It changes hands on a frequent basis. At the moment, it belongs to a bandit named Hardhand Bigclub. You can force your way through the gap or take a 150-mile detour to the east."

McKee ordered the drone to pull back. "Roger, that . . . What's your present situation? Over."

"I'm surrounded," Storytell replied. "I killed three of them, but I'm running out of bullets. It's only a matter of time before they nail me."

That was very bad news indeed. McKee needed the Naa in order to find Truthsayer. "Hang in there . . . Help is on the way. Over."

"I'm glad to hear it," Storytell said. "Tell your drone to land. Otherwise, they're going to—"

McKee never got to hear what the Naa was going to say. She heard a clang and saw an explosion of light. That was when the transmission cut to black, and a tone sounded. Drone 2 was dead.

CHAPTER: 2

The first method for estimating the intelligence of a ruler is to look at the men he has around him.

NICCOLÒ MACHIAVELLI
The Prince
Standard year circa 1513

PLANET EARTH

Over thirty-six years, Carlo Veneto had risen from street urchin to gigolo. Then, powered by a clever mind, he made the nearly impossible journey from a wealthy matron's bedroom to her drawing room. That's where he dazzled her friends with his wit and made a name for himself. From there it was a small leap into the Byzantine world of royal politics—and a carefully engineered "chance" encounter with the equally rapacious Princess Ophelia. It was what one critic called "A match made in hell."

The attraction was mutual and quickly consummated in Ophelia's bed. Veneto became her secretary a few weeks later. And from then on he had her ear. Not her mind, however. Because close though they were, Ophelia knew better than to give anyone full access to her thoughts. So there was a line that Veneto was never allowed to cross. Nor did she expect him to sleep with her every night. And that suited him just fine.

Because valuable though his relationship with Empress Ophelia was—Veneto had come to regard the physical aspect of it as something of a chore. So the freedom to pursue more intense sexual experiences was welcome indeed. And, as Veneto's long, grueling workday finally came to an end, the opportunity for some relaxation was very much on his mind.

After donning street clothes, Veneto examined himself in a full-length mirror. It was something he did frequently and for good reason. The thick, curly hair, the strong blade-like nose, and the sensuous lips were important assets.

Confident that his good looks were intact, Veneto strode through the richly decorated living room to the private elevator that carried him up to the roof. Ophelia and her son Nicolai occupied most of the palace, but that still left room for the three-thousand-square-foot apartment that Veneto had all to himself.

A pair of bodyguards were waiting. They were on his payroll rather than the government's—and were experts at a number of martial arts. Both men had been subjected to psychological loyalty programming in return for large amounts of money. Given his destination, a larger force would have been nice—but too many escorts could attract the kind of trouble he hoped to avoid. Because, according to a popular axiom, "Anyone worth guarding is worth attacking."

Veneto entered the air car and sat in the back. The leather-upholstered seat began to squirm in an effort to make Veneto feel comfortable, and his favorite drink appeared at his elbow. It was dark, and as the car lifted off, Veneto could see the lights of Los Angeles spread out all around. Over the years, the metroplex had grown to encompass more than one thousand square miles. Some of that was relatively flat, but there were thickets of buildings that soared hundreds of feet into the air. Lights representing thousands of air cars, buses, and other flying vehicles wound their way between such structures and battled each other for space.

Not Veneto's limo, though. Thanks to its owner's importance, and the coded transmissions associated with it, the air car's pilot was free to go wherever she chose. A wedge-shaped high-rise glowed up ahead. The tower was hundreds of stories tall and clad with solar panels. The limo's running lights blipped across rows of highly reflective windows as it circled prior to coming in for a landing.

The bodyguards exited first, with their long dusters open to reveal the stubby assault weapons that dangled under their arms. Then, having assured themselves that the pad was safe, the taller of the two waved Veneto forward.

Veneto paused to pull a formfitting mask down over his head before exiting the car. Anonymity was important both for the sake of Ophelia's reputation and his own safety. Some criminals, especially members of the so-called Freedom Front, would shoot him on sight. Other less political gangs would hold him for ransom. Neither prospect had any appeal.

The high-rise belonged to a wealthy family who wanted to know what Ophelia was going to do before she did it so they could invest their money accordingly. A service Veneto was happy to provide up to a point. He knew better than to take the service too far—and his friends were happy to take what they could get.

Veneto stepped up to a reader, so that the building's security system could scan his retinas. A thumbprint was required to complete the process. Doors parted, and the bodyguards entered. Veneto waited for a hand signal before stepping aboard.

The doors closed with a whisper, and the platform fell so fast that Veneto felt a couple of pounds lighter. It slowed after thirty seconds or so and coasted to a gentle stop. The doors slid open, and Veneto followed the bodyguards into a tiny lobby located two levels beneath the streets. A four-digit code was required to enter a narrow passageway that led out into the Deeps. Multicolored signs crawled, slid, and blipped across the structures around him. Neon glowed, spotlights roamed, and ad blimps floated above.

Veneto knew that the power required to run the businesses around him had been obtained by tapping into LA's grid. Ophelia could put a stop to that . . . But it would take an army to do so, and the government had a lot of other priorities at the moment. The alien Hudathans being primary among them.

Veneto pushed work out of his mind so as to take everything in. He loved the bars, the strip clubs, and the sleazy ambience of it all. The Deeps reminded him of the environment he'd grown up in, the difference being that most of New York's combat zone was aboveground.

So as Veneto walked past the beggars, the robotic Sayers, and the hookers who waited in doorways, it was like a symbolic homecoming. The locals noticed him. How could they fail to? But none dared approach the man in black. Not with two bodyguards in tow.

The two-block journey to the Sweet Dream Sim Salon was delightfully uneventful. Unlike most of the establishment's patrons, Veneto had enough money to buy a sim system and have it installed in his apartment if he wanted to. But if he did so, Ophelia would learn about the purchase within a matter of hours and disapprove. Besides, the weekly visit to the Deeps was part of the fun.

Anyone could stroll through the front door and into the sleekly furnished lobby beyond. But then it was necessary to enter a kiosk and provide a nine-digit alphanumeric code before being allowed to enter "The Inner Sanctum." That was where a scantily clad hostess was waiting to take Veneto to a "dream box."

Secure in the knowledge that his bodyguards would remain outside and be there to protect him, Veneto followed the young woman into the boxlike room. Then it was time to remove his ankle-length cloak and hang it up before stretching out on the couch. The hostess was waiting. "Are you ready, sir?"

"Yes."

Veneto could smell her perfume and see her nipples as she leaned forward to insert the lead into the very expensive socket hidden under the hair near his temple. Then he was gone . . . Carried away on a wave of euphoria. Thanks to computer-driven virtual-reality generators, the sim world was a place where *every* experience was available no matter how obscure or perverted it might be. And such scenarios were so realistic, they were indistinguishable from what sim designers referred to as "Set One." Their designator for the real world.

There were all sorts of things clients could do while immersed in the sim world. Some chose to live life as an ant, or a flower, or a bird of prey. But most chose some form of sex. Sadomasochism, rapes, and orgies were common. And Veneto had tried most of them.

But before he could choose one of the icons floating in front of him—what sounded like the voice of God reverberated through his seemingly disembodied mind. It wasn't the *real* voice of God of course—but it felt that way. "Good morning . . . Or is it evening? Who knows down here? Not that it matters. My name is Colonel Red."

Veneto felt a stab of fear. *Colonel Red?* He knew that name. Millions of people did. Colonel Red was the nom de guerre of the man who led the Freedom Front. A rebel group that claimed responsibility for having assassinated Earth's governor months earlier. Veneto struggled to take control of his body. If he could pull the plug . . .

Laughter echoed as if from somewhere far away. "No, you

can't break free. Not until your half-hour sim is over. Yeah, we spent a lot of money following your movements and hacking this system. But it was worth every credit. Now you're mine. Any questions?"

Veneto knew that the system could "hear" him and assumed that Colonel Red could, too. "What . . . What are you going to do to me?"

"What the hell do you *think* I'm going to do to you?" the voice demanded angrily. "You and the bitch you work for killed thousands of people including my brother and my sister-in-law. I'm going to kill you."

"*No*, don't do that," Veneto said desperately. "I can pay you . . . I can . . ."

"You can *suffer*," Colonel Red said darkly. "Just a little at first. Then more and more until the pain generates enough stress to stop your heart."

That was when Veneto found himself on a conveyor belt. He was unable to get off but discovered that he could raise his head just enough to see the glowing oven. Then came the heat. Nothing too severe at first—just enough to make him sweat. But as Veneto neared the open door, he felt hot. *Very* hot. And thirsty. Then his clothes caught fire, and the *real* pain began. Indescribable, searing, burning pain. He could smell his own charred skin as the fire consumed his legs and approached his genitals. Then Veneto screamed, and the sound was so loud that his bodyguards heard it. They looked at each other and grinned. The boss was having a good time.

Tarch (Duke) Hanno had just arrived in his office and was preparing to wade through the e-mails that were waiting for him when one of his subordinates entered the room. Her name was Crystal Kemp and her expression was bleak. "Sorry to interrupt you, sir . . . But I have some bad news. Secretary Veneto was assassinated last night."

Veneto was no great loss. Not to Hanno anyway . . . But the fact that someone had been able to successfully target Ophelia's private secretary was of considerable concern for the government and his department in particular. Especially if it turned out that the assassin or assassins were on the list of people the Bureau of Missing Persons had been ordered to kill. That would be something his enemies could blame on him. So Hanno had a reason to look concerned. "Why, that's terrible! Please . . . Sit down. Do they have the assassin?"

Kemp was a carefully-put-together fortysomething blonde with a reputation for ruthless efficiency—and a perfect fit for a high-level position in the Bureau. As Kemp perched on the arm of a guest chair, she shared what she knew. It seemed that Veneto had been killed while on a sex safari in the Deeps. The body was discovered by a Sim Salon attendant and reported to Veneto's bodyguards shortly after the secretary's "dream" came to a close. There were no signs of violence, so all three of them assumed their client had died of natural causes.

But as the body was being transported up to the surface, the Freedom Front issued a statement detailing the circumstances of Veneto's death and the way the assassination had been carried out. That was followed by a lengthy screed accusing Empress Ophelia and her government of mass murder plus a long list of other offenses.

Hanno thanked Kemp, and she was leaving as the comset on his desk began to chirp. His secretary's face was visible on a small screen. "Excuse me, Tarch Hanno . . . But a priority one security meeting has been scheduled for 10:00 A.M."

"Okay, tell them I'll be there." Hanno glanced at his watch. It was 9:21. He'd have to hurry. "And call for my car."

Hanno hated the government complex located north of the metroplex and had gone to considerable lengths to make sure the Bureau's offices remained downtown. Now he had to pay the price for that by hurrying up to the roof, where an air car swooped in to pick him up. However, thanks to a priority routing from LA's air-traffic-control computer, the car's pilot was able to put the vehicle down with minutes to spare.

Hanno hated to be late for meetings but didn't want to look hurried either. So he was careful to maintain a normal pace after he passed through a checkpoint and stepped onto the moving sidewalks that carried him through a maze of gleaming passageways to the Security Center. Then it was necessary to undergo a second check prior to being admitted.

It was a big room, twice as large as it needed to be to accommodate the seventeen people who were present, eighteen now that Hanno had arrived. There were the usual greetings including one from Lady Constance Forbes, Director of the Department of Internal Security (DIS), and his main rival. She thought the Bureau of Missing Persons should be part of the DIS and sought to undercut him whenever she got a chance. Hanno offered a half bow and took a seat across the oval-shaped table from her.

Minister of Defense Tarch (Duke) Ono had responsibility for chairing such meetings. Ono's head was shaved, and his suit looked as if it had been spray-painted onto his chemically enhanced body. He nodded to Hanno. "Now that everyone is here, let's begin with a review of what we know so far."

What followed was a recitation of what Hanno already knew, except that it was supported with vid clips, still photos, and preliminary lab reports. All of which suggested that the Freedom Front's claims were true. Veneto had been assassinated and in a very unusual way. But as Hanno scanned the faces around him, he was unable to find any that looked especially sad. Veneto had been someone to fear not love. "So," Ono said, as the presentation came to an end. "The empress is very upset. Secretary Veneto was not only an important member of her staff but a close personal friend as well."

Ono didn't say, "lover," and didn't need to. Everyone knew. And Hanno wondered how the empress felt about Veneto's visits to the Deeps. Because she had to know. Even if Veneto thought she didn't. "At this point," Ono continued, "our task is to formulate a recommendation. Should Veneto's death be characterized as an assassination? To do so would give Colonel Red and his followers a propaganda coup. On the other hand, such an admission could be used to justify the sort of crackdown that is long overdue. Every garden must be weeded from time to time."

The moment that Ono mentioned Colonel Red, Hanno knew what to expect. Forbes cleared her throat. She had perfectly cut bangs that fell to her eyebrows, high cheekbones, and cold eyes. *"Colonel Red?"* she inquired innocently. "Isn't he on the list of people that the Bureau of Missing Persons is supposed to find and neutralize?"

All of the officials turned to look at Hanno. And there wasn't much he could say since all of his efforts to find Colonel Red had been for naught. So all he could do was launch a counterattack. "Lady Forbes is correct . . . Colonel Red *is* on our list. And it's true that we've been unable to capture or kill him. That's because he, like thousands of other criminals, continues to live in the Deeps. The very place where Secretary Veneto was killed and the DNI was supposed to sterilize months ago." Point and counterpoint. All eyes went to Forbes. But, before she could respond, Ono stepped in.

"Amusing though this game is—we don't have time for it. Both of you are correct to some extent—and both of you share responsibility for this debacle. That brings us back to the question of how we want to position Veneto's death with the public."

"We could take it in the opposite direction," the woman in charge of the Department of Public Information offered.

"Veneto had a secret life and died as a result of a sim-induced heart attack. That would keep the Freedom Front from calling his death a victory."

"True," Forbes allowed. "But it would suggest that Veneto wasn't properly vetted—and would reflect negatively on the empress. Why didn't *she* know? Why didn't *we* know? That's what people would ask themselves."

Hanno decided to seize on what looked like an opportunity. "I agree with Lady Forbes. The first option is best. Let's call the assassination what it is—and use it to justify an all-out attack on the Deeps. Maybe we can bag Colonel Red and clear the cesspool out for good."

Even Ono looked at Forbes. She nodded. "I agree. Our sewers are full of rats. Let's exterminate them."

The alarm began to beep, so Rex slapped it. Then he yawned and swung his bare feet over onto the cool floor. A short walk took him into the bathroom, where he stared at the bleary-eyed image in the mirror. There were gray streaks in his otherwise black hair, bags under his eyes, and a deathly pallor to his skin. Sun. He needed sun. But there was no day or night down in the Deeps. It never rained, it never snowed, and it was never too cold. Some people professed to like that, but Rex Carletto wasn't one of them. He ached to go up top and feel whatever was waiting to be felt.

But visits to the surface were rare, and had to be, since he was a wanted man. Did the government know that Rex Carletto and Colonel Red were the same person? No, he didn't think so. But Rex was number 2998 on the list of people the Bureau of Missing Persons was looking for, just ahead of his niece Cat, who was 2999. So he had to remain hidden. That didn't mean he was helpless though . . . The Veneto assassination proved that.

The thought made him feel better. So Rex went to work

scraping the stubble off his cheeks. He was almost finished when Hiram Hoke's voice came over the intercom. "Hey, boss . . . Are you awake?"

"Yeah, what's up?"

"Nothing good. A large force of heavily armed people is closing in on the club."

"The club" was a night spot that the Freedom Front had taken over a couple of months earlier. A lot of renovations had been done, and some were still under way. Rex felt the first stirrings of concern as he ran a washcloth over his face. "Who are they?"

"That's the strange thing," Hoke replied. "Rather than a single gang, it looks like all of them are coming after us. The Sayers, the Combine, and hundreds of street people."

Now Rex was worried. Gang raids were a common occurrence in the Deeps. Most were aimed at taking over some real estate or looting an especially prosperous business. But if the Sayers *and* the Combine had joined forces against him, there had to be a larger and more compelling reason behind it since they had countervailing interests. "Okay," Rex said. "Pull the lookouts back, activate the perimeter defense system, and sound the general alarm. I'll be there shortly."

Rex chose to put on combat gear rather than street clothes. Doing so reminded him of all the years spent in the Legion—and all the battles he'd fought for the empire. Now, with Ophelia on the throne, it was time to fight against rather than for it. He chose an assault rifle from the wall rack in his bedroom and left for the front of the club.

There was no such thing as high ground on Level 3 of the Deeps. And with three shared walls, plus a ceiling and a floor, there were five directions from which an enemy could attack. All they had to do was blow a hole through a partition and charge through. That's why all the rooms could be sealed off, and a fast-response team was waiting to respond to any breach. Still, if an enemy created enough holes and was prepared to create more, they would be able to enter. And that was true of every business on every level.

As Rex entered the security center, he saw that Hoke was present along with Percy. Hoke stood six-three, weighed 225, and had a twelve-gauge shotgun slung across his back. Percy had a spherical body held aloft by an ARGRAV unit. After being "killed" in battle, the Legion brought him back to life as a cyborg. Percy had been retired when Ophelia murdered her brother, and like Rex, had called himself back to duty. Servos whined as he pointed a skeletal tool arm at a bank of security monitors. "Check it out, boss . . . All of 'em want a piece of us."

Rex looked and saw that Percy was correct. A row of waist-high pipes fronted the club. Under normal circumstances, that's all they were. But a blue force field jumped and crackled between them now—and threatened to kill anyone who tried to pass through it. That was keeping the mob at bay for the moment. Thanks to spotlights controlled by his forces, Rex could see robotic Sayers in their black robes, gray-clad members of the Combine crime syndicate, and street rabble all milling about. Were they going to attack the club? That's the way it looked. But *why?*

The answer came in the form of a com call. "Hey, boss, Mr. Vas is on line two," one of the com techs said. "He wants to speak with you."

Rex made his way over to the console, where Vas could be seen with part of his office in the background. He was the elected head of the Combine and a strange-looking creature indeed. His head was clean-shaven, his eyes were violet, and his nose had been minimized to little more than a bump. Most striking of all, however, was skin that seemed to be lit from within. The crime boss nodded as Rex appeared. They had met on previous occasions—the most recent being to discuss the possibility of an alliance. Discussions that went nowhere. "Mr. Vas."

"Colonel Red."

"What can I do for you?"

"You may have noticed a crowd out front."

"I assumed they were customers . . . Hoping to buy a drink."

Vas laughed. The sound was dry and raspy. "Ah, if only that were the case. What the crowd actually wants is *you*."

"*Me?* Whatever for?"

"They . . . *We* believe that the recent assassination of Secretary Veneto was a huge mistake. Killing Governor Mason was bad enough. But Veneto was *here*, in the Deeps, when you canceled his ticket. Ophelia won't tolerate that. She'll send an army. A *real* army this time. And her soldiers will kill anything that moves. Unless we give her a reason not to, that is."

"Which would be me."

"Precisely. So here's your choice . . . Surrender to us, and we will leave your followers alone. But if you don't, we'll attack, take your head, and send it to Ophelia on a platter. That may or may not be sufficient to stave off an attack. But it's certainly worth a try."

"Not too surprisingly, I disagree," Rex replied. "What we should do is band together and get ready to fight the bastards if they venture underground. But, since you chose to send a mob, I'll deal with that instead. Good-bye, Mr. Vas." And with that, he touched a button. The scene snapped to black.

Rex turned to Hoke. "Seal the building, drop the flood doors, and start pumping. Those people need a bath."

Hoke nodded and turned to a control panel. The club had come under fire by then. A hail of bullets hit the duracrete façade as rockets destroyed three vertical pipes, and the defensive force field went down.

But as the crowd surged forward, watertight doors dropped all around, thereby fencing some of the attackers out—and sealing the club off from the rest of the neighbor-hood. That was when valves opened, and water began to pour in. Now the people directly in front of the club were trapped in a box that was quickly filling with water. Seeing that, they turned, looking for a way to escape. "Open one door," Rex said. "Let them go."

"They'll be back," Percy warned.

"Probably," Rex conceded. "But if we murder them, we will become the thing we're fighting." People poured out of the trap along with a knee-high wave of water. But the momentary victory was just that: momentary. Was Vas right? Would Ophelia attack? Probably. And then every hand would be turned against the Freedom Front. It was time to run.

Preparations for the attack began at 1:00 A.M. The first step was to announce a "National Defense Exercise," impose a no-fly zone over the city of Los Angeles, and use a squadron of aerospace fighters to enforce it. That would prevent Colonel Red and his fellow criminals from getting away. Then Tarch Ono sent sanitation crews in to seal storm drains and spot-weld the city's manholes in place.

Once those preparations were complete, the Minister of Defense stationed contingents of soldiers at every known entrance to the Deeps and issued orders to kill anyone who tried to escape. That included any nobles or other prominent citizens who had the misfortune to be in the Deeps on that particular night. Because, according to the way Ophelia looked at it, to consort with criminals was to be one.

To counter the risk that, once cornered, the rats would use the World Wide Web to distribute antigovernment propaganda, Ono cut all the com links in and out of LA. Not forever, he promised, just for six hours, as part of the National Defense Exercise.

At that point, government officials felt confident that half the battle was won. It wouldn't be long before the rats realized they were in a trap and couldn't escape. Then the bleating would begin as some of them tried to negotiate, surrender, or plead for mercy. But it wouldn't work. All of them were going to die, with the possible exception of Colonel Red who could surrender if he wanted to and would be executed on a live broadcast.

Then Ono had eighteen so-called "penetrators" airlifted in and placed at key locations. Parking lots mostly—and a couple of parks. It took more than three hours to prepare the drill rigs and position troops next to each. Once the holes were drilled, Imperial troops would drop through. That would force the rats to divide their forces. Assuming they were unified to begin with—which Ono's spies said they weren't.

Engines roared, drill bits turned, and as the sun rose in the east, the penetrators broke through. Tarch Hanno was standing twenty yards away from Penetrator 12. As soon as the still-rotating shaft was withdrawn from the ground, he faced the scary prospect of dropping through the hole. Because even though he had ordered hundreds of deaths, he'd never fired a gun at somebody who could shoot back.

No one expected him to enter the Deeps with the troops. But if he did so, Hanno knew that word of his bravery would reach Ophelia, and she would be suitably impressed. Could he snatch the DNI away from Forbes? That was too much to hope for. But in the wake of a successful raid, Hanno felt certain that his present position would be secure. *If* he survived the fighting.

To that end, Hanno was wearing full-body armor, had armed himself with a pistol, and was accompanied by a couple of synth bodyguards. The Bureau employed thousands of the machines and relied on them to find and kill people like Colonel Red. But, since they didn't know the criminal's true identity, it was impossible to track him down through friends and relatives.

The robots were Human in appearance but only vaguely so, and that was no accident. Each head was made of metal. They were broad in front and tapered to a ridge in back. Red eyes were set into deep sockets, and each droid had a bulge where a Human nose would have been. Their bodies had a sleek, stripped-down look. And rather than clothes, they wore urban camo paint jobs.

Frightened though he was, Hanno took comfort from the fact that the synthetics were present and knew that if they failed him, cowardice would play no part in it. As for himself, well, the challenge was to look brave.

Twelve soldiers, all bulky in their combat gear, dropped through the hole on ropes. Hanno heard the sound of gunfire followed by two muffled explosions. A noncom waved him forward and clipped a rope to the harness he wore. Then it was time to back into the abyss. Hanno fell, and the darkness took him in.

Rex was in his office, checking to make sure that all of the organization's records had been destroyed, when Elf appeared. She had big eyes, biosculpted elf ears, and could communicate with the dead. Or so she claimed. Elf was carrying *two* Samurai swords. One more than usual. A hilt could be seen over each shoulder. "So what's the situation?"

"It ain't good," Elf replied. "This one is for real. They even went so far as to seal the storm drains and manhole covers."

"How about penetrators?"

"There are at least a dozen. It's hard to tell from the radio chatter. Rumors are flying every which way. But from what I can make out, the bastards own Level 1 and most of 2. The

Combine put up a fight, but they're losing . . . And when people try to surrender, the Imperials cut them down."

Rex winced. There had been attempts to invade the Deeps before, but nothing like this. Vas was right . . . Ophelia was out to get him. "Okay, we'll follow the old subway line north. Once we leave the city, we'll find a way up and out."

Elf's eyes were huge. "Sorry, boss . . . The Sayers took a run at that. A company of troops was waiting for them."

Both were silent for a moment. Automatic fire stuttered in the distance. "So," Rex said, "what do the dead people have to say?"

Elf's eyes were luminous. "They're waiting for us."

Rex knew she was waiting for him to adjust . . . To accept the inevitable. "And the others?"

"They know."

"Okay, then let's give the bastards something to remember. We'll head for the nearest penetrator hole and use their ropes to climb out."

They would never make it. Both of them knew that. But it was an objective—a reason to move. "I'll tell them," Elf said, and left.

Rex thought about Macy, the woman he loved, and was thankful for the fact that she was in Chicago. And Cat . . . Brave Cat. He'd said things to her. Stupid things. *I'm sorry, Cat. I really am.* Vive la legion.

Then he turned and left the office. Hoke, Percy, Elf, and all the rest were waiting for him. Twenty-three in all. Rex left through the front door, and the rest streamed along behind him.

The Imperials could have cut power to the Deeps but had chosen not to. Rex thought he knew why. While the incoming soldiers would have night-vision technology built into their helmets—the locals knew every nook and cranny

of their subsurface world by heart. So there was very little
reason to turn the lights off. That meant all of the garish
signs continued to glow, ads for services that would no longer be available crawled the walls, and text messages continued to zigzag along the floors.

Then all such thoughts were put aside as a mob of locals
flowed down from Level 2, clearly desperate to reach Level 3.
The crowd broke around the column of Freedom Front
fighters and surged past them. "Turn back!" a woman yelled.
"There are hundreds of them."

A few seconds later, Rex arrived at the top of a ramp that
led into an open area occupied by bars, restaurants, and tat-
too parlors. A large shaft of sunlight came down through a
hole in the ceiling and splashed the floor. It was surrounded
by a cordon of troops, placed there to defend the drop zone
from people like Rex. A dozen soldiers were rappelling from
above. The time to kill them was *before* they could land and
get their bearings.

Rex shouted, "Grenades!" and threw one of his own. It
landed, bounced a foot into the air, and exploded. There was
a flash followed by a loud boom as pieces of shrapnel cut
three Imperials down. More grenades followed, and Rex
waved his people forward. Speed . . . That was the key. That
plus the element of surprise.

So they charged out into the open, firing as they ran.
Hoke fired his shotgun and *more* soldiers fell. But the battle
was far from one-sided. Percy was flying about twelve feet
above the floor, firing his laser at targets of opportunity,
when a rocket struck his spherical body. There was an
orange-red explosion, and what remained of the cyborg's
body hit the floor and rolled. Rex shot the man with the
launcher. He was closer by then. Much closer. Maybe, just
maybe, some of his people could escape.

Then a Human appeared up ahead. He was flanked by

two synths armed with machine pistols. They fired, and Rex staggered as a hail of bullets struck him. Then he was falling . . . And reaching for something important. Something that would prevent them from identifying his body. Something that would protect Cat. The only gift he had to give.

A synth stepped forward, and as Rex looked up, he could see the machine's ruby red eyes staring down at him. That was when he pulled the pin, and there was a bright flash as the thermite grenade went off. Rex was cremated, the rest of his grenades went off, and shards of jagged metal tore the synth apart.

Hanno's visor went dark to protect him from the bright light, he felt a sharp pain as something sliced through his left arm, and blinked as his vision was restored. A patch of blackened duracrete marked the spot where the man had been immolated and little pools of molten metal continued to burn. *I stood my ground,* he thought to himself. *They couldn't make me run.* Then he felt dizzy, and the floor came up to meet him. The darkness took him in.

Empress Ophelia woke up in a good mood. She rolled out of bed, made her way over to the French doors, and threw the floor-length curtains out of the way. Once the doors were open, she stepped out onto a large veranda. A breeze caught her nightgown and whipped it around her well-shaped legs. The sun was shining, and the surface of the Pacific Ocean glittered as if dusted with gold. And there, out on the horizon the vague outline of a floating hab could be seen, gradually cruising north. All was right with the world. *This* one anyway. Others were less fortunate. But that could and would be corrected.

Three days had passed since the army had gone down into the Deeps and killed 99 percent of the scum who lived there. A few, including a crime lord named Vas, had been captured. And once the DIS interrogators were finished with him, he would be executed. A very satisfying outcome indeed.

The glitch, if there was one, had to do with the army's failure to find Colonel Red. The Freedom Front leader had been there . . . That's what Vas claimed. Unfortunately, the army had been unable to recover a body that matched Red's description. Still, there had been a number of intense fires, and there was the very real possibility that the rebel had perished in one of them. Most convincing of all was the fact that Colonel Red had been silent since the raid.

Yes, things were going very well indeed. She did miss Veneto, though. Not the sex so much as the rest of it. She'd been able to talk to him—to share some of her problems. Realizing that it was important to maintain at least some distance from everyone she knew. Especially lovers.

But Veneto had been stupid and paid a steep price for his stupidity. So she would put him and all memories of him aside. There was work to do, starting with the meeting scheduled for 10:00 A.M. Ophelia took a moment to savor the sea air, turned, and went back inside.

The synth that had been watching over her from the roof above notified the rest of the security team. A gray-and-white seagull rode the wind, drifted in toward shore, and floated there. The android "saw" it, compared the bird to its operational parameters, and made the logical decision. Just because the seagull *looked* like a seagull didn't mean it was one. The synth brought its rifle up and fired. The bird exploded, and pieces of it fell out of the sky. The empress was safe.

A shadow flitted over the buildings below as Tarch Hanno's air car flew north. His arm ached, but he didn't care. The raid . . . That was the important thing. It had gone well, and body or no body, everyone agreed that Colonel Red was dead. That took the pressure off and made it very unlikely that Forbes would be able to seize control of the Bureau.

So he felt as good as a man with a lacerated arm could as the car put down, and he made his way to the Security Center. This meeting was to be different from the last one and for a very good reason. Empress Ophelia was going to participate. And as he entered the room, Hanno saw that she was already there.

Heads turned. Ophelia saw him and broke away from a group of admirers in order to come over and greet him. Her long dark hair hung down to her shoulders, and there was a smile on her heart-shaped face. "Tarch Hanno! I didn't expect to see you here . . . How do you feel?"

"Quite well, Majesty," Hanno replied. "Thank you for the gift basket by the way . . . What a wonderful selection of wines."

"I'm glad you like it," Ophelia said, as she took his good arm and escorted him over to a chair. "Going down into the Deeps was both unnecessary and foolhardy. But brave as well. I daresay we'll have to come up with a suitable commendation of some sort. How does Knight of the Empire sound? That might suit the situation."

It was more recognition than Hanno could have hoped for. Especially since he had done little more than drop through the hole and get wounded. Lady Constance Forbes was on the other side of the table, and, judging from the expression on her face, had doubts regarding the extent of Hanno's heroism.

Tarch Ono brought the meeting to order, welcomed Ophelia, and thanked those present for their roles in the successful attack. With the formalities out of the way, Ophelia took over. She was seated at one end of the table, and her eyes probed the faces around her. "I would like to add my thanks to those already expressed by Tarch Ono. Sterilizing the Deeps was an important accomplishment.

"However, I think you'll agree that this is no time to rest on our laurels. Even though the Freedom Front has been decapitated, there are like-minded organizations on other planets. And while the Hudathans were driven off of Orlo II, they represent a constant threat. So this is the time to strengthen our hold on the inner worlds. Tarch Ono, Lady Forbes, and Tarch Hanno all have roles to play in that effort. But force isn't everything. We need to win hearts and minds.

"So I plan to make a grand tour of the empire, starting with Orlo II. Each time I arrive, there will be receptions, parties, and parades. All of which are opportunities to communicate why the empire is relevant to their lives. Who else can facilitate trade? Who else can protect them from the Hudathans? And who else can ensure that they aren't cut off from the rest of Humanity? The trip will also provide an opportunity to strengthen my relationships with governors and leading royalists. I'd like to hear your opinions."

Ophelia's proposal was met with universal approval. Some people, like Ono, seemed to actually believe in the concept. Hanno was less sanguine. He feared that Ophelia's visits would trigger bloody protests. But with a knighthood in his pocket, he wasn't about to object. Besides, Ophelia's absence would be equivalent to a vacation.

Hanno's eyes drifted into contact with Forbes's. She smiled for the first time in recent memory—and that was when Hanno realized that they might have something in common. Maybe Forbes was looking forward to a break as well—or maybe she saw Ophelia's impending absence as an opportunity. A chill ran down his spine.

CHAPTER: 3

I don't know what effect these men will have on the
enemy, but, by God, they frighten me.

THE DUKE OF WELLINGTON,
on a draft of troops sent from England
during the Peninsular Campaign
Standard year 1809

PLANET ALGERON

Andromeda McKee was riding Corporal Sam Vella, and he
was running full out. And she was experiencing a wild mix
of emotions. There was fear, and for good reason since she
and a small group of riders were about to attack some Naa
bandits; but there was more. McKee was conscious of the
cold air that blew in around her visor, the wild thumping of
her heart, and the guilty joy of riding into battle. It was
stupid. McKee knew that. Because the excitement was often
followed by grief.

Knowing made no difference. The unrepentant sense of
joy was still there, as was the broad expanse of sun-streaked
sky and the spiky rock formations ahead. That's where
Longtalk Storytell was holed up. Could they reach him in
time? McKee hoped so. Because if anyone could help her
find the chief of chiefs, Storytell was that person. So the
mission could very well depend on what took place during

the next few minutes. "This is Alpha-One," McKee said.
"Go in hard. Fire at will. Over."

The heavily rutted road took a turn to the right, and a
flurry of gunshots were heard, as Corporal Smith yelled,
"Contact!" Sparks of light could be seen in among the rocks
as the bandits fired. Sureshot shouted something in Naa,
and two warriors followed him as he dropped down along
his dooth's massive neck and galloped straight ahead. As
bullets kicked up geysers of dirt all around, one of Sureshot's warriors fell. He was trampled by the dooth coming
along behind.

"Go left and flank 'em," McKee ordered via the intercom,
and Vella obeyed. McKee brought her assault weapon up
and fired as a bandit broke the skyline. Meanwhile, Vella
rounded an outcropping of rock and spotted a group of
dooths. The frightened animals were milling around while
three Naa attempted to mount up. The T-1 fired his .50
caliber machine gun. A bloody mist floated over the scene
as the indigs and their animals died. When Vella came to a
stop McKee took a moment to put a dying dooth out of its
misery. Corporal Smith's voice filled her helmet. "Alpha-
Three to Alpha-One . . . We have what's-his-name. Over."

"This is One. What kind of condition is he in? Over."

"No holes. Over."

McKee felt a sense of relief. She looked forward to hear-
ing what Storytell had to say. But first things first. They
were in enemy territory, the column was coming up behind
her, and the light had begun to fade.

The next half hour was spent locating a spot where a
ridge of rock offered protection from the south, and the
company could laager up around a well-established fire pit.
It was a regular stop then . . . A place where north- and
southbound caravans paused to eat and grab some sleep.

Once the company's defenses were complete, McKee
asked Jivani to accompany her on a full circuit of the perim-

eter. It was dark by then, and a scattering of fires lit the campground. McKee paused to speak with each group. She was wearing a translator but knew Jivani would pick up on the sort of subtleties that a machine couldn't.

The Naa preferred to camp upwind of the Humans, whom they privately referred to as "stinks" or "slick skins." Something not lost on the Human bio bods, who routinely called the Naa "digs" and "fur balls." It was a schism that McKee hoped to bridge.

Once the tour was over, McKee told Jivani to get some chow and went looking for Storytell. McKee found the guide crouched in front of a small blaze, with Sureshot sitting across from him. That was both annoying and potentially dangerous since she didn't trust either one of them. But if the Naa were plotting against her, there was no sign of it as Sureshot rose to introduce her. "This is Lieutenant McKee . . . My people call her Nofear Deathgiver."

"It's a pleasure to meet you," Storytell said as he stood. "I heard the story of Doothdown from a northerner named Quickword Spellbind. It's a wonderful tale, and I was hard-pressed to offer a story of equal value in return."

McKee accepted the forearm-to-forearm grip and was thankful for it. It was nice to know that Storytell was willing to take her seriously. "Thank you. I'm glad you came through the fight unharmed."

"They killed my dooth," Storytell said sadly. "I will miss her."

"We captured two of their animals," Sureshot put in. "You can take your pick."

"Thank you," Storytell said. "No offense . . . But why is that thing watching us?"

The Naa pointed, and McKee turned to see that Andy was staring at them from the edge of the firelight. Recording? Yes, probably. "Ignore it," McKee said, as she turned back. "It was sent to document the mission."

"If you say so," Storytell said doubtfully, and sat down. The other two joined him, and it was a chance for McKee to tuck into one of the MREs that a private dropped off. Sureshot opened his. But Storytell preferred to carve slices off a chunk of jerky. "So," she began. "You know why we're here?"

"To find Truthsayer," Storytell replied.

"And how do you feel about that?"

Light flashed off steel as Storytell carved another slice of meat. "My father was from the north . . . And my mother was from the south. We were *Noogin*. Wanderers. So while I have no reason to hate Truthsayer—I have no reason to love him, either."

That was a good thing if true, and McKee paused to eat some stew before asking the most critical question. "So, where is he?"

Storytell eyed her across the fire. "I can tell you where he was—but only the gods know where he *is*. Eighty-one days ago, he was in the City of Pillars. My cousin saw him there. But he could be anywhere by now."

McKee tried to do the math in her head. If she was correct, eighty-one local days were equivalent to something like nine standard days. So Storytell was correct. By the time the column entered the City of Pillars, *if* they were allowed to enter the City of Pillars, the chief of chiefs could be long gone. But what choice did she have? Even if Truthsayer had left she might be able to pick up his trail or figure out a way to contact him. But first she had to get there. "Tell me about Graveyard Pass."

Storytell shrugged. "Travelers must pay to pass through it. That's the way it has always been. I don't know Hardhand Bigclub. Maybe he would allow you to pass through for the right price. Or maybe he hates slick skins."

"I could talk to him," Sureshot volunteered. "Or try to."

It was a generous offer and one that involved no small amount of risk for Sureshot. McKee nodded. "Thank you.

Let's get some rest and give it a try. I would prefer a peaceful passage if such a thing is possible."

Once the meal was over, McKee took one last tour of the perimeter and spent a few minutes going over the watch schedule with Larkin. "I plan to have some of our people on duty around the clock," the noncom said. "And I told the squad leaders to keep an eye on the fur balls."

McKee understood Larkin's perspective—but felt obliged to stress the need for unity. "Remember Desmond, we're all on the same team."

Only half of Larkin's face was illuminated, but she could see the look of surprise. McKee rarely called the legionnaire by his first name, and when she did, there was a reason. In this case, to take the sting out of her comment. He nodded. "I hear you. But I plan to handle things the way you would have . . . Back before they pinned that bar on you! And there's no way in hell that *Sergeant* McKee would let a bunch of indigs stand watch alone."

McKee couldn't help but laugh. "I stand corrected. Carry on, Sergeant. And get some rest. Something tells me that we're going to need it."

The bandits fired on the company twice during the next five hours but did so from a distance. McKee woke up on both occasions but didn't think the outlaws were serious. And when no one came to get her, that opinion was confirmed. So she went back to sleep.

Then, after what seemed like no more than a minute or two, it was time to get up. Her morning shower consisted of a wipe down with a premoistened towelette followed by the application of some spray-on deodorizer. Then it was time to down a mug of hot coffee before going out to join Ridefast Trickshot's funeral ceremony. The location was the makeshift graveyard that was adjacent to the camp. Judging from the rows of crude headstones, dozens of Naa had been buried there over the years.

As the rest of them listened, Sureshot told the gods how Trickshot had been killed, how brave he was, and why they should welcome him. Then, as the blanket-wrapped body was lowered into the ground, Sureshot led the rest of the Naa in a chant that Jivani didn't need to translate. The sadness and regret inherent in the rise and fall of the words was universal. The company had suffered its first casualty—and McKee was left to wonder how many would follow.

Twenty minutes after the ceremony, Sureshot and two of his warriors were armed and ready to ride. McKee was there to see them off. "I will carry my father's totem," Sureshot said solemnly. "Bigclub would be foolish to fire on it."

"Good," McKee replied. "If you run into trouble, use your radio. The third squad will come a-running."

"That's good to know," Sureshot said. McKee saw the familiar look in the warrior's eyes and knew he was thinking about something other than war. Males. They were so predictable.

McKee placed the entire company on standby as Sureshot rode out. By standing on a rocky outcropping, she could watch as Sureshot and his companions followed the road south and disappeared into a ground-hugging mist. There were no gunshots, and no calls for help, so it seemed safe to assume that Bigclub was willing to talk.

An hour passed. And as night began to fall, McKee was beginning to worry. What if Sureshot and his warriors were dead? All killed by arrows or some other means? At what point should she attack? Jivani believed that the warriors were having tea, a ritual that involved a good deal of socializing before either party could discuss the matter at hand. And McKee understood that. But an hour and a half?

That's what she was thinking when Larkin's voice came over the radio. "This is Alpha-One-Three . . . We have Sureshot on Drone 3. He's on his way back. Over."

McKee said, "Roger," and climbed up onto the rock. The

sun was an orange smear in the western sky, but there was still enough light to see by. And sure enough . . . Three riders were headed her way. The pace was deliberately slow, so as to signal nonchalance. It took every bit of McKee's self-control to hide the impatience she felt as the negotiating team finally entered camp.

But once Sureshot dismounted and turned her way, she knew the negotiations had been successful. It was visible in the way he held his body. "I have good news," Sureshot said confidently. "Bigclub will allow us to pass."

"And the price?"

"A RAV, a construction droid, and a hundred thousand rounds of ammunition."

McKee's spirits fell. There was no way she could or would pay that price. But, before she could reply, Jivani spoke up. "That's what he *asked* for . . . What price did you get him down to?"

Sureshot grinned. "One thousand rounds of ammo, ten grenades, and a case of MREs."

McKee laughed. "Nice job. I hate to provide bandits with arms, but we'd be forced to use even more ordnance to launch an attack, and we would take casualties as well."

McKee had no intention of taking the company through the pass at night. So the hours of darkness were used to eat another meal, review contingency plans, and break camp. By the time the sickly yellow sun was two fingers off the eastern horizon, they had cleared the rocks and were halfway to the hills.

Sureshot and his dooth led the way with a pack animal. It was loaded with the ammo, grenades, and food required to pay Bigclub. Sureshot was followed by alternating squads of Naa and legionnaires, with RAVs and construction droids behind them. The rear guard consisted of Larkin and the members of the third squad.

McKee noticed that a T-1 named Sal Toto was carrying

two shoulder-mounted rocket launchers rather than Sergeant Rico Sager. *He* was sitting astride the last RAV. That was Larkin's doing—and not in keeping with the order of march she had approved.

McKee thought about calling the arrangement into question and knew Larkin would lose face if she did. It was the sort of "I'll do it my way" approach Sergeant McKee had been known for . . . And now it was coming back to bite her. McKee smiled. She would talk to Larkin later . . . *After* they cleared the pass.

Sureshot started upwards, and the rest followed. McKee rode at the head of squad one, behind the first group of Naa. Storytell, Jivani, and Andy were nearby. At the beginning, the road had been wide enough to accommodate two dooth-drawn carts. Now it was starting to narrow, and as that occurred, rocky hillsides rose to the right and left. And as McKee looked up, she saw ledges. Each occupied by at least one of Bigclub's ragged-looking warriors, all of whom were staring down at the column.

By that time, McKee could *feel* the hostility they projected and realized that she'd been stupid. *Very* stupid. They were riding into a trap. Bigclub had lied to Sureshot who, being young and relatively inexperienced, believed the bandit.

McKee chinned her mike and opened her mouth but never got the opportunity to speak. Because that was when one of the bandits fired a rifle, and Sureshot toppled out of the saddle. All hell broke loose immediately thereafter. Both hillsides sparkled as dozens of bandits opened fire. Bigclub wasn't about to settle for a pittance. He planned to take *everything*.

It seemed to occur in slow motion. There was only one way to go, and that was straight ahead. So McKee shouted, "Fire at will! Charge!"

It was impossible to know if Sureshot's warriors were following her order or their own instincts as they kicked their dooths into a trot. They were firing back and doing so with deadly accuracy.

Bullets pinged against Vella's armor as the T-1 raised his fifty. The short, three-round bursts were computer-controlled—and nearly every slug found a target. McKee was firing, too. Her 4.7 mm Axer Arms L-40 Assault Weapon could fire two thousand rounds per minute in the three-round-burst mode. Her job was to keep the Naa from closing in on Vella.

As McKee looked up, dark bodies were silhouetted against the gray sky. She fired, and fired again. A body landed in the center of the road and popped when Vella stepped on it. McKee knew she should be monitoring what was taking place behind her—but was forced to fight for her life as they passed a hidden alcove, and bandits surged out to attack them. Even though they were on foot, the bandits managed to pull two warriors off their dooths. There were screams as knives flashed, and McKee fired at them. But it wasn't enough.

A Naa had hold of Vella's machine gun and was heavy enough to weigh it down. McKee could hear Jivani firing her pistol and sensed that Storytell was fighting back as well. She triggered a burst, heard her AXE click empty, and was reaching for a magazine when something unexpected occurred.

Andy surged into the mob, put a Naa down with a perfectly timed head butt, and snatched the bandit's rifle. Then the robot began to kill with the ruthless efficiency of what it was . . . A machine. And not a moment too soon because the column had bunched up behind the first squad by that time and was taking casualties. "Keep moving!" McKee shouted. "Up the hill! Kill the bastards!"

Only three of the ten Naa who had been leading the way were still alive. But they and the legionnaires in the first squad continued to battle their way up the hill. At least two dozen bandits had been killed by then, and the incoming fire had begun to slacken. For one brief moment, McKee thought the worst of it was over. Then a heavy machine gun began to fire at them. The Naa were torn to shreds and a T-1 named Gan went down with his bio bod on board.

McKee swore and waited to die. Bigclub shouldn't have a heavy machine gun. *Couldn't* have one unless . . . Yes! As McKee looked upslope, she could see a turret poking up out of the soil and knew what was underneath. A combat car had been lost to the enemy during the battle for the mesa, and there it was, half-buried at the top of the pass. "Grenades!" McKee shouted, as she fumbled for one. "Destroy that gun!"

But the range was too great, and the grenades fell short. Geysers of dirt flew up where they landed and did no harm. Meanwhile, the big gun continued to chug as Vella fired, and a curtain of dirt rose around the armored turret.

Then a whoosh was heard, and the combat car took a direct hit from a rocket. The first explosion was followed by a second. It produced a flash of light and a resounding boom. The turret shot fifty feet straight up into the air and seemed to pause there for a moment before crashing down. A column of fire rose from what remained of the combat car, and McKee heard a series of loud bangs as stray rounds of .50 caliber ammo cooked off.

Her head swiveled left and right as Vella carried her upwards, and the company's remaining drones appeared. Energy beams sizzled as the flying robots entered the fray. That was when McKee remembered that Sal Toto was carrying shoulder-mounted rocket launchers. Why? Because Larkin didn't trust fur balls, that's why. Thank God for that. Thank God for him.

As Vella passed the burning combat car, McKee saw the stone fortress off to the right. It was a one-story affair, with a flat roof and rifle slits all around. Puffs of smoke were visible as the surviving bandits fired from within. Was Bigclub in there? Bullets kicked up dirt all around, so McKee ordered Vella to back up a bit.

She hadn't had time to tally the butcher's bill but knew it was going to be extensive and didn't want to lose more lives if that could be avoided. So she ordered the column to stop. And since the road led up through a ravine, the bandits inside the fort couldn't see them. That left both the legionnaires and Naa free to help their wounded while McKee sent for Private Toto. The T-1 arrived a few minutes later. The so-called cans on the cyborg's shoulders had been reloaded by then, so he was ready to fire twelve independently targeted rockets. "Take the fort out," McKee ordered. "But don't use any more ordnance than you have to."

Toto nodded his huge head. "Yes, ma'am."

Thanks to her HUD, McKee had a Toto-eye view as the T-1 topped the rise and went to work. He fired the rockets one at a time. Each was targeted on a rifle slit. And it wasn't long before a large hole appeared in the fort's east wall. Toto sent two missiles through the gap. One followed the other so closely, she heard what sounded like a single boom. The explosion was so powerful that a section of roof went airborne, and jets of fire shot out through the rifle slits. It appeared that the fort's main magazine had gone up, and McKee ordered Toto to stop firing.

McKee waited to see what would happen next and felt relieved when there were no further signs of resistance. So she sent what remained of the first squad forward to clear the fort, ordered the column up onto the ridge, and began the process of assessing how badly the company had been mauled.

Thirteen Naa had been killed. Fourteen, counting Sureshot. And three legionnaires were dead, two of whom were T-1s. A serious blow indeed—and McKee blamed herself for it. Allowing Sureshot to handle the negotiations had been a serious error in judgment. And the realization made her sick to her stomach.

There were wounded, too . . . Seven in all. Two of whom were in critical condition, a Human and a Naa. So McKee sent for a com tech and told her to request a dustoff, plus replacements, and some more supplies.

Night was on the way. So McKee told Larkin to establish observation posts (OPs) on both slopes—and to set up a quick-reaction force comprised of both Humans and Naa. She had been afraid that the indigs would pack up and leave in the wake of Sureshot's death. But Jivani had been talking to the Naa, who assured her that they planned to stay. "They know your reputation," the civilian said simply. "And they want revenge." That suited McKee just fine.

The fly-form arrived half an hour later. McKee half expected a senior officer to be aboard. Cavenaugh perhaps . . . Come to tell her how stupid she had been. However, when the cyborg landed, it was empty except for the flight crew and two medics. But, after giving the matter some additional thought, McKee realized that made sense. The situation would look innocent enough to a person who read her preliminary report but hadn't been on the ground. Sureshot negotiated a deal, Bigclub went back on his word, and the company fought its way up onto the ridge. No big deal if you were sitting in a chair drinking coffee.

So there weren't any senior officers, and no reinforcements, either. Fortunately, her request for supplies had been honored. Part of it anyway . . . And as a squad of legionnaires carried cases of ammo off the fly-form, another carried bodies onto it. Bodies plus two brain boxes. McKee wanted to cry but couldn't allow herself to do so.

The casualties went aboard last. McKee said good-bye to them, thanked the crew, and left via the ramp. Grit flew in every direction as the fly-form lifted off. The people on board would arrive at Fort Cameron in less than an hour. Not just a place, but a whole different world, filled with luxuries like hot showers, palatable food, and real beds.

Finally, having met everyone else's needs, McKee had a moment in which to reflect on everything that had occurred. The fort was little more than a pile of rubble, so she took an MRE and a mug of hot caf out to a point where she could lean on a rock and look out to the mountains beyond. The Towers of Algeron had a pink hue thanks to the quickly rising sun.

The beautiful sunrise and the hot meal combined to lift McKee's spirits a bit. And as McKee spooned rice and beans into her mouth, she carried out a blow-by-blow review of the battle. Never mind the *why* of it . . . What had gone well? And what hadn't? Larkin had stepped up—and so had the troops. And then there was Andy . . .

McKee's spoon stopped halfway to her mouth. There hadn't been time to think. But how had a combot been able to kick so much ass? As far as she knew, such machines weren't programmed for combat—and if they weren't programmed for something, they couldn't do it. What did that suggest? What felt like an injection of ice water entered McKee's veins. The answer was obvious. Andy wasn't a combot—Andy was a synth. Sent to check on her. Sent to kill her if necessary.

McKee's appetite had disappeared. She put the bowl down and stuck her spoon into the quickly congealing pile of rice and beans. It made sense. She'd been forced to kill *three* government operatives over the last few months. One had been assassinated, while the others had been neutralized in less obvious ways. So it seemed reasonable to believe that the people at the Bureau of Missing Persons didn't *know* she was someone other than who she claimed to be . . . But they suspected as much. And, rather than send a synth that looked like what it was, they had chosen to send a synth disguised as a combot.

The substitution could have fooled her for a long time. But unlike combots, synths were programmed to defend themselves when attacked, so when the bandits charged out of their hiding place, Andy did what it was supposed to do. And that was a good thing. McKee knew the truth now. So, what to do? Find a way to terminate the robot? Or attempt to fool it?

McKee tried to remember anything she might have said or done that would give her identity away. She couldn't. But there were other possibilities. After they murdered her parents, it was reasonable to suppose that government agents had orders to harvest DNA samples from their bodies. So what if Andy had taken samples of her DNA? It would be easy enough to do. All the machine had to do was swab her coffee mug or the equivalent thereof.

Where did that leave her? If Andy had a fatal accident, that would look suspicious. Especially in light of her recent history. And if she allowed the robot to deliver a DNA sample to the BMP she would wind up dead shortly thereafter. It was a lose-lose situation and one that would require additional thought.

After eight hours of rest and maintenance, the company was ready to head south. That meant McKee had to face a difficult decision. Should she leave enough troops to hold the pass? So as to secure her line of retreat? Or should she take everyone with her—and hope for a dustoff later? Both strategies had inherent advantages, but after giving the matter some thought, McKee decided to keep her force intact. She couldn't afford to leave more than two squads behind and was painfully aware of the fact that such a small group wouldn't be able to hold the pass against a force of fifty or sixty Naa. And because the company might have to fight its way south, McKee wanted to keep as much firepower as she could.

So the column formed up and followed the drones down

the south side of the pass into a rock-strewn valley. Trees grew in small clumps, streams tumbled down steep hillsides, and the road was a series of switchbacks. Eventually, the valley widened out, and a multitude of streams joined forces to create a river. It flowed through a succession of boulder gardens and accompanied the road south. Two miles later, they came to a campsite reminiscent of the one on the north side of the pass. It, too, had its own graveyard.

There were no signs of life other than a pair of long wings riding the thermals high above. And that was fine with McKee. As the short day wore on, the previously barren valley began to green up, and signs of habitation appeared. The first was a solitary finger of smoke signaling the presence of a distant hut. And that got McKee's attention. They were likely to encounter a village soon. And when they did, the drones would scare the crap out of the locals. So she had the robots pull back and sent an advance party forward to replace them. It consisted of Storytell, Jivani, and a Naa warrior. Her hope was that the trio could gather Intel and prevent misunderstandings.

Storytell's role was to let the locals know what was coming. Jivani was there to keep him honest, and the warrior's job was to provide the others with security. Would it work? McKee hoped so . . . But she was ready to send the first squad forward if things got dicey.

Night came and went. The test came shortly after a nondescript dawn. The morning light found its way down through a thick layer of clouds to fill the valley with an uncertain glow. Columns of gray smoke could be seen up ahead and signaled the presence of a village. "Alpha-One-Five to Alpha-One. Over."

Jivani had been quick to pick up on the Legion's military-radio procedures, and McKee was proud of her. "This is Alpha-One. Go. Over."

"We're just outside a small village. Storytell is schmoozing the local chief. Twelve of his warriors were killed during the attack on the mesa, and he hates slick skins. Over."

"Uh, okay . . . That sounds bad, over."

"It *is* bad. But Storytell is getting ready to dispense some of the loot we captured up in the pass. That could make a difference. I suggest that you hold off on entering the village. Let's give negotiations some more time. Over."

"That makes sense," McKee agreed. "Keep me informed. Over."

Jivani clicked her mike twice by way of a response.

McKee posted a drone to the east and west, put out pickets, and let the rest of the company take a bio break. The better part of thirty minutes passed before Jivani contacted her again. "Alpha-One-Five to Alpha-One. Over."

"Go Five. Over."

"We have a deal . . . Chief Digdeep accepted our gift and will no doubt send word of his negotiating prowess south. That means we'll have to pay off every strongman between here and the south pole. Over."

McKee smiled. "It beats fighting them . . . Tell Storytell to keep the gifts small, or we'll run out of loot. Over."

"Understood," Jivani replied. "Over."

The column got under way shortly thereafter and passed through the village of Fastwater ten minutes later. It was little more than a clutch of twenty huts surrounded by a rotting palisade. Two T-1s would have been sufficient to destroy it. But McKee was glad to avoid that. She felt badly about the locals who had been killed attacking the mesa. Their loss would be felt for many years to come.

The deeply rutted road was lined with ragged-looking villagers, all of whom stared at the column as it passed by. McKee saw one warrior finger the hilt of his knife, but other than that, there were no signs of overt hostility.

The sun set half an hour later, but McKee couldn't stop. Not with such short days to work with—and so many miles to cover. So she pulled the advance team back and put the drones on point with a couple of T-1s to back them up. The cyborgs could "see" any Naa who might be in the area regardless of how much light there was.

There were some contacts, and that was to be expected. The Naa had no choice but to work through a couple of night cycles each day. Two local cycles later, it was time to stop and fort up. Like thousands of military commanders before her, McKee chose to camp on a hill. A defensive ditch was dug, lined with sharpened stakes, and seeded with computer-controlled crab mines. The missing element was a source of water. But even that problem was resolved when it began to rain. A steady drizzle continued for the next five hours.

So when the time came to depart, the compound was a quagmire and there was half a foot of water in the defensive ditch. Fortunately, the crab mines could be disarmed and summoned with a handheld remote. The T-1s had to be careful not to step on the devices as they scurried in from all directions. Each one had to be inspected and wiped clean before being placed in a special container. Only when all of them were accounted for could the box be loaded into a RAV.

And that wasn't all. The mud meant that *everything* took longer than usual. But eventually the troops were fed, the shelters were torn down, and the column was ready to depart. As before, McKee sent the advance party out first, followed by alternating squads, the RAVs, the construction robots, and the rear guard. Larkin was tired of riding drag but understood the necessity. If the column was cut in two, both halves would require leadership. But that didn't keep him from bitching.

Meanwhile, as T-1s and dooths plodded down the road, Andy struggled to keep up. The mud would have made that difficult anyway—but the fact that it had been ordered to carry an eighty-pound pack made the task that much more difficult. The plan was to slow the robot down.

There had been a protest, needless to say. But Andy couldn't refuse an order that fell within the list of tasks that a combot could be ordered to do. Not without revealing its true nature. McKee not only took a childish delight in that—but hoped the additional stress would cause some sort of malfunction. Then, if the problem was sufficiently serious, she could order a legionnaire to destroy the machine. Would it work? Probably not. But some sort of plan was better than no plan at all.

The rain stopped just as night was falling, but the road was still muddy, and the rivers were full. That made for some very wet crossings. McKee was soaked, her skin was cold, and she knew the rest of the bio bods felt the same way. At some point, the possibility of hypothermia could force them to stop—but she was determined to make as much progress as possible.

Adding to the misery was the need to pause every now and then while Storytell and Jivani went forward to negotiate with yet another chieftain. Then, once an agreement was struck, the march resumed. Halfway through the next local day, they came to the largest village they'd seen yet. It was called Gooddirt. A name which, though far from poetic, described why the Naa lived there.

This time the advance party was met by a large group of armed warriors. It seemed that they knew the column was coming and were waiting for it. So McKee called a halt and took the first squad forward. She noticed that none of Gooddirt's delegation looked surprised. That seemed to indicate that the villagers had seen Humans and T-1s before. At the mesa? Yes, that made sense.

Storytell had his pitch down by then. So he told the villagers that while they were looking for Truthsayer, they had no desire to hurt him, only to speak with him. It was an inquiry that hadn't produced meaningful results up to that point. But in this case, the statement stimulated a strong response. The local chief was named Beathard Metalshaper. His voice was still strong in spite of the fact that he appeared to be old and frail. "Truthsayer?" he demanded. "Naaslayer is more like it . . . My son took two hundred warriors north to fight, and only three of them returned. I would kill you right now except that doing so would bring down fire from the sky."

"Understood," Storytell replied. "But what about Truthsayer? Where is he?"

Metalshaper spat, and a big glob of yellow sputum landed halfway between them. "I heard that the worthless pook is south of here . . . In the City of Pillars. You're welcome to him."

Storytell offered a gift and was refused. "You look like a Naa but smell like a slick skin," Metalshaper said. "Keep your blood money and leave my village."

Jivani translated. They were brave words, possibly foolish words, but McKee had no intention of attacking Gooddirt for reasons of pride. Fortunately, none of Sureshot's warriors were close enough to hear. McKee knew they had a very strict code of conduct where matters of honor were concerned—and would have been duty-bound to kill Metalshaper. Or try to anyway.

The march continued. The information gleaned from Metalshaper squared with what Storytell had been told earlier. Truthsayer was, or had been, in the City of Pillars.

McKee requested an uplink, got it, and ordered a sat map of the area ahead. The City of Pillars was hard to miss. It was considerably bigger than the largest village she'd seen. And, at their present rate of speed, they would arrive in three local days.

But the encounter with Metalshaper was an eye-opener. It seemed that Truthsayer wasn't as popular as he had been, not after the slaughter up north, a possibility Colonel Caven-augh had neglected to mention. Or never thought of. Not that it mattered since McKee's orders were clear: Find Truthsayer and bring him in. Or, failing that, kill him. How the locals felt about the chief of chiefs was irrelevant.

But marching her troops into the City of Pillars wasn't likely to get the job done. That could provoke an attack. What she needed was an out-of-the-way place to hide the company. Then she could go in and gather Intel without triggering conflict. That was the theory anyway. So McKee sent Storytell and two warriors out to scout the countryside. The call came in two hours later. "McKee."

"This is Alpha-One. Please use radio procedure. Over."

"Sorry," Storytell said. "I found it. Over."

"Tell me more, over."

"We're on an island in the middle of the river. There are the remains of some old huts, but nobody lives here any-more. Over."

McKee eyed her HUD, saw the icon that marked Story-tell's position, and the irregular outline of an island. The river must be fairly shallow, or Storytell and his warriors wouldn't have been able to get out there. Still, the need to wade through a current would slow attackers down and pro-vide defenders with a free-fire zone as well. "Is there any cover? Over."

"Trees . . . And some rocks. Over."

"Okay . . . Hold your position. We're on the way. Over."

There was no, "Roger that." Just a click.

It took two hours to reach the river, cross it in the dark, and take possession of the island. McKee knew it was very likely that a farmer or hunter had seen the column pass. And if one person knew about them, all of the locals would. So they couldn't hide on the island. But they could prepare to defend it. McKee ordered the construction robots to dig both fighting positions *and* bunkers in case the locals brought some catapults or captured artillery to bear. That, plus the need to perform maintenance on the T-1s, would be enough to keep the legionnaires busy.

So McKee went looking for Storytell. He was sitting on his haunches, sharpening his knife. The whetstone made a rasping sound as it slid the length of the blade. McKee sat on a rock. The sun was rising, and the sky was clear. "I want to enter the city," she said. "If Truthsayer is there, I need to locate him."

Storytell looked up at her. "And if he isn't?"

"Then I need to find out where he is."

"I can go," Storytell said. "But a Human? That's impossible."

"No," McKee said. "It isn't. I'll wear a hooded cloak . . . Like the ones Naa females use to keep warm. And I'll wrap a scarf around my face."

Storytell looked skeptical. "And where will you obtain this cloak?"

"Jivani has one. She wore it the other day."

"We would need warriors. Just in case."

McKee took note of the "We." "Eatbig and Highstep would be perfect."

Storytell made the knife disappear. "Can you ride a dooth?"

"I guess I'll have to."

Storytell nodded. "I will notify Eatbig and Highstep."

After borrowing the cloak from Jivani—McKee went to see Larkin. Naa females rarely carried rifles, so she couldn't either. The solution was to borrow Larkin's sidearm. That allowed her to carry *two* concealed pistols plus a combat knife. Grenades, one each, went into her side pockets. A hidden radio would allow her to stay in touch. "You know what to do," McKee said. "Keep a low profile, don't shoot anyone you don't have to, and call for air support if the situation turns to shit. Oh, and don't under any circumstances send people into the city after me. That's an order."

Larkin looked at her. She could see the concern in his eyes. "Be careful . . . It takes a long time to train an officer."

McKee frowned. "Don't go soft on me, Desmond. And use Jivani to stay in touch with the Naa."

"Yes, Mommy."

McKee grinned. "That's better . . . I'll see you soon."

Larkin watched her walk away. The cloak made her look smaller. His voice was pitched too low for her to hear. "Take care of yourself," he said. "And watch your six."

McKee, which was to say Cat, had done some horse riding in her younger days. But the dooth named Bigfoot was so big that Highstep had to boost her up onto its back. Then, once McKee managed to throw a leg across the animal's spine, it felt as if her feet were sticking out sideways.

That made staying aboard even more difficult as her fellow riders urged their mounts into the river. All McKee could do was hold on to the equivalent of a saddle horn as Bigfoot carried her through the current and up onto the opposite bank. So far so good.

Then the animal broke into a trot as it hurried to catch up with the other dooths. That's when the up-and-down pounding began—and continued as Storytell led the group through the verdant countryside. Farmers waved as they passed, and the traffic increased once they turned onto the main road. Now they were part of a parade of pedestrians and dooth-drawn carts all headed for the City of Pillars.

In order to enter the town, it was necessary to pass through a palisade constructed of vertical logs. It spanned the gap between two rocky hills and looked very sturdy. There was no line to get in, and the gate was unguarded. That seemed strange.

Where were the beggars, food vendors, and assorted ruffians that should be hanging around the entrance to the city? McKee looked at Storytell, and he shrugged. Hooves made a *clop, clop, clop* sound as they made contact with worn cobblestones. Except for that, an eerie silence hung over the city, and the only sign of life was the skinny pook that eyed them from an alleyway and ran away. Others were present, however. McKee could *feel* their eyes on her. Staring through door cracks, peeking from windows, and eyeing her from heavily shadowed alleys. *But where were the rest?* The city felt empty.

By that time, McKee could see the sandstone pillars from which the city took its name. Most were about a hundred feet tall and too spindly to have any practical value. But a few were crowned with shrines or tattered banners that snapped in a light breeze.

McKee thought the formations might have been shaped by a powerful flow of water at some point in the past. But whatever the mechanism, they gave the city an exotic feel, and McKee wished that Jivani could see it. Her thoughts were interrupted by Storytell. He was speaking via a wire-thin boom mike and a low-power squad-level freq. His voice was tight. "We're being followed."

McKee felt adrenaline surge into her bloodstream. She looked back over her shoulder. There were six mounted warriors, and they were hanging back. Was that simply a matter of coincidence? Or were they there to prevent McKee and her companions from turning around? "There's *more*," Bigeat rumbled. "Left and right."

McKee looked and sure enough . . . Riders were converging on the main thoroughfare from the surrounding side streets. She was about to issue an order when a group of warriors appeared up ahead. They blocked the street. She thought about the pistols . . . And the grenades. But resistance would be futile. There were too many of them. "Pull up," she ordered. "Don't fire. We'll try to talk our way out of this."

None of her scouts answered, but none went for their weapons, either. A warrior mounted on a battle-ready dooth came forward. The Naa was big and armed with a Legion-issue assault rifle. When the Naa was about thirty feet away, he pulled back on the reins. "My name is Stinkkiller," he said matter-of-factly. "But I like to kill Naa, too . . . Especially those who whore themselves out to the slick skins. What do they call you, old man? Assuming you have a name."

Storytell was reaching for his rifle when McKee said, "Stop!" And the voice that emanated from the translator was loud enough for Stinkkiller to hear. McKee threw the hood back, pulled the scarf away, and looked the Naa in the eye. "My name is Nofear Deathgiver . . . And I'm here to speak with Chief of Chiefs Truthsayer. Take us to him or get out of the way." The silence hung heavy in the air, and McKee could feel the weight of Stinkkiller's gaze as her right hand slid toward the butt of her pistol.

CHAPTER: 4

Honor is a fragile, elusive, and subjective thing.
Yet nothing is more important.

WAR COMMANDER OHA WORA-SA
A Treatise on the Clan Wars
Standard year 1947

PLANET HUDATHA

Admiral Dor Nola-Ba stood with hands clasped behind his
back as he stared out through a narrow window. The sky
had been clear an hour earlier. Now a bank of gray clouds
had rolled in from the west, and the temperature had
dropped twenty degrees in a matter of minutes. Such a
change would have been regarded with alarm on a planet
like Orlo II but constituted a nice day on Hudatha.

The extreme changes in the weather were due to the fact
that Hudatha rotated around a star that had a core temperature so high that it resulted in rapid nuclear fusion. The result
was that the sun was well on the way to becoming a red giant.

And making the situation even more complex was the
fact that Hudatha was in a Trojan relationship with a Jovian
binary. The Jovians' centers were separated by roughly
174,000 miles, which meant that their surfaces were only
68,000 miles apart.

If there hadn't been any other planets in the system, Hudatha would have followed the Jovians in a near-perfect orbit. But there *were* other planets. And they tugged on Hudatha enough to make it oscillate around the following Trojan point. The result was a wildly fluctuating climate, a race that had evolved to cope with nearly impossible conditions, and a need to find some new real estate to live on. And that had everything to do with why Nola-Ba was back on his home planet staring out a window. He'd been in command of the fleet sent to cleanse Orlo II and prepare it for colonization.

Nola-Ba's ships had engaged the Human navy, destroyed sixteen of their ships, and chased the rest away. Once that was accomplished, War Commander Tebu Ona-Ka had taken a brigade of troops down to the surface and attacked the city of Riversplit.

Nola-Ba had been powerless to determine how things went subsequent to that. So the fact that most of the brigade had been wiped out wasn't his fault. But would the court of inquiry see it that way? No, probably not, since Ona-Ka had been killed in the fighting, and his uncle was a member of the court.

Nola-Ba's thoughts were interrupted by the sound of a loud knock. It was good manners to announce oneself prior to entering a room. And to do otherwise was dangerous since all male Hudathans were not only armed but extremely paranoid. The latter being an excellent survival trait on a very unpredictable world. Nola-Ba turned. "Enter."

The Arrow Commander was young, of average size, and dressed in his best uniform. It consisted of a waist-length blue jacket, leather cross straps, and white pantaloons. They were tucked into knee-high boots. A holstered sidearm and a back-sword completed the outfit. "I am Arrow Commander Ora-Sa," the youngster said formally. "It would be my honor to escort you to the command chamber."

"Thank you," Nola-Ba replied. "My sword is on the table."

It was called Ka-Killer. A name assigned to it during one of the ancient clan wars. The hilt was worn as befitted an heirloom blade. But the scabbard looked new, having been replaced by Nola-Ba a few years earlier.

Ora-Sa had to carry the weapon because Nola-Ba couldn't. Not unless the court chose to return it. Ora-Sa lifted the weapon off the table without touching the hilt. That was something only a member of the Ba clan could do. "Thank you," he said solemnly. "Now, if you are ready, we will depart."

"Lead the way," Nola-Ba said gravely. "I will follow."

Ora-Sa preceded Nola-Ba out into a generously sized hallway. It was, like most public thoroughfares, just wide enough for four columns of soldiers to march through. A design that harkened back to ancient times when clan wars were frequent, and the government changed hands every two or three years. A continual stream of military personnel passed them headed in the opposite direction. Nola-Ba was a very senior officer, so most of them were obliged to salute. But regardless of rank, all of them could see the sword that Ora-Sa carried cradled in his arms and knew what that meant. Did they pity him? Some did. As for the rest, well, many of them would be happy to see an admiral go down. Especially if they were members of the navy. An open slot at the top of the naval hierarchy would allow as many as half a dozen officers to climb one rung higher on the ladder of promotion.

A pair of elite star guards crashed to attention as Nola-Ba approached, and the iron-clad wood doors opened as if by magic. The chamber beyond was large enough to hold a hundred Hudathans, but no more than a dozen were present. Three of them were members of the tribunal who would judge him. The one Nola-Ba feared the most was War Commander Ona-Ka's uncle. His name was War Commander Ruma-Ka. He was a brutish-looking officer whose eyes lurked below a heavy supraorbital ridge.

The other two officers included a much-decorated army officer named War Commander Duma-Da and Grand Admiral Dura-Da. He was the senior person present, a well-known naval officer, and Nola-Ba's best hope. All wore dress uniforms complete with rows of decorations and clan crests.

The panel was seated behind a sturdy wooden table. They watched impassively as Nola-Ba's sword was laid out in front of them. The fact that it was there, well within reach, was symbolic of the power they had over its owner.

A gong sounded, signaling that the court of inquiry was officially under way. In response to a gesture from Admiral Dura-Da, a military clerk stepped forward to read the charges. "During the attack on the Human world Orlo II, Admiral Dor Nola-Ba had responsibility for naval operations, and reported to War Commander Tebu Ona-Ka. Unfortunately, War Commander Ona-Ka was killed during the fighting on the planet's surface. At that point, Admiral Nola-Ba chose to withdraw, leaving thousands of Hudathan troops stranded on the surface of Orlo II."

Even though he was already familiar with the charge Nola-Ba felt a sudden surge of anger. He was tempted to snatch the family blade off the table and take heads. Given the way it was written, the charge amounted to an allegation of cowardice. And it didn't require a genius to figure out that certain highly placed individuals were trying to protect the Ka clan's reputation. The after-action reports were clear . . . The terrible losses on the ground had been the direct result of errors made by War Commander Ona-Ka.

But Nola-Ba's entire life had been an exercise in discipline. So he sought to suppress the rage and focus his mind. A battle was about to take place, and it would be fought with words rather than razor-sharp steel. "The charge has been read," Grand Admiral Dura-Da intoned. "Both the court and the defendant have had full access to all of the relevant reports. Now, before a formal judgment is reached, oral arguments will be heard. Judicial Officer Ree-Da will speak on behalf of the prosecution."

Ree-Da was an older officer with stooped shoulders and the manner of a clerk. He stood and shuffled forward. He read the words off a data pad without looking up. "As put forth in the final charge, and documented via a written brief, Admiral Nola-Ba failed to provide adequate support for ground troops during the battle for Orlo II. As a result of Admiral Nola-Ba's willful negligence, more than a thousand troops were left behind when the navy was forced to withdraw."

There it was . . . The whitewash the Ka clan was hoping for. If they could blame Nola-Ba for the calamity on Orlo II, their honor would remain unblemished. And because the Ka clan had more political clout than the Ba clan did— there was an excellent chance that the bastards were going to get away with it. Nola-Ba felt light-headed. "In light of the charge leveled against him," Ree-Da continued, "the chief prosecutor recommends that Admiral Nola-Ba be relieved of his command and reduced to rank of warrant officer."

"So noted," Grand Admiral Dura-Da said. "Judicial Officer Duba-Sa will speak for Admiral Nola-Ba."

Duba-Da was young and relatively inexperienced. But he was enthusiastic and the son of a retired naval officer. So Nola-Ba hoped for the best as Duba-Da rose and stepped forward. He looked good in his uniform and spoke without referring to a data pad. "The charges against Admiral Nola-Ba are just that—charges. What the allegation neglects to mention is that Admiral Nola-Ba's vessels were under attack by advance elements of an incoming fleet even as the battle raged on the ground. Because the admiral's ships had to defend themselves, they weren't free to provide the amount of support that War Commander Ona-Ka demanded. Later, as even more Human ships arrived, the admiral had no choice but to withdraw or risk the loss of his entire squadron."

"Thank you," Dura-Da said. "At this time, the court will withdraw to make a final decision."

The members of the court rose, and so did everyone else, except for those already on their feet. The gong sounded, and that meant Nola-Ba could sit. Duba-Da came over to say some encouraging words, but Nola-Ba had seen the look on Ruma-Ka's chiseled face and knew that the army officer was determined to bring him down. Could he face the shame of being broken to warrant officer? It was either that or commit suicide—and Ruma-Ka would like nothing more.

Conscious of the fact that others were watching, Nola-Ba sat with his head up and his back straight while the minutes ticked away. Ten, fifteen, twenty . . . It seemed as if the wait would never end. Finally, after what seemed like an eternity, the court of inquiry reentered the room. Did Ruma-Ka look pleased? Or was that Nola-Ba's imagination?

All he could do was stand and wait as the gong sounded, and the members of court took their seats. "The court has made its finding," Grand Admiral Dura-Da announced. "It is our judgment that the arguments put forward by the defense are largely correct. Admiral Nola-Ba's actions were in keeping with the written as well as verbal orders given to him by War Commander Ona-Ka."

Nola-Ba felt a tremendous wave of relief only to have it snatched away as Dura-Da continued to speak. "However," he said gravely, "had Admiral Nola-Ba assigned a small portion of his force to evacuate stranded troopers, it might have been possible to save hundreds if not a thousand lives. Therefore, it is the finding of this court that Admiral Nola-

Ba's rank be reduced to vice admiral—and he will be relieved of his present command. That is all."

Nola-Ba watched in a state of shock as the officers trooped out of the room, and the gong sounded. Did the finding represent their true opinion? Or was it the result of a compromise in which he had been punished so that the Ka clan could save face? That was the way it appeared.

"Your sword, Admiral," Arrow Commander Ora-Sa said as he returned the weapon. He looked embarrassed.

"Thank you," Nola-Ba said as he took the blade. It felt heavier somehow.

ABOARD THE LIGHT CRUISER *INTAKA* (DEATHBLOW)

Vice Admiral Nola-Ba was seated in one of the high-backed chairs located to either side of the cruiser's U-shaped control room. The captain, pilot, and navigator were positioned at the bottom of the U, where they could view a mosaic of ever-morphing screens on the bulkhead opposite them.

Nola-Ba had been a captain himself and knew what it felt like to have a senior officer present while conning a ship. So he felt some sympathy for Captain Po-Ba but not much. Anyone who couldn't deal with that sort of situation was too weak for command.

The better part of two standard months had passed since the court of inquiry and his day of shame. That had been followed by weeks of politicking as he tried to secure a command. Not an office in the basement of naval headquarters but a *real* command. The kind of assignment that might offer him a chance at redemption.

And finally, after more than a month of worry, the orders came through. He was, in the stilted language of the admiralty, ". . . To take command of Battle Group 761, establish a presence on the planet Savas, and form alliances with the indigenous peoples that would prevent or hinder further colonization of said planet by Humans."

There was more of course. Thirty pages of it. But the essence of the situation was that the Savas system was located at a point where the Hudathan and Human empires overlapped. Eventually, it would be necessary to eradicate both the beings indigenous to Savas and the Humans— because any variable that could be controlled should be controlled. But that would have to wait for a while.

In the meantime, there were only so many resources to work with, and there were thousands of potentially strategic planets, so it wasn't realistic to occupy low-priority worlds like Savas. Not while the Human empire continued to flex its muscles on planets like Orlo II. So Battle Group 761 had been sent to secure Savas until such time as a Class II Occupation Task Force could be sent to "process" the planet.

But first, Nola-Ba had to reach Savas. And that meant slipping through a screen of robotic picket ships. A network of such machines protected the Human empire and was programmed to launch message torpedoes in case of an attack. And, should such a vessel fail to report in on schedule, a navy task force would be dispatched to check on the situation.

So Nola-Ba's first task was to pass through the early-warning system undetected. Failure to do so would result in a swift and most likely fatal naval battle since the increasingly edgy Humans would respond to such an incursion with overwhelming force.

The battle group's fate was in Captain Po-Ba's hands as he gave an order, and the *Intaka* began to accelerate. For Nola-Ba's idea to work, timing would be critical. The plan was for his ships to accelerate in concert, match velocities with the long-period comet that was due to pass through the area, and hide in its tail. If the plan was successful, the Human computers would ascribe sensor anomalies to the comet's passage.

Would it work? Nola-Ba was gambling his life and the

lives of all the people in the battle group that it would. He worked to keep his face blank and forced his body to relax while his ships slid in behind the comet and took up stations on it. The biggest threat to his plan was an old hulk called the *Head Hunter*. He had plans for the destroyer—but were her ancient drives up to the task? So far so good.

It wasn't long before the nearest picket ship showed up on the *Intaka's* detectors. And if the cruiser could "see" the picket ship—then it could "see" the Hudathan vessel as well. And if the picket ship launched a message torp, Nola-Ba would know that he had failed. At that point, they could run or wait for the Humans to arrive. And running was unthinkable.

Every minute felt like a year. Finally, after half an hour had passed, Captain Po-Ba spoke. "Since there was no launch, it seems safe to assume that the trick worked. Secure from battle stations."

Nola-Ba gave no outward sign of the elation he felt because to do so would be to communicate the possibility of defeat. He released the harness and stood. "Very well . . . Carry on." And with that, he left the bridge.

Battle Group 761 had been inside Human-dominated space for the better part of a standard week when Flight Officer Homa-Sa entered the ship's Command Center and crashed to attention. The semicircular space was large enough to accommodate six officers although only three were present. They included Nola-Ba, Captain Po-Ba, and the battle group's Intel officer Spear Commander Aro-Sa. All sat with their backs pressed into shallow niches intended to make them feel more secure because no Hudathan would sit with his back exposed if that could be avoided. "At ease," Nola-Ba said. "Commander Aro-Sa tells me that you had a very successful mission. What did you see?"

"The Humans are present," Homa-Sa said, his eyes on a point over Nola-Ba's head. "But there is only one small settlement."

"The Humans call it Savas Prime," Aro-Sa said contemptuously, as aerial photographs morphed onto the screens around them. "A sty fit for animals."

Nola-Ba had done battle with the "animals," and Aro-Sa hadn't. So as he eyed a dozen roofs and some poorly laid-out streets, he wasn't so dismissive. Some of the Humans were worthy adversaries. "What sort of vehicles did you see?"

"There was a single spaceship," Homa-Sa said. "Plus a couple of air cars and some ground vehicles."

"And that was all?"

"Three message torpedoes and two satellites are orbiting the planet," Homa-Sa responded. "I left them untouched."

Nola-Ba could destroy the town, the torpedoes, and the satellites whenever he chose to. So he had given orders to leave them alone for the moment. "And the moon?"

"The moon was uninhabited. I saw no signs of activity there."

"Good. We can use it," Nola-Ba said.

Po-Ba frowned. "Use the moon? For what?"

"A moon base would enable us to respond quickly if Human ships arrive and to fire on the planet's surface if that becomes necessary," Nola-Ba replied. Po-Ba was a good navy officer, and as such, had a tendency to focus on his ship. He would learn.

Nola-Ba looked at Homa-Sa. "Was your presence detected?"

"No, Admiral. I don't think so."

"Good job. Thank you. Dismissed."

Homa-Sa did an about-face and left the room. "He's a good pilot," Aro-Sa said thoughtfully. "We could use more like him."

"We could use more of *everything*," Nola-Ba said absently.

"Let's take a look at those surface images again . . . We need to establish a base, and I don't want to put it near that town."

After two standard days of preparation, the invasion of Savas began. The first step was to destroy the Human message torpedoes and the satellites that were orbiting the planet. That process took all of forty-six seconds.

Aro-Sa wanted to level Savas Prime, and that would have been easy to do, but Nola-Ba refused. Not out of a sense of compassion but because it might be instructive to interrogate the Humans before killing them.

So instead of destroying Savas Prime, Nola-Ba elected to land a couple of thousand miles away. Not in an assault boat but aboard the elderly *Head Hunter*. The ancient destroyer wasn't designed to land on planetary surfaces, so it would be a one-way trip.

But if the plan was successful, Nola-Ba would have one of the things he needed most, and that was raw materials for the fort he had orders to build. Metal salvaged from the *Head Hunter*'s hull would be used to construct the base, the ship's drives would supply the power to run it, and its weapons would keep the fort safe from harm.

The *Head Hunter*'s commanding officer had been chosen because he was experienced enough to do the job but still qualified as expendable. His name was Spear Commander Ana-Ka and he had chosen to con the ship himself. The destroyer started to shake as it entered the atmosphere. The frame groaned, welds broke, and an alarm began to moan. The sound was similar to what a dying beast might produce. Nola-Ba was of the opinion that officers should never show emotion but couldn't blame Ana-Ka as the retros fired, and he uttered a joyous bellow. The deck tilted, the shots on the screens disappeared, and the *Head Hunter* hit hard. "Shut the drives down," Ana-Ka ordered, "but leave the emergency power on."

Then, with the swagger typical of young officers everywhere, Ana-Ka turned to Nola-Ba. "Welcome to Savas, Admiral . . . I hope you enjoyed the ride."

THE GREAT PANDU DESERT, PLANET SAVAS

The sun was still in the process of parting company with the eastern horizon, the vast expanse of sky was streaked with pink light, and the air was deliciously cool. It was Pudu's favorite time of day. And that was fitting because he was chief of the northern tribe, also called the dawn people. His was the tribe that followed their katha eternally east while the southerners traveled west. The arrangement gave the grass path time to grow tall in between visits.

So there he was, sitting on a one-legged stool and drinking Jithi tea, when a rider approached from the south. The reddish zurna he rode galloped through the sprawl of domed tents and skidded to a stop not far from Pudu's hoga. Guards offered salutes but made no attempt to intercept the rider.

Even at a distance, Pudu could recognize the lanky confidence typical of his firstborn son. His name was Ro Bola, and he was brave to a fault. Would he be chief one day? Sadly, no. That honor would fall to Pudu's number two son.

But Bola didn't know that and entered his father's encampment with the swagger of the proven warrior that he was. Bola was more than six units tall. He had a bony, heat-dispersing head crest. It had been notched three times . . . And each notch symbolized a confirmed kill. His eyes were protected by semitransparent side lids designed to keep dust and sand from getting into them.

Bola paused to give his mother a wildflower that had probably been plucked while riding at full speed. Pudu had been capable of such feats in his younger days—and could remember the way the ground rushed past as he dangled from his zurna.

Having paid his respects to his mother, Bola made his way over to the spot where his father waited. A young female, one of dozens eager to capture Bola's attention, hurried to bring a second stool. Bola thanked her and accepted a cup of tea from a second maiden before turning to his father. "Greetings, wise one . . . I see the light in your eyes. May it never grow dim."

Pudu signaled acknowledgment. "It *will* dim . . . But not today. Welcome home."

Bola took a sip of tea. "I bring news."

Pudu knew that. Why else would his son make the long ride up from his station to the south? But a formal request would please the youngster, and he was willing to oblige. "How interesting . . . Please share it."

"A huge starship landed next to Unda's Belly," Bola said, his eyes bright with excitement.

Because the northerners had been circling Savas for thousands of years, there had been plenty of opportunities to name each river, valley, and, in this case, a softly rounded hill. The crest of which resembled a belly. Or would if the person to whom it belonged was lying on his back and half-buried in the soil. That was the way the god Unda was said to sleep. Then, when Unda decided to roll over, the ground would shake.

So based on his son's description Pudu knew where the landing had taken place. But *why*? The round heads had been content to live in the jungle until now—and their flying machines were rarely seen. Were the off-worlders planning to take more land? If so, that couldn't be tolerated.

All that and more flickered through Pudu's mind as Bola awaited a response. "This is important news indeed," Pudu said gravely. "You were correct to come here as quickly as possible. Tell me everything you saw."

So Bola described the ship which, even allowing for some exaggeration, was clearly larger than anything the northerners had seen before. But of equal importance was the way he described the creatures who emerged from the machine. "They were *huge*," Bola said. "I estimate that each one of them weighs the amount that *two* warriors would! And they have head crests, like we do, only less pronounced."

"So they aren't Human."

"No, they look different," Bola replied. "But they have lots of machines—and what I took to be powerful weapons."

That was very interesting indeed. At present, there were two types of weapons on Savas. Those manufactured by the jungle-dwelling Jithi—and those the round heads brought in. He knew that doing so was illegal according to Human laws, but that didn't seem to stop them.

So if the newcomers planned to sell weapons, it was important to not only acquire some but prevent the southern tribe from doing likewise. And the most obvious way to accomplish those objectives was to kill the star creatures and take what he wanted. That wouldn't be easy, of course . . . But *everything* was hard. He would think. Then, when the time was right, the sword would fall.

SAVAS BASE 001

Two standard weeks had passed since the landing. Engines growled as the Hudathans worked to improve their new base. Thanks to the crawlers that had been stored inside of the *Head Hunter*'s hangar bay, Admiral Nola-Ba's ground party had been able to slice the top of the hill off. Now, having paved the raw surface with tilelike metal gratings, the Hudathans had a landing pad. It was large enough to handle two shuttles at once, which meant Nola-Ba could rotate personnel with the ships orbiting above. And that was good for morale. Especially given how primitive the planet was.

The troops were holding up well, however, thanks to skin that turned to a reflective white when exposed to the desert sun. So conditions that might have brought Humans to their knees had done very little to slow the work, a fact that was very much in evidence as Nola-Ba continued his daily walkabout.

Tons of soil removed from the top of the hill was spilling down its flanks. By that time, tunnels had been driven into the heart of the mound. The walls were reinforced with sheets of durasteel salvaged from the *Head Hunter*. And once the passageways were completed, the effort to create spaces for the ship's fusion reactors, armory, and living quarters would begin.

As Nola-Ba's walk took him past the steadily dwindling destroyer, he arrived in front of a specially designed tower. It was being used to drill a well, and the water was there, or so his engineers claimed. And once they tapped the aquifer, the liquid would be pumped into the hill via a system of buried pipes.

Out past the drill rig, Nola-Ba came to the spot where an earthen embankment was under construction. The plan was to use material removed from the hill's interior to complete the barrier. Once the berm was finished, it would encircle the hill. Then it would be time to remove six energy cannons from the *Head Hunter* and install them in hardened bunkers. Power for the weapons would be supplied by fusion reactors inside the hill. At that point, the first element of Nola-Ba's orders would be complete.

Of course, building the fort might be the easy part. He was also supposed to establish positive relationships with the indigenous peoples—and members of the Paguumi species had been lurking around the area since the landing.

Nola-Ba's thoughts were interrupted by a radio transmission from Captain Ana-Ka. "The executive officer on the *Intaka* informs me that a dust storm is headed our way. I recommend that we pull the patrols in and stop work until it passes."

That was regrettable since Nola-Ba wanted to use every minute available to him. But he knew that Ana-Ka was right and gave the necessary orders. All of the personnel on the ground were to take cover in what remained of the *Head Hunter* and stay there until the storm had passed. That included him. The wind had already begun to pick up, and Nola-Ba was being pelted with grains of sand by the time he reached the safety of the destroyer.

Originally, there had been only a few ways in and out of the hull. But thanks to all the salvage work, Nola-Ba could enter through any number of holes now. Guards were posted at each, and Nola-Ba acknowledged a salute as he stepped through a rectangular opening. From there, it was just a few paces to an internal hatch and the corridor beyond. The lifts had been removed, so it was necessary to climb an emergency ladder to reach the main deck. About half of the controls on the bridge were lit. The rest were permanently dark.

Captain Ana-Ka saw Nola-Ba enter and pointed at one of the few screens that were still operational. The camera was pointed toward the drilling rig, which was almost entirely obscured by flying sand. "It's getting worse. According to the *Intaka*'s XO, the dust cloud is about five thousand feet tall and fifty miles wide."

Nola-Ba nodded. "I hope such storms are the exception rather than the rule. What about our patrols? Have they returned?"

"Yes, Admiral," Ana-Ka replied. "All of our people are accounted for."

"Excellent. I'll be in my cabin if you need me." After Nola-Ba left the bridge, he took advantage of an emergency ladder to reach the deck below. The emergency lighting flickered occasionally but was sufficient. Once in his cabin, Nola-Ba had to use a hand torch in order to see.

It was impossible to get any work done the way things were—so Nola-Ba gave himself permission to enjoy a rare nap. It felt good to stretch out on the narrow bunk and close his eyes. It wasn't long until sleep pulled him down into a wonderful dream. He was young again . . . And walking through one of the many villages that belonged to the Ba clan. Things weren't entirely right, however. He could see people he'd known from childhood, but they couldn't see him.

Still, it was pleasant to walk up the path past the granary and the blacksmith shop to the barns and the stronghold beyond. It was made of stacked stone and was the place to which his ancestors could retreat when another clan attacked. He followed a walkway up the front door and pushed it open. Apparently, his father could see him because he spoke. "Admiral Nola-Ba? Can you hear me? We're under attack!"

Nola-Ba awoke with a jerk as Captain Ana-Ka said his name again. "Admiral Nola-Ba . . . The locals are inside, repeat *inside* the ship, killing the crew." The words were followed by the staccato rattle of gunfire and a bellow of pain. Then the intercom went dead.

Nola-Ba swore, rolled off the bunk, and was forced to confront the truth. The mistake was his. What was the saying? "To overestimate oneself is to underestimate the enemy." The beings he had written off as primitive nomads had been watching for days. What's more, they understood what Nola-Ba intended to do and were trying to prevent it.

So rather than attack a clearly superior force, the indigs

waited for the kind of storm they not only understood but were evolved to cope with. Then, using the flying sand for cover, they'd been able to approach the destroyer unobserved. And with more than a dozen entrances to choose from, all they had to do was kill a sentry and enter the ship. It was a possibility that could have and should have been anticipated.

But the full extent of Nola-Ba's self-recrimination would have to wait. The first order of business was to grab his weapons and join the fight. Nola-Ba's pistol belt was hanging from a hook. After buckling it on, he turned to a locker. Ka-Killer was waiting inside. He pulled the weapon free of its sheath and opened the hatch.

That was a mistake. Nola-Ba felt a searing pain as a spear slid along his left side. The Hudathan parried the shaft with his sword and kicked the Paguumi with a huge boot. The force of the blow sent the local backpedaling into the opposite bulkhead. The warrior was a fierce-looking creature with a head crest, bladelike nose, and a black eye patch.

Nola-Ba heard a grunt of expelled air as the Paguumi hit the steel bulkhead and took the opportunity for a follow-up. Ancient steel punctured alien flesh. Nola-Ba gave Ka-Killer a twist to maximize the internal damage. Then he jerked the weapon up before pulling it free. The Paguumi clutched his abdomen and collapsed.

It had been a long time since Nola-Ba had killed anyone face-to-face, but the skills were still there—and Nola-Ba heard himself utter the traditional Hudathan war cry: "Blood!" The war cry was echoed from down the corridor, which meant that others were still in the fight.

Nola-Ba shouted, *"To me!"* And seconds later, two crew members appeared out of the gloom. One was armed with a combination fire axe/crowbar acquired from a damage-control locker—and the other was clutching one of the short, three-barreled shotguns kept in racks throughout the ship. "Follow me," Nola-Ba said grimly. "It's time to hunt." The crewmen replied with growls of approval.

Having heard fighting over the intercom, Nola-Ba figured that the bridge would be a good place to go, both to engage the enemy and regain control of the ship. So he led the crewmen over to a ladder and began to climb. The rungs were slippery with blood.

As Nola-Ba arrived on the main deck, he could hear bursts of automatic fire, interspersed with the *pop, pop, pop* of single-shot weapons and warbling war cries. As Nola-Ba emerged from the alcove where the ladder terminated, he found himself behind a group of Paguumi warriors. They were facing the bridge, which remained under siege.

Nola-Ba drew his pistol and opened fire. Two warriors fell, and the rest turned. As they fired, Nola-Ba heard something buzz past his right ear. So he pulled the trigger again, heard the handgun click empty, and allowed it to fall. The crewman who had been armed with the axe was down, but the rating with the shotgun remained on his feet. They moved forward together.

A warrior came to meet him, and Nola-Ba felt the impact as the sword struck the Paguumi and sliced through his neck. There was a momentary fountain of blood as the animal's head flew free. That was followed by a meaty *thump* when the body hit the deck.

The shotgun was firing by then, and the last warrior was torn to shreds as dozens of lead slugs tore through his flesh. He staggered, lost his balance, and fell into a pool of blood.

Nola-Ba stepped over the corpse. Half a dozen bodies representing both races were sprawled outside the control area. Consoles, screens, and the surrounding bulkheads were pockmarked with bullet holes and splashed with blood.

Captain Ana-Ka was lying on the floor with *two* spears protruding from his chest, and an engineering officer lay facedown on the deck. The only member of the bridge crew to survive was the navigator. He emerged from behind the holo tank holding a pistol. His voice sounded like a rock crusher in low gear. "Sorry, Admiral . . . They took us by surprise."

And whose fault was that? Nola-Ba asked himself. The answer was obvious. His. But, much as it troubled him to do so, he would have to blame Ana-Ka for the debacle. It was either that or accept the blame himself, and that would be pointless. Plus it was a way to get back at the Ka clan. A group of five troopers arrived, and one of them saluted. "The ship is secure, Admiral."

"Good. How many people did we lose?"

"It's too early to say for sure," the noncom replied. "But I've seen at least twenty Hudathan bodies—not counting the ones here."

Nola-Ba winced. More than twenty dead. He would avenge them.

CHAPTER: 5

There can be no doubt that the slick skins wanted north to fight south and opened the tunnel through the Towers of Algeron for that purpose.

LOOKBACK THINKSEE
A History of My People
Standard year 2727

PLANET ALGERON, CITY OF PILLARS

McKee could feel the sun on her face, smell the sweet-sour stink of the dooths around her, and hear the wild thumping of her heart. The warrior named Stinkkiller was staring at her. Had he killed Humans? Yes, if his name was any indication. People she knew? Possibly. Her hand was hidden beneath a long cloak. It was in contact with one of two concealed pistols. "There are stories about a female slick skin named Nofear Deathgiver. They say that when Fastblade Oneeye and his warriors attacked the village of Doothdown, she held them off with a handful of soldiers."

"*And* females," McKee said. "Their mates had gone south to take part in the Battle of Bloodyriver. They fought with knives, with axes, and with shovels."

"I fought in the Battle of Bloodyriver," Stinkkiller said. "Your soldiers were poorly led. We killed many slick skins that day. And your machine people, too."

"So maybe the killing should stop. That's why we're here . . . To speak with Chief of Chiefs Truthsayer."

Stinkkiller was silent for a moment. Then he nodded. "Follow me."

McKee's hand came off the pistol as Stinkkiller pulled his dooth around and led the procession of riders deeper into the nearly empty city. Stone pillars rose here and there, some bare, some topped with wind-ripped flags. The streets turned and twisted without any apparent rhyme or reason, and it would be easy to get lost.

McKee expected her guide to lead them to a large structure commensurate with Truthsayer's rank and reputation. Such was not the case. When they arrived, it was at a modest, two-story structure notable only for the number of heavily armed males hanging around. The warriors watched with considerable interest as Stinkkiller pulled up in front of the building, slid to the ground, and invited McKee to do likewise. She felt lonely and frightened as her boots hit the ground. Could she count on Storytell? Maybe . . . And maybe not. Venturing into the City of Pillars without a squad of T-1s had been foolhardy. She realized that now but couldn't back out. All she could do was look confident and hope for the best.

A group of warriors were blocking the front door—but they hurried to get out of the way as Stinkkiller approached. As McKee passed between them, she could feel their hatred. And that was to be expected in the wake of the incredible slaughter that had taken place to the north.

Hinges squealed as Stinkkiller pushed the wooden door open, and McKee followed him into a dimly lit interior. It smelled like beer, food, and dirty clothes. A circular stairway led down to a subterranean living area, which was lit with lanterns and dominated by a central fireplace. A small dooth-dung fire burned on the hearth, and the smoke rose through a funnel-shaped flue. And there, sitting on a wooden chair, was a small Naa with a hunched back. He was reading a leather-bound book and looked up as the visitors descended the stairs.

McKee assumed he was a scholar, one of Truthsayer's advisors perhaps, until Stinkkiller made the introductions. "Chief Truthsayer . . . This is Nofear Deathgiver. She would like to speak with you on behalf of her leaders."

Truthsayer put the book aside and stood. In marked contrast with most adult males, he stood no more than five and a half feet tall. Black markings interrupted his otherwise orange fur, and his eyes were exceptionally large. McKee saw what might have been amusement in them. "Not what you were expecting?" he inquired. "Well, the feeling is mutual."

McKee laughed and felt herself drawn to the chief as he honored her with the forearm-to-forearm grip. "You are known to me," he said. "Come, join me by the fire."

So they sat by the fire while Stinkkiller, Storytell, and the others looked on. Regardless of what happened, there wouldn't be any secrets. Stories would be told. "So," Truthsayer began, "were you at the mesa?"

"Yes."

"Your people fought bravely."

"As did yours."

"But we lost."

"Yes."

"So what is there to talk about?"

McKee shrugged. "I am not authorized to negotiate with you. Only to invite you to negotiate."

Truthsayer frowned. "But if they sent you, they must have something in mind."

"I hope so," McKee replied fervently. "Lives were lost bringing this message to you."

"Yes," Truthsayer said sadly. "It seems that everything must be paid for with blood."

McKee broke the ensuing silence. "So? Would you be willing to go north? To meet with General Vale?"

Truthsayer's eyes came back to meet hers. "Your troops are camped on Fishtrap Island. Can you reach them by radio?"

McKee swallowed. She had assumed that the locals would notice the company's presence—but it was a shock to find out that *everyone* knew where they were. "Yes, I can."

"Good. I suggest that you order them to move. There's an old mill just north of town. You can meet them there. I will give you my answer by tomorrow morning."

All sorts of thoughts chased each other through McKee's mind. Was Truthsayer trying to trick her? Trying to send the company to a place where he could attack it?

Truthsayer smiled knowingly. "No, Deathgiver . . . It isn't a trick. Battles have consequences. Especially for those who lose. I still have a strong following. But other chiefs want what power I have left or want to punish me for our defeat. A coalition has been formed, and they know I'm here. In a day, two at most, they will arrive here. That's why most of the city's residents left. So I have no choice but to accompany you or to begin a journey to nowhere. Either way, it would be prudent for you to head north quickly. Do I make myself clear?"

The last was spoken not in the manner of the scholar that Truthsayer appeared to be but with the hard-edged assurance of a general. And what he said squared with what McKee had heard during the trip south. There were those who hated Truthsayer. Still, his explanation could constitute a distortion if not lie. All she could do was make a decision and hope for the best. "We'll be there," she said. "At the mill."

Truthsayer looked into her eyes. "Leadership is difficult."

"Yes, it is. But why wait? You could make the decision now."

"The decision isn't up to me alone," Truthsayer answered simply. "I must consult with others."

That made sense. McKee stood. "It was an honor to meet you."

"The honor was mine," Truthsayer said. "Go to the mill. Then, one way or another, it will be time to ride."

McKee could feel the hostility around her as she left the building—and heard the warriors laugh as she struggled to climb up into the saddle. Then, with Storytell leading the way, McKee and her companions followed the winding streets back to the north gate.

During the trip, McKee contacted Larkin and ordered him to take a look at the latest satellite imagery. She figured that if Truthsayer was preparing an attack, there would be some sign of it on the aerial photos.

It took about thirty minutes to reach the old mill. It was sited next to a stream. While part of the old waterwheel was still in place, the interior of the building had been ravaged by fire. But the walls were thick enough to make the building defensible, and McKee hoped that was a sign of good faith on Truthsayer's part.

It was starting to get dark by that time, and the group was too small to defend itself against even a dozen attackers, so McKee ordered the Naa to take their dooths inside. All the party could do was remain alert and wait for the company to show up. Were they under observation? McKee would have been willing to bet that they were.

A good hour passed before Larkin made radio contact. The satellite imagery was clean, and the company was on the way. A drone arrived ten minutes later, speared McKee with a beam of light, and proceeded to explore the ruins.

McKee felt a profound sense of relief as Larkin and lead elements of the company arrived soon thereafter. Now, come what may, she was with her command. Once the defensive perimeter was in place Larkin came looking for her. "There's a possibility that Truthsayer will join us in the next hour or so," McKee told him. "If he does, good. If not, we'll head north. So feed everybody and tell them to be ready."

There had been a time when Larkin would have said something snarky as a way to push back against authority, any authority, even hers. But responsibilities that went with his new rank had begun to change him. "We did as much maintenance as we could. Most of the T-1s are in pretty good shape. Oso's right arm actuator is acting up though . . . I'd appreciate it if you could take a look."

Cat Carletto had a degree in cybernetics, which meant Andromeda McKee could make repairs that most techs couldn't. That was both a blessing and a curse. A blessing when it kept a cyborg running—and a curse when it cost her some much-needed sleep. McKee was about to agree when she heard movement behind her. She turned to find Andy standing there. "Hold that position," the robot said. "I'll get a two shot."

McKee sighed. Andy would have to be dealt with. The question was *how?* The combot accompanied her as McKee and Jivani made their rounds.

Once the circuit was complete, McKee inspected Oso's actuator and realized that it would have to be replaced. And, given the fact that Truthsayer could arrive at any moment, there wasn't enough time in which to make the repair. So she waited. But thirty minutes passed without any sign that the Naa leader planned to come. Maybe she should have given him a radio. But that would enable the Naa to monitor the company's communications.

McKee was still thinking about that when a distant boom was heard, and a column of black smoke rose over the City of Pillars. Truthsayer's enemies were shelling the town. Preparing to invade it. That's the way it appeared anyway, and it wouldn't be long before they realized that the place was undefended. So what did that mean to her? Since Truthsayer's enemies were *her* enemies, they would pursue the company and attack it. Should she run? Hell yes, she should run.

But what about the mission? What if Truthsayer had been delayed for some reason? Worse yet, what if his enemies captured him? All because she left too quickly? Thirty minutes. That was the answer. She would wait for another half an hour, and if Truthsayer hadn't arrived by then, she would leave.

So as time passed, McKee switched back and forth between the pictures the drones sent back hoping to see the riders she was waiting for. Andy was staring at her, so she ordered it to get some pictures of a dooth's rear end, and laughed as the robot departed. Finally, after what seemed like forever, the half hour was up. And Truthsayer was nowhere to be seen.

The shelling had stopped, and a steady stream of refugees was pouring out of the city via the north gate. They were herding animals, pushing handcarts, and carrying packs. These were the people who had stayed behind hoping that the attack would never take place. Now, as a pall of gray smoke drifted over the city, it appeared that at least part of it was on fire. So the time had come to leave. McKee knew that but couldn't bring herself to do it.

Instead, she sent Storytell out to speak with the refugees in hopes that they might know where Truthsayer was. But none of them did. By the time he returned, another fifteen minutes had elapsed, and darkness was starting to fall. So McKee summoned Larkin and gave the necessary orders. "Take the company about twenty miles north. Look for a place that we can defend and throw a high berm around it."

"And what will *you* be doing?" he inquired pointedly. There was no "ma'am" in the sentence and never would be whenever they were alone.

"I'm going to wait a bit longer. I'll keep the Naa warriors. You take Jivani."

Larkin frowned. "This is bullshit . . . You know that."

McKee grinned. "We're legionnaires, remember? *Legio bullshit nostra.*"

Larkin laughed. Then he looked serious again. "Don't get killed, McKee . . . Our people are counting on you, and I'm not good enough to get them back on my own."

It was the most honest thing Larkin had ever said to her, and McKee knew it was probably true. Larkin was willing to follow orders most of the time, and to force others to do so as well, but he wasn't very imaginative. "That isn't true," she lied. "But don't worry . . . It's hard to get rid of me."

So Larkin took the RAVs, robots, and legionnaires north while McKee, Vella, and the Naa remained behind. And that's where they were, waiting near the mill, when Andy appeared out of the gloom. Apparently, the robot realized that out of sight was out of mind and was determined to stay close. And that, she knew, was what any synth would do. The damned thing was a threat and one she would have to neutralize.

McKee's thoughts were interrupted by a flurry of gunshots. Refugees scattered as a group of riders appeared. They were whipping their dooths, and the reason was obvious. *More* Naa could be seen in the distance, firing as they came.

The light was nearly gone, but McKee could see Stinkkiller in the lead with a diminutive figure on a dooth slightly behind him. *Truthsayer!* She gave orders over the radio as she waved her Naa back into the shadows. "Let the first group pass—kill the rest."

McKee spoke to Vella over the intercom as Truthsayer and his party thundered past. "Fire a grenade followed by the fifty."

"Roger that," Vella replied.

McKee switched to night vision and chinned the radio to the company freq. "Get ready," she said. "Don't fire until Vella does."

The oncoming warriors were so intent on catching up with the chief of chiefs that they weren't aware of the ambush until Vella's grenade landed immediately in front of them. There was a brilliant flash of light followed by a boom—and the shrill screams that dooths made as they went down.

The next rank of warriors was largely untouched but moving so fast they couldn't stop. The mounts tripped over bodies and fell, throwing their riders onto the ground. That was when McKee opened fire, and her Naa companions did likewise. They were from the north and quite happy to slaughter southerners. The whole thing was over seconds later. "Cease fire!" McKee ordered. "Save your ammunition . . . We're going to need it."

Then, with Vella leading the way, the party streamed north. Stinkkiller, Truthsayer, and their warriors were waiting half a mile up the road. Once greetings had been exchanged, Truthsayer spoke. "You waited."

"Yes."

"Thank you for what you did . . . Although it pains me to see more southerners die for nothing."

"Maybe the negotiations will go well."

"Maybe," Truthsayer said doubtfully. "I was trying to convince two chiefs of that when their warriors attacked the city. The talks were a trick . . . A way to keep me busy while they attempted to surround me."

"But it didn't work."

"No, we fought our way clear."

"I sent most of the company north," McKee said. "We need to catch up."

"They will follow," Truthsayer warned. "And there will be hundreds of them."

"Understood," McKee said. "Let's ride."

They rode through the rest of that night and into the early morning, pausing only to water the dooths and check their back trail. Meanwhile, McKee had been on the radio to Larkin. "Get the duty officer at Fort Camerone on the horn," she instructed. "Tell him or her that we need a dustoff. Over."

"How soon? Over."

"Let's make it for 1500 hours standard. We'll send Truthsayer and his people out first. So tell them to have Colonel Cavenaugh or the equivalent thereof on the first fly-form. Then we'll need a Titan or two Vulcans to bring the rest of the company out. Over."

"Roger that," Larkin replied. "Over."

As McKee and her companions neared the end of their journey, the rising sun revealed a layer of ground fog that lay like a gauzy shroud over the land and shivered when a breeze slid in to touch it. The hill the company had camped on seemed to float above the mist. Raw earth marked the berm Larkin had thrown up. And there, at the very top of the mound, broken columns marked the spot where a temple once stood.

The ground fog parted in front of them as McKee led the party up the slope and over a timber bridge. She saw that T-1s were posted around the perimeter, fighting positions had been dug behind blocks of granite, and the excavation work was still under way. Larkin had done an excellent job, and McKee made a mental note to tell him that. He was mounted on a T-1, and as the noncom came forward, his expression was grim. "Uh-oh," McKee said. "What's wrong?"

"Fort Camerone is socked in. It'll be at least four hours before they can launch aircraft. Maybe more."

McKee looked up at broken clouds and patches of blue sky. It appeared that the problem was up north. "Damn . . . At least some of the bad guys will be here by then."

"Yeah."

"Okay, we'll make the best of it. You chose an excellent site—and I like the way the defenses are laid out. Let's place the RAVs so we can take full advantage of their firepower—and equip four T-1s with shoulder launchers."

Larkin nodded and eyed the group behind her. "I'm glad you're back," he said simply. "And I hope the bastard is worth it." Then he was gone.

McKee jumped to the ground and went over to explain the situation to Truthsayer. He listened and shrugged. "We will fight. The gods will decide."

McKee wasn't about to place her fate in the hands of the capricious gods. So she sent Stinkkiller and his warriors south to act as pickets. She considered sending more but figured that mixing northerners with southerners was a recipe for disaster. Then it was time to make the rounds and check to make sure her squad leaders were up to speed.

McKee had just completed a full circuit when Jivani appeared with two MREs. They sat on a block of granite, and McKee listened as the xenoanthropologist talked about an ancient religion she'd heard of. It was, she felt certain, connected with the ruins. And that's why she had spent the last few hours taking hundreds of pictures. Images that could be compared to those of sites elsewhere on the planet. "What if all of them were similar?" Jivani wanted to know. "What if the ruins in the north matched those in the south? That would imply an ancient civilization that spanned both hemispheres!"

Jivani's enthusiasm was contagious, and for a moment, McKee found herself caught up in a grand vision of what might have been. Then she remembered where she was and why. The poop was about to hit the fan . . . And the dustoff would give her an opportunity to ship the civilian out.

The first sign of trouble came when a flurry of gunshots were heard from the south, and Stinkkiller came galloping

back from the woods with his warriors streaming along behind. Hooves clattered over wood as the dooths crossed the
bridge and entered the compound. Then, with nowhere to
go, the animals began to mill around.

"They're coming," Stinkkiller proclaimed as he dropped
to the ground. "All but two of them. They're dead."

It was said with the same élan a general might use to
announce a major victory. McKee managed to repress a
smile. "Excellent. How many are there?"

"At least fifty, with more arriving every minute."

"Well done. Please put someone in charge of your mounts
and take the rest of your warriors to the north side of the
perimeter."

"Why *north?*" Stinkkiller demanded haughtily. "The
enemy is gathering to the south."

"Because I expect some of the enemy to circle around,"
McKee explained patiently. "And we'll need some of our
finest warriors there to meet them."

Stinkkiller was oblivious to the blatant flattery. "Yes," he
said. "That makes sense."

"Good. And please do everything in your power to keep
Truthsayer alive."

Stinkkiller frowned. "He will insist on fighting."

"I assumed as much. Please do what you can."

The Naa nodded soberly. "I will."

Night had fallen once more, and any sign of light was
bound to draw sniper fire. The cyborgs had their sensors to
rely on. But if the Legion's bio bods weren't inside one of the
two carefully shielded cooking stations, or in the command
bunker, they had to wear their helmets in order to navigate
the compound. Which was why everything McKee saw had
a ghostly green glow.

After completing her rounds, McKee followed a dirt
ramp down into the command bunker. That's where the
first-aid station, the com center, and the ammo box labeled

"CO" were located. McKee didn't have time to sit on the box but wished she did.

The com tech spotted McKee and shook her head. "Nothing new, ma'am. Fort Camerone is still socked in."

McKee thanked her and paused to chat with the senior medic before heading back up. She arrived on the surface just in time to see a fireball rise from the south, climb like a miniature sun, and start to fall. "Catapults!" someone shouted, and McKee swore. Such weapons might be primitive, but the Naa had used them to good effect in the past. There was a splash of fire as the artificial comet landed twenty feet short of the defensive ditch.

That stimulated shouts of derision from legionnaires and Naa alike. But McKee knew the enemy would make the necessary corrections, and the chances were good that the next fireball would land inside the perimeter. "This is Alpha-One to Alpha-Five . . . Target that launcher and take it out. Over."

Larkin had placed Sergeant Rico Sager in charge of the T-1s that were armed with rockets. He said, "This is Five . . . Roger that. Over."

A minute passed. Then *two* fireballs rose in concert. Each T-1 carried an onboard computer. And they could commutate with each other. That meant they could link up, share observed data, and calculate where the catapults were located. Once a consensus was reached, one cyborg fired two rockets. Two, because there was no reason to expend more ordnance than was absolutely necessary.

The fire-and-forget weapons shot out of the cyborg's shoulder "cans" and disappeared into the night. Twin booms were heard even as the incoming fireballs landed. One splashed the ditch, and one came down inside the compound, where it scored a direct hit on a Naa warrior. He screamed and ran in circles until his best friend shot him in the head. McKee winced but understood. The liquid fire couldn't be extinguished with water and had already burned its victim beyond the point where he would be able to recover. So she turned her attention back to the south. McKee waited, and after three minutes had passed, she chinned her mike. "Alpha-One to Alpha-Five and team. Well done. Over."

Outside of occasional harassing fire, the rest of the night passed without incident. As dawn approached, McKee gave the order to "Stand to." For thousands of years, Human beings had chosen to attack at dawn, hoping to catch the enemy sleeping. Or if not sleeping, then groggy and therefore vulnerable. And it had been no different on Algeron.

So as the sun raised its fiery head, McKee was anything but surprised as hundreds of dooth-mounted warriors poured out of the tree line to the south. They screamed incoherent war cries as they fired on the run. "Pick your targets," McKee said calmly. "Ready, aim, fire!"

The massed fire from the Legion's bio bods and the Naa warriors was effective by itself. But the bursts of .50 caliber fire from the T-1s were simply devastating. Dooths and warriors alike fell in a welter of blood as more Naa joined the fray. They were riding in a counterclockwise fashion, and each rotation brought them closer to the berm. Humans and Naa alike fell as a hail of bullets swept across the top of the hill. McKee chinned her mike as she fired at the nearest attacker. "Use grenades! Make 'em pay."

And pay the attackers did, as explosions blew bloody gaps in the circling horde. As the enemy began to pull back, a com tech spoke into McKee's ear. "This is Alpha-Five-Four . . . We have a Titan inbound. ETA twelve minutes. Over."

"This is One," McKee responded. "Advise the pilot that the LZ is hot. Over."

"Roger that," the tech replied. "Over."

McKee half expected to hear that the Titan had turned

back, but that wasn't the case. And as the tubby VTOL appeared out of the north, it was a sight to see. The cyborg's miniguns burped intermittently as his or her waist gunners fired at ground targets.

As McKee switched frequencies, she could hear the pilot talking to her com tech. "Get your people ready to board. Wounded first. I'll give you three minutes, then I'm outta here. Over."

Larkin was getting things ready. Uninjured dooths were being herded out of the LZ while the construction droids towed two dead animals away. McKee ran over to the spot where a small group of walking wounded and three stretchers were waiting. Truthsayer was ready to go. "My warriors want to take their dooths!" he shouted, as the huge fly-form arrived over the compound.

"That's a negative," McKee said emphatically. "There isn't enough room, and we don't have time to secure them even if there was."

Truthsayer nodded as the fly-form touched down, and the artificial wind created by its rotors blew dust in every direction. "Thank you," Truthsayer said, as he extended a hand. "You are worthy of your name."

McKee accepted the forearm-to-forearm grip and looked him in the eye. "As are you, Chief . . . As are you."

The stretchers were going aboard when a heavily loaded Jivani arrived to give McKee a hug before turning to trot up the ramp. Truthsayer and his warriors were the last on, and as McKee watched them board, she saw Colonel Cavenaugh. He was dressed to the nines and apparently eager to receive the chief of chiefs. That made sense, of course, since the opportunity to deliver Truthsayer to General Vale was too good to pass up.

Engines roared as the ramp went up, and the cyborg took off. The fly-form made a huge target, and McKee could hear dozens of telltale pings as dozens of bullets hit the VTOL.

That was followed by the stutter of automatic fire as Mc-Kee's legionnaires responded in kind.

Then the Titan's miniguns went to work as the fully loaded cyborg began a ponderous turn. And that was when a streak of light jumped out of the trees and struck the ship. There was what sounded like a clap of thunder as the number three engine exploded, and McKee was left to watch in horror as the fly-form began to heel over, and went in hard. Severed rotors scythed through the air, the fuselage broke in two, and a fuel tank exploded into flame.

It didn't take a genius to realize that the ship had been destroyed by a shoulder-launched missile. Booty captured from a Legion outpost most likely—and saved for just such an opportunity. McKee felt sick to her stomach but she couldn't allow herself to barf, cry, or ask why. There might be survivors. If so, every second would count.

McKee chinned her mike. "This is Alpha-One . . . First squad to me. We're going to check the wreck for survivors. Alpha-One-Three will assume command in my absence. Let's go. Over."

Though not a member of the first squad, Vella appeared at her side. And as McKee took her place on his back, Sergeant Payton and the remaining members of his unit appeared. Foy and Gan had been killed back at Graveyard Pass. But the noncom still had two bio bods and three cyborgs under his command. It would have been nice to take a larger force, of course. But, if the southerners launched still another attack, Larkin would require every fighter he had left.

"Okay," McKee said over the squad freq. "We're going to run out there, search for survivors, and haul ass. Any questions? No? Let's do this thing."

Vella led the rest of them over the wooden bridge and down the slope beyond. It appeared that the southerners were so stunned by their own success that they had been slow to follow up. But now, dooth-mounted warriors were starting to emerge from the tree line and clearly intended to take possession of the wreck and the booty it might contain. Vella ran to cut them off. He fired, and McKee did as well.

A dooth and its rider went down, but the contest was far from one-sided. Puffs of dirt flew up all around, and McKee could hear bullets striking the T-1's armor as *more* riders appeared. By then it was apparent that McKee had bitten off more than one squad could chew. So she was going to abort the mission and run like hell when a series of explosions marched along the tree line. Trees, parts of trees, and what might have been body parts were tossed high into the air only to come cartwheeling down.

Rockets! Larkin had ordered the T-1s back in the compound to fire on the woods. And the barrage gave her legionnaires the opportunity they needed. They swept in to take up positions bordering the south side of the crash site. "This is Alpha-One . . . Three-One and Three-Three will dismount and help me search for survivors. Everyone else will defend the wreck. Over."

So with Payton in charge, and four T-1s to do his bidding, McKee felt the situation was under control as her boots hit the ground. Corporal Deon Smith arrived seconds later, closely followed by Private Flo Hyatt. "Smith, I want you to go forward. Find the emergency access hatch, open it up, and jerk the pilot's brain box.

"Hyatt . . . You and I are going in. Keep your head on a swivel and run your recorder. The Intel people are going to run this stuff frame by frame."

Smith took off at a trot, while McKee led Hyatt toward the crash site. Scraps of the fiber-composite fuselage were scattered everywhere. What remained of engine three lay thirty yards west of the main wreck and was still burning. The Titan's cigar-shaped fuselage had been bent into the shape of a Chinese fortune cookie. The split between the two halves offered a way in.

A headless body had been thrown clear. It was dressed in a flight suit so McKee knew it belonged to the crew chief or one of the door gunners. She checked to make sure that her camera was on and recording as she scanned the legionnaire's name tag. ORKOV. The graves registration people would want to know.

AXE at the ready, McKee stepped over the corpse and approached the badly contorted hatch. If any passengers had survived the crash, they would be armed and understandably trigger-happy. So she called out. "This is McKee! Don't shoot . . . We're coming in."

There was no answer other than the occasional groan of tortured metal as the wreck continued to settle. McKee heard a burst of gunfire from behind her and knew that Sergeant Payton and his T-1s were earning their pay.

There was a profound emptiness at the pit of McKee's stomach as she brushed past the pintle-mounted minigun and entered the hull. If there were survivors, where were they? She called out again, but there was no response.

McKee turned left and was barely able to squeeze through the narrow gap that opened into the cargo hold. Sunlight streamed in through dozens of ragged holes to form pools of gold on the bodies sprawled within. It looked like a slaughterhouse.

The first thing McKee noticed was that Naa bodies had been tossed every which way. That didn't make sense at first. Then she remembered that the ride on the Titan was a first for the locals . . . And someone, Stinkkiller came to mind, might have objected to wearing a safety harness. Perhaps he thought it would be a sign of weakness—or maybe he was afraid of what the Humans might do to the warriors if they were restrained.

Whatever the reason, McKee found the Naa's body with

a stretcher laid across it. Stinkkiller's head was turned at an unnatural angle and it looked as though his neck was broken. Tears ran down McKee's cheeks as she spotted Jivani. The civilian was strapped in the way she should be. But a shard of bloody metal was protruding from her chest. The xenoanthropologist's eyes were open and staring at McKee, who paused long enough to close them. "I found Truthsayer," Hyatt said from ten feet away. "It looks like a locker fell on him."

McKee swore and was forced to step over a legionnaire named Nix in order to join Hyatt. Judging from all the blood, Nix might have been dead *before* the crash. Truthsayer was still recognizable even though the ammo locker had crushed his rib cage. A quick check confirmed that the chief of chiefs was dead. There would be no negotiations or prospects for peace.

Then McKee noticed some khaki under some wreckage and pulled a ceiling panel aside to reveal Colonel Cavenaugh's body. Had he been up out of his seat when a piece of shrapnel tore his arm off? It appeared that way. Then, while he was in the process of bleeding out, the Titan hit the ground. The impact could have bounced him off the ceiling and crushed his skull. Not that it made any difference. McKee's thoughts were interrupted by a blast of static and the sound of Payton's voice. "Alpha-Three to Alpha-One . . . They're massing for an attack. We've got to pull out. Over."

"Copy," McKee said. "We're on the way. Over."

She turned to Hyatt. "You heard the man . . . It's time to amscray."

Hyatt said, "Yes, ma'am," and turned to go. McKee was immediately behind the private when she saw an arm shoot up out of a pile of bodies. A survivor! She hurried to help. And there, much to her amazement, was Andy! It appeared the synth had completed the task it had been sent to do—or it figured that McKee was going to die in battle.

Whatever the reason, the robot had slipped aboard the Titan and been cut in half during the crash. McKee almost made the mistake of trying to help the machine. Then she realized how stupid that would be and removed a thermite grenade from a pouch on her chest protector. Knowing that her helmet cam would capture everything she did, McKee pulled the pin and dropped the grenade where Andy wouldn't be able to reach it. "No!" Andy said. "Help me!"

"Sorry," McKee replied, as she backed away. "We have to pull out, and I can't allow you to fall into enemy hands." Then she turned and ran.

A flash strobed the bulkheads around her as the grenade went off, and she knew that the thermite would turn Andy into a puddle of metal and prevent the machine from submitting a report to the Bureau of Missing Persons. Vella was waiting as McKee cleared the wreck. "Smith got the pilot . . . She's alive."

"Thank God for that," McKee said, as she strapped in. "Alpha-One to Alpha-One-Three . . . Let the digs close in on the wreck. Once they do, destroy it. Over."

The response came from squad leader Sergeant Joi Ling. "This is Alpha-Four . . . Roger that. Over."

This time it was Payton and his T-1 who led the way, with McKee and Vella bringing up the rear. The squad circled out and around the west side of the crash site as they followed the slope upwards. And when they entered the compound, Ling was there to greet them. She waited for McKee to dismount before delivering her report. "At least a dozen of the bastards are inside the wreck," Ling said. "With more gathered outside."

"Let them have it," McKee said coldly, and stepped up onto a block of granite so she could see better. Rockets sleeted into the sky, fell downwards, and hit the wreck in quick succession. A second salvo followed the first. The fly-form shook in response to a series of overlapping explosions.

A new sun was born a second later. It produced what sounded like a clap of thunder, collapsed in on itself, and sent a column of black smoke billowing up into the sky. All that remained was a shallow crater and a large field of debris.

McKee turned to Ling. "Well done. Where's Sergeant Larkin?"

The noncom's expression was grim. "He took a bullet . . . Zapata's working on him now."

It was too much. More than McKee thought she could take. It took all of her strength to maintain the icy composure that the job required. "Where is he?"

"In the command bunker."

McKee ran across the compound and followed the ramp down into the dimly lit chamber below. Larkin was laid out on a folding table. A bloodstained battle dressing was wrapped around his head. A medic was taking his blood pressure. McKee made her way over to the corner. "Is he conscious?"

Zapata had a buzz cut, brown eyes, and cheeks covered with black stubble. He removed the stethoscope from his ears and let it hang. "Sometimes."

"What happened?"

"Something hit his helmet, he took it off to see how much damage had been done, and a bullet creased his skull. But, if we can get him to Fort Camerone, there's a good chance he'll make it."

"Don't let him die," McKee said harshly. "Do everything you can. Do you read me?"

The words sounded shrill, even to McKee, and she could see the fear in Zapata's eyes. That was when she realized that the AXE was pointed at him. She pulled the barrel up so it was pointed at the roof before turning to face a wide-eyed com tech. "Give me a sitrep . . . We need a dustoff."

The com tech was opening her mouth to speak when a

voice came over a small speaker. "Alpha base, this is Fox-Four, Six, and Seven inbound. ETA three minutes. I understand you could use some air support. Over."

McKee went over to snatch the hand mike. "This is Alpha-One. Roger that. Most of the targets are in the woods a half mile south of our location. Over."

"Understood," came the reply. "Take a break . . . We'll tidy up. Over."

"We need a dustoff," McKee said. "And we need it *now*. Over."

"This is Bravo-Two-Two," a new voice said. "Roger the dustoff. Prep the LZ for two Vulcans. Over."

"You'll have to land one at a time," McKee responded. "But we'll be ready. Over."

There was a muted roar as the fighters passed overhead and began their bombing runs. McKee returned to the surface in time to witness the resulting explosions, the tidal wave of fire, and the roiling smoke. If even one Naa survived the aerial onslaught it would be a miracle.

The fighters circled above as the first Vulcan came in for a landing. Larkin's stretcher went on first, followed by the brain box Smith had pulled out of the Titan, and three walking wounded. Four T-1s, the construction droids, and the RAVs completed the load. McKee would have preferred to stay with Larkin, but that wasn't possible. Her place was on the ground until the last member of her company had been loaded.

There was a wait as the first fly-form took off and disappeared to the north. Then the second Vulcan came in for a landing. The crew chief began to talk about a potential overload as more T-1s clomped aboard but stopped when McKee pointed her AXE at him. Finally, after one last look around, McKee walked up the ramp. The mood was somber inside the cargo compartment, and no one spoke.

The engines wound up tight as they struggled to lift the

overloaded fly-form off the ground. The hull wobbled as the Vulcan took to the air and steadied as the pilot switched to horizontal flight. That was when McKee closed her eyes, watched the Titan crash all over again, and wished that officers were allowed to cry.

CHAPTER: 6

In Flanders fields the poppies blow.
Between the crosses, row on row.

JOHN McCRAE
"In Flanders Fields"
Standard year 1917

PLANET ORLO II

A temporary platform had been set up on a rise that looked
out over the new cemetery. From where John Avery was
standing, he could see more than a thousand white grave
markers. They stood in precise rows, each representing a life
lost. Avery had known some of them, fought next to them,
and seen them die.

Dignitaries were present, too, a couple dozen of them,
along with contingents of military personnel representing
the Legion, navy, Marine Corps, and the planet's Militia.
They stood at attention as a military chaplain read a speech
peppered with phrases like, "These fine men and women,"
"the best the empire had to offer," and "for the greater
good."

All of which was bullshit, but no one was going to call
the chaplain on it, since the empress was about to speak. She
had arrived to much fanfare three days earlier and was slated

to remain on Orlo II for two additional weeks before continuing her tour of the empire.

And thinking about Ophelia inevitably reminded Avery of Cat Carletto, or Sergeant Andromeda McKee as she was now known. The footage of her receiving the Imperial Order of Merit had been sent to all of the colonies and played endlessly over the government-run media outlets. And Avery never tired of watching the vid in order to see her face. What was McKee thinking when she accepted the medal? he wondered. Nothing good, that was for sure.

They had fallen in love during very trying circumstances, which made the bond even stronger. But he was an officer, and she was enlisted, and that made their love affair illegal. And the ever-present threat of discovery had been difficult to live with.

That was bad enough, but there was another problem as well. The Bureau of Missing Persons had sent synths out to find Cat and kill her—and there was reason to believe that he was under suspicion, too. Not because of McKee, or his actions, but based on things his brother had said back on Earth.

Avery's thoughts were interrupted by loud applause. After being introduced, Empress Ophelia was climbing the stairs that led to the stage. As she stood behind the bullet-proof podium, a pair of synth bodyguards took up stations on either side of her. The sleek machines wore spray-on uniforms and carried submachine guns. It was just one aspect of the additional security precautions put in place after the Veneto assassination on Earth.

Two cameras swooped in to capture Ophelia's words as a gentle breeze ruffled her hair. "Good afternoon," she said. "First let me say that it's a pleasure to visit this beautiful planet. And nowhere is that beauty more apparent than in the vast forest that you call the Big Green. It was there that I was introduced to a Droi named Insa. It told me that while many issues are left to be settled, there is no reason why all the peoples of Orlo II can't live in peace . . . And I agree. Now that the recent civil unrest is behind us, we can come together. That's what the men and women buried in this cemetery were fighting for . . . Peace and our glorious empire."

That was a load of crap. And Avery was glad to be standing at attention. That meant he didn't have to clap with the rest of them. The truth of the situation was that Empress Ophelia raised imperial taxes by 12 percent shortly after seizing power from her brother.

The increase led to noisy protests. Then, fearful that things were starting to get out of hand, the so-called loyalists requested that marines be sent in to restore status quo. Their request was granted, and that resulted in a civil war, with loyalists on one side and secessionists on the other. And since there weren't enough marines to impose order by themselves, the empress sent the Legion to help.

Meanwhile, having spotted what they saw as an opportunity, the Hudathans attacked. That forced the Legion to fight the loyalists and the aliens at the same time. And both wars had been won. Not easily and at great cost. So the truth was that the loyalists, rebels, and Droi were *still* at odds, and it was the presence of the Legion that kept them from clashing.

As for the Hudathans, they had been driven out of the solar system but would almost certainly return one day. And they would bring an even bigger fleet next time.

There was another five minutes of royal drivel followed by thunderous applause as the empress left the podium. How many new graveyards would be commissioned during her reign? Avery wondered. Enough to hold a brigade? A regiment? An army?

Moments after the empress left the stage, a sergeant major bellowed, "Dismissed!" That was the signal for military personnel to either break formation or march off to the trucks that were waiting for them. Avery was about to fade when Colonel Rylund stopped him. He was a good if somewhat eccentric officer, whose leadership had been critical to the recent victory. "Not so fast, John . . . General Ashton and I would like to have a word with you."

Avery frowned. "This wouldn't be in regards to some sort of shit detail would it, sir?"

Rylund chuckled. "Why yes, it would. Is there any other kind?"

"No, sir."

"Good. That's settled then. Come on. The general is going to give us a ride into town."

Like Ashton herself, the staff car had arrived after the fighting was over, so there wasn't a scratch on it. Rylund opened a door and gestured for Avery to enter. Once inside, the legionnaire found himself with his back to the driver, facing the general. He'd been introduced to Ashton at a reception but had never exchanged more than a few words with her until then.

She was a large-boned woman who was known as a straight talker, a bodybuilder, and an enemy of the cavalry. The very branch that Avery belonged to. The reasons for her bias weren't entirely clear but probably stemmed from more than twenty years spent in infantry regiments. Or, what the ground pounders liked to refer to as "the *real* Legion." Their eyes met and she nodded. "Good afternoon, Major . . . We met once before I believe."

Ashton had probably been introduced to a thousand people since her arrival on Orlo II, so Avery was impressed. "Yes, ma'am. We met at the reception that followed the change-of-command ceremony."

Rylund entered the car and closed the door. "Yes . . . Avery distinguished himself on a number of occasions—not the least of which were his efforts to forge an alliance with the Droi."

"A touchy business indeed," Ashton observed, as the hover car rose off the ground, then turned on its axis. "And that's one of the reasons why we think you're the right officer for the job at hand."

Avery looked from Ashton to Rylund and back again. "Thank you, ma'am. And what job would that be?"

"The empress needs a military attaché," Rylund answered. "A person who can provide Her Highness with assessments of military readiness on each planet she visits—and offer tactical advice should that become necessary."

"Yes," Ashton put in. "If the empress is going to have a military attaché—then who better than one of *our* officers?"

The inference was obvious. The Legion, navy, and Marine Corps were locked in a perpetual battle for resources. So rather than cede the slot to another branch, the general wanted to place one of her officers where he or she could suck up to the empress on behalf of the Legion. And Avery had been chosen for the job. It was an especially odious task given the fact that Ophelia wanted to kill the woman that Avery was in love with. "Yes, ma'am," Avery said obediently. "But I haven't spent much time on staff. Surely someone with more experience could do a better job."

Ashton laughed. "That's what Colonel Rylund told me you would say. Nice try, Major . . . But no cigar. I hear the empress has a preference for *real* soldiers. The kind who have been in action. And, in spite of the fact that you mistakenly chose the cavalry over the infantry, I think you have the right credentials. Pucker up, Avery . . . It's time to kiss some ass."

More than a week had passed since the conversation with Colonel Rylund and General Ashton. During that time, Avery had to pare his belongings down to the ninety-six pounds he would be allowed to take aboard the ship, find his way through the labyrinthine checkout process, and say good-bye to a special place.

In a city where housing was hard to come by and overnight accommodations were almost impossible to find, the apartment where Cat and he had spent their last night together was absurdly expensive. But he stayed there anyway and drank the bottle of wine by himself. Cat wasn't there, of course, but the memories were, and they haunted his dreams.

When morning came, Avery made himself a light breakfast before packing the B-1 bag and hauling it down to the street. A mere major didn't rate a vehicle like the one assigned to Ashton—but a beat-up scout car had been sent to pick him up. The driver had the old-young face typical of so many legionnaires. He was wearing a white kepi, crisp camos, and a pair of mirror-bright boots. He snapped to attention and offered a salute. "Good morning, sir. Corporal Sanko reporting as ordered. Where are we headed?"

Avery dumped the bag in back and took one last look around. He didn't expect to see any of the surrounding buildings again. "We're going to the new spaceport."

"Yes, sir."

Avery swung into the well-worn passenger seat and made good use of the grab bar as the car bounced through a succession of potholes. Avery could see signs of the recent fighting as the vehicle wound its way down the hill to the recently scoured floodplains below. There were lots of shot-up buildings, charred ruins, and bomb craters, most of which were half-full of rainwater.

Because of all the damage, a new spaceport was being built south of town. To get there, it was necessary to follow the arrow-straight road past a row of burned-out Hudathan tanks to the hills beyond. There was lots of traffic going in both directions, but the driver proved to be an expert at dodging in and out between big transports and delivered

Avery to a security checkpoint in what might have been record time.

After being waved through, the driver guided the car up the side of what had been a hill until the men, women, and cyborgs of the famed Pioneers sliced the top of it off. As they arrived on the newly created mesa, Avery saw that all sorts of heavy equipment were being used to create rows of landing pads. Only two were in service at the moment, however, and repellers roared as a boxy-looking assault boat lifted off.

The so-called terminal building was little more than an inflatable hab with four dusty vehicles parked outside. "This is it," Sanko announced as he pulled into an empty slot. "I'll get your bag."

But Avery was used to handling such chores himself and waved the offer off. After thanking Sanko for the ride, he carried the bag inside. There was a crowded waiting area off to the left and a line straight ahead. It led to a sign that said, CHECK IN. So Avery fell in behind a navy ensign and began what turned out to be a fifteen-minute wait. Eventually, it was his turn to approach the counter. A harried-looking petty officer looked up from his terminal. "Name please."

Avery gave it, the sailor typed it in, and everything changed. A smart-looking chief petty officer (CPO) appeared, took charge of the B-1, and led Avery over to a door that bore a handwritten sign. VICTORIOUS. That said it all.

Everyone knew that the *Victorious* was a light cruiser that had been reconfigured to serve as the royal yacht. That meant everyone associated with the vessel received special treatment. Even obscure majors like John Avery.

So rather than wait with the horde out front, Avery found himself in a small VIP lounge that was equipped with six seats, a coffeepot, and a tray of stale pastries. Eventually, a couple of sailors were shown in, and in keeping with their ranks, sat as far away from the officer as they could. Shortly thereafter, the natty-looking CPO came to get the group.

Avery hoisted his bag and followed the noncom out to a gleaming shuttle. It looked brand-new, wore the royal coat of arms on its flawless fuselage, and was taking on cargo. Supplies probably bound for the *Victorious*.

The sailors were sent into the cargo compartment, where they would ride with the flight crew. But Avery's status as an officer entitled him to sit on a leather-upholstered seat just aft of the cockpit. The copilot welcomed the legionnaire aboard, the crew chief offered some rudimentary refreshments, and a sailor took charge of the bag.

Avery had no way to know if other ships were waiting for a clearance to take off but suspected that they were. That made no difference, however, because the moment the aircraft was ready, the pilot announced, "All personnel to fasten their safety harnesses," and gave them thirty seconds to do so before firing the shuttle's repellers. The ship went straight up and swiveled to the north. Then, having received the necessary clearance, it took off into the wind.

There was nothing remarkable about the trip up through the atmosphere, and that was a good thing. It took the better part of two hours to enter orbit, match speeds with the *Victorious*, and enter her cavernous launch bay. Avery had done a little bit of research so he knew that the LC 8654 (Light Cruiser) *Victorious* was more than two miles long. The ship could carry twelve fighters, twelve shuttles, and boasted a crew of a thousand men, women, and robots.

But raw statistics didn't capture what made the ship different from other ships of the same size. Because although the cruiser was armed, the *Vic* was more luxury liner than warship. A fact that became immediately apparent once the bay was pressurized, and Avery could disembark. Except for the unavoidable scorch marks on the gray decks, everything else was perfect.

The bulkheads, directional signs, and even the mainte-

nance droids looked as if they'd been painted the day before.
Even the air that had been pumped into the bay was scented
lest the acrid stench of ozone offend sensitive nostrils. Not
Avery's nostrils, nor the crew's, but Ophelia's. Was she
aboard? Or still on the surface? There was no way to be
sure as a smart-looking ensign offered a perfect salute.
"Major Avery? I'm Ensign Neely. Welcome aboard, sir. If
you would be kind enough to follow me, I will take you to
your quarters."

"Thank you," Avery replied. "I have a bag here somewhere."

"Yes, sir," Neely said. "It will be delivered to your cabin.
See the yellow lines? For your own safety, please stay within
them."

Avery followed Neely through a lock, into a corridor, and
onto a lift. It carried them up to what she said was C deck.
The closest thing to a common area on the ship. Neely told
him that A deck was devoted to command and control functions. Empress Ophelia and her retinue were situated on B
deck, and crew quarters were on D deck. The engineering
spaces occupied the levels below.

The corridor that ran the length of C deck was crowded
with people. As Neely led him along, Avery saw deck officers, weapons officers, engineering officers, flight officers,
supply officers, all manner of ratings, camo-clad marines,
and a variety of robots all walking in both directions. Glow
panels marked off regular six-foot intervals, the conduit-
lined bulkheads were navy gray, and multicolored decals
identified where first-aid kits, damage-control stations, escape pods, weapons blisters, node points, and access panels
could be found. A constant stream of routine announce-
ments could be heard as they walked along.

"Here we are," Neely said as she led Avery into a side
corridor. "This is officer country. You were assigned to cabin

C-231." Neely stopped in front of a hatch marked C-231 and waved a keycard. There was a hissing sound as the door slid open.

Avery was pleasantly surprised as he entered. The cabin was equipped with a bunk, a storage unit, and a tiny fresher with toilet. There was a fold-down desk and data terminal as well. All in a space roughly eight-feet-by-eight-feet in size. That was small, but Avery had been forced to share such spaces with other officers on troopships. After giving the keycard and a pocket com to Avery—Neely told him to report to the ship's executive officer (XO) at 1500 hours. Then she left.

That gave Avery plenty of time to unpack, visit the officer's mess, and explore C deck. So by the time his appointment rolled around, he knew where to go. There was a short wait in the anteroom outside the XO's office before a laconic droid sent him in. Avery took two steps into the compartment, came to attention, and announced himself. "Major John Avery, reporting as ordered, sir!"

The man on the other side of the desk had black hair worn so short he looked bald. He had dark skin, a moon-shaped face, and a big body. Thanks to the silver oak leafs on the naval officer's shoulders Avery knew he was a commander—a rank equivalent to a lieutenant colonel in the Legion. The XO said, "At ease," and came forward to greet his visitor. "My name is Max Honto. Welcome aboard."

Avery could feel the other man's strength as they shook hands. "Thank you, sir."

"Have a seat," Honto said, as he sat on a corner of the desk. "As far as I know, you're the only member of the Legion on the ship. A regular one-man army."

Avery smiled. "I'll try to live up to that."

Honto smiled. "I suppose you're curious regarding your duties."

"Sir, yes, sir."

"Well, so am I," Honto confessed. "The empress hasn't required a military attaché up until now, so we'll learn as we go. Please document what you're required to do so we can create an appropriate job description."

"Yes, sir."

"Okay, I guess that's it. Her assistant will give you a call when the empress needs you. Its name is Daska. That means Earth—or so I've been told. Should you receive a message from Daska, I suggest that you respond promptly regardless of what you may be doing at the time."

Was that a threat? A friendly warning? Or both? Avery scanned Honto's face for clues and came up empty. "Yes, sir."

A couple of minutes of small talk followed, but Avery could sense that the meeting was essentially over. So when the com set began to buzz, he took the opportunity to salute and withdraw.

Days of boredom followed. There was a flurry of activity when the ship broke orbit, and Orlo II was left behind. But there was nothing for Avery to do except eat, work out with the marines, and sleep. But finally, two days into the journey, his pocket com buzzed. Avery fumbled the device out into the open. "This is Major Avery."

The voice on the other end of the call was clearly synthetic—but was being processed so as to sound feminine. "This is Daska. Please report to compartment B-14."

Avery felt his heart start to race. *The empress!* The woman who wanted to kill McKee . . . And would have him shot if she knew what he really thought about her. Avery's chest felt tight. "Thank you. I'm on my way."

Avery heard a click and was thankful that he hadn't been working out when the call came in. Knowing he was on call, the legionnaire had been careful to wear a freshly pressed Class B uniform when he wasn't exercising—and that habit was about to pay off as he entered an elevator and pushed B.

He'd been on C deck. A short ride took him up a level.

When the doors parted, he stepped out into an ornate lobby. A pair of synths stepped forward to check Avery's ID and pat him down. They stepped aside as Empress Ophelia entered the reception area.

Avery was about to bow when the royal spoke. "My name is Daska," the android said. "Please follow me." He was looking at a body double! Still another way for Ophelia to protect herself.

Daska passed a palm over a scanner, and a hatch hissed open. Avery followed the robot into a wood-paneled corridor. The fittings were gold, or appeared to be, and his shoes sank into the thick carpet. The hatches were labeled military style, and Daska opened the door to compartment B-14 without knocking.

As Avery followed the android into the room, he was surprised by what he saw or didn't see. There was no sign of Ophelia or the kind of furnishings one would expect an empress to have. A raised platform occupied the center of the compartment. It was roughly the size of a pool table. And there, sitting on top of it, was a make-believe battlefield, complete with two miniature armies. They were located at opposite ends of the table and separated by an artistically executed mountain range. Avery frowned. Surely the empress wasn't going to plot strategy using toys?

He was about to ask Daska a question when a second hatch whispered open and a five- or six-year-old boy entered the compartment. He had tousled hair, inquisitive eyes, and wore a navy uniform. "This is Prince Nicolai," Daska informed him. "You will bow when he arrives and address him as Your Highness in public. Here, however, during private sessions, you are permitted to address him by his given name. Do you have any questions?"

Avery bowed. It felt awkward. His head was spinning. The toys, the prince . . . Everything was coming together. Had he been brought aboard to play games with Nicolai? To substitute for the playmates the boy didn't have? The answer was yes; shock soon gave way to embarrassment and anger. He wanted to leave. But what would the penalty be? Avery knew that Ophelia was capable of anything and everything, so it was important to control himself. He was groping for something to say when Nicolai intervened. "You're a major."

"Yes," Avery replied awkwardly. "My name is Avery. Major John Avery."

The boy's eyes were big. "Should I call you sir?"

"No," Avery replied. "First because you are a prince . . . But, since you are wearing the uniform of a navy captain, you outrank me in that respect as well."

"Oh. Can I call you Major John?"

"Yes. And I'll call you Nicolai."

Avery looked up to discover that Daska had left. There were bound to be surveillance cameras, however. He wanted to look for them but was careful not to. "So you're interested in the military."

"I'm going to be an emperor," Nicolai said matter-of-factly. "So I need to kill people and stuff like that."

The boy said it so casually that it made Avery's blood run cold. Here, right in front of him, was a megalomaniac in the making. Avery was careful to choose his words with care. "Yes, well, being part of the military involves a lot more than killing people. There's strategy to consider . . . And logistics . . . And . . ."

Nicolai looked bored. "Can we play now?"

"Sure," Avery replied, as Nicolai led him to the platform. The raised step that ran all the way around the display allowed the boy to access the tabletop. "I'll be the marines," Nicolai said brightly, "and you can be the Legion. Mommy says legionnaires are bad people."

Avery thought it best to let the comment pass. As he examined the miniatures that were laid out on the battlefield, he realized that they were moving. Not much, just a little, as if to signal that they were in play. "Use the laser pointer," Nicolai said. "Zap a unit in order to activate it—then zap the place where you want it to go."

Avery picked up a laser pointer, aimed it at a three-inch-tall Trooper I, and touched a button. Then he chose a point directly behind a perfectly executed clump of trees and marked it with a blip of light. Tiny servos whined as the toy advanced. It was armed with shoulder launchers, and its head turned right and left as if scanning for danger. It was fun, and Avery was starting to get interested. He discovered that after activating a unit, he could use the laser pen to draw a winding route through a series of obstacles, and the toy would follow it.

"See?" Nicolai demanded. "It's easy. You're supposed to try to cross the mountains while I do the same thing. Then, if you reach the other side, you can try to capture the dome at my end of the table. *If* General Crowley lets you do that . . . Which he probably won't."

General Crowley? An imaginary playmate perhaps? No, there *was* a General Crowley . . . An officer who had distinguished himself by suppressing a revolt on Mars twenty years earlier. "So General Crowley might join us?"

"He's here now," Nicolai replied. "In my head. Not the real one, a copy. Mommy gave him to me. I don't like it when he argues with Tarch Senta."

It sounded as if Ophelia had found a way to clone selected personalities and install them in her son's mind. Or maybe the boy was all mixed up. Avery thought it best to play along. "Two against one . . . That's not fair."

Nicolai frowned. "I'm five, and you're a grown-up. That isn't fair, either."

The line was perfectly delivered, and Avery couldn't help but laugh. "Good point. Okay, let's see who can get over the mountain range first." The answer was Nicolai and General

Crowley. While Avery was still learning how far each piece could move, and how to "fire" their weapons, his opponents took control of all three mountain passes by landing aircraft on them.

Then, as Avery began to advance, they fired salvos of heat-seeking missiles over the mountains and destroyed his cyborgs one by one. And that's where the battle stood when Daska reappeared. "Playtime is over, Your Highness. It's time for lunch."

"But I don't *want* lunch . . . We're having fun. Aren't we, Major John?"

"Some of us are having fun," Avery said with a smile.

"Maybe you'll do better next time," Nicolai said.

"I will certainly try."

Nicolai waved as the robot led him away. Avery was free to go.

The play sessions became part of the daily routine after that. Avery would receive a call, make his way up to B-14, and spend an hour with Nicolai. The only thing that changed was that Avery managed to cross a mountain pass on the third day, and was close to capturing a second one, when Daska entered the compartment. It wasn't until Nicolai ran over to her that Avery realized the truth. Instead of the body double, he was looking at the empress herself! "Mommy! Major John is winning, and General Crowley is mad at him." Having had some practice, Avery managed to bow without making a fool of himself.

Empress Ophelia ruffled her son's hair as she looked at Avery. Her voice was identical to Daska's. Or the other way around. "So," she said. "I understand your brother doesn't like me."

The comment was like a bolt of lightning out of the blue. Avery was stunned but knew he shouldn't be. A synth named Snarr had cautioned him about his brother's intemperate remarks months earlier. Which meant the government knew about it. So why had his nomination been approved?

Ophelia smiled. "Never fear, Major . . . I know how brothers can be."

That was true. The difference was that Ophelia's brother had been murdered on her orders. Avery forced a smile. "Thank you, Highness."

"Nicolai looks forward to the daily sessions," Ophelia said. "But I suspect they are a trial for you."

Avery looked at Nicolai and back to her. "I have come to look forward to the sessions, Highness." And it was true.

Ophelia smiled knowingly. "That was well said. And I believe it. As you know, we will enter orbit around Worber's World in a couple of days. And when we do, Nicolai will have to share you with his mother. The governor of Worber's World claims that all is well on his planet. My intelligence people say otherwise. I would like you to accompany me. Your job will be to look and listen. Then, when our visit is over, I will ask for your impressions."

There was only one thing Avery could say. "Yes, Highness. I would be honored."

"Good. Come on, Nicolai. Let's have lunch."

PLANET WORBER'S WORLD

Worber's World was an earthlike planet that had been quick to declare its fealty to Ophelia upon the death of her brother but was also experiencing some "social upheaval." Which was a polite way of saying that a significant portion of the population didn't care for the empress or the new 12 percent "mutual welfare and defense" tax that had been imposed on all of the colony worlds. So whom to believe? Video of huge protests captured by Ophelia's intelligence people? Or the governor? Who claimed that the civil disobedience was limited to a few cities—and not representative of the citizenry in general.

Ophelia was understandably gun-shy in the wake of the civil war on Orlo II. And Avery assumed that his analysis would constitute but a single tile in the mosaic of intelligence reports the empress would receive from a variety of sources. In any case, it felt good to function as something more than a glorified babysitter for a change.

In his role as military attaché, Avery got to ride in Ophelia's lavishly equipped shuttle along with her synth security detail and a handful of key advisors, all of whom treated Avery with haughty disdain. He was a commoner, after all, a mere major, and a Legion major at that. The Legion being the lowest form of military life there was where the courtiers were concerned. But Avery didn't care. All he wanted to do was complete the assignment and return to regular duty. Somewhere near McKee if he could wrangle it.

Avery expected some pomp and ceremony once the shuttle put down but was unprepared for the totality of what followed. A crowd of five thousand people was waiting in the drizzle, many of whom held identical welcome signs aloft. A band played, dimly seen aerospace fighters passed overhead, and Governor Judd delivered a flowery speech. He was a portly man with a florid face and an ingratiating smile. Avery didn't like him and could tell that Ophelia didn't either.

But she played her part and waved to the clearly partisan crowd as she and a small retinue climbed into the bubble-topped limo that had been brought down to the planet's surface six hours earlier. Avery was among that group and had been told that the rain-streaked duraplast could stop a .50 caliber bullet.

But that wasn't all. The car was equipped with running boards, and two synths rode on each. There was a military escort as well, plus snipers stationed on rooftops all along the parade route. None of the buildings were more than five or six stories high, so Avery had a clear view of the marksmen and the armed air cars that kept pace with the limo.

There were discrepancies, however—differences between various elements of the militia that Avery found interesting. So, much to the annoyance of the economic advisor seated next to him, he whispered comments into a wire-thin boom mike as spectators cheered and pelted the car with identical bouquets of flowers.

Maybe it was the cloudy sky and the incessant rain, but Avery thought the city of Newport was a depressing place and was thankful when the journey ended two miles later. The governor's mansion was a sturdy-looking affair surrounded by a blastproof perimeter wall, a water feature that could double as a partial moat, and narrow, slit-shaped windows. Were the soldiers on duty around the mansion a bit sharper than those guarding the intersections in town? Yes, Avery thought so . . . But it would make sense to put the best people at critical locations. There were other things however—things that bothered him.

At least there would be a good meal, or so Avery assumed. But first it was necessary to endure the reception, where, given his status as military attaché, Avery was expected to chat with a gaggle of officers all eager to curry favor with Ophelia's pet major.

Finally, having survived the reception, Avery was given a chance to eat what turned out to be an excellent lunch. The only distractions were the woman on his right who wanted to know what Ophelia wore every day—and the geezer on the left who assumed the legionnaire was a criminal. "Did you murder someone?" he demanded. "And if so, why?"

Once lunch was over, one of Ophelia's air cars plucked the party up off the roof of the mansion and flew it back to the spaceport. The empress was scheduled to attend a number of events over the coming days but preferred to spend the night aboard the *Victorious*. "So I can care for my sick son," she told Governor Judd even though Avery knew that Nicolai was in good health.

Avery was beat by the time he returned to his quarters on the *Vic*, and about to get ready for bed when his pocket com buzzed. It was Daska . . . And she informed Avery that the empress wanted to speak with him. He was surprised, but only mildly so, and glad that he had taken the time to review his notes on the trip up into space.

A couple of synths were waiting outside the elevator. Daska watched impassively as the other robots patted Avery down. Then it led him down a corridor he hadn't been in before to a hatch marked B-3. It opened as if by magic as Daska led Avery into a beautifully furnished room. There were fresh flowers from Worber's World, gilded mirrors, and art on all of the walls. Ophelia was seated on an off-white couch that was part of a well-conceived conversation area. She was dressed in a beautiful but modest synsilk robe and sat with her feet tucked under her. Avery bowed. Ophelia gestured to the chair across from her. "Have a seat, Major . . . Would you like a drink? I know I would."

Avery said "Yes," rather than risk offending her, and wound up with something called a Blue Comet. It packed a punch, and he resolved to have only one.

"So, Major," Ophelia said, once he'd been served. "Tell me what you noticed during our visit. And Major . . ."

"Yes?"

"Don't tell me what you think I *want* to hear. Tell me what you honestly believe."

The whole thing was ironic. Avery was seated across from the dictator who was responsible for thousands of murders, including the deaths of Cat's parents. A woman who would have McKee killed were she to learn of the legionnaire's true identity. And he was going to provide Ophelia with what might or might not be valuable assistance. But what choice did he have? Other than to turn himself in. He took a sip and felt the cold liquid trickle down his throat. "I noticed two things, Highness. The first is that although they *look* new—every military vehicle I saw was at least ten years old. And some were older than that."

Ophelia frowned. "And that's important because?"

"That's important because your brother provided Governor Judd with ten billion credits to modernize the local militia two years ago."

Ophelia's eyebrows rose. "And Judd did so . . . I read the readiness reports."

"I'm sure you did," Avery agreed. "But if the governor had new vehicles, why use the old ones? Especially for a royal visit? It's my guess that the new equipment was never purchased."

A hardness Avery hadn't seen before appeared in Ophelia's eyes and found its way into her voice. "You're saying that he stole the money."

"Not all of it," Avery replied. "That's the second thing . . . There are *two* militias on Worber's World. The *real* one, and the militia within the militia, which is probably comprised of paid mercenaries."

Ophelia stared at him. "How can you tell the difference?"

"The real militia is out of shape, sloppy, and poorly armed. The mercs are in great shape, well disciplined, and armed with assault weapons so new your marines haven't received them yet."

Ophelia looked puzzled. "But *why*?"

"I don't know," Avery answered honestly. "But, if I had to guess, I'd say half of the ten billion credits is stashed on one of the rim worlds waiting for the governor to retire. As for the militia . . . They're the ones you'd expect to restore order if the population rose up against Judd. Except that his mercs could eat them alive. Then he'll jump on a ship and run. Or maybe I'm wrong."

"It fits," Ophelia said angrily. "It fits with other things I know. And now that I can tell people what to look for, they can verify your theories. Thank you, Major. Thank you very much. Why didn't my other officers notice those things?"

"Because they don't belong to the Legion," Avery answered. "Most of our people know something about crime."

When Ophelia laughed, it was surprisingly loud. Avery had a feeling that Governor Judd was going to wind up dead pretty soon. Did that bother him? Hell, no. The people of Worber's World deserved better. Would they get it? Not while Ophelia was empress. Chances were that she would replace Judd with someone worse. He finished the drink. It had a bitter taste.

There was no way to ascertain whether Governor Judd had billions of credits stashed on a rim world. But it didn't take Ophelia's agents long to confirm that the militia's vehicles were as old as Avery said they were. And, after a bit of digging, they learned that 80 percent of the militia's elite Ravager battalion were not only from off-planet but were full- versus part-time soldiers.

Avery half expected Ophelia to line Governor Judd and his family up against a wall and shoot them. But she was smarter than that. The truth was that the *Victorious* and her escorts weren't carrying enough marines to land, duke it out with the mercs, and keep the civilian population under control at the same time. So Ophelia was pleasant to Judd—and left Worber's World just as she'd found it. But Avery figured that Judd would wake up one morning to discover that a fleet was orbiting his planet, dropships were on the way down through the atmosphere, and a team of synths were knocking on his front door.

Once in space, the sessions with Nicolai resumed. They had moved on to other games by then, and Avery enjoyed the time he spent with the boy. Would Cat and he have children? It was an intriguing question and something he hadn't considered before.

The *Victorious* was bound for Clone World BETA-018 at that point. The mission was to let the Alpha Clones know that Ophelia hoped to continue the friendly relationship they had enjoyed with her brother. As usual, the majority of the voyage would be spent in the never-never land of hyperspace, a dimension in which enemies couldn't even see each other, much less fight.

That's how it was *supposed* to work, at any rate. But such journeys often involved the need to exit hyperspace at what were commonly referred to as jump points, or places where a ship's NAVCOMP could recalculate the next leg of the journey, before plunging back into hyperspace. And for reasons too technical for Avery to comprehend, the best jump points were not only well charted but used by a wide multiplicity of sentient races. That meant it was possible for a warship to wait at such a spot and ambush vessels as they arrived.

Everyone knew that, of course, so it was SOP to down-jump with weapons systems hot and all personnel at their battle stations. That's why Avery was strapped into a chair at the very back of the command center. He didn't have anything to do, but Commander Honto figured he had an obligation to put the military attaché somewhere near the action or run the risk that the empress would complain.

Avery had experienced dozens of jumps during his career and knew they could go wrong. So the possibility of an accidental death was enough to keep him from feeling bored. The command center was located forward of the bridge and half a level down. The semicircular space was organized around a large holo tank. It was dark and would remain so until the *Vic* reentered normal space. Then it would come back to life and provide the crew with information about who or what might be in the neighborhood.

Avery yawned as the ship's NAVCOMP began the countdown. "Three, two, one . . . Reentry is complete." The shift to normal space triggered the usual moment of nausea, the holo tank lit up, and a host of alarms went off. Avery sat up straight as the NAVCOMP launched into its report. "There are three, make that *four* ships located within twenty thousand miles of the jump point. All of them are a 98.4 percent match to known Hudathan profiles. Tracking, tracking, tracking . . . Sensors have detected *twelve* enemy torpedoes, estimated time to impact one minute thirty-seconds. Fighters launched. Shields up. Electronic countermeasures on."

Captain Suzuki sounded calm. "Inform our escorts . . . We will engage. Kill those torpedoes and launch ship-to-ship missiles using standard threat protocols. What are we up against?"

"The ridgeheads have a Ka-Class battleship," the ops officer said tightly. "Plus a cruiser and two tin cans."

"We're outgunned then," Suzuki said clinically. "Prepare to . . ." He never got to finish his sentence. The Hudathan battleship fired a salvo of energy bolts from its projectors and the *Victorious* shuddered as they struck. Now a new and even more strident voice was added to the existing chorus of alarms.

"The ship's energy shields are down," the NAVCOMP announced. "We can reload the accumulators, but it will take thirteen minutes and seven seconds, assuming the ship sustains no further damage."

The hull shook as two torpedoes struck and exploded. At that point, even a cavalry officer could tell that the *Victorious* was in trouble. "We can't duke it out with a battleship,"

Captain Suzuki said. "We'll have to jump. Inform our escorts. Tell them to hold until the empress is in hyperspace. Then they can pull out."

There it was. Brave men and women were going to die to buy time for a mass murderer. It made Avery sick, but there was nothing he could do about it.

"What about our fighters?" the operations officer asked hopefully. "Can we retrieve them first?"

"No," Suzuki said woodenly. "We don't have enough time. Tell the pilots to contact our escorts. Maybe they can help."

Avery felt an emptiness where his stomach should have been. What would that be like? he wondered. To launch your fighter, defend your ship, and be left behind? Aerospace fighters weren't equipped with hyperdrives. So, unless an escort managed to take them aboard, the pilots would be killed by the Hudathans or die of asphyxiation when they ran out of oxygen.

Avery clutched the armrests on his chair as the NAV-COMP began the countdown, and the holo tank went dark. That should have been the end of the danger but wasn't. Avery listened as the chief engineering officer spoke from her control room deep inside the ship. "This is Collins. We took a serious hit, sir . . . The hyperdrive's cooling system was damaged, and it's running hot. I recommend that you down-jump ASAP."

"Roger that," Suzuki replied. "Give me some options."

"The next down jump would place the ship in the Altari system," the NAVCOMP responded.

"Who owns it?"

"Both the Human *and* the Hudathan empires lay claim to the system's only inhabitable planet," the computer answered. "It's called Savas."

"Settlements?"

"One Human colony."

"Okay," Suzuki said. "Savas it is. Execute."

"Sixteen minutes and counting," the NAVCOMP responded calmly.

Avery thought about Ophelia, Nicolai, and the rest of the crew. So long as the ship's hyperdrive continued to function, they would be safe. And if it didn't? Then all of them would be adrift in a dimension from which none of them could escape. Eventually, after a few months, they would fight each other for food. Would Ophelia's synths win that battle on her behalf? Perhaps. But even if they did, she would still starve to death. And that would be a good thing. Unfortunately, Nicolai would die as well. Because Avery liked the little boy even if he was a monster in the making.

The minutes seemed to crawl by. Avery thought about all the things he'd done and hoped to do. Not by himself but with Cat. She was smart, funny, and brave. But she was sad, too . . . And plagued by guilt. If they could escape the empire, maybe he could make her happy again.

The NAVCOMP's voice overrode his thoughts. "Stand by . . . The down jump will take place in ten seconds. Eight, seven, six, five, four, three, two, one."

Avery felt a moment of nausea, watched a planet appear in the holo tank, and saw it start to rotate. Savas. He'd never heard of the place before. Except for caps of white, both hemispheres were primarily tan in color, separated by a wide belt of green that encircled the globe's midsection. Puddles of blue marked large lakes, but none were big enough to qualify as oceans.

"We'll park the ship in orbit," Suzuki declared. "Then we can evaluate the full extent of the damage and send a message torp to Earth."

No sooner had Suzuki outlined his plan than the chief engineer killed it. "Collins here . . . I'm sorry, sir . . . But the standard drives are off-line. Both the primary and secondary control systems were damaged."

"That is correct," the NAVCOMP confirmed emotionlessly. "Given the ship's inertia, and with no means to brake, the *Victorious* will enter the atmosphere."

Avery heard the words, but it took him a moment to fully understand what they meant. After the *Victorious* entered the atmosphere, and with no way to slow down, the cruiser would crash. And since it wasn't designed to land on a planetary surface, there would be a very large impact. One that few if any of them were going to walk away from. Savas dominated all of the screens by then, and the surface was coming up quickly. Somebody said, "Oh, shit," and the countdown began.

The *Victorious* shuddered as she entered the upper atmosphere, did a slow roll, and went in at a steep angle. Through the skillful use of the cruiser's steering jets, the pilot managed to pull the bow up. That acted to slow the rate of descent and made the possibility of a survivable crash more likely. The shields were back up by then, and they flared in response to the heat.

Avery closed his eyes and wished he had something to do as the *Victorious* bucked, performed another nauseating roll, and began to groan. The hull had never been intended for the sort of stresses that were being applied to it—and there was a very real possibility that it would fail before the vessel smashed into the ground. Then, after what seemed like an eternity, the *Victorious* began to level out. "Hang on," Suzuki said, "we're going in hard."

And it *was* hard. The ship hit, bounced up into the air, and hit again. Then it slid. Loose items flew through the air as the hull struck the ground. A stainless-steel coffee mug whizzed by Avery's head and clanged off the bulkhead. Gee forces pushed him into the seat. Someone screamed as the *Victorious* took the top of a hill off, belly flopped onto a plain, and skidded toward a low-lying mountain. Avery saw the obstruction grow to fill the screen, heard himself shout, "No!" and felt his head jerk forward as the ship slammed to a halt. Every possible type of alarm was beeping, bleating, and wailing. Avery didn't care. He was alive.

CHAPTER: 7

When I die, and parachute into hell, the members of the 2nd REP will be there waiting for me.

COLONEL JOSE FUENTES,
Commanding Officer 2nd REP
Standard year 1936

PLANET ALGERON

As McKee looked up, she saw that the sky was gunmetal gray. It was snowing, and as each flake fell, it added substance to the shroud that lay over the village of Doothdown. The hamlet was deserted and had been ever since the devastating attack months earlier.

McKee was standing on what remained of the eastern wall. It consisted of vertical poles that had been harvested on the neighboring hillsides and dragged into the valley using dooths. Fireballs had been fired into the village, so a substantial portion of the palisade had been reduced to charred wreckage.

From where McKee stood, she could see the main street. After forcing their way in through the main gate, the southerners had been gathered at the north end of the town, preparing for a final push, when Larkin marched straight at them, firing two assault weapons at once. It was a brave not to mention a crazy thing to do. McKee smiled. He was at Fort Camerone now . . . Bedridden and bitching to anyone who would listen. That was something to be grateful for.

As for her, she was on leave. That was the problem of being stationed on Algeron. There were two choices. You could hang out in the fort or visit Naa country, most of which was off-limits. But after some lobbying, she had been able to wrangle a green-zone pass. Meaning permission to camp in "pacified areas." The reality was that one had to be careful *everywhere*. Especially when traveling alone.

McKee was about to leave the top of the wall when she heard a faint tinkling sound. Bells? Or something else? McKee brought a pair of binoculars up to scan the area to the north. Another short day was coming to an end, so the light had begun to fade.

But as McKee swept the glasses from left to right, she saw a hint of movement. Then a tall, gangly figure emerged from the screen of falling snow and paused to look around. He was wearing a robe with an attached hood. That suggested a Human rather than a Naa because the fur-covered indigs made very few concessions to the snow.

McKee couldn't see the man's face. He was too far away for that. But there was no mistaking the eight-foot-long fighting staff. It was sheathed in metal and topped with the iron loop that symbolized the holy man's faith. And bells? Yes, she could hear them tinkle as he made his way toward the shattered gate. It was a good idea to let people know you were coming on Algeron. Especially if you were Human.

McKee smiled, slung the AXE over her shoulder, and made her way to a rickety ladder. Moments later, she was on the ground and walking up the street. Her boots made a crunching sound—and the only tracks to be seen were hers.

Ramirez waved when he saw her. McKee waved back and gave him a hug when they met at the center of the village.

Ramirez had a gaunt, skull-like face. He smiled. "Nofear Deathgiver."

"Crazyman Longstick." They laughed.

"We meet again," Ramirez said. He'd been present during the battle of Doothdown and fought at her side.

"Yes. How did you know I was here?"

"Everyone within fifty miles of this spot knows that Deathgiver is camped here."

"I haven't seen anyone."

"They don't want to be seen. But six warriors keep watch over you day and night. This area is relatively safe—but there's no way to know when bandits will pass through."

McKee felt a lump form in her throat and managed to swallow it. "Come on . . . I'm using an abandoned hut. It's warm there."

The hut was a short distance away, and like the majority of such dwellings, most of it was underground where the fire in the central hearth was still burning. The original owners had relied on dried dooth dung for fuel. But McKee didn't have any of that, so she was using scraps of wood instead. Her sleeping bag was laid out on one of three curved benches that fronted the fireplace. "Make yourself to home," she said, as Ramirez descended the ladder. "Are you hungry? I have lots of MREs."

"I can't believe I'm saying this," Ramirez said, as he shrugged the pack off. "But an MRE sounds good."

So they made what turned out to be dinner. And when Ramirez asked about what she'd been up to, McKee found herself telling him about the mission to find Truthsayer, the disastrous crash, and the extraction that followed. "So," Ramirez said as he sipped some instant caf, "what happened when you returned to Fort Camerone?"

McKee was silent for a moment. "They debriefed me. I told them everything I knew. And helmet footage served to verify my report."

"And then?"

"Nothing. They thanked me, said it was too bad the way things turned out, and cleared me for a return to duty."

Ramirez eyed her over the steaming cup. "And you didn't like that?"

McKee frowned. "Are you a licensed psychotherapist?"

"No. But I was an officer once."

McKee made a face. "That counts, I guess . . ."

"So, like I was saying, you didn't like that. At some level, you thought you deserved to be punished. Some sort of cleansing."

McKee shrugged. "I failed. People died."

"And you succeeded. People lived."

"Not enough of them."

"It's never enough," Ramirez replied soberly. "But think about it . . . Was there someone else? Someone who could have done better? And be honest."

McKee thought about it. Larkin? No. Sergeants Payton, Ling, or Sayer? All good noncoms, but no, no, and no.

Ramirez smiled. "Your silence says it all. You aren't perfect, McKee. None of us is. But you aren't so flawed as you think you are either. And you're learning."

"So that's why you came here? To straighten me out?"

"Hell, no. I came to get a free meal."

McKee laughed, threw a piece of wood onto the fire, and watched a constellation of sparks disappear up into the clay chimney. The pain was still there—but more bearable somehow. They slipped into their sleeping bags shortly thereafter—each claiming one side of the fire. Wood crackled and popped. Light danced the walls. And for the first time in days, McKee fell into a deep dreamless sleep.

The sun was up by the time McKee awoke, threw the last of the wood on the fire, and had to go looking for more. Plus it was a chance to take a pee and look around. The sky was clear, and a fresh layer of snow obscured the tracks that she and Ramirez had made earlier. A sure sign that there hadn't been any visitors. Snow crunched under her boots, and her breath fogged the air as she approached the remains of the watchtower.

The old axe was right where she'd left it, so she put her assault weapon down, and went to work. The axe produced a satisfying *thunk* as it bit into a piece of wood, and there was a sharp, cracking sound when a section split in two. It was hard but satisfying work because a well-aimed blow produced a predictable result. And that's what McKee was thinking about when a humming noise caused her to turn with the axe raised.

Unlike the drones she had employed during the mission to find Truthsayer, this one was larger, shaped like a cigar, and equipped for long-range missions. It hovered four feet off the ground, and McKee could feel the envelope of heat that surrounded it. The voice was clearly synthetic. "Are you Lieutenant McKee?"

McKee felt a sudden flood of anxiety as she lowered the axe. They were looking for her. *Why?* Because they knew her true identity? Or because some supply officer wanted an accounting of all the gear she'd left in the field? Not that it mattered. Chances were that the robot knew the answer to its own question. "Yes, I'm McKee."

"Please stand by."

McKee swore under her breath. Who was being summoned? The answer turned out to be someone she didn't know. "Lieutenant McKee?" a female voice said. "I'm Captain Olson. I'm sorry to cut your leave short, but we need you here at the fort. Remain where you are. A Vulcan will pick you up within the next hour."

McKee swallowed. "May I ask why?"

"Sorry," came the reply. "That will have to wait until you return. Suffice it to say that we have an assignment for you."

"Yes, ma'am."

"Report to me when you arrive." The words were followed by a click.

The drone rose and took up station fifty feet over her head as McKee made her way back to the hut. That was offputting, but McKee chose to take comfort from the little bit of information she had. If Olson had a shit detail with her name on it, then chances were that her true identity was safe. It could be a trick, of course . . . But why bother? They could order the drone to kill her and send a graves-registration robot out to deal with the carcass.

Ramirez was up and around by the time she dumped the load of firewood into the underground chamber and lowered herself down the ladder. He took one look at her face, and said, "Uh-oh. What's wrong?"

"They called me back for some sort of assignment."

"That sucks," Ramirez replied. "So, you have a radio?"

"No. They sent a drone."

Ramirez produced a low whistle. "Must be important. Are you going to hike out?"

McKee had stacked the firewood and was opening an MRE. "Nope. They're going to send a Vulcan."

Ramirez muttered some words and traced a circle in the air. He meant well, but the fact that the holy man felt the need to deliver a blessing was more than a little unnerving. "I'll leave the rest of the MREs," McKee said.

"Thank you. I'll think of you each time I eat one."

"Please do me a favor, Father . . . Tell the warriors who have been guarding me that I said, 'Thank you.' "

"I will," Ramirez promised.

McKee finished her meal, packed her gear, and was about to climb the ladder when Ramirez came over to deliver a hug. "Take care of yourself, Andromeda. And remember . . . You did your best. No one can do more than that."

McKee gave him a peck on the cheek and shouldered her pack. The ladder creaked under her weight. Once she was up on the surface McKee took a look around. The drone was gone.

Rather than ask the fly-form to land in the confines of the village, McKee made her way out into the open, where there were no obstructions to worry about. And that's where she was when the Vulcan appeared off to the west. It circled the village before coming in for a landing. Steam rose to envelop the machine as repellers stabbed the ground, and McKee hurried forward. The ramp bounced slightly as she made her way up to the point where the fly-form's crew chief was waiting to greet her. "Good morning, ma'am . . . Where's the rest of your patrol?"

"There is no patrol . . . Just me."

There weren't very many legionnaires wandering around Algeron by themselves—and the chief gave her a strange look as servos whined, and the ramp came up. McKee turned to look, saw that Ramirez had come out to see her off, and tossed a salute at him. He waved in return and disappeared as the ramp came up. The flight to Fort Camerone took about forty-five minutes but seemed longer. Were they going to send her south again? Or assign her to some godforsaken outpost? There were lots of possibilities and no way to guess which one might be correct.

There was a *thump* as the Vulcan put down on one of the fort's landing pads. McKee was up and ready to disembark as the ramp hit duracrete. A choice had to be made. Would it be best to clean up first? Or report to Olson in a filthy uniform? Something about the brief interaction seemed to suggest that the second course was safest. "Report to me when you arrive." That's what Olson had said, so that's what she would do.

Once she was inside the fort, McKee consulted an electronic directory and discovered that Captain Olson was attached to the 2nd REP—or 2nd Regiment Etranger De Parachutistes. A much-celebrated airborne outfit known for their daring special-operations missions. That didn't make much sense since McKee was a cavalry officer, but then what did? Perhaps some sort of joint operation was in the offing.

McKee made her way through a maze of busy corridors and into the area occupied by the 2nd REP. A smart-looking corporal was seated behind the reception desk and eyed McKee's muddy uniform with obvious distaste. "Good morning, ma'am. How can I help you?"

"I'm looking for Captain Olson."

"Yes, ma'am. I'll tell her that you're here."

McKee waited while the corporal mumbled something inaudible into the wire-thin boom mike positioned in front of his mouth. "You can go back, Lieutenant. Take the first right. Captain Olson is in the second office on the left."

McKee made her way back to the office with a sign that read CAPT. OLSON next to the open door. Then she shrugged the pack off and placed it on the floor next to her assault rifle. Her knuckles produced a rapping sound as they hit the block of wood placed there for that purpose. Then she waited to hear a voice say "Enter," before taking three paces forward. "Lieutenant McKee reporting as ordered, ma'am."

The office was small, and Olson was seated behind a gunmetal gray desk. She wore her hair in a flattop, and had white sidewalls, with two ears stuck out at nearly right angles. Her narrow-set eyes were bright with intelligence— and when she spoke, her slitlike mouth barely moved. "At ease. Close the door and grab a chair."

McKee did as she was told. "So," Olson began. "Welcome to Special Operations Team One-Five."

McKee could tell that she was supposed to ask, so she did. "Thank you, ma'am. I don't believe I've heard of Special Ops Team One-Five."

"That's because it's secret," Olson said primly. "As is everything I'm about to tell you. The team is a company-strength unit under the command of Major Brett Remy. I am his executive officer. For reasons that will soon become clear, the decision was made to cut one platoon of infantry from the One-Five and replace it with a platoon of cavalry. You will be in charge of that platoon."

Even though nothing had been said, McKee got the distinct feeling that Olson was opposed to replacing infantry with cavalry—and that wasn't too surprising given her background. "Yes, ma'am."

Olson's chair made a squeaking sound as she leaned back in it. "You have a very interesting record, McKee . . . You joined the Legion on Esparto, rose to the rank of sergeant in record time, and received an Imperial Order of Merit from the empress herself. Then you won a battlefield commission here on Algeron. As it happens, Major Remy likes jackers. He believes that ex-noncoms make excellent officers."

Olson paused to create a steeple with her fingers. "I have a different opinion, however. I believe that most jackers are worthless, ass-kissing con artists, who know how to take credit for the things they didn't do and are a disgrace to the Legion. So be warned. I will watch you—and I will document what I see. Understood?"

McKee was careful to keep her voice neutral. "Yes, ma'am."

"Good. Now that we understand each other, let's talk about the mission. Empress Ophelia left Earth about a month ago to tour the colonies."

All it took was the mention of Ophelia's name to make McKee's heart beat faster. But it was important to keep her face blank, and she did.

"Her first stop was on Orlo II," Olson added. "And by all accounts, that visit went well."

Memories of the planet and the battles fought there came flooding back. Suddenly, McKee was lying on her back looking up at John Avery from six inches away. *Focus,* she told herself. *Pay attention.*

"The next stop was Worber's World," Olson continued. "Then, after a brief stay, the empress left to visit the Clone Hegemony. But she never arrived. A Hudathan battle group was lying in wait at Jump Point 897632, and a battle ensued."

Olson had McKee's full attention at that point. And it was time to ask the obvious question. "Did the ridgeheads know she was coming?"

"We don't think so," Olson replied. "But there will be an investigation. You can be sure of that. The *Victorious* made an emergency jump and her escorts remained behind to prevent the Hudathans from following her.

"Shortly thereafter, the *Victorious* exited hyperspace in the vicinity of the planet Savas. However, due to extensive damage suffered during the ambush, it was impossible to control the ship's in-system drives. So the planet's gravity pulled the *Vic* down. We know this because the commanding officer launched a message torp just before the ship entered the atmosphere."

Though no expert on such things, McKee knew that large warships weren't designed to land on planetary surfaces. So whatever happened next wouldn't be pretty. "That sucks," McKee said, hoping Ophelia was dead. "Did anyone survive?"

"We don't know," Olson answered. "All we can do is hope. Our job is to reach the crash site, find the empress if she's still alive, and protect her until a naval task force arrives."

"And if the empress is dead?"

"Then we will protect her body. And her son if he's alive."

McKee had met Nicolai and liked him. "Yes, ma'am. When do we lift?"

"At 0100," Olson replied. "I'm sorry, but time is of the essence. You weren't available, so I was forced to select your platoon for you."

The last thing McKee wanted was to have a ground pounder choose her team. Especially for a mission like this one. But judging from the look in Olson's eyes, she was just waiting for McKee to object. And doing so would be pointless. So McKee limited her reply to a "Thank you. How about supplies?"

"I delegated that responsibility to your platoon sergeant. He has an excellent record and seems to be quite capable."

McKee thought about Larkin and made a note to visit him if only for a few minutes. "Yes, ma'am."

"All right, then," Olson said. "Pull your gear together and be on Pad 8 at 1245 hours. We'll use the trip out to train up. Any questions?"

"No, ma'am."

"Dismissed."

McKee rose, offered a salute, and received one in return. She felt a fierce sense of determination as she executed an about-face and left the office. If they found Ophelia, and the bitch was alive, she wouldn't be for long.

With less than twelve hours left to lift off, McKee had to make good use of her time. The first stop was to see Larkin who, according to the lead medic, was an enormous pain in the ass. Hardly a surprise from McKee's point of view. His bed was positioned in a row of beds, some of which were invisible behind pulled curtains. The legionnaire still had a bandage wrapped around his head, but his face lit up as she approached. "McKee! You're back . . . That's great. Tell the pill pushers to turn me loose."

McKee grinned. "I come bearing good news . . . According to the medic out front, they plan to discharge you in a couple of days. *If* you continue to improve. So lie back and get better."

Larkin made a face. "Okay . . . But keep my slot open."

McKee shook her head. "I'm sorry, Desmond . . . I'd like nothing better. But I have orders."

"Shit. Where are you going? I'll find a way to get there."

"I'm not allowed to say."

They looked at each other. There was a moment of silence. Larkin spoke first. "I'm going to miss you, McKee. Watch your six."

McKee felt a lump form in the back of her throat. Ever since boot camp, there had been one thing she could count on—and that was the certain knowledge that Larkin would be there to watch her back. "I will, Desmond, I will. You too."

And then, fearful that she would start crying, McKee turned and left. There were other people she cared about—but none she felt compelled to say good-bye to. So she made her way to the tiny room that constituted her quarters and went to work sorting her gear. She could take about sixty pounds' worth of stuff with her. The balance would go into storage. Would she return to claim it? She pushed the thought away.

The rest of the day passed quickly. Then, after a three-hour nap, it was time to get up. A hot shower and a simple breakfast were followed by McKee's carrying her gear through a maze of corridors to a lift that took her up to the flight center. Her breath fogged the air as she emerged, and there was nothing to see but darkness out beyond the fortress.

After clearing a security checkpoint, McKee followed an elevated walkway to Pad 8, where a shuttle sat crouched under the glow of two overhead lights. It looked as though the third light had been shot out by a sniper stationed on High Hump Hill. The Naa couldn't see the shuttle, or the ground crew, thanks to a protective wall. But the bastards took pride in popping the perimeter lights when they could.

Wisps of vapor drifted away from the manta-shaped shuttle as a petty officer came down the ramp to help with her gear. He was wearing a helmet, a navy blue flight suit, and combat boots. The salute was crisp. "Welcome aboard, ma'am. The pilots tell me we're going to lift on time. That'll put you on *Io* in three hours or so."

McKee thanked the sailor and followed him up the ramp into the dimly lit hold. Cargo modules occupied most of the space, but a trio of legionnaires was settling in as well. One of them said, "Atten-hut!" But before the others could stand, McKee said, "As you were," and went over to introduce herself. The ground pounders wouldn't be reporting to her, but it made sense to know everyone in the unit. All of them wore rakish green berets and the winged-hand-and-dagger emblem they took so much pride in.

Once the introductions were complete, McKee chose a seat, strapped in, and was asleep before the shuttle lifted off. When she awoke, it was to find the crew chief looming over her. "Lieutenant? We're on the *Io*. Your gear is at the bottom of the ramp."

McKee rubbed her eyes and yawned. "Thank you."

The petty officer smiled. "We aim to please." Then he was gone.

Once McKee reached the bottom of the ramp, she saw that a legionnaire was waiting for her. He snapped to attention. "Platoon Sergeant Jolo, ma'am. Welcome aboard." The salute was picture-perfect. Jolo had dark skin, serious eyes, and a square chin. McKee hadn't had an opportunity to study his P-1 file but liked what she saw. And that was important because Jolo was going to be her second-in-command.

She returned the salute and extended her hand. "Captain Olson has nice things to say about you."

Jolo grinned. "Who am I to argue with the XO? Speaking of which, Major Remy is holding a meeting in half an hour, and we're invited. Here . . . I can help with your gear."

The outer hatch was closed, and the hangar was pressurized. As Jolo led McKee over to a lift, she quizzed him about the ship. According to the information available on-line at the fort, the *Io* was an SSML or Supply Ship Medium Load. That suggested a small freighter. But the *Io* didn't *feel* like a freighter, and when she said as much, Jolo laughed. "No, ma'am. The *Io* is a special-operations dropship. She's about half a mile long, carries a 150-person crew, and can deliver up to 150 pods."

McKee looked at him. "As in 'climb-inside-a-capsule-and-fall-out-of-the-sky' type pods?"

"Yes, ma'am. I'm looking forward to it. The green hats tell me it'll be one helluva ride."

McKee didn't like the idea but thought it best to keep such reservations to herself. By the time they reached her tiny cabin and placed her gear inside, it was time to leave for the meeting.

The wardroom was located on A deck and barely large enough to accommodate the nine people who were present. They included Olson, who acknowledged McKee with a nod prior to making an introduction. "Major Remy, this is Lieutenant McKee."

Remy had bushy brows, penetrating eyes, and a cleft chin. He was no taller than McKee, but he had a firm grip and a strong physical presence. "Welcome to the One-Five, McKee . . . You've had the briefing, so you know where we're headed. There's no telling what we'll run into, and we're damned lucky to have a cavalry officer of your experience."

After that, McKee was introduced to the other platoon leaders, the company sergeant, and two platoon sergeants. All of whom were members of the 2nd REP. "Okay," Remy said. "Find places to sit. We will break orbit shortly. That will be the beginning of a seven-day, two-jump run to Savas."

Remy waited until all of them were situated before continuing. His expression was serious. "All of you know that the empress was aboard the *Victorious*. What you *don't* know is that according to data gathered by an unmanned recon ship, the Hudathans have a base on Savas."

McKee heard the platoon leader seated on her right say, "Oh, shit," and Remy nodded.

"Thank you, Lieutenant Ellis . . . That's my sentiment as well. And the Hudathans have everything to do with why a dropship was chosen for this mission. In addition to the base, it looks like the ridgeheads have a battle group stationed off Savas.

"Ideally, the navy would attack those ships and put a battalion of marines on the ground. And ultimately it will. But our forces are stretched thin at the moment. So while the people on Earth pull the necessary resources together, the *Io* is going to swoop in and drop us onto Savas. Then she's going to run like hell. The hope is that she can make a hyperspace jump before the ridgeheads can nail her."

Remy's eyes probed the faces around him. "We will find ourselves in a challenging situation regardless of what happens to the *Io*," he said. "Once the Hudathans realize what took place, they will start to search for us. Lieutenant Sokov . . . I can tell that you're itching to ask a question."

Sokov had a shaved head, a prominent brow, and a 2nd REP emblem dangling from one ear. "Sir, yes, sir. Do the Hudathans know about the *Victorious*?"

"That," Remy said heavily, "is a very important question. And we don't know for sure. But it seems safe to assume that they do."

"So if the empress is alive, they might have her," Olson pointed out.

"Shit, shit, shit," Ellis said.

"The lieutenant has a limited vocabulary," Remy said dryly, "but an excellent grasp of the situation. That brings us to the week ahead. Lieutenant McKee hasn't been introduced to any of her people with the exception of Sergeant

Jolo here. Nor has she, or any member of her platoon, completed a drop. So they'll have to hit the virtual-reality system hard during the coming days."

Olson cleared her throat. "Permission to speak freely, sir?"

Remy smiled grimly. "Of course."

"We're still in orbit, sir. In the light of what you said, I recommend we request an additional platoon from the 2nd REP and dispense with the cavalry. It would take six to eight hours to effect the change—but the payoff would be worth the delay."

If Olson's proposal caught Remy by surprise, there was no sign of it on his face. His eyes swung over to McKee. "How about it, McKee? Should we trade you and your platoon for more green hats?"

McKee felt mixed emotions. The mission Remy had described verged on the impossible. And who could blame her if she chose to side with Olson? Her people lacked the necessary training, and no amount of VR time would make up for the deficit. But what if the empress was alive? The mission might give McKee an opportunity to kill her . . . And that would be a very good thing indeed. She met Remy's gaze.

"I understand Captain Olson's point of view, sir . . . But I think the benefits of keeping my platoon on the team outweigh the potential problems. Once on the ground, each one of my T-1s will provide firepower equivalent to an entire squad of green hats. That, plus our ability to travel at up to 30 MPH over flat terrain and our heavy weaponry, will provide the One-Five with a much-needed edge should the unit be forced to engage a numerically superior force. Sir."

Remy grinned. "I couldn't have said it better myself . . . So we're going to roll the dice on this one. Okay, that's it for now. Go check on your people. Make sure they're ready for departure. Lieutenant McKee . . . A moment of your time, please."

"I'll take care of the platoon," Jolo said as he slid past her. "We're on C deck."

McKee thanked the noncom and watched Olson say something to Remy before leaving the compartment. Was the XO okay with the major's decision? Hell, no. Would she find a way to make McKee's life suck? Hell, yes. That was life in the Legion. McKee sighed.

Once the rest of them were gone, Remy turned to McKee. "Welcome to the team, Lieutenant . . . I can see that you have a good grasp of why I requested a cavalry detachment. What may not be so obvious is why I requested *you*. We need an officer who can think on her feet—and has a lot of combat experience. You have those qualities plus one more . . . You are the only person on the team who has been eyeball to eyeball with the empress."

McKee frowned. "Sir?"

"If she's alive, and if we find her, the fact that she knows you could come in handy," Remy said. "The empress is used to giving orders—but she lacks tactical experience."

There it was. The *real* reason why McKee had been selected over more senior officers. Remy was understandably worried about what it would be like to try and manage a famously dictatorial monarch under stressful conditions. "I only spent a few minutes with her," McKee put in.

Remy nodded. "True. But during those minutes, she presented you with the Imperial Order of Merit. That's something she isn't likely to forget. So if you make a suggestion, there's a very good chance that she will listen to it."

"And if she's dead?"

Remy shrugged. "I have photos . . . But someone will have to identify the body. A mistake could be disastrous."

That was true. Should the team find a female body and mistakenly identify it as Ophelia's, only to have the real monarch surface somewhere else, that would not only end

Remy's career but put his life in danger. A possibility he was clearly aware of.

Would she be able to recognize Ophelia's dead body? Barring major disfigurements, McKee thought she could. More than that, it was a sight she *wanted* to see. She nodded. "Yes, sir. Roger that, sir. You can count on me."

The work began the moment the *Io* broke orbit and entered hyperspace. The first thing McKee wanted to do was meet each person in her platoon, get Jolo's impressions of them, and study their P-1 files. The good news was that Remy and Olson had clearly gone to considerable lengths to draft bio bods and cyborgs who had better-than-average service records. The bad news was that some of the best legionnaires McKee knew were screwups like Larkin. Difficult to manage? Yes, but frequently worth their weight in gold when the poop hit the fan.

There was another problem as well. Rather than draft an existing platoon, Remy and Olson had plucked "volunteers" from a variety of units. That meant McKee's people didn't know each other—and had no experience working as a team. To compensate for that, McKee put her legionnaires through dozens of VR drills covering standard combat situations. Things went poorly at first but had begun to improve by day four.

By that time, McKee was under a great deal of pressure from Olson to practice high-altitude drops. So even though she would have preferred to spend additional time and effort on standard tactics, McKee was forced to switch. And because the drop scenarios were custom-designed by Olson, they were consistently difficult. That was good in a way since the landing on Savas would be tough.

But it seemed as if the XO was determined to make sure

that every make-believe mission ended in failure. That was hard on morale. During the latest drop, the entire platoon landed in a virtual swamp so dangerous it reminded McKee of boot camp on Drang. Half her people were KIA by the time she aborted the mission, ripped the VR leads off, and told her people to take a break.

McKee made the trip from C deck to Olson's cabin on A deck in record time. The hatch was open, and she entered without knocking. Olson looked up from her computer, frowned, and was about to speak when McKee beat her to it. "Permission to speak freely, ma'am."

Olson smiled as if she knew what was coming and looked forward to it. "Permission granted."

"As regards the VR simulations for my platoon, ma'am . . . While I understand the need for tough training prior to the insertion, my team has never worked together before. So they have no record of past successes to fall back on. By creating scenarios in which they never succeed, you are working contrary to the best interest of the One-Five. I request that you provide my platoon with some exercises in which they have an opportunity to do well. If you fail to do so, I will go over your head."

It looked as though all the blood had drained out of Olson's face. Her eyes were wide, and her lips moved, but nothing came out at first. "How dare you! I am going to document what you said and charge you with insubordination. It's just as I suspected. You aren't a *real* officer . . . You're a jumped NCO who happened to be in the right place at the right time, won an IOM she didn't deserve, and thinks she can throw her weight around."

McKee took three paces forward, placed both fists on Olson's desk, and bent forward. Their faces were inches apart. "Listen, bitch . . . This isn't a fucking game. Have you ever gone up against a ridgehead? No? I didn't think so. Well, I have, and they're tough. If we run into them, the odds are that both you and I will wind up dead. So do you think I give a damn about your silly-assed charges? Hell no, I don't. And if you want to take this to Remy, I would welcome that. So think things over. And make some changes to the way you put those VR scenarios together. Because if you don't, I will come up here and personally kick your skinny ass. Do you read me?"

There was fear in Olson's eyes by then, and her voice was little more than a whisper. "I read you."

McKee came to attention. The salute was perfect. "Good. Thanks for listening." And with that, McKee left the compartment. The next VR scenario was difficult but survivable.

The succeeding days seemed to fly by even though they were long and tiring. There were VR exercises to take part in, but more than that, actual preparations to complete, including a review of every item that the legionnaires would take with them. Because once on the ground, they weren't likely to receive more supplies until the theoretical relief party arrived.

Fortunately, Jolo had used team One-Five's high-priority clout to requisition so many spares that the platoon wouldn't be able to carry all of them. But some components had a tendency to wear out faster than others. So McKee had her bio bods replace such parts no matter how new they were in an effort to ensure that her T-1s remained operational for as long as possible.

There was one glitch, however, or what could have been a glitch, and that had to do with the three supply pods allotted to the cavalry platoon. After inspecting them, McKee discovered that they had been loaded by category. All of the food in one, all of the ammo in another, and so forth. That meant that if one container was lost, then *all* of something would be lost with it.

So McKee had all three pods repacked, making sure that

all her supplies were spread around. Would the green hats make that kind of mistake? McKee didn't think so. But ever since her tête-à-tête with Olson, the XO had been hands off. That was the downside of telling her off—and caused McKee to wonder what problems had been missed.

Then time ran out. The *Io* left hyperspace and began the run in toward Savas. Odds were that at least one of the Hudathan ships would be close enough to "see" the dropship and respond. That meant there would be no second chance.

With that in mind, Major Remy ordered his people into their pods *before* the *Io* left hyperspace. There were a hundred drop tubes on D deck, seventy-eight of which were loaded with pods. The plan was to launch all of them simultaneously, so that they would land within a few miles of each other. But there were a lot of variables to contend with, and having been through ten virtual insertions, McKee knew that the so-called "spread" could cover a much larger area.

Some of the containers were packed with supplies, some carried RAVs, and the rest were filled with people. Twelve pods were what the hats called "deuces," meaning they were loaded with a bio bod *and* a corresponding cyborg, so that each two-person team would hit the dirt together.

So as the *Io* entered the planet's gravity well and bucked her way down through the atmosphere, McKee found herself seated across from a ten-foot-tall T-1 named Leo Bartov. They were almost knee to knee thanks to the fact that she was perched on a storage compartment full of .50 caliber ammo. The ceiling was low, the inward-curving walls felt oppressively tight, and the LEDs on the control panel to McKee's left glowed green.

Bartov gave her a gigantic thumbs-up, and she answered in kind. He was, according to what McKee had read, guilty of killing his wife and her lover. With a baseball bat if she remembered correctly. And, when given a choice, had chosen to live life as a cyborg rather than face the big nothing. But unlike many of his peers Bartov seemed to enjoy life as a T-1. Or, as he liked to put it, "I'm the baddest badass on the block."

McKee's thoughts were interrupted as the pilot's voice flooded her helmet. "All personnel, stand by for launch . . . Check onboard NAV functions and reboot if necessary. Thirty, twenty-nine, twenty-eight . . ."

Remy's voice overrode the pilot's. "Okay, people . . . It's time to earn that drop pay. And remember . . . Those pods belong to the government, so don't soil them."

That produced a chorus of guffaws as the countdown resumed. "Sixteen, fifteen, fourteen . . ."

McKee gave thanks for the helmet and visor. It was nice to know that Bartov couldn't see how scared she was. "Three, two, one."

McKee felt a sudden jerk as the *Io* leveled out and fired the pods straight down. Her stomach performed a flip-flop as the pod fell clear of the ship's ARGRAV field, and the steering jets fired. McKee couldn't see the activity but knew the *Io* was dumping chaff into the atmosphere along with the pods as a way to confuse the Hudathans. Which blips were pods and which weren't? It would be tough to tell. The deuce began to vibrate as an envelope of hot plasma formed around it. She could feel the temperature inside the module start to rise as layer after layer of protection was burned away. Then the deuce flipped and flipped again as the steering jets fired. "We're having some fun now," Bartov rumbled.

McKee was about to reply when the main chute deployed, and she felt a violent jerk. The sensation was identical to what she had experienced during the VR training, and that was reassuring. The pod swayed from side to side, and a downward-pointing camera fed video to McKee's

HUD. That was when she saw the lake and realized that the deuce was going to hit the water. "Get ready," she said. "We're going to . . ." And that was when the pod hit.

It sank at first. Then, being airtight, it bobbed to the surface. That was the good news. The bad news was that the pod had no means of propulsion—and couldn't be opened without allowing water to rush in.

Meanwhile, as the pod floated on the surface of the lake, it was an inviting target for anyone who wanted to shoot at it. Fortunately, no one had. Not yet anyway. McKee tried to remember a VR session that dealt with such a predicament but couldn't. Remy's voice sounded in her ears. "This is Charlie-Nine . . . It looks like we have three floaters. Blow your pods, salvage what you can, and get to shore. We'll cover you. Over."

McKee chinned her mike two times and eyed her HUD. The other floaters belonged to her. She switched to platoon freq. "This is Charlie-One to Charlie Four-One and Charlie-Five. You heard the major. You can swim, and your borgs can walk along the bottom of the lake if they have to. Be sure to remove your supplies from storage *before* you blow your pods. Once your T-1 is loaded, blow the pod. Over."

There was very little room in which to maneuver. But McKee managed to open the compartment she'd been sitting on. Bartov leaned forward to pull two waterproof containers out. There was a forty-pound backpack for McKee and a larger chest pack for him. With help from McKee, he was able to strap both to his body. The weight distribution was all wrong but would be okay for the relatively short walk to shore.

Once that was accomplished, McKee flipped a protective cover out of the way and thumbed a button. There was a loud bang, both halves of the pod separated, and the sky appeared. That was followed by a sudden influx of water. It was cool but not that cold.

McKee threw herself clear and Bartov waved as he sank. Fortunately, McKee was only a hundred yards from shore. But she was wearing combat gear and carrying her AXE. All being too precious to shed.

So she floundered forward, sank, and battled her way to the surface again. But it wasn't going to work. She was going to drown. Then McKee felt something grab her combat vest from behind and lift. Suddenly, she was halfway out of the water and still kicking her feet as Bartov carried her ashore. As the cyborg put her down, Remy appeared out of the brush that bordered the water. His visor was open, and there was a smile on his face. "Welcome to Savas, Lieutenant. If we survive this mission, I'll rate you as drop-qualified . . . A signal honor for a cavalry officer." The Legion had landed.

CHAPTER: 8

It is difficult to say which I hate more, the round heads, or the change skins. Both bring death.

CHIEF SOTH NENGAR
The northern Paguumis
Standard year 2761

PLANET SAVAS

The air was cool, and the sky was a beautiful violet color as Avery exited the wreck and paused to look around. But off to the east, the orange-red sun was about to break company with the horizon and would soon make itself known. By midday, the temperature would climb to a toasty ninety-five degrees. That was why he wanted to climb the mountain early. Marines and sailors were posted around what remained of the ship. One of them said, "Good morning, sir," as the officer passed by.

Avery waved as he followed boot prints toward the base of the mountain. Or was it a large hill? Not that it made any difference. More than a week had passed since the crash landing. Ophelia and her son had survived, along with most of the people on the upper decks, but hundreds had been killed down below, where the force of the impact crushed a hull never intended for a planetary landing.

The marines on D deck suffered a disproportionate number of casualties, and that included the loss of their commanding officer, Major Conklin, which was how Avery wound up in command of all ground forces. That included most of the sailors since their regular jobs didn't exist anymore. With nothing else to do, the survivors were waiting for the rescue force that was sure to come, assuming that Captain Suzuki's message torp made it through.

Avery let his AXE dangle from its sling as he started up the steep trail. The path wasn't new, or he didn't think so, and for good reason. Many of the sentients who lived on Savas were nomads. So it seemed likely that they had passed through the area many times and placed lookouts on the hill just as he had.

It took the better part of twenty minutes to follow the switchbacking path up to the summit, where Outpost Oscar was situated. The OP consisted of a large tarp supported by metal poles, a well-dug fighting position, and a team of six. The idea was to make sure that two people were awake and scanning the surrounding countryside at all times.

A row of empty five-gallon water containers sat ready to be picked up later that morning. Two of the ship's maintenance bots were being used to hump five-gallon containers of water up to the summit—and without them, Outpost Oscar wouldn't have been possible.

The NCO in charge of the OP was a cheerful sergeant named Rucker. Like the rest of the detachment, he was dressed in shorts, boots, and very little else. Having missed his weekly haircut, his red hair was getting longer. "Good morning, Major . . . It's nice to see that the Legion is finally up and around."

"Good morning, Sergeant. Look at that hair . . . You're a disgrace to the Marine Corps." Both men grinned and shook hands.

Then Avery made the rounds, pausing to talk with each

marine or sailor before returning to the point where a pair of tripod-mounted 30-160x70 binoculars had been set up. "So, Rucker, what are the buggers up to this morning?"

"They're all around us, sir . . . Just watching so far. See the pointy rock out there? You can see a couple of digs down at the base of it."

Avery stepped up to the glasses, swung them onto the rock, and tilted down. That's when he saw two cloth-wrapped heads and what might have been a rifle barrel. The locals had the wreck under surveillance all right. The question was *why*? Were they merely keeping an eye on the off-worlders? To make sure they stayed where they were? Or were they preparing to attack?

Avery took his eyes from the binoculars in order to survey the surrounding terrain. It was open. That was a good thing because it meant the digs wouldn't have much cover if they tried to take a run at the wreck. But how many fighters could they bring to bear? A hundred? A *thousand*? That was Avery's greatest concern. The remaining marines weren't equipped to deal with a situation that no one had foreseen. Had it been otherwise, he could have placed artillery and mortars on the hill ready to sweep the open area with plunging fire. But such wasn't the case. All they had were small arms and a few crew-served machine guns. *A squad of T-1s,* the legionnaire thought to himself. *A single squad of cyborgs could make a huge difference.* But he might as well have wished for a battalion of tanks.

Closer in, near the foot of the hill, he could see the wreck. Most of the bow was buried under the tidal wave of dirt that had been pushed up during the ship's three-mile journey across the planet's surface. The top half of the hull was exposed, but the lower decks were inaccessible from the outside. And there, leading away from the stern, was the fifty-foot-deep furrow that ran east to the recently decapitated hill. No wonder the digs were watching. The ship's arrival would have been hard to miss. "All right," Avery said, as he turned to Rucker. "Keep your eyes peeled. And call me if something changes."

Rucker nodded. "Got it."

"Okay, give me a couple of empty water containers. I might as well take 'em down with me."

"Finally," Rucker said. "A task the Legion is good for."

Avery laughed. "I'll send your relief up at 1800 hours."

The trip downhill was a lot easier than the climb up had been. Even with a plastic container in each hand. Fifteen minutes later, Avery was on flat ground and could feel the heat beating down on his back. He said "Hello" to a fire team comprised of sailors as he passed through the security perimeter, dumped the empties onto a pile outside the hatch, and waited for a petty officer to descend the make-shift ladder that led up to Emergency Hatch 016. Once her boots hit the ground, he was free to climb up and enter the hull.

It was cooler inside and would remain so through much of the day, thanks to the hull's thickness. The engineering spaces were located at the very bottom of the ship and would have been crushed like everything else had it not been for the heavy-duty girders and the shielding that surrounded the drives. So Chief Engineering Officer Collins and some of her techs had survived the landing. And, thanks to their efforts, the *Victorious* still had some power. Just enough to keep the emergency lighting on, to power the water-purification system, and send juice to a single energy cannon that sat atop the hull.

So there was light to see by as Avery made his way up a series of access ladders to A deck and from there to the bridge. The morning meetings with Ophelia and Captain Suzuki had become a daily routine. And all of the ship's surviving department heads were present when the empress arrived at 1017 hours. Rumor had it that her cabin was air-conditioned. She looked calm, cool, and collected as she took a seat.

As was the custom, Captain Suzuki opened the meeting with a readout on the ship's steadily deteriorating condition. It was all he had left to do—and each report was worse than the last. Then it was Avery's turn. He told them what he'd seen from the top of the hill and concluded the presentation with the usual admonition. "This position cannot be defended against anything other than a minor attack by poorly armed locals. I recommend that we pack up, find a more defensible location, and reestablish ourselves there. Thank you."

"Major Avery is nothing if not predictable," Ophelia said as she eyed the faces around her. "However, I think it's time for us to take his advice. Help has not arrived as quickly as we had hoped. And if our message torp went astray, assistance may *never* arrive. So the logical thing to do is pack up, destroy the ship, and make our way to Savas Prime. I know it's a small town, but ships call there, and the residents might have a message torp up in orbit. If so, we'll use it to summon help. Are there any objections?"

The final sentence was directed to Suzuki, who was not only the senior military officer on Savas but had been the primary advocate for staying put. Avery waited to see what would happen. Judging from the way the proposal was worded, the empress had given the matter a lot of thought. Would Suzuki lay out an equally convincing counterargument? Or, after spending more than a week in the desert, was he ready to abandon the wreck?

Suzuki was in his midforties and looked at least ten years older than that. While in space, he had an answer for every problem. But on the ground, he was like a fish out of water. And rather than undertake what he saw as a risky cross-country trek, he wanted to remain with the thing he understood best. And that was his ship.

But like all senior officers, Suzuki was a part-time politician and a good one. That's why he had what amounted to a plum command—and was slated to become an admiral in the not-too-distant future. So Suzuki knew what he had to say and forced himself to say it. "Her Highness is correct. The time has come to abandon ship."

Suzuki's reward was a royal smile. "We are all in agreement then," Ophelia said. "So, Captain . . . How long will it take to prepare?"

Suzuki frowned. "At least two days, Highness. We'll need to decide what to take, devise ways to carry our supplies, and prepare our personnel for the journey."

Avery knew he should remain silent for political reasons but couldn't bring himself to do so. "Excuse me, sir . . . But I think we should carry out the necessary preparations in *one* day. The ship could come under attack at any time."

If other people hadn't been present, Suzuki might have listened. But he had already been overridden by the empress and wasn't about to accept the same treatment from a subordinate. "Thank you, Major," Suzuki said coldly. "Your suggestion has been noted. But since there was no mention of an imminent attack in the report you gave earlier, a two-day interval seems appropriate. And given that most of the preparatory work will fall on *your* shoulders—I suspect you'll thank me later."

Ophelia smiled thinly and chose to remain silent. That left Avery with no choice but to obey Suzuki's orders. "Sir, yes, sir."

"Good, it's settled then," Suzuki said. "Let's get to work."

And there was plenty of work to do. It began with a hurried inventory of what they had. Then it was necessary to agree on what they would take. The final task was to pull everything together and load it onto improvised pack frames. The work went on and on, so that by the time Avery collapsed on his bunk, he was exhausted. Sleep pulled him down.

The second day was equally grueling. And by the time Avery finished inspecting the security perimeter at 1900 hours everything was ready. So he returned to the ship, took a much-needed sponge bath, and went to bed dressed for the day ahead.

There were dreams. A lot of dreams. And Cat played a part in some of them. They were fighting something, battling it side by side, when she began to moan. Then the moan morphed into the mournful sound of the ship's emergency Klaxon.

Avery rolled off the bunk, stood, and slipped his arms through the corresponding holes in the load-bearing vest. It was equipped with a pistol, ammo, and some grenades. He made a grab for his assault weapon and heard a cacophony of radio traffic as he pulled his helmet on.

"There are *thousands* of them!" an excited voice proclaimed. "Over."

"Thousands of *what*?" another person demanded.

"They're like cattle," a third voice chimed in. "But different."

"There are some digs too," the first voice added. "Riding the cattle."

"This is Major Avery," the legionnaire said. "All personnel will use proper radio protocol from now on. As for the riders, shoot the bastards—and secure all the hatches. Over."

"It's too late," a desperate-sounding female voice said. "Sorry . . . This is Riley. They're in the corridors! I shot one of them, but there are more. *Shit!* They're everywhere!" That was followed by a short burst of automatic fire and silence.

Avery swore under his breath. From the sound of it, the

locals had used some sort of cowlike animals to stampede through the area, ridden them in, and taken most of the sentries by surprise. He stepped out into the corridor and saw an indig coming toward him. The warrior was bipedal, had a crested head, and was armed with what Avery recognized as a Hudathan pistol. The weapon was so large it was difficult for the warrior to handle. And while he was fumbling with it Avery shot him. The dig jerked spastically as the 4.7 mm slugs hit his chest and knocked him off his feet.

Avery had to go that way anyway, and paused long enough to grab the pistol and shove it into a pocket as he took a left. The access ladder was directly in front of him. The sound of firing could be heard as he climbed upward. Avery wanted to rally the crew . . . But *where?* And was it too late?

He stepped off the ladder onto B deck. Maybe it was safe . . . *If* they could seal it off. Then he saw Ophelia and Nicolai hurrying toward him. "Major Avery," she said urgently, "please get us out of here."

All sorts of thoughts whirled through Avery's mind. Get them out . . . *How?* Especially under the circumstances. Plus, here was the perfect opportunity to kill the bitch . . . For Cat and all the others. "Major John?" Nicolai said. "Can I have a gun? I want to fight."

Avery swore. He was about to reply when a sign caught his eye. EMERGENCY POD B-14. "Get in," he ordered, and pointed his weapon at the hatch.

Ophelia flipped a protective cover out of the way and hit the big red button with the heel of her hand. There was a whoosh as the air inside the capsule equalized with the ship's atmosphere. The empress sent her son in first and followed him. Then she turned and motioned for Avery to enter.

It had been his intention to seal the royals inside and defend the entrance. But a new possibility had occurred to him. Pods weren't equipped with power plants. They were propelled out and away from a ship by a powerful blast of compressed air. Would the system work? And, if it did, where would the capsule land? Outside of the combat zone? Or right in the middle of it? There was no way to be sure—but he figured it was worth a try.

Avery couldn't go though . . . His responsibility was to defend the ship. "Lock it!" he shouted. "I have to stay."

That was when Suzuki's voice filled his helmet. "This is the captain. They have Empress Ophelia," he said dully. "We can't let them capture the *Victorious*. All personnel are to abandon ship. The demo charges will blow in sixty seconds."

Avery wanted to object, to explain, but there was no time in which to do so. He turned to the pod, stepped inside, and told the royals to sit down. As Avery fell into a chair, a well-padded cage folded around him.

Controls were available at each seat. Avery flipped a transparent cover out of the way and pushed the FIRE button. Like the rest of the crew, he'd been forced to participate in regular abandon-ship drills, and that knowledge was about to pay off. Or so he hoped as an outer hatch opened and a powerful blast of air threw the capsule up into the sky. "Hang on!" he shouted. "We're going to hit hard."

And he was correct. Avery felt a brief moment of weightlessness followed by a fall and a heavy impact. His jaw hit his chest, and the unsecured AXE almost struck Ophelia's head before bouncing off a bulkhead and hitting the deck.

The protective cage hugged Avery even more securely as the pod bounced up into the air. But the second ride was mercifully short. It ended when the capsule hit the ground and rolled for a distance before finally coming to a stop. Nicolai's eyes looked huge and his lower lip was starting to quiver. "I want my mommy."

That was when Avery opened his mouth to say, "She's

right here," looked at Ophelia, and realized the truth. Suzuki was correct. The empress *had* been captured. And he was looking at Daska. The robot nodded. "The empress was outside when the attack came."

Avery swore. Somehow, he had wound up on the surface of a hostile planet with a five-year-old boy to take care of. And that was when the future emperor began to cry.

The sun was high in the sky, the air was heavy with the stench of animal feces, and Admiral Dor Nola-Ba was seated inside a Paguumi hoga. The shade was welcome. His back was exposed, however—and the swill his host called "tea" made his stomach churn.

But those irritations were nothing when compared with the frustration that stemmed from Chief Imeer Oppo's failure to move against the Human ship in a timely fashion. Nola-Ba's battle group had become aware of the vessel shortly after it dropped hyper and approached Savas.

Nola-Ba was alarmed at first, fearing that a landing similar to his own was about to take place, but it was only a matter of minutes before the actual situation became clear. The alien ship was out of control and about to crash. So all Nola-Ba had to do was watch it hit the planet's surface, skip like a stone on the surface of a pond, and slam into a large hill. Shortly thereafter, some survivors appeared but made no attempt to leave the wreck.

The Hudathan's first reaction was to swoop in and take control. But then what seemed like a better plan entered his mind. What if *more* Humans were on the way? If so, the wreck could serve as bait. Then he would attack once the would-be rescuers were on the ground.

But then he had *another* even better idea. After the attack on the *Head Hunter*, Nola-Ba had sent scouts out to speak with the local nomads and, based on their reports, had a basic knowledge of local politics. It seemed that there were *three* groups of Paguumis—all descended from common ancestors hundreds of thousands of years earlier. But two of them were of primary concern. They included the northern tribe, which was responsible for the attack on his base, and the southern tribe, led by Chief Oppo.

So, given that his orders directed him to forge alliances with the indigenous peoples, Nola-Ba decided to befriend the southern Paguumis, knowing that they hated the northerners. And what better way to cement the new alliance than to give them the Human wreck? A rich source of what the locals valued above all else, and that was metal. The single caveat was that his intelligence people would be allowed to survey the ship before the locals took it apart. And if the Humans arrived, so much the better . . . While they were busy killing the natives, he would attack them!

Oppo was thrilled to receive title to the bounty that had fallen out of the sky. In fact, he had even gone so far as to sign a thousand-year peace treaty with the Hudathan Empire. A largely meaningless document, of course—but one Nola-Ba would submit as proof of his success on Savas. All of which was good except for the fact that Oppo was a very cautious creature who, rather than dash in to capture the wreck shortly after it was brought to his attention, insisted on watching it for days while gathering his forces.

Then, after what seemed like an eternity Oppo did something rather clever—and that was to send thousands of herd animals stampeding through the area where the wreck was located. The unconventional attack had the effect of neutralizing most of the Human's defenses. Meanwhile, warriors who were mounted on the four-legged beasts had been able to get in close and finish the job.

But then, in a move worthy of Nola-Ba's race, the Humans destroyed both themselves and their ship, killing more than a hundred warriors in the process. A terrible loss to be sure . . . But one that in no way weakened Oppo's position as chief since the attack netted more metal than his tribe knew what to do with. So what if they had to go out and gather the far-flung pieces? It was still an incredible haul.

The result was that they were drinking tea while Oppo talked nonsense, and Nola-Ba seethed with anger. Due to Oppo's failure to act expeditiously, what could have been a significant intelligence coup had been lost. Would he be blamed for allowing that to occur? Of course he would.

That's what the Hudathan was thinking about when Oppo said something important. Something so significant that it broke through his chain of thought. The electronic translator had a tendency to render everything in a monotone, but there was no mistaking the meaning of what was said. "So," Oppo said, having concluded a long tirade, "we plan to execute the Humans tomorrow . . . Would you like to watch?"

Oppo's head crest had been notched so many times that it resembled a saw blade. His skin was like old leather, a rakish-looking patch covered the hole where his left eye had been, and most of his front teeth were missing. But he was a clever old bugger and had been waiting to drop that piece of news on him! The southerners had prisoners . . . And, not content with a fortune in alien metal, Oppo was determined to squeeze even more out of his off-world allies.

"I never tire of watching Humans die," Nola-Ba replied truthfully. "But on my world, we like to ask prisoners a few questions prior to removing their heads. I'm sure it's the same with you and your people."

Oppo nodded agreeably as he gummed a piece of dried fruit that his wife had presoftened for him. He was seated on a beautifully woven carpet with a large cushion to support his back. "This is so," the chieftain said. "Unfortunately, what might otherwise be a routine matter is made more complicated by the deaths of so many warriors. Their families are very sad, but some speedy executions will serve to lift their spirits."

Nola-Ba clenched his considerable jaw in an effort to control the anger he felt. Most, if not all of Oppo's warriors would still be alive had the old geezer attacked right away. Now the chieftain was trying to squeeze what amounted to reparations out of Nola-Ba. And, much as he didn't want to, the Huda-than would have to bend. Not because he believed that interrogating the Humans would produce a treasure trove of intelligence—but because he could use the resulting transcripts to paper over the loss of the Human ship.

So Nola-Ba repressed the desire to kill Oppo with his bare hands and offered him a deal instead. "There's no way in which one can make up for the loss of a father, brother, or son. But life continues. Perhaps I could make that life a little easier."

Oppo seemed to perk up. "Really? What does the honored emissary from the stars have in mind?"

"You have metal now," Nola-Ba replied. "A great deal of hard metal and no efficient way to cut it."

Though no expert on Paguumi facial expressions, Nola-Ba could tell that Oppo hadn't considered that. And now that the idea had been planted in his head, he was worried. "How true," the Paguumi said, as if the issue had already occurred to him. "We would welcome whatever help you could provide."

"We have special saws," Nola-Ba said, conveniently ignoring the fact that his troops were equipped with plasma torches as well. "Saws that can cut through the toughest metal. Could it be that the joy associated with receiving such saws would be great enough to render the executions unnecessary?"

Oppo produced a frown. "Yes," the Paguumi chief allowed, "a thousand such saws would improve morale. There's no doubt about it."

"I'm sure they would," Nola-Ba answered smoothly. "And I hope a hundred blades will suffice. That's all we have beyond our own needs."

Nola-Ba could tell that Oppo didn't believe it—but knew better than to push his luck. "More tea," the Paguumi ordered imperiously. "We must seal the agreement. A hundred saws it is."

Nola-Ba waited for Oppo's wife to pour, raised the bowl high, and drank the contents. For some reason, the bitter brew tasted better than it had before.

THE GREAT PANDU DESERT

A warrior mounted on a proud-looking zurna led the way, followed by twelve Human prisoners. One of them was Empress Ophelia Ordanus—and she was in crudely forged chains. Her right ankle was bleeding where a rusty bracelet had rubbed it raw. The trail wound its way through a scattering of boulders, up over a ridge, and onto an area of reddish hardpan. The sun was a malevolent presence in the sky—and beat down on the Humans as if determined to suck them dry of moisture.

More than a day had passed since the attack on the wreck. After being cooped up inside the hot, muggy ship all day, Ophelia and Nicolai had gone out for a stroll. Daska and two additional synths had been along for protection. It was dark, but the moonlight offered enough light to see by, and the air was delightfully cool. So Ophelia allowed her son to play hide-and-seek with Daska.

After an hour or so, she ordered the synth to take her son into the ship and put him to bed. The cross-country hike was slated to begin first thing in the morning, and it was important for Nicolai to be rested. He complained but was led away. That was the last time she'd seen him. Had he been killed inside the ship? Yes. Were it otherwise, Nicolai would be among the prisoners. Tears cut tracks through the dust on her cheeks and evaporated within seconds.

Twenty minutes after Nicolai left, Ophelia heard what sounded like thunder and began to make her way back to the ship. But it wasn't thunder. A fact that soon became clear as the marines fired flares from the top of the hill, and Ophelia saw that a large number of animals were running toward her. Animals that were urged on by riders who cracked whips and shouted words she couldn't understand.

The ship was still too far away to reach in time, so the synths boosted Ophelia up onto a large rock and turned to confront the bawling horde. The robots fired their machine pistols, and Ophelia heard grunts of pain. But the small-caliber bullets had very little stopping power, and the tidal wave rolled over the machines and kept on going.

At that point it was up to the marines and sailors to stop the stampede, and they tried. Ophelia saw muzzle flashes and heard the stutter of automatic weapons as sentries attempted to cope with the unexpected threat. That was when the energy cannon on top of the wreck began to fire. Ophelia saw blips of coherent energy stutter out only to be absorbed by the seething herd of animals around her. How many died? Hundreds—maybe more.

There was an urge to run but no place to go. Ophelia had never felt so helpless before. Normally, she was in charge. That's what Ophelia was thinking about when the ship exploded. She was outside of the blast zone, but the flash of light took her night vision, and a shock wave blew her off the rock. She hit hard and rolled to her feet. The moon had set, but fiery pieces of wreckage were still twirling down out of the night sky.

While lots of indigs had been killed, others were mounted on the herd animals. One of them spotted her, stood, and jumped from back to back. It was a display of athleticism unlike anything Ophelia had seen before. She turned and began to run as a secondary explosion lit up the night. Ophelia hadn't traveled more than twenty feet when the warrior took a dive off one of the rampaging beasts and drove her to the ground. She struggled but to no avail. The Paguumi jerked the Human to her feet, tied her wrists, and led her away.

The rest of the night was spent in a ravine where a small fire provided what little warmth there was—and three guards kept a close eye on Ophelia and two other prisoners. More captives trickled in until there were twelve in all. That was when a blacksmith arrived to fit them with leg irons and chains. The fact that such things existed said something about the locals and their culture.

By the time the sun rose over the eastern horizon, the column was under way. Chains rattled, and when somebody tripped, all of the prisoners were whipped. Time lost all meaning as the sun arced across the achingly blue sky, and the shadows cast by the rock formations grew longer. Then, as the Humans rounded a low-lying hill, Ophelia spotted what looked like an inflatable hab up ahead. A mirage? Probably. That's what she assumed until they were about a hundred feet away.

That was when the entrance irised open, and a Hudathan emerged. Ophelia knew he was a Hudathan because she'd seen pictures of them. And he was *huge*. But for some reason, the alien's skin was white instead of gray. A reaction to the heat? Yes. But details like that didn't matter. What *did* matter was that the Hudathans had a presence on Savas and were on friendly terms with locals. That came as a shock.

The Hudathan was equipped with a translator. It was set to let him talk with the locals, so Ophelia couldn't understand a word of what was said. The alien's hand gestures were eloquent enough, however. Based on his instructions, the locals herded the prisoners into the shade provided by a cluster of jagged rocks. Then they were given bowls of brackish water and allowed to drink as much as they wanted. After some gulps, Ophelia swished the liquid around the inside of her parched mouth before letting it trickle down her throat. Had wine tasted so good? If so, she couldn't remember it.

By that time, Ophelia had begun to think about strategy. It looked as though the indigs were about to hand their prisoners over to the Hudathans. If so, should she admit to who she was? Or would it be better to keep her identity secret? That would prevent the aliens from using her as leverage. On the other hand, she was likely to receive far better treatment if the Hudathans knew who she was. Besides, the other prisoners were likely to rat her out even if she ordered them not to. Especially if they were subjected to torture.

No, all things considered, Ophelia thought it would be best to announce herself and hope that her subordinates on Earth would negotiate a release. Or perhaps she could cut a deal of her own. But with *whom*? Ophelia figured that question would answer itself before too long.

There wasn't much conversation among the prisoners, and Ophelia knew why. The sailors and marines were afraid to speak with her. But that was a blessing since she had nothing worthwhile to share. What could she say? Don't worry—we'll be fine? That was bullshit, and they would know it. So it was better to remain silent, allow the heat to sedate her, and to sleep if she could.

So Ophelia was slumped forward, with her chin resting on her chest, when the shuttle passed overhead. There was a roar followed by a miniature dust storm as the machine turned and landed not far from the hab.

A few minutes later, a ramp was lowered and some Hudathan troopers clomped down onto the ground. Ophelia saw what she assumed to be a noncom point in her direction—and wasn't surprised when four of the Hudathans came over to collect the prisoners.

A series of grunts, hand gestures, and the occasional shove were used to guide the Humans up the ramp and into the shuttle. Once aboard, their chains were shackled to O-rings set into the deck. *They're taking us up to one of their ships,* Ophelia thought to herself.

After the shuttle took off, it stayed low instead of climbing up out of the atmosphere—and followed the contours of the land in what Ophelia thought was a northwesterly direction. There was nothing to do, so her thoughts turned to Nicolai, the man he might have been, and the sudden reversal of fortune that led to his death. How could this be? she wondered. Bad things happened to other people. Never to her. The engines made a droning sound, and Ophelia felt numb.

SAVAS BASE 001

The blazing-hot sun was beating down on his broad shoulders but, thanks to a body that was equipped to cope with Hudatha's wildly fluctuating climate, Nola-Ba barely noticed. He was about to complete a full circuit of the newly completed base. An almost daily ritual that would no longer be necessary.

The top of the hill had been removed to provide space for two landing pads. And down inside the hollowed-out core were a pair of fusion generators, living quarters, and *six* energy cannons. All of which had been taken out of the skeletonized *Head Hunter.* But that wasn't all. Now that the defensive ditch was complete, the Paguumis wouldn't be able to use their herd animals as part of an attack on the base.

So that part of Nola-Ba's mission was complete, and he was in a good mood as he crossed one of four narrow footbridges and entered the fort via a sally port. A corridor led into the heart of the hill and the center of the base. One of two large lifts carried Nola-Ba up to Deck 3 where the command's administrative functions were housed.

Nola-Ba's desk was positioned so that his back was protected by a wall. And as the naval officer sat down, his data screen came to life. There was a long list of messages waiting for him but one was flashing on and off. Nola-Ba touched it with a blunt forefinger and saw Spear Commander Aro-Sa appear. He was, according to the caption at the bottom of the screen, on the Light Cruiser *Intaka* (Deathblow). Having heard a tone, the Intel officer turned from what he'd been doing and looked into the camera. "Admiral."

"Spear Commander."

"You will recall that a Human ship passed through the upper atmosphere a few days ago and went hyper before we could intercept it. It was too small to constitute a warship of any significance, so we assumed it to be a scout or a freighter. A smuggler perhaps, which, having detected one of our ships, reentered hyperspace."

Nola-Ba nodded. "And?"

"And, after further analysis, we believe the vessel was a Human dropship."

Nola-Ba felt his pulse quicken. A dropship! The kind of vessel used to literally "drop" special-operations teams into enemy-held territory. So odds were that the Humans knew about the wreck—and had sent a team to search for survivors. "So," Nola-Ba said, "did they drop troops, or didn't they?"

"We believe they did."

Nola-Ba nodded. "Find them."

"Yes, Admiral. After the dropship reports in, the Humans will send a battle group."

"And we'll be here to greet them. I assume that Captain Po-Ba and you are ready to spring the trap."

"We are."

"Excellent." Nola-Ba speared the line of flashing text and the intelligence officer disappeared. Things were getting interesting.

Ophelia opened her eyes as the deck started to tilt and the engines began to work harder. Moments later, the shuttle seemed to stall, made the switch to repellers, and went straight down. There was a soft landing followed by a sudden flurry of activity. Chains rattled as they were pulled through O-rings, and the Humans were ordered to stand. From there they shuffled out into bright sunlight. It caused Ophelia to squint, and she could feel the sun's strength through the cotton shirt she wore.

Ophelia followed the prisoners in front of her across the badly scorched landing pad to a steel hatch. It looked like the sort of airtight door commonly used on spaceships, and as they waited for the barrier to cycle open, Ophelia had an opportunity to look around. She was struck by how elaborate the base was. It looked as if the ridgeheads were planning to stay. That would stretch their navy even more and make them vulnerable elsewhere. Maybe there was a way to take advantage of that. Then Ophelia remembered that she wasn't in charge anymore, and the question of what to do next would fall to someone else. But *who?* There was no heir apparent. And that was no accident.

Ophelia's thoughts were interrupted as the hatch cycled open, and the prisoners were ordered to enter. The interior felt cool, which came as a relief. Chains scraped across the metal deck as the POWs were herded down a corridor into a lift. All of the doors and fittings seemed to be larger than necessary. So much so that Ophelia felt small.

The lift took the Humans down to one of the lower levels, where they were shoved, prodded, and kicked into a nearly featureless room. Then the door closed, and the prisoners were left to their own devices. Some spoke to each other in low tones, and others took naps. One sailor rocked back and forth and sang to himself.

Which person would the aliens interrogate first? Ophelia figured the Hudathans would choose a male since the Hudathans had a male-dominated culture, and that assumption proved to be correct when a pair of troopers entered the room about twenty minutes later. One of them pointed at a chief petty officer (CPO), who smiled engagingly. "*Me?* You're asking me to the prom? Where's my corsage?"

The comment made no sense but caused all the rest of the prisoners to laugh. The Hudathans didn't understand, of course, and one of them frowned. That's how Ophelia chose to interpret the expression anyway. *I'll be next,* she thought to herself, as they took the noncom away. *So be ready.*

That prediction came true approximately half an hour later when the CPO returned. One eye was swollen shut, there was a cut on his upper lip, and he refused to meet her gaze. The prisoners were silent as he sat down, and a guard pointed at Ophelia. "You." He was wearing a translator now—so it seemed reasonable to think that he had taken part in the interrogation.

Had the CPO told the Hudathans that Empress Ophelia was among the prisoners? Yes, of course he had, just as she expected him to. More than that, *wanted* him to. She stood. And when the Hudathan gestured for her to exit the room she did. What were the others thinking? She didn't care.

Ophelia was frightened but mustered all the dignity she

could as she boarded a lift and was carried upwards. When the platform coasted to a stop, she was escorted down a hall and into a sparsely furnished room. Three Hudathans were present, and all of them were seated behind a kidney-shaped table with their backs to a slightly curved wall. The one in the middle spoke first. "I am Admiral Dor Nola-Ba. And you are?"

"Empress Ophelia Ordanus."

A moment of silence followed as a wall screen came to life. What looked like motes of light swirled and took shape. "Here it is, Admiral," the Hudathan to Nola-Ba's left said. "It's the only footage we have."

As the picture locked up, Ophelia saw herself delivering a speech on Earth. Had a copy been captured somewhere? That seemed likely. "And so," the slightly younger Ophelia said, "it will be necessary to increase taxes on the colony worlds in order to defend them." A Hudathan pointed a remote, and the screen and video froze.

All three Hudathans looked at Ophelia, looked at her likeness, and looked back again. "It appears that you are telling the truth," Nola-Ba said.

"Yes, I am," Ophelia agreed. "And from this point forward, I insist that you treat me with the same level of respect due to a member of your triad."

The triad was the three-person triumvirate that ruled the Hudathan Empire, and as Nola-Ba stared at the ragged-looking Human, he could hardly believe his luck. Now, after being shamed, he was about to get the full measure of his honor back.

How would the authorities on Hudatha use the leverage he was about to give them? What demands would they make of the Humans? He didn't know or care. All he had to do was record the ensuing interrogation, upload it to a message torp, and send it off.

Would they restore his previous rank? Or make him a Grand Admiral? If they did, he would use the position to destroy War Commander Ruma-Ka. The idea pleased him, and had Nola-Ba been capable of smiling, he would have done so. "It's an honor to meet you," Nola-Ba lied. "I have questions . . . A lot of them. So let's get started."

CHAPTER: 9

What makes the desert beautiful is that somewhere it hides a well.

ANTOINE DE SAINT-EXUPÉRY
The Little Prince
Standard year 1943

PLANET SAVAS

Empress Ophelia was alive! That was the good news for everyone except McKee. Because it had been her fervent hope that the bitch was dead. The announcement came the day after the team landed and just before they were about to head out. With the exception of those who had guard duty, the rest of Special Ops Team One-Five were gathered around the flat-topped rock on which Major Remy stood.

"I have some good news for you," Remy said, as he eyed the faces around him. "The empress is alive. We know that because a tiny locator beacon was inserted under the skin behind her left ear roughly nine months ago. At the time it was seen as a precaution that would help authorities find Ophelia in the unlikely event that she was abducted. The existence of the implant is classified because if assassins knew about it, they could use the signal to track her movements. In any case, the beacon is programmed to fail if she's killed and, since we are receiving a strong signal, it's safe to conclude that she's still alive."

The announcement prompted applause, lots of positive comments, and an immediate improvement in morale for everyone except McKee. Remy smiled and nodded. "That's the good news. The bad news is that she's more than three hundred miles northeast of here . . . So a long hike lies ahead of us."

Now, three days later, they were forty-five miles into the journey that Remy had warned them about, and a cloud of insects was swirling around McKee's head as she elbowed her way forward. Sergeant Roy Feng was next to her, while Bartov and the rest of the squad were concealed in a ravine a hundred yards to the rear.

The legionnaires wormed their way up over a rise and paused so that McKee could use her binoculars. There was a ragged-looking tree line in front of them, and McKee knew that she was looking at a peninsula of equatorial jungle that jutted out into what their maps called the Great Pandu Desert. The battle between the jungle and the desert had been under way for a long time. Given enough rain, the green stuff would hurry to colonize new territory. Then, when a dry spell came along, the desert would recover the ground it had lost.

In any case, Remy was eager to reach Ophelia as soon as possible. And in order to do that, it would be necessary for the company to push its way through two fingers of jungle before committing itself to the desert for the balance of the journey. Having fought in the Big Green on Orlo II, McKee knew what they would be in for once they entered the forest. The overarching canopy would block a lot of the sunlight. Animals they'd never seen before would scamper through the branches over their heads—and there would be frequent bouts of rain.

Still, after days spent crossing an arid wasteland, a little bit of precipitation would feel good. But that was to come. The immediate challenge was to make sure that the company didn't walk into an ambush. "See anything?" McKee said from the corner of her mouth.

"Nope," Feng replied as he peered through the scope on his weapon. *"Nada."*

"Okay, send the drone in for a look-see."

Charlie Company had three drones—one for each platoon. McKee's was affectionately known as Can-Three, or C-3, because of its shape and the "3s" painted on both flanks.

C-3 hummed as it passed over their heads and made straight for the jungle beyond, where it passed between two trees and disappeared. McKee brought the drone's video up on her HUD—and found herself flying through the sun-dappled forest. A Paguumi subrace called the Jithi represented the immediate threat. According to the briefing materials, the Jithi had split away from the nomadic Paguumis thousands of years earlier—and taken up residence in the planet's equatorial rain forests. In contrast to their desert-dwelling cousins, the Jithi had light green skin, their hair resembled dreadlocklike fronds, and they had prehensile tail-tentacles. That's what they were supposed to look like anyway—although the off-worlders had yet to see any of them.

Not having spotted any Jithi, Paguumis, or Hudathans, McKee stood and called for the second squad to come forward. Rather than reclaim her perch on Bartov's back, she ordered the other bio bods to dismount and cross the intervening patch of ground on foot. If the legionnaires didn't like it, they would soon change their minds as they entered an environment where anyone riding a T-1 would be forced to battle low-hanging branches all day.

The other option was to find a trail, assuming that such a thing existed. Then the bio bods would be able to ride.

But, since an established path was the perfect place to set an ambush, the soldiers would have to be extremely vigilant. "Stay within sight of each other," McKee advised, as vines brushed past her face, and a thick carpet of detritus gave under her boots. "And remember . . . The Jithi can travel through the treetops."

Something screamed as if to emphasize that point, and some foliage shook violently as whatever the creature was fled the monsters below. But there were no signs of threats, so McKee called a momentary halt. "Charlie-One to Charlie-Nine. Over."

Remy was quick to respond. "Nine here . . . Over."

"We're thirty yards into the green and haven't seen any hostiles yet. Over."

"Roger that. Look for a spot where we can spend the night. Over."

McKee chinned her mike button two times. Now it was up to her to find a place where there was access to water, and the company could defend itself. Given what the Jithi were capable of, that seemed to suggest a clearing. So C-3 was sent forward to search for an opening in the jungle—and McKee instructed the squad to proceed single file. That was all she said, leaving it to Feng to assign people to the point and drag positions. A decision that would signal her confidence in Feng's leadership.

C-3 offered up a number of potential camping spots before McKee saw one that she liked. A stand of dead trees marked the spot where some sort of disease had left its mark. By cutting those down, the legionnaires could clear a site large enough to accommodate the entire company, and the logs could be used to construct a palisade. And there was a rock formation off to one side. It rose thirty feet into the air. That made it the perfect place for a lookout.

So McKee sent a bio bod named Perodi up to the top with orders to keep her head on a swivel. Then she sent C-3 out to patrol what would become the perimeter at treetop level. Once those precautions were in place, work began.

The first step was to clear the dead trees, a task made easier by the use of the multifunction plasma torch that each squad carried. Feng made the cuts himself, dropped the trees in quick succession, and went to work trimming the branches off. Once that task was accomplished, it was a simple matter to chop the trunks into eight-foot lengths and plant them in the three-foot-deep trenches that two of her cyborgs were digging. The work would have gone even faster had McKee assigned *all* of her cyborgs to the task— but she wanted to keep at least half the squad ready to fight should the need arise.

The rest of the team arrived fifteen minutes later. The green hats were good—McKee had to give them that. In fact, had it not been for a call letting her know that they were closing in on her location, she would never have known that they were in the vicinity. The legionnaires seemed to materialize around the clearing. But rather than order them to pitch in, Olson put the troops on standby while she took a tour of the area.

Although that was consistent with the XO's responsibilities, it also signaled a lack of faith in McKee's judgment. Was that intentional? McKee assumed that it was—but knew she should expect some sort of retaliation after the confrontation on the ship.

So McKee kept her mouth shut as Olson paused to sample water from the stream that flowed through the area, tested a freshly cut log to make sure that it was solid, and eyed the beginnings of a latrine. Finally, having found no faults of the sort that would disqualify the site, the XO was forced to issue a terse, "Carry on."

The work went quickly after that and was completed well before sundown. As the sun went down, and diurnal creatures began to give way to their nocturnal counterparts, a different set of sounds could be heard. The night creatures were a noisy bunch that liked to gibber, screech, and howl while they looked for food. McKee had been through it before and preferred the peace and quiet of the desert to the cacophony of jungle noises.

Olson had assigned McKee to the 1200–0200 watch for three nights running by then. A form of harassment that forced her to sleep, get up, and try to sleep again. A practice so obvious that it had been the subject of commentary from her peers. "What's with the XO?" Ellis inquired at one point. "I get the feeling she'd have you dig latrines if she could."

"Been there, done that," McKee replied. "I was a private once." And that, McKee knew, lay at the heart of the problem. Olson didn't approve of jackers and never would.

Noisy though it was, the night passed without incident and, consistent with Remy's orders, the company was ready to depart by 0700. As before, McKee's people were on point except that she was traveling with Sergeant Mo Hiller and the third squad this time. The second had been rotated back to the drag position, with the first serving as a fast-reaction force that was positioned halfway down the column.

The sun was still in the process of climbing up off the eastern horizon, so it was murky on the jungle floor. The minimum goal was fifteen miles per day and, in order to achieve it, McKee had to push hard. Even though moving faster increased the possibility of walking into an ambush.

A front moved through at 1136. It dumped half an inch of rain onto the jungle in half an hour and left it steaming. The humidity was terrible, and since every leaf was laden with moisture, the bio bods were soaked in minutes.

McKee was splashing through a puddle when C-3 made its report. The drone was flying at treetop level about half a mile ahead. Its voice had a harsh, mechanical quality. "Three targets are headed your way. They are a 97.6-percent match with the indigenous species called the Jithi. Fifteen, that is one-five, targets are pursuing them. They are a 98.6-percent match to the Paguumi profile. Estimated time to first contact is approximately two minutes. Over."

McKee had to take action and do it fast because if she took the time required to ask Olson or Remy for orders, the incoming targets would be practically in her lap. All she could do was make some decisions and hope they were the right ones.

"This is Charlie-One," McKee said. "You heard C-3. Take up defensive positions in a line abreast. Allow targets one, two, and three to pass through. If they open fire, then smoke 'em.

"Fire warning shots over the pursuers and try to stop them. If that doesn't work, then grease 'em. Charlie-Five and I will hang back and try to intercept targets one through three. Over."

There were lots of clicks as the first Jithi appeared. He or she charged out of the underbrush, spotted a T-1, and skidded to a halt. That was when McKee activated her translator and overrode the PA systems on all of the cyborgs. "Keep coming . . . We won't harm you. And we won't let the Paguumis harm you either."

The words boomed through five speakers and were followed by a flurry of gunshots as the Paguumis fired. The Jithi surged forward, and McKee was waiting as they passed through the line. They had shaggy green hair, prominent cheekbones, and none of them were more than six feet tall. The shimmery scales on the leather jerkins they wore seemed to blend with the background. "Halt!" McKee said. "Place your weapons on the ground and step back."

The Jithis stopped and turned to look at each other. One of them spoke emphatically. Then, with considerable care, the Jithis laid their long, beautifully crafted rifles on the ground. McKee made eye contact with Bartov. "Guard them."

Then she turned and ran a few feet to the moss-covered log where Hiller and his squad were waiting to confront the Paguumis. No more than a couple of seconds passed before the Paguumis emerged from the jungle undergrowth with their weapons raised. That was when they spotted the T-1s and fired. It was a serious mistake. The cyborgs triggered their fifties, and the desert tribesmen were swept away by a hail of bullets. Hiller, conscious of the need to conserve ammo, shouted "Cease fire!" He had to repeat the order three times before the last T-1 obeyed.

"Chow!" McKee yelled. "Count the bodies and do it fast. Popov . . . Watch her six."

Gun smoke hung heavy in the air as McKee went back to speak with the Jithi. They were right where they had been, eyes wide with what might have been apprehension, waiting to find out what fate held in store for them. McKee wanted to say something reassuring but didn't have enough time. "How many?" she demanded. "How many were there?"

"Fifteen," the Jithi in the middle said.

McKee was on the squad freq. She chinned her mike. "Chow . . . What have you got?"

"Twelve bodies, Lieutenant."

"Shit! Three got away. Hiller, take over here. Bartov, let's go. If those bastards get away, we'll be ass deep in indigs by this time tomorrow."

Bartov waited for McKee to climb aboard and strap in. A slap on the right shoulder sent the cyborg running toward a moss-covered log. He jumped over it and kept going. McKee had to duck lest the tree branches take her head off. She chinned her mike. "Charlie-One to C-3 . . . Three locals are headed east. Find and report. Over."

"This is Three," the drone replied emotionlessly. "Understood. Over."

Water flew as Bartov pounded through a stream, the sun played hide-and-seek up above the treetops, and a flock of fliers exploded into the air as they hurried to escape the monster below. "This is Three," the drone said. "I have them."

McKee took the feed up on her HUD and found herself looking down on the forest canopy. She could see C-3's shadow blipping over the jungle and could make out some movement down below. According to the data that was crawling across the bottom of the image, the fugitives were half a mile ahead, and Bartov was closing fast.

So everything was looking good until something landed on McKee's back, sank its claws into her flesh, and screeched in her ear. It wasn't that heavy but she could feel it nudging her helmet, looking for a way in. So she let the AXE dangle in order to reach back and grab the creature. Her reward was a painful bite. And when McKee brought her hand back it was bleeding from two tiny puncture wounds. Poison? She hoped not as she made a grab for the pistol. It was holstered on the left side of her combat vest. After pulling the weapon free, she pointed the barrel back over her right shoulder and pulled the trigger. Whatever the thing was made a screeching sound and fell away as Bartov tripped on a thick root and fell forward.

The T-1 took McKee down with him. They hit hard, and her visor bounced off the back of Bartov's head. Fortunately, the helmet protected her from injury so that McKee could hit the harness release and roll free. The cyborg was still struggling to stand when the Paguumis emerged from the brush. Rather than let the aliens run them to death, they were going to fight.

McKee heard the reports and saw a geyser of dirt jump up in front of her as the warriors fired. The AXE seemed to fire itself in short, efficient bursts. Two indigs were dead by the time Bartov killed the third. And that's where she was, swaying slightly on her feet, as Major Remy appeared. McKee was about to greet him when she fainted.

Prince Nicolai was crying—and Avery didn't know what to do. Days had passed since the attack on the wreck, the desperate escape in the pod, and the hard landing that followed. Fortunately, the sphere-shaped container had been thrown well clear of the animals used to overrun the crash site. Then the pod hit, bounced, and hit again. All three of the passengers were thrown about. But, thanks to the way their seats clutched them, none were injured. The moment they came to a stop, Avery triggered the charge that blew the hatch open, and Daska ventured out with its machine pistol at the ready. Avery hated synths, but it was nice to have one of the machines on *his* side for a change.

The robot gave the all clear moments later. So Avery sent Nicolai out while he searched for the pod's emergency supplies. They consisted of a good first-aid kit, five days of rations for four people, and a built-in tank filled with twenty gallons of water. The bad news was that he couldn't take it with him. Still, the other stuff was better than nothing, and Avery hurried to toss it out through the hatch.

Once outside, Avery could see the flicker of a fire off in the distance. A dull boom marked a secondary explosion as something blew up deep inside the wreck. There was enough starlight to see by, and that was good, since they needed to clear the area before the sun rose. Once that occurred, more locals would flood the area searching for loot. Even so, it was necessary to pause and try to comfort Nicolai. Avery knelt next to him. "I want my mommy," the youngster said, "and I want her *now.*"

It was a royal command but one Avery couldn't comply with. Ironically enough, Daska was the spitting image of

Ophelia, but that didn't help. "I'm sorry, Nicolai . . . But your mother isn't here—and I don't know where she is. But there's one thing I *do* know. Some bad people are looking for us, and we need to hide."

There wasn't much light, but Avery had been able to see the youngster's frown. "Kill the bad people. That's what Mommy does."

Avery looked at Daska and back again. The boy had that right. His mother would kill anyone she considered to be "bad." He cleared his throat. "Yes," he agreed. "That's true. But there are more bad people than Daska and I can kill by ourselves. So we have to retreat and live to fight another day."

Nicolai was silent for a moment. Then he nodded. "General Crowley says that you are correct."

Avery knew the general pretty well by then, having played war games with him aboard the *Victorious*. And now, as one of the so-called "advisors" Ophelia had downloaded into her child's brain, Crowley could help or hinder. "Good," Avery said. "Hop up onto Daska's back. It will carry you. I'll bring the supplies."

It was obvious that the problems presented by the current situation had never occurred to the designers of the escape pod. And why would they? The vehicle was made for use in space. So there were no carrying straps on the bags containing the emergency supplies. Just handles. That forced Avery to sling the AXE and carry them like a pair of suitcases as he led the others in a southwesterly direction. Not because he truly believed that they could hike to Savas Prime but because they had to go *somewhere*.

They had some food, and the fact that Daska didn't need any would make what they had last that much longer. Water was the most pressing necessity. That and a place to hide during the day. The time when the digs would be most likely to spot them.

As time passed, and a violet glow appeared along the eastern horizon, Avery became increasingly concerned. Now he realized that he could have, and should have, had the boy drink as much water as possible before parting company with the pod. But it was too late for could-haves. Daska's voice interrupted his thoughts. "There's some vegetation up ahead. That would suggest the presence of water."

Avery peered into the early-morning gloom. He couldn't see anything beyond a hundred feet or so. "Really? How can you tell?"

"I'm looking at it via a satellite," the robot answered evenly. "It was damaged somehow . . . So most of its functionalities are off-line, but the infrared sensors still work, and I can see patches of bright red where vegetation exists."

Avery knew synths had all sorts of capabilities, so the fact that Daska could uplink to a satellite and hack into it wasn't too surprising. And, like most officers, he'd been trained to interpret various types of sat scans. That included Color Infrared Imagery (CIR). So he knew that Daska's readout made sense. Even though it was counterintuitive, vegetation would appear to be red. So there was reason to hope. If they could reach the vegetation in the next couple of hours, they might find some water . . . Or a dozen warriors camped around a well! But all they could do was try. "Okay, well done. Who does the satellite belong to?"

"The Savas Prime Business Association," Daska replied.

"Can you communicate with them?"

There was a pause. "No. Like I said, it was damaged, and my radio isn't powerful enough to reach them without a relay."

Avery swore. It would have been nice to call for help. But that wasn't going to happen. So all they could do was put one foot in front of the other. Progress was steady, however. After two-plus hours, they arrived at an oasis. Avery was relieved to find that it was unoccupied at the moment. Only for the moment, though, since three fire pits could be seen along with hundreds of overlapping animal tracks.

As the sun rose, the Humans drank their fill before retreating to some thick underbrush to rest and come up with a plan. The problem was simple. Although Avery and his companions had a source of water, odds were that they would be discovered if they stayed in the oasis for very long, yet they couldn't travel without canteens. So what to do? Take the canteens from the locals . . . Some of whom were likely to arrive at any time. Problem solved. Assuming they could overwhelm some Paguumis.

Avery shared the plan with Daska. And, since the concept was consistent with the robot's programming, it had no objection. The wait began. The shade protected them from the worst of the heat—and furtive trips to the well served to slake their thirst.

But by the time the sun made its daily trip across the sky and set in the west, there had been no sign of the indigs Avery had been hoping for. He did see one thing, however . . . Something that was sufficient to produce a combination of hope and fear. That was the appearance of three white claw marks on the azure sky. They were contrails. But *whose*? Humans, come to rescue the empress? Or Hudathans bent on conquest? Both were possible.

As darkness fell, and Daska stood watch, the Humans made a meal of emergency rations. The dry fiber bars made MREs look good. But there was plenty of water to wash them down with—and Avery took the opportunity to teach Nicolai some basic camping skills. The princeling had never spent any time in the outdoors, and the chance to carve shavings off a dry stick and to light a carefully shielded fire kept his mind occupied for a while.

The process caused Avery to think about children. Would McKee want any? Some of their time together had been spent having sex—but there hadn't been much conversation about the future. Just a vague plan to leave the Legion and settle on a rim world. And that made sense since there was no way to be sure that either one of them would survive their current enlistments.

Avery pushed such thoughts aside and prepared a depression for Nicolai to sleep in. Then he covered the boy with an emergency blanket and waited for him to fall asleep. At some point, Avery drifted off as well. He remained asleep until a touch caused him to sit upright and reach for the AXE. The air was cool, the sun was starting to rise, and he could hear voices. "Quiet," Daska cautioned from inches away. "There are fourteen of them. Too many for us to kill. We must wait."

Avery's first thought was for Nicolai. Though normally clean, he was grubby now and looked like a street urchin rather than a prince. The boy was sitting on his haunches chewing a ration bar, and Avery knew he'd be thirsty as a result. And, with the natives gathered around the well, Nicolai wouldn't be able to drink. It was the sort of thing a robot wouldn't think of.

However, there was nothing they could do except hide and hope the digs would leave soon. A fire had been lit, and Avery could smell what he assumed was food, so he hoped they would eat and leave soon thereafter.

Once the meal was over, the locals posted a couple of sentries, spread mats out under the trees, and went to sleep. Travel at night and rest during the day. It made sense. Could they sneak up on the guards, kill them silently, and open fire on the others while they slept? They could try . . . But Avery didn't like the odds.

Fortunately, neither one of the sentries felt the need to explore the oasis and were satisfied to groom their mounts, clean their weapons, and chat with each other. Not long thereafter, Nicolai began to complain of being thirsty, demanded to see his mother, and started to sulk. Avery gave him a pebble to suck on—knowing it would moisten his mouth. That was all he could do.

The sentries were relieved during the middle of the day, and as they lay down, one of the newly awoken warriors walked toward their hiding place. Avery was preparing to shoot him, and kill as many of the sleepers as he could, when the dig stopped to urinate. Once that was accomplished, he returned to the well. Avery gave a sigh of relief and thumbed the safety on. It was a reprieve. How many would they get?

But with the exception of the close encounter, the rest of the day was uneventful. Finally, as the sun began to set, the sleeping warriors got up and went about making another meal. The process seemed to take forever. Eventually, after a good deal of messing about, the Paguumis rode away.

Nicolai wanted to run straight to the well, but Avery made the boy wait for a full five minutes to make sure that none of the riders returned. They didn't.

"Come on!" Avery shouted. "I'll race you to the well!" Nicolai took off running—and Avery grinned as he followed along behind.

After drinking their fill, eating ration bars, and drinking more water, the Humans prepared for bed. If a patch of bare ground could be dignified as a "bed." And as Avery lay there, he went over the day in his mind. What was to prevent the same thing from happening again? Nothing. But what could he do? Silly though it seemed, they were wedded to the well until a smaller group of travelers arrived.

Knowing that Daska would keep watch and couldn't fall asleep, Avery allowed himself to drift off. He awoke several times during the night. Once to take a pee—and once because he heard voices. Or thought he did.

But the night passed uneventfully, and when morning came, there were no visitors. It was frustrating, and rather than wait any longer, Avery decided to leave once the sun went down. According to Daska, there was another oasis about fifteen miles to the west. It would be a long hike, but maybe they could make it.

Rather than run the risk of being caught out in the open, the threesome retreated to their hiding place as the sun rose higher in the sky. Avery and Nicolai made armies out of stones and passed the time attacking each other. Games that were made more interesting when General Crowley chose to participate. And that's what they were doing when four warriors galloped into the oasis, skidded to a stop, and jumped to the ground. There was a good deal of grunting and belching as the animals drank from the well.

The digs were in a hurry, judging from their decision to travel during the heat of the day and the fact that they weren't setting up camp. A rest stop then . . . Before continuing on their way. "These are the ones," Avery whispered to Daska. "They will leave soon, so we must act quickly. Don't kill the animals if you can avoid it. They could come in handy."

Avery turned to Nicolai. "Stay here, son . . . Don't move. Either Daska or I will come for you." Nicolai knew enough to be scared. His eyes were big as he gave a short, jerky nod.

The boy would be helpless if both he and Daska were killed. Avery knew that. But it was a chance he'd have to take.

Avery turned back to Daska and motioned the synth forward. There was nothing especially subtle about the attack. Avery was counting on the element of surprise, and it worked. The warriors turned to stare as two strange-looking apparitions broke cover and ran straight at them. They were still trying to process the situation when Avery shot one of them in the head.

As the body fell, the others began to move, and one reacted quickly enough to fire a shot. Avery felt the slug tug at his left sleeve as Daska opened fire. In order to use the machine pistol effectively, the robot had to get in close. But once in position, the synth was deadly. Short bursts took two warriors down.

Meanwhile, Avery had a problem on his hands. Having been startled by the first shots, a big quadruped had interposed itself between Avery and warrior four. A nimble fellow who took the opportunity to grab onto the saddle-horn-like prominence located to the rear of the beast's neck and pull himself up off the ground. Then, with a series of yips, he urged the animal into motion. The dig was about to escape, and if he did, would soon return with some of his friends.

Avery swore and did the only thing he could. He led the mount slightly, pulled back on the trigger, and fired half of the assault weapon's fifty-round magazine. The bullets stitched a bloody line along the animal's flank until they found a vital organ. The warrior managed to jump free as the beast fell. He was busy trying to bring his long-barreled rifle to bear when Avery shot him in the chest. He backpedaled and fell. Avery sensed motion and turned to discover that Daska was standing next to him. "You aren't supposed to shoot the animals," the robot said critically.

"And you aren't supposed to be a pain in the ass," Avery replied. "But you are."

The sun beat down on his shoulders as he walked over to where the dead beast lay. What looked like a wineskin hung from the largely decorative saddle. He cut the object loose. It was still wet after being immersed in the well and clearly filled with water. Mission accomplished.

Further investigation produced a purse full of what appeared to be uncut gemstones—although Avery knew next to nothing about such things. It turned out that the other warriors were carrying similar pouches. Were such stones common on Savas? Or had the warriors stolen them from somebody? Either was a possibility. Avery poured all of the stones into a single pouch and buttoned it into a pocket.

The next twenty minutes were spent gathering everything that might come in handy, including three additional water bags, a couple of curved knives, and one of the single-shot rifles. The theory was that, primitive though the firing mechanism was, a long-range weapon could come in handy.

The original plan had been to ride the captured animals. But one lay dead, one had been wounded, and the others were anything but cooperative. Any attempt to climb aboard was met with loud grunts, shrill screams, and an effort to buck him off.

The reason for that soon became apparent as Avery studied one of the creatures. The blanket on its back was just that—a blanket. The *real* saddle consisted of the concave mass of bone and cartilage that lay underneath. It was equipped with what appeared to be a socket. And if Avery's guess was correct, it was evolved to receive the short, tail-like tentacles that each warrior had. A symbiotic relationship? Yes, he thought so. And that being the case, the chances of successfully riding one of the animals was zero.

Fortunately, the beasts were equipped with small panniers that could be used to haul their belongings. Because even if the animals couldn't be ridden, they could be led. So Avery turned the wounded mount loose, loaded the other two with supplies, and waited for darkness to fall. And that was when Nicolai began to cry. It seemed natural to hold the boy, to let him sob, and to give him assurances that everything would be okay. Even if that was very unlikely indeed.

When McKee came to, she was lying on her back looking up through a screen of foliage to the patches of blue sky beyond. And she was moving. Not gliding, because the movement was too jerky for that, but traveling at what seemed to be a pretty good clip. How could that be? McKee attempted to sit up, felt an explosion of pain in her head, and fell back. Darkness reached up to pull her down.

Eventually after what might have been a day, week, or month McKee awoke once again. As before, she was lying on her back. But the surface underneath her was steady this time. And instead of foliage, she was looking up into an alien countenance. She would have been frightened if it hadn't been for the fact that she recognized the creature as one of the Jithi they had rescued from the Paguumis. A translator dangled from his neck.

"Greetings, Lieutenant. You were bitten by a claw wing. The poison it injected into your bloodstream is very toxic. But you are better now. It seems the extract made from Ibumi tree bark works on Humans as well as Jithi. Praise be to the great one."

McKee tried to speak, but her mouth was too dry. She croaked "Water," and felt grateful when the Jithi helped her to sit up. The water he offered her was cool and felt heavenly as it trickled down her throat. "What's your name?" McKee inquired.

"They call me Kambi."

"Thank you, Kambi. How long has it been since the wing bit me?"

"Four days."

"Where are we?"

"We are ninety passems, or about sixty of your miles northeast of the point where my companions and I were ambushed. Major Remo wanted to place you in one of the RAV machines, but Sergeant Jolo said that the members of your platoon preferred to carry you, which they did."

McKee remembered looking up into the branches as she was carried along. Carried by a couple of T-1s? She thought so. And the fact that her platoon would do that for her caused a lump to form in the back of her throat. "What about *you*?" she inquired, eager to change the subject. "Tell me about the ambush."

Kambi produced something very similar to a Human shrug. "There were five of us. We came north to sell jewelry to the Paguumis. Their females are hungry for such baubles. And a certain amount of gifting is required prior to the wife-taking ceremony. So the males want to buy.

"But we were waylaid by a party of warriors who planned to take what they wanted. Rimbee was killed. So was Koshi. So we ran. That's when we saw your cyborgs and you called us forward. Later, after the wing bit you, Major Remy hired us to act as guides."

Guides would come in handy . . . There was no doubt about that. "Help me get up," McKee demanded.

"Take it slowly," Kambi advised. "You'll need time to get your full strength back."

It didn't take long to realize that the native was correct. Getting up and leaving the Jithi-style lean-to took a lot of effort. McKee's legs felt wobbly as she made her way out into the main encampment. The nearest legionnaires turned to look at her—and their applause was both unexpected and gratifying. Having heard the ruckus, Remy came forward to greet her. "Lieutenant McKee! It's good to see you up and around."

McKee mumbled something she hoped was appropriate before allowing Kambi to lead her back to the shelter. Then it was time to take a pee on her own and eat a few bites of food before going back to sleep.

The next time McKee awoke was just before 0500 as the company began to stir. That was her cue to extricate herself from the sleep sack, take a couple of pain tabs, and totter off to a female latrine. All of the people she ran into both going and returning were clearly glad to see her—and that served to lift McKee's spirits as she packed her gear. It turned out to be an unexpectedly difficult task, and she was only half-done when Sergeant Jolo appeared with a steaming-hot mug of tea and a lukewarm MRE. "Good morning, ma'am. I heard you were up and around. Here's a bite to eat."

McKee thanked him and was surprised to discover how hungry she was. Jolo was packing her gear by that time and replied to her questions with short, efficient answers. It seemed that the T-1s were starting to experience all of the maintenance issues that one would expect after a prolonged period in the field. But nothing critical as yet. That was a relief, and as McKee put the MRE down, she felt better. Good enough to mount up? Yes, she thought so, even if Jolo disagreed.

Twenty minutes later, McKee was up on Bartov's back as the company got under way. But rather than take the point, McKee chose to ride with the reserve squad. She wasn't ready to take the lead and knew it.

The jungle was beginning to thin out as the company neared the point where it would be forced to leave the protection of the forest and cross what Kambi called "the grass path." Or, the planet-girding swath of grass the Paguumis' katha fed on. The desert lay beyond that.

McKee knew there were two ways to proceed. Remy could continue to travel during the day on the theory that while his unit would be easier to see, the heat stored in the sand, dirt, and rocks would help conceal the team's infrared signature. And according to what their Jithi guides had heard, the huge aliens were definitely on the ground.

On the other hand, if the legionnaires traveled at night, they would be less visible to the Hudathans and indigs alike. The problem was that their heat signatures would be clear to see from orbit. Still, it was more comfortable to travel during the hours of darkness, so that was a factor, too.

So Remy ordered a halt at the point where the jungle gave way to desert. The plan was to rest until evening and march all night. McKee was tired by then and grateful for the break. But she was also determined to resume her duties. With that in mind, she went to see Remy.

The major was seated under a tree. He was speaking into

his hand comp. Keeping a record of their progress? Probably. And for good reason. If the mission failed, he could be blamed, court-martialed even, and would have to defend himself. But if they were able to locate Ophelia? And bring her out alive? Then Remy would receive a promotion, a really important medal, and be free to write a book about his exploits. So long as it cast the empress in a good light, that is. Remy saw McKee and waved her over. The comp went into his pack. "Just the person I wanted to see! Please, have a seat."

The only seat available was a box labeled AMMUNITION, .50 CAL. So she sat on it.

"Damn," Remy said. "We were very worried about you. Nice job with the Paguumis by the way. Had one of them managed to return home, we would have been ass deep in digs shortly thereafter. As things stand, we made it this far without having to fight a major action. Although that may change once we track the signal to its source."

McKee frowned. "Signal, sir? Meaning Ophelia's signal?"

Remy smiled. "Sorry, McKee . . . I forgot that you've been out of the loop for a while. No, not Ophelia's beacon . . . This is something different. Two days ago we began to pick up a standard distress signal. You know, the kind you'd expect from a downed shuttle or something similar.

"It's about twelve miles north of our present position. We know the Hudathans are here, and it sounds like they plan to stay, but one of our weather sats survived an attack by the ridgeheads. In any case, a tech managed to hack into it so we had a chance to eyeball the area using infrared sensors. There are no obvious signs of a trap."

"So we're going in tonight?"

Remy nodded. "Damned right we are."

"I request permission to resume all of my duties sir."

Remy eyed her. "Are you sure?"

"Yes, sir."

Remy grinned. "I had a feeling you would say that. Permission granted."

"Can I speak freely, sir?"

"Of course."

"We have to respond to the signal. I get that. If some swabbies survived, we need to help them. But it smells like a Hudathan trap. How come the beacon came on *after* we landed?"

Remy looked grim. "Captain Olson and I share your concern. Believe me we do."

"So," McKee said, "if it's a trap, maybe we can turn that to our advantage."

Remy's eyebrows rose. "Please continue."

McKee groped for words at first, found them, and spoke for the better part of two minutes. And when she was finished, a big grin appeared on Remy's face. "You know something, Lieutenant? I like jackers. Especially ones who can think outside of the box."

By the time the sun began to set, and violet haze settled over the desert, the company was ready to set forth. In keeping with McKee's suggestion, the hats went first, with the RAVs and two squads of cavalry bringing up the rear. The others, four in all, were half a mile out in either direction where they could protect the column's flanks. And on her orders, all of the bio bods were on foot. That included McKee herself—and she knew the twelve-mile hike was going to be difficult for her. But she couldn't ask others to do what she wasn't willing to do herself.

As the sun vanished, and a dusting of stars appeared in the sky, there was no noise other than the steady whir of servos, the crunch of boots on gravel, and the rasp of her own breathing. Bartov was carrying her pack, for which she was grateful—because her body was still recovering from the effects of the wing toxin. But there was nothing she could do other than drop another stim tab and keep walking.

At least the terrain was flat, which meant they could expect to arrive in about three hours.

Time seemed to drag as the moon rose and threw an eerie white glow over the desert as they wound their way between outcroppings of rock, down through gullies, and up over wind-scoured hills. It was like marching through a dreamscape.

But all dreams must end, and such was the case as Remy spoke over the company's alternative infrared com net. It was set on "scatter," which meant that the legionnaires didn't have to establish a line-of-sight connection in order to communicate with each other. Though not appropriate for enclosed spaces like buildings, the system was perfect for the desert, and almost as secure as a wired connection would have been. "This is Nine. Company, halt. Platoons 1 and 2 will take up defensive positions. Platoon 3 will prepare for Operation Sucker. Eight, you are a go. Over."

Charlie-Eight, which was to say Captain Olson, was under orders to lead a team of hats forward to scout the situation out. What was waiting for them up ahead? A downed shuttle with some sailors hiding inside? Or a Hudathan trap? McKee didn't envy the other woman. But if the prospect bothered Olson, there had been no sign of it during the premission brief. She might be a bitch, but she was part of team One-Five for a reason.

Now there was nothing any of them could do but wait. The minutes seemed to crawl by as the XO and her people elbowed their way forward. Finally Olson's voice was heard. "This is Charlie-Eight . . . There isn't any shuttle. What we're looking at is a standard escape pod. The kind they use on navy ships. But that's really weird because . . ."

None of them got to hear why the pod was weird because that's when there was a flash of light, a loud boom, and the object in question ceased to exist. As did Olson and her three-person team. The trap had been sprung.

The purpose of the explosion was to not only kill the team sent to investigate the pod but to create a flash of light that would ruin any survivors' night vision. That part of the strategy wasn't very successful because the bio bods were wearing helmets that dampened their visors. And McKee's T-1s weren't bothered in the least.

They'd been warned of such a possibility and weren't "looking" at the pod. Their sensors were focused on the night sky, their onboard computers were linked to create a joint fire-control system, and the cans mounted on their shoulders were hot.

So when they detected two aircraft approaching from the east, there was no need for McKee to give an order. Two preselected T-1s fired twelve heat-seeking rockets each. Weapons that would have been equally effective against ground targets had some Hudathan tanks been positioned in the area. The results were spectacular.

Both of what were later determined to be Hudathan assault boats were transformed into momentary suns, overlapping claps of thunder were heard, and the legionnaires were treated to a fireworks show as pieces of flaming debris twirled down from the sky. McKee chinned her mike. "This is Charlie-One. Both targets were destroyed. AA team 2 is armed and ready to fire. Over."

"I don't think that will be necessary," Remy said somberly, "but remain on standby. The second squad, first platoon will search for remains. We lost four legionnaires tonight but, when our time comes, we'll see them again."

A voice said, "CAMERONE," and was answered by all the rest. *"CAMERONE!"* Blood had been drawn—and the enemy would respond.

CHAPTER: 10

Sadly, there have been many occasions on which
we battled ourselves.

GRAND MARSHAL NIMU WURLA-KA (RET.)
Instructor, Hudathan War College
Standard year 1956

PLANET HUDATHA

The message torp exited the nowhere land of hyperspace
and appeared fifty thousand miles off Hudatha. The vehicle announced itself a few seconds later. Recognition codes
were exchanged, permission was granted, and the torpedo
was allowed to enter orbit. Once the proper command was
sent to the torpedo, the data in its memory banks was
downloaded to the planet below. Minutes later, an unen-
crypted report was hand-delivered to both Grand Admiral
Dora-Da and War Commander Ona-Ka.

But even though Admiral Nola-Ba's message was labeled
"urgent," hundreds of such communications arrived each
day. And when the staff officer charged with managing
Grand Admiral Dura-Da's inbox saw that the report had
originated from a low-priority system out on the frontier, he
assumed that the "urgent" classification had been applied to
the communication by an officer who hoped to jump the

queue by labeling a routine message as "urgent." It was a common practice and one he was determined to stamp out. So he gave the message a much lower priority and passed it on. Maybe, if the staff meeting concluded on time, the admiral would read it before he left for home.

Meanwhile, in an office nearby, the same message was received in a very different way. War Commander Ona-Ka's attaché was named Hosep Ma-Ka. And when he saw that the urgent message was from Admiral Nola-Ba, he gave it an even higher priority, knowing that Ona-Ka *hated* Nola-Ba and was interested in everything the officer did. And, as luck would have it, Ma-Ka happened to be present when Ona-Ka opened the message and Nola-Ba's holographic likeness appeared over the war commander's desk.

Ma-Ka thought the admiral looked tired but excited as well, judging from the way he was leaning forward. "Greetings. I have exciting news to report," Nola-Ba said importantly. "It seems that one of our battle groups set an ambush near a commonly used jump point. A flotilla of Human ships blundered into the trap and most were destroyed. But among the vessels that managed to escape was a light cruiser called the *Victorious*. And that ship was carrying none other than Empress Ophelia Ordanus herself!

"After an emergency hyperspace jump, the *Victorious* entered normal space in the vicinity of Savas, which is presently under my, that is to say *our*, control. Because of damage suffered during the ambush, the Human vessel was forced to make a crash landing. Many crew members were killed on impact, but the empress survived, and I have her in custody."

Nola-Ba paused at that point as if to savor the moment. "Grand Admiral Dura-Da, War Commander Ona-Ka, I give you Empress Ordanus."

The holo broke up into a thousand multicolored chips of light that swirled and flew back together again. Then a

Human appeared. There were some contusions on the alien's face. Other than that, the female looked like the pictures he'd seen. The Humans struck him as small, seemingly defenseless creatures who would be easy to eradicate. Why that effort had proved to be so difficult was a mystery to him. When the empress spoke, her words were translated into Hudathan by the holoplayer. "My name is Empress Ophelia Ordanus. Free me or die."

War Commander Ona-Ka had been silent until then. Now his fist fell on the desk causing various objects to jump into the air. "Did you hear that? The Human dares to threaten us!"

Ma-Ka *had* heard it. And thought her statement was quite courageous given the circumstances. He wasn't stupid enough to say that, however, and held his tongue as Nola-Ba reappeared. "By now you may be wondering if the Human is who she claims to be. I lack the means to carry out DNA testing on the Human but have corroborating testimony regarding her identity from a number of survivors, all of whom were subjected to various types of torture. Based on that, I think there is an extremely high probability that the creature is who she claims to be.

"I am sending notification via message torpedo because it seems unwise to transport such a high-value prisoner with anything less than a battle group—and I have orders to hold this system. However, if you'd like me to bring her to Hudatha using the force at my disposal, please send an order to that effect. It seems likely that the Humans are searching for the empress, so time is of the essence."

Ona-Ka swore as the holo collapsed in on itself. "The clanless bastard!"

Ma-Ka was mystified. Surely there was reason to praise Admiral Nola-Ba rather than curse him. "I'm sorry, War Commander . . . I don't understand."

Ona-Ka was on his feet by then and pacing back and

forth in front of a large window. "Nola-Ba could have sent her here on one of his ships. The nonsense about the need for a battle group was just that . . . Nonsense. His *actual* purpose was to let Grand Admiral Dura-Da and the Da clan's allies know that he's holding a prize which could have an effect on the upcoming elections. Imagine! If he delivers the Human empress to Hudatha, the populace will go wild!

"He had to inform me, or ignore the chain of command, and open himself to *more* charges. By now you can be sure that Dura-Da is conferring with his advisors about how to best exploit the news."

Ona-Ka stopped and looked at Ma-Ka. "Contact the clan council and inform them that we must meet in two hours. Tell them that time is critical. Go." Ma-Ka went.

The extended Ka family maintained what amounted to a fortress in the City of Blades. It was part keep, part armory, and part social center. A home away from home for any male who happened to be visiting the city. As such, it was large and much given to thick walls pierced with loopholes that dated back to the era of black-powder weapons. All of which made it the ideal location for the sort of secret meeting Ona-Ka had requested.

The meeting began right on time. In light of the short notice, only five members of the seven-member clan council could attend. But that was sufficient, and as Ona-Ka waited for Council Leader Sak-Ka to open the meeting, he was pleased with the quality of the turnout. Every council member had been in the military and would understand the gravity of the situation. "And so," Sak-Ka said, as he eyed those seated around the circular table, "War Commander Ona-Ka has important news for us. War Commander?"

Ona-Ka nodded. "Thank you. I have important news indeed . . . The essence of which is that a ship carrying the

Human empress was forced to crash-land on the planet Savas, where she was captured by Admiral Nola-Ba."

Ona-Ka heard a collective groan followed by all sorts of commentary. "Savas? Where's that?" one member inquired.

"Nola-Ba?" another demanded. "He's a disgrace."

"Since the Ba family is aligned with the Da clan," one of the council members observed, "this development will make Triad Uba-Da's position that much stronger."

"*And* prevent us from securing another seat on the triad," another put in.

The triad was the triumvirate that ruled the Hudathan empire. At the moment it included members of the Ka, Da, and Ra clans. So a *second* Ka would allow that clan to control the empire. Ona-Ka saw the opportunity and took it. "That's correct . . . Once the public learns of the capture, it will be seen as an enormous accomplishment for the Da clan and its allies. And, with the general election nearly upon us, that will ensure Uba-Da's place on the triad. Assuming the fool is still alive, that is—and capable of performing his duties."

That comment produced a long moment of silence followed by a sudden stir and the traditional cry of "BLOOD!" from a grizzled veteran. The battle cry was soon echoed by all the rest.

But once the noise died down, Council Leader Sak-Ka was there to sound a cautionary note. "War Commander Ona-Ka is correct . . . Given this news, Uba-Da's place on the triad will be secure if we fail to take action. But if the Ka clan, or any member of the clan were to assassinate Uba-Da, public sentiment would turn against us. That could cost us the seat we *do* have."

Ona-Ka had anticipated such an objection and was ready with an answer. "Council Leader Sak-Ka is correct . . . But, like the Da clan, we have allies, too. And one such relationship has been secret for more than a year now."

"The Sa clan!" a council member named Ro-Ka said excitedly. "They owe us! And honor binds them."

"Yes, it does," Ona-Ka said judiciously. "And you may recall that the Sa clan is home to the Brotherhood of Night Stalkers . . . Which is to say, a group of very skilled assassins."

"I am satisfied," Sak-Ka proclaimed. "Let he who objects speak, or this deed will be done."

There was a moment of silence followed by the cry of "BLOOD!"

A HUNDRED AND TWENTY-TWO UNITS
NORTHWEST OF THE CITY OF BLADES

War Commander Ona-Ka was crouched in among a copse of wind-twisted trees. Members of the Sa clan's Night Stalker battalion were all around him, speaking in low tones and making final preparations for the attack. The sun had set, and it was beginning to snow. Not much, but enough to provide the assassins with some additional cover as they made the perilous journey across a fallow field to attack Triad Uba-Da's hunting lodge. The low, pie-shaped structure had originally been a family fortress back during the times when every warlord had a stronghold no matter how modest.

But things had changed over hundreds of years, and the round keep, as the locals referred to it, was less of a fort now and more of a fortified home. It still sat atop a hill; the moat had been filled in, and the outermost ring of walls had been allowed to deteriorate.

That said, the Triad's country estate would still be a difficult objective to take. Airborne drones roved the property, the keep was protected by a twelve-foot-tall inner wall, and Uba-Da employed a force of fifty warriors, all of whom were members of his clan.

Nevertheless, the keep would be easier to deal with than Uba-Da's castle would have been. So the fact that he was in the country hunting tuskers amounted to a lucky break. And thanks to the advantage of surprise, Ona-Ka believed that the Sa clan's force of one hundred highly trained warriors would be able to blow a hole in the defensive wall and use it to enter the lodge. Especially since the Da clan had failed to reinforce the keep in the wake of the latest news. That puzzled Ona-Ka, but he was willing to put the mistake down as incompetence.

"We're ready," Spear Commander Ra-Sa growled as he appeared next to Ona-Ka. The soldier was shrouded in a cloak made of a high-tech metamaterial that could bend light, heat, and radio waves so that they flowed around objects rather than bouncing off them. That made him more of a presence than a clearly defined form. The Night Stalkers weren't supposed to have access to the top secret cloaks, but, thanks to Ona-Ka, they did.

"Kill him," Ona-Sa said, "and the debt will be paid. More than that, something will be owed by my clan to yours."

"So be it," Ra-Sa agreed, and turned away. There was a soft rustle as the Night Stalkers literally disappeared. Ona-Ka wished that he could go with them and be present for the kill. But that was impossible since any hint of the Ka clan's involvement might result in the loss of what power they had.

Ona-Ka looked up as he heard the sound of engines, and what might have been an assault boat passed over his head. The running lights were off. A sure sign that the Da clan had finally gotten around to reinforcing the hunting lodge. That last-minute arrival of more defenders was unfortunate—but a handful of warriors wouldn't make much difference to the Sa. A curtain of snow fell as Ona-Ka picked his way through the trees to the dirt road where his ground car was parked. His job was complete. It was time to return home.

THE ROUND KEEP

The assault boat's engines roared as it dropped through whirling snowflakes to land on the pad inside the complex. They had arrived in time, or so Admiral Dura-Da assumed, since there had been no requests for assistance from Triad Uba-Da's bodyguards. Dura-Da was still angry regarding the low priority that one of his officers had placed on Admiral Nola-Ba's dispatch, a decision that could result in disastrous consequences. Perhaps an extended tour of duty on a remote mining world would serve to focus the fool's mind.

But, given the extra time, why hadn't there been a response from the Ka clan? One possibility was that they were arguing over what to do. That would be understandable since the magnitude of Nola-Ba's accomplishment left them with very few choices. They could sit back and watch Uba-Da enjoy the adulation that would be heaped upon him by the public, or they could try to kill him. What then? The citizenry would rise up against the Ka clan, and they would be worse off.

Such were Dura-Da's thoughts as the boat landed and the cargo ramp dropped to the ground. The naval officer was the first person to disembark, closely followed by twelve armed warriors. One of Uba-Da's aides was there to receive Dura-Da and was clearly peeved. "Good day, Admiral. This is a surprise."

"Good," Dura-Da replied tartly. "If you're surprised to see me, maybe the Ka clan will be as well. Take me to the Triad and prepare to leave. We will use the assault boat that I arrived on."

The aide was used to dominant personalities and had one

of his own. He stood his ground. Their eyes locked. "And why," the civilian inquired, "would we want to leave?"

Dura-Da was about to say, "Because I told you to," when a flash of light strobed the compound, an explosion was heard, and a large chunk of flying debris hit the assault boat. Engines screamed as the aircraft flipped over onto its side. A siren began to wail as a flare went off high above. "Come on!" the aide shouted. "Follow me." He took off at a trot, and Dura-Da followed, with his warriors trailing along behind.

It was Dura-Da's first visit to the keep, so everything was new to him. The aide, a functionary named Ra-Da, led him into a narrow corridor. It was barely wide enough for a single adult to pass through. That meant individuals traveling in the opposite direction would have to step into a wall niche, unless they were of higher rank, that is, in which case *he* was the one who would stand aside.

Dura-Da had seen the design used in other strongholds and knew there were probably half a dozen such hallways all radiating out from a central core. That would force invaders to proceed one at a time and make it possible for a handful of warriors to defend the heart of the fortress. Assuming there was a well at the structure's core, a feudal lord and his retainers could hold out for days or even weeks while they waited for help to arrive.

Ancient though the system was, Dura-Da knew it could still be effective. Something that the officer in charge of security was clearly counting on. Because as Dura-Da and his commandos arrived in the Star Chamber, he saw that Uba-Da was already there, along with members of his family and a small group of warriors. Dura-Da assumed the rest of the triad's bodyguards were outside, trying to prevent the invaders from entering the compound.

Uba-Da was *huge*, even by Hudathan standards, and armed to the teeth. If he was afraid, there was no sign of it on his craggy face or in the timbre of his voice. "Dura-Da! Just in time it would seem . . . Who's trying to kill me this time?"

"The Ka clan," Dura-Da responded, "or so I assume."

After listening to a brief report regarding Nola-Ba's stunning accomplishment, Uba-Da nodded his massive head. "That would explain it. The Ka clan hopes to kill me before word gets out, but we'll have none of that. Blood!"

"BLOOD!" the warriors around him shouted, even as a head flew off, and one of them fell. He had been positioned in front of corridor number five, and as Dura-Da looked in that direction, he saw the air shimmer.

"Ghost cloaks!" he shouted. "They're wearing ghost cloaks—and they're in the room!"

And it was true. The Sa had forced their way into the Star Chamber, which became apparent when Uba-Da fired at what looked like a blur and was rewarded with a hit. The assassin's cloak flared wide as he went down—giving the defenders a glimpse of the warrior within.

That was the beginning of a desperate battle as Dura-Da and his naval commandos formed a protective ring around Uba-Da and his family. Bullets seemed to come out of no-where. Swords swung through empty air. Bodyguards fell one after another. And it was impossible to tell how many opponents they were up against. "Automatic weapons!" Dura-Da shouted, as he raised his own. "Fire!"

It was a reckless, almost suicidal thing to do. Because as all of the defenders opened up the majority of the bullets they fired struck stone walls and bounced back at them. They buzzed, sang, and made slapping sounds as they struck flesh. One slug struck Ra-Da between the eyes and killed him instantly. Another hit Uba-Da's seven-year-old son in the shoulder. The impact spun the youngster around and sent him reeling to the floor. A third projectile grazed the triad himself.

But not all of the slugs hit the walls. Some struck assassins and with devastating effect. They fell, and as they did so, additional bullets were fired into their bodies just to make sure. Prisoners were a luxury the defenders couldn't afford.

Silence descended on the scene as smoke eddied in the air and a file of six bodyguards entered the chamber. They were led by a noncom. His right arm was bloody and hanging limply by his side. When the soldier saw Uba-Da, he came to attention. His expression was bleak. "The grounds have been secured—and reinforcements are on the way. My troops and I request permission to die."

"Permission denied," Uba-Da said, as he came forward to throw a huge arm around the noncom's shoulders. "If you kill yourselves, who will I drink with? Medic! Take care of this warrior's wounds. Then see to my son . . . He's leaking."

The next few hours were spent resecuring the lodge, searching the dead assassins, and running identification checks on them. None of the intruders were carrying IDs. But it didn't take long to figure out that they belonged to the Sa clan and were members of that family's Night Stalker battalion.

That was puzzling at first since Dura-Da expected the attackers to be from the Ka clan. But after consulting with the head of Internal Security, Dura-Da learned that there was evidence of a secret pact between the Sa clan and the Ka clan, the exact nature of which was unknown. So while it was likely that the Ka clan was responsible, it looked like the Sa were willing to take the blame, and would do so without admitting to a relationship with the Ka.

Thus, in spite of all the deaths on both sides, the Ka clan was not going to obtain another seat on the triad. And given the explosive nature of the news that would be released first thing in the morning, it was possible that *another* Da would join the ruling triumvirate. The prospect gladdened Dora-

Da's heart as a navy shuttle carried him back to the City of Blades. *War is hell,* he thought to himself, *but politics is far worse.*

THE HALL OF HEADS IN THE CITY OF BLADES

The Hall of Heads had originally served as a La clan monastery. Then, after the Common Blood Treaty of 1108, it had become the place where clan leaders came to air grievances, get drunk, and occasionally kill each other. Eventually, in 1297, the spot was officially designated as the seat of government for the first Clan Alliance and it had been the empire's most important government building ever since. The original structure now sat at the center of three wings, each housing a triad and his staff.

In order to attend the hastily called conclave in the Hall of Heads, it was necessary for Uba-Da and his bodyguards to leave his office at the far end of wing two and march all the way to the center of the complex, where only the Triad himself was allowed to enter. The practice had been adopted after a brawl involving all of the triads and their security personnel some 243 years earlier.

Panels of clear duraplast formed a dome through which rays of momentary sunlight streamed down to form a pool of gold on top of the three-sided conference table that occupied the center of the room. The walls were lined with shelves on which hundreds of Hudathan skulls had been arranged. Some heads had been taken in combat, others had been lopped off in retribution for crimes real or imagined, and a few had been harvested after a peaceful death. There were only three of them.

All of the skulls had one thing in common, however—and that was the fact that they had once belonged to triads. And as Uba-Da entered the hall, he knew that his own head would grace the room one day. *But not today,* he told himself, *or anytime soon.*

Triad Tu-Ra was already present and came forward to greet Uba-Da. Tu-Ra was a rarity among triads since he was a scholar rather than a warrior, and Uba-Da liked him. Yes, Tu-Ra could be counted upon to advance the interests of his clan and its allies, but usually with an eye to the greater good, a fact that accounted for the many attempts on his life. "Uba-Da! It's nice to see that your head remains on your shoulders! What did you do to offend the Sa clan?"

"I have no idea," Uba-Da confessed. "But whatever it was, I hope they will simply send me a message next time. I promise to open and read it."

Tu-Ra laughed, but both of them knew the truth. It was the Ka clan that stood to benefit from Uba-Da's death and was somehow behind the attack. It wouldn't do to say that however. Not without proof.

The conversation was interrupted by the arrival of Triad Isa-Ka. He was significantly smaller than the average Hudathan, and a good deal more vicious, which had a lot to do with how he had risen to prominence. And judging from the expression on Isa-Ka's face, the events of the night before had done nothing to improve his famously grumpy demeanor. "All right," Isa-Ka said. "I'm here. Let's get on with it."

"It," was the news that the Human empress was a prisoner and how to best leverage it. There was a loud scraping of chairs as the triads took their seats and, as was often the case, Tu-Ra took it upon himself to lead the discussion. "All of us have read Nola-Ba's report, so there's no reason to go over it. If the empress were a Hudathan, she'd be dead by now—since her clan wouldn't waste money or lives to free a hostage. But the Humans are different in that regard. Though strong in some ways, they are weak in others, and could be willing to negotiate."

"They have no honor," Isa-Ka said flatly as he sat slumped in a chair that was much too large for him.

"Of course they don't," Uba-Ba agreed. "They're *Humans*." The way he spoke made it clear that the aliens were inherently inferior.

"Honorable or not, they still forced us off Orlo II," Tu-Ra cautioned. "So it would behoove us to take them seriously."

"Whatever," Isa-Ka said carelessly. "Get to the point."

"The point is that we have an opportunity," Tu-Ra replied. "Or a couple of opportunities. We could trade her for something . . . Orlo II, for example. Or we could enter into protracted negotiations and make use of the time to strengthen the navy."

"I like option one," Uba-Da said, knowing Isa-Ka would oppose whatever he put forward.

The Ka clan's leader was predictable if nothing else. "I favor option two," he said. "We need new ships."

Then, just as Uba-Da knew he would, Tu-Ra chimed in. "I agree with Isa-Ka . . . We need time more than we need Orlo II."

"You see?" Isa-Ka demanded triumphantly. "You need to think more strategically."

"Point taken," Uba-Da said. "Now what?"

"Now we send a message to the Humans," Tu-Ra replied. "We tell them that we have the royal on Hudatha, so they won't send a battle group to Savas, and we demand that they cede Orlo II to us. But the *real* objective will be to buy time. Then, once we're ready, we'll send the Human's head to Earth in a message torp."

"Ha!" Isa-Ka responded enthusiastically. "I like it!"

"Sounds good," Uba-Da agreed. "But we need to bring the Human *here*. And quickly."

"Of course," Tu-Ra said. "We'll send ships to replace those already in orbit, and Nola-Ba can bring her back."

Isa-Ka knew that would result in a flood of positive publicity for the Da clan and its allies but there was nothing he could do to prevent it. And the decision was, insofar as the surrounding skulls were concerned, just one of thousands they had witnessed. They stared down from their shelves silently.

PLANET EARTH, CITY OF LOS ANGELES

Tarch Hanno hated meetings. *All* meetings including staff meetings, budget meetings, and personnel meetings. Worse yet were mysterious meetings. The kind one had to participate in without knowing what the subject was, who would be there, or what was at stake. And that was the sort of meeting he'd been told to attend.

So as his official air car entered a high-priority "lane" and headed north, Hanno was busy considering the possibilities. And most of the possibilities were bad because if the Minister of Defense had good news to share, why would he keep it secret? No, maybe Ophelia was dead . . . Or maybe the Hudathans were going to attack Earth! Or maybe another official had been assassinated.

But such ruminations were a waste of time, and Hanno knew it. All he could do was wait to see what sort of bad news was in the offing and deal with it. So he stared out the window, marveled at how vast LA was, and wondered when it would stop growing.

The car put down fifteen minutes later. And as Hanno stepped out of it, he felt an ocean breeze tug at his clothes. It felt good, and he wished he could be at the beach.

First he had to clear security before entering the main building and making his way through a labyrinth of busy hallways. Then it was necessary to pass through another security checkpoint before entering the heart of the building.

The conference room was the same one Minister of Defense Ono had reserved for previous meetings. And if that official's expression was any indication, they were in for a grim session indeed. Lady Constance Forbes was present, as were a couple of her staffers, both of whom were dressed in black business suits.

The bodyguards were unusual and, when Forbes looked at him, she smiled. Hanno couldn't remember her smiling at him before, and that sent a chill down his spine. If Ono was unhappy—why would Forbes be in a good mood?

Hanno offered Forbes a half bow and what he hoped was a cheerful "Good morning," before choosing a seat two rows behind her. As people continued to filter in, Hanno realized that a large contingent of military personnel were in attendance. That was ominous. Maybe the Hudathans *were* going to invade.

Once everyone was seated, Ono called the meeting to order. "I can't say, 'Good morning,' because it isn't. We received a message from the Hudathans about seven hours ago. I'll play it. Then we'll talk."

The room was equipped with a theater-quality holo player. Motes of multicolored light swirled, sought each other out, and coalesced into the image of a Hudathan. He was seated behind what looked like a slab of black granite. And when he spoke, there was little or no relationship between the movement of his jaw and the words they heard.

"Greetings. I am Triad Tu-Ra, speaking on behalf of the Hudathan government. As you are aware, Empress Ophelia Ordanus is missing and has been for some time. What you don't know is that she's here, on Hudatha, having been captured on the planet Savas. Naturally, you will want proof. Here it is."

The picture disintegrated and was replaced with a shocking image. Ophelia was wearing filthy clothes and standing in front of what looked like a durasteel bulkhead. There were obvious contusions on her face, her wrists were chained, and Hudathan guards stood on both sides of her. But dire though her circumstances were, her voice was steady. "I am Empress Ophelia Ordanus. My ship was attacked near a jump point and suffered significant damage during the ensuing battle. In order to escape certain defeat, the captain made an emergency hyperspace jump. We emerged near the planet Savas and were forced to make a crash landing. A significant number of the crew were killed on impact. Those who survived fortified the wreck. But when the locals attacked a few days later, we were overwhelmed. I was taken prisoner and transferred to the Hudathans."

The empress looked as if she was about to say something more, but the holo swirled and flew back together. Tu-Ra reappeared. "Listen, and listen carefully, Humans," the triad said. "We will free the empress in return for the planet Orlo II. If you refuse, or if you fail to respond within two standard weeks, we will kill Ordanus and ship her head to you in a message torpedo. Then we will attack."

The holo collapsed at that point, and the lights came back up. Ono was ready and waiting. "Well," he said grimly. "There is one thing to be grateful for—and that is the fact that Her Highness is still alive."

The statement was met with various expressions of enthusiastic agreement. Ono nodded in agreement. "During the last seven hours, the holo has been analyzed by experts from a number of different fields. They agree that the images you saw are genuine—and the facts as laid out by Empress Ophelia are consistent with what we know. With that in mind, here are the possible strategies we could pursue. First, we could agree to the Hudathan demands."

That statement produced a chorus of "No's," "Never's," and an emphatic "Over my dead body" from an admiral.

Ono nodded. "I concur. The second option is to let the Hudathans kill Empress Ophelia."

That possibility produced howls of protest, and Hanno was quick to add his voice to all the rest. Not because he thought the option was out of the question but in order to ensure his personal safety. There were fanatics in the room, and any sign of disloyalty could be punished.

Ono held up a hand. "I know, I know, all of us agree. But if the empress were here, she would insist that every possibility be examined. No matter how distasteful it might be."

Hanno knew that was true. Had Ophelia's recently deceased brother been in similar circumstances, he felt sure she would have allowed the poor bastard to "Sacrifice himself for the good of the empire."

"We lack the means to attack Hudatha," Ono continued. "And they would kill the empress if we did. So that leaves us with the third choice. We can stall. And there are some excellent reasons to do so. Some of you may have noticed the setting in which Empress Ophelia's statement was recorded. It could have been anywhere, including on the surface of Savas. For all we know, the Hudathans are lying. Maybe they captured her, as they claim they did, but for some reason haven't been able to move her. If so, there's a chance that the special-operations team led by Major Remy will reach and free her.

"Secondly, a battle group consisting of eight ships left for the Savas system three days ago. That's because the ship carrying Major Remy and his team detected the presence of Hudathan naval units in orbit around Savas just prior to going hyper. That's consistent with what the empress said about being handed over to them. So if she's still on the planet, and the task force arrives quickly enough, it may be possible to keep the Hudathans from moving her off-planet."

The Minister of Agriculture was seated to Hanno's right. Her hand shot up. "But what about the empress? If we destroy some of their ships, the Hudathans might kill her."

Ono's expression was grave. "That's true . . . But we

didn't know a Hudathan message torpedo would arrive days after the battle group departed. Unfortunately, that's the hand we were dealt—and that's the one we'll have to play."

"What about the public?" the Minister of Public Information wanted to know. "Are we going to tell them?"

"No," Ono said emphatically. "Not yet. So far as they know, the empress is still on her tour of the colonies. So unless someone leaks the information to the press, we'll be able to keep the lid on for a while longer. And should a leak occur, I can assure you that the penalty will be quite severe."

All of them knew what that meant. The person or persons who were responsible for the leak would be killed. The meeting ended shortly thereafter, and it was a very subdued crowd that filed out of the conference room and returned to their offices, most of which were located in the same building. Hanno was the exception since his headquarters were downtown. A statement of independence that Ophelia had been willing to tolerate in order to recruit what she believed to be the right man. And Hanno took comfort from that.

There were potential dangers, however. What if the Hudathans sent Ophelia's head to Earth in a message torp? A power struggle was sure to ensue. And remote though the possibility might be, a person connected to one of Hanno's victims might rise to power. What would happen to his carefully crafted kingdom then? And more importantly, to *him*?

Dark thoughts followed Hanno to his air car and accompanied him on the trip downtown. Some sort of backup plan was in order. A second identity on a rim world perhaps, complete with a nice place to live and a fat bank account. He could use his agency to create it. No, that was too obvious. And too dangerous. He would use a different channel.

Such were Hanno's musings as the air car settled onto the top of the building that housed the Bureau of Missing Persons. The BMP's administrative offices were located on the twenty-sixth floor. But the so-called crypt was down in the basement. That was the place where Earth-based sanctions could be monitored live and the computers were located.

Normally, Hanno began each day with a visit to the crypt so that his staff could brief him on current operations before he went upstairs. And Hanno saw no reason to vary his routine.

So he entered an elevator that carried him down to the basement. A pin code plus a thumbprint were required to exit the lift. Cool air flooded the car as the doors hissed open. Hanno stepped out into a small but tastefully furnished waiting room. The lighting was subdued, and abstract paintings graced the walls.

Beyond that, and placed so as to block entry to the hall beyond, sat a curved reception desk. Hanno frowned. The receptionist was a retired marine named Murdock, and he was nowhere to be seen. This was highly irregular, not to mention annoying, because Hanno had given strict instructions that the desk be manned at all times. If Murdock needed to take a pee, he was supposed to call for another employee to come out and sit in for him.

Hanno made his way over to the desk and circled around it. That was when he saw Murdock lying on the floor staring at the ceiling. There was a blue-edged bullet hole between his eyes, and judging from the bloodstain on his chest, he'd been shot there as well. A double tap. The sure sign of a professional.

Suddenly, there was an empty place where the bottom of Hanno's stomach should have been. Where was the killer? In back? Hanno knelt next to the body, fumbled under Murdock's blue blazer, and located his pistol. He removed the weapon and stood. A quick check served to confirm that there was a bullet in the chamber.

Should he call police? No, they weren't cleared to enter the top secret facility. DIS then? Hanno remembered the way Forbes had smiled at him and felt a chill run down his spine. Was this *her* work? No, she wouldn't dare! Or would she? Ophelia was being held for ransom and might never return . . . What if Forbes knew that *before* the meeting? And, as chief of the DIS, she probably had. If there would ever be a time for Forbes to strike, this was it.

Hanno entered the dimly lit hallway with the pistol extended in front of him. Small workrooms lined both sides of the corridor. Controllers used them to monitor field operations.

The first room on the left was empty and the equipment was dark. But, as Hanno stepped into the one on the right, he saw two brightly lit computer screens and Samantha Yang. Her body was slumped forward, and judging from the blood, she'd been shot in the back of the head. Hanno swore under his breath. Samantha was one of his favorites. A young woman slated for promotion. Now this.

He stepped out into the hall. Was the killer or killers still in the basement? Or had they left? Blood pounded in his head as he advanced. More horrors awaited him. Controller Mark Bowers had been shot in the chest and looked surprised.

Computer tech Reba Dann was sprawled facedown in the hallway. Hanno had to step over her body to enter the open area generally referred to as the tank. That was when he encountered the first sign of resistance. Crystal Kemp lay on her back with a small semiautomatic pistol lying inches from her dead fingertips. Her blond hair was fanned out behind her head, and the front of her white blouse was red with blood.

Then, as Hanno's eyes came up, he saw the letters that had been spray-painted onto the wall. "FF." The Freedom Front. Had the man called Colonel Red come back to life? No. Hanno sensed that this was the *second* part of Forbes's plan. Having been unable to seize control of the BMP, she was going to destroy the organization and blame the slaughter on the Freedom Front. A strategy that would not only eliminate a competitor but further justify the need for her department! It was a brilliant plan. And Hanno knew that footage of the scene, supposedly shot by Freedom Front commandos, would soon appear on the net. Or maybe it was there already.

Hanno turned a full circle with weapon raised. But there were no targets to shoot at. The DIS agents had completed their mission and left. Then it occurred to him. If the DIS agents were gone, and he was there, Forbes would . . .

Hanno never got to complete the thought. Four carefully placed charges went off. Everything in the crypt was destroyed by a flash fire and buried under tons of rubble as the upper floors of the building collapsed. More than a hundred office workers were killed.

Forbes watched the whole thing from many miles away, made a note to eliminate the BMP personnel located on other planets, and went to lunch. All in all it had been a very successful morning.

CHAPTER: 11

There is, between lovers, an attraction more powerful than gravity itself.

AUTHOR UNKNOWN
A Dweller folk saying
Standard year circa 2349

PLANET SAVAS

Thanks to night-vision technology, the team could travel during the hours of darkness when it was cooler, and they were less likely to be seen by people on the ground. The Hudathans could see their heat signatures from the air, of course, if they were passing over and paying attention. But that was a chance the team had to take.

Now, having been on the move for more than six hours, the sun had broken company with the eastern horizon, and the temperature was about to rise. It would approach a hundred degrees by noon—so it was necessary to find a place where they could hole up. One that offered both protection from the sun and a source of water would be ideal.

Fortunately, their Jithi guides had traveled that way many times and knew the area well. And, according to Kambi, the ruins of an ancient city lay directly ahead. According to legend, the metropolis had been built on the banks of a river during a time when the equatorial jungle dominated the area. But eventually the desert sand moved south, the river dwindled to a stream, and the population declined. Finally, when the water withdrew below the surface, the once-thriving metropolis was reduced to a ghost town.

However, some water was still available thanks to an underground well. That was the good news. The bad news was that the ruins might be occupied by one of the Paguumi caravans that paused there from time to time. A small group wouldn't be a problem. But the mission was to find and rescue Ophelia, not get into meaningless firefights, so Remy wanted to avoid a potentially costly battle if he could.

With that in mind, he sent Kambi and a squad of hats forward to reconnoiter. They searched the ruins, determined that they were empty, and radioed in. At that point, McKee's platoon was sent forward to secure the area. She ordered Mo Hiller and his squad to circle wide and take up positions north of the ruins. Then McKee led the rest of them through what had probably been a well-fortified entrance back during the city's heyday. Her thoughts went to Bindali Jivani. Had she been there, the anthropologist would have been fascinated by the ruins and eager to explore every nook and cranny. Most of the city had been reduced to little more than sand-drifted streets, waist-high adobe walls, and piles of rubble. But fragments of buildings remained—and who knew what lay buried below?

Kambi and the recon team came out to greet the newcomers. The Jithi pointed to what might have been a temple. "Stairs lead down into the lower level," he explained. "It was hot, so more people lived belowground than above it. That's where the well is."

McKee ordered her people to establish a security perimeter by hooking up with Hiller's squad. Once it was safe to do so, she gave the go-ahead for the rest of the company to enter the city. Then it was time to make the rounds. The key was to find shade and concealment for each person, while maintaining interlocking fields of fire, and paths that would allow them to fall back if necessary.

Once the task was complete, she went looking for Remy. A sand-drifted street led her back to what she thought of as the temple. That's where Sergeant Major Hadley and some of his hats were busy unloading a RAV. "He's down below," Hadley said, as he pointed to some stairs. "Inspecting the well."

McKee thanked him and followed the well-worn steps down into near darkness. The air was noticeably cooler, which was consistent with Kambi's claim that the majority of the city's residents had chosen to reside there.

The light from a distant glow stick served to guide McKee down a broad corridor to a circular chamber, where a number of other passageways met. Half a dozen legionnaires were gathered around the crude framework that straddled a hole in the ground. Remy turned as McKee arrived. "How did it go?"

"The ruins are defensible," McKee replied. "Assuming that the digs don't throw an army at us and the ridgeheads don't attack from above."

Remy grinned. "That's a lot of ifs, Lieutenant."

"Yes, sir. Perhaps you would like to walk the perimeter. I would value your opinion."

"I'll be up in a minute or two," Remy replied. "We're waiting for the first bucket of water to come up. If it's potable, we'll stay. If not, we'll have a difficult decision to make. The next source of water is about twelve miles away."

There was a squeaking sound as a legionnaire turned a crank. Hand-plaited rope wound onto a piece of wood as another soldier aimed a light down into the hole. McKee noticed that, while there was a sizable pile of trash about twenty feet away, the area immediately around the well was scrupulously clean. A cultural norm perhaps? Because all the locals depended on such wells? It was the type of question Jivani delighted in.

When the water appeared, it was in a large leather bucket complete with a hoselike arrangement at the bottom. Once opened, it would allow the contents to drain into smaller containers. The tube was controlled with a spring-loaded clamp. "My people made that," Kambi said proudly, as Remy held a mug under the hose.

A legionnaire squeezed the clamp. Once the cup was full, Remy brought it up to his lips where he took a sip and was seen to swirl the liquid around his mouth. Then he spit the water onto the ground. "It's brackish," Remy declared, "but I've had worse. We'll purify it and top off the canteens."

By the time McKee and Remy were done touring the perimeter, the temperature was at least eighty degrees, and McKee was sweating. It felt good to duck into some shade and drink the cool well water.

Remy set the watches, and McKee wound up in charge of the third. That meant she was able to enjoy nearly five hours of sleep before returning to the surface. Once she arrived, Lieutenant Sokov could go off duty, and he reported that everything was fine. A single contrail had been seen an hour earlier, and that was all. Though less than threatening, it was a reminder that the Hudathans held the high ground. A sobering thought indeed.

The sun moved with what seemed like excruciating slowness as it arced across the sky before eventually sinking into the west. The air would start to cool in an hour or so. Then it would be time to roust those who were asleep, eat a meal, and leave. In the meantime, McKee kept busy by circling the perimeter while pausing occasionally to eyeball the horizon through her binoculars. And that's what she was doing when Remy arrived. McKee heard movement and turned to look. She thought he looked tired, but all of them looked tired, and would until the mission was over. "Lieutenant."

"Major."

"I've got a job for you."

The last thing McKee wanted was a shit detail—but there was only one thing she could say. "Yes, sir."

"The signal continues to be strong, but we're moving too slowly," Remy said. "Maybe Ophelia is in hiding—or maybe the Paguumis have her. But what if the Hudathans get their mitts on her? They'll take her off-planet and out of reach. So speed is of the essence, and while your cyborgs can run all day at thirty-miles an hour, my people can't. And making a bad situation worse is the fact that we're spending an hour a day looking for water.

"So to recover that time, and speed things up, I'm going to send you forward. Kambi will show you the way. Your job will be to find water and mark the location for us."

McKee knew Remy was correct. Each day that passed made it less likely that they would find the empress alive. And while that was fine with her, the rest of them wouldn't agree. "Yes, sir. I can act as a scout as well."

"Exactly," Remy responded. "But it's important to keep radio communications to an absolute minimum. Otherwise, the Hudathans will use your transmissions to track us down."

McKee nodded. "Yes, sir. Can I have three T-1s? One for me, one for Kambi, and one to carry supplies?"

"Yes," Remy agreed. "And you can take C-3 with you as well. It will come in handy. Go out, secure the next two sources of water, and wait at the third. Good luck."

McKee spent the next hour getting ready. She chose Nick Riley from the second squad to carry Kambi—and Peter Popov from the third to hump supplies. That left both of the squad leaders shorthanded, but it couldn't be helped. As an extra precaution, McKee had shoulder launchers mounted on Popov. That would give the detachment at least some chance of defending themselves against an attack by Hudathan aircraft.

After handing the platoon off to Jolo, McKee followed C-3 out of the city, closely followed by Kambi on Riley and Popov in the three slot. According to Kambi, the next source of water was about twelve miles ahead, and McKee planned to get there quickly. Then, after reaching that goal, she hoped to arrive at the Oboli Oasis by dawn. It was sixteen miles beyond objective one. That meant they would have to cover twenty-eight miles in all. A difficult if not impossible goal for the hats—but a stroll in the park for her T-1s. Barring mechanical difficulties or a run-in with the Paguumis, that is.

As Bartov continued to increase speed, McKee looked over to see how Kambi was doing. Theoretically, all the Jithi had to do was to bend his knees, lean back, and relax. But like most beginners, the Jithi was holding on for dear life with knees locked. McKee smiled. He would learn.

The country that lay northeast of the ancient city consisted of dry riverbeds, scattered boulders, and occasional outcroppings of rock. As darkness fell, and McKee's night-vision gear came on, her surroundings took on a ghastly green appearance. But she was used to that and welcomed the additional cover that nighttime gave her.

Low-power infrared communications were safe unless the ridgeheads were extremely close, so McKee could make occasional use of the squad freq. C-3 led the way, followed by the three cyborgs. They covered the twelve-mile trip in half an hour and would have arrived even sooner if it hadn't been for the difficult terrain. Kambi was wearing a borrowed helmet and was using the night-vision technology without difficulty. "We must stop here," Kambi said, as the group skidded down the side of a ravine and into the bottom of a gully.

"Okay," McKee responded. "But where's the water?"

"It is here," Kambi insisted. "We must dig for it."

After releasing their harnesses, McKee and Kambi dropped to the ground, where the legionnaire replaced the graspers that Bartov and Riley were wearing with shovel hands. Meanwhile, lest someone sneak up on them, C-3 and Popov were standing watch.

Once their shovel hands were locked in place, the T-1s began to dig. Given the fact that they were down in a ravine and out of sight, McKee thought it was safe to let the cyborgs use their headlamps. The resulting pool of light was focused on a patch of dry, rocky-looking soil. The ground was hard, which meant it was slow going at first. That was understandable. But after fifteen minutes of digging, the hole was still bone dry. "So where's the water?" McKee wanted to know.

"It's there," Kambi insisted. "Sometimes it flows just below the surface and sometimes it's farther down."

Bartov and Riley had paused to watch the debate, and McKee put them back to work. "You heard him . . . Keep digging." So dirt, gravel, and rocks continued to fly. Bit by bit the hole grew wider as well as deeper. Eventually, the borgs had to kneel in order to work. Then it became necessary to stand in the hole.

Six feet deep. That was as far as McKee was willing to go. That's what she was thinking when Bartov spoke. "We're in sand now . . . And it's damp."

"I told you so!" Kambi said triumphantly. "Keep going."

The cyborgs obeyed, and gray water rose to fill the bottom of the hole thirty seconds later. "Well done," McKee said. "Let's make it bigger so the company won't have to."

That produced some grumbling, but the cyborgs continued to dig, and it wasn't long before they had a small pond. McKee ordered C-3 to take pictures of the water hole and send it, plus the coordinates, to Remy via an encrypted "squirt" transmission. A signal so brief the Hudathans weren't likely to notice it—and wouldn't be able to trace it if they did.

Then McKee removed an eight-foot-by-eight-foot tarp from the gear that Popov was carrying. The plan had been to use it to provide shade once the sun came up, but it would have to serve a different purpose now. Kambi helped her spread the sheet of plastic over the well and anchor the corners with rocks. Thanks to the desert camo pattern printed on the tarp it would be very difficult to see—and McKee sprinkled sand over the cover in hopes of disguising it further.

The process of digging the hole had consumed more than an hour. But McKee thought they could still reach the Oboli Oasis before dawn and was determined to try. So with C-3 in the lead, they set off in a northwesterly direction. Broken ground gradually gave way to hardpan and desert. That meant the legionnaires could travel faster, but it also meant that they were exposed.

Finally, as the sky began to lighten in the east, McKee called a halt near an outcropping of rock. They'd been lucky so far. But wells were like magnets. And the very fact that the Oboli Oasis had a name was a good indicator of how important it was.

Assuming Kambi's estimate was correct, their destination was about a mile away, and if a large group of Paguumis was present, McKee figured they would post pickets halfway out. That opened the possibility that they could blunder into a sentry and trigger a firefight. In order to avoid that, McKee ordered C-3 to stay high, *very* high, and check the place out.

As the drone departed, McKee opened her visor in order to take a bite of a dust-dry energy bar. Then she had to close it again to see the HUD and monitor C-3's progress. The drone was in the thermal-imaging mode and cruising along at two hundred feet. That was lower than she would have liked but close to the machine's maximum ceiling.

There wasn't much to see at first. Just patches of cooler ground and rocks that still retained some warmth. Then, as McKee swallowed a bite, she saw what looked like a thick carpet of undulating heat. What the hell was it?

"Switch to image enhancement," she ordered, and C-3 obeyed. Suddenly, McKee found herself looking down on a large herd of animals. Were these the kudu she'd heard about? That seemed likely. And the guess was confirmed when she saw a warrior mounted on a huge quadruped. "Pull back," McKee said urgently, "and stay high."

Then it was time to hold her breath until the drone appeared out of the night. The T-1s had been monitoring the whole thing. "Now what?" Bartov wanted to know.

"Now we ask the major for orders," McKee replied.

The squirt transmission went out and the reply came back five minutes later. "Meet the team at water hole one." McKee wasn't surprised. Remy hoped to avoid a fight.

Riley was unhappy. "Damn. We just got here."

"Yeah, the Legion sucks," Bartov said heartlessly. "But you can always quit and hitchhike home."

Unfortunately, the trip back to the water hole in the gully was just as tiring as the trip out had been. But it was blessedly uneventful, and with a mile left to go, McKee knew they would appear on the team's sensors soon. It was hard to imagine how T-1s could be perceived as anything other than what they were—but when people are keyed up, accidents can happen. So rather than take chances, McKee chinned her mike. "This is one. We are a mile out and closing. Over." She heard two clicks as someone keyed a mike.

The sun was up by then, and it wasn't long before McKee spotted a legionnaire standing in the shade cast by an outcropping of rock with a T-1 beside him. She recognized the bio bod as Bill Dixon and the borg as Eno Ellis. Both were members of the first squad. They waved as Bartov trudged past.

The company was camped inside an earthen berm that had been thrown up by the cyborgs. Large sections of camouflage netting had been erected to hide the legionnaires from eyes in the sky and to provide a modicum of shade. It was hot, though, and bound to get worse as the sun arced higher. That would make sleep difficult if not impossible. And sleep was what McKee wanted most.

Various people waved, and Sergeant Major Hadley was there to meet them as they entered the compound. Twin puffs of dust exploded away from McKee's boots as she dropped to the ground. "Welcome back. The old man's over there," Hadley said as he pointed at the largest tent.

McKee said, "Thanks," before turning to face the cyborgs. "You did a good job . . . Take a break. And have somebody run a full set of diagnostics on your systems. If there are any problems, let's find them now."

McKee could feel the sun beating down on her shoulders as she made her way over to the camo netting and ducked under it. It was cooler underneath in the shade but not by much. She was walking toward the tent when she heard the high piping sound of a child's voice. "Sergeant McKee! It's Nicolai . . . Do you remember me?"

McKee felt a chill run down her spine as she turned to confront Prince Nicolai. It had been many months since she'd met him at his mother's estate near LA on Earth. Was he a bit taller? Maybe. One thing was for sure. The tousled hair was nearly blond, and he had a tan. And there was something else too . . . A sense of confidence that hadn't been there before.

All of that crossed her mind but was quickly subsumed by the sudden realization that Ophelia was not only alive but had been rescued. McKee's mouth felt dry and it was difficult to speak. "Of course I remember. You were wearing grav skates."

"They're at home," Nicolai said. "But I have something new. Do you want to see it?"

"Yes," McKee said, "I do."

"Here it is," Nicolai said, as he pulled a small folding knife out of his pocket. "Major John gave it to me."

McKee was processing that when a male voice said, "That's right . . . He's a bit young, but every boy should have a knife. Especially here."

McKee knew that voice and whirled around to find that both John Avery *and* Major Remy were standing a few feet away. "Major Avery tells me that you two served together on Orlo II," Remy said. "It's a small Legion, isn't it?"

McKee felt her face flush as her heart sought to beat its way out of her chest. Avery was tanned. Very tanned. And somewhat gaunt. But she could see the warmth in his eyes and some caution as well. Both of them knew that their relationship had to remain a secret. So she did what any junior officer would do and came to attention. Both men returned the salute. "Come on," Remy said. "It's at least one degree cooler inside the tent."

McKee's head was spinning. *Avery!* There on Savas! There was so much she wanted to say. And so much she wanted to know. All of which would have to wait until they could be alone.

Remy led the way into the tent, and that was when McKee saw Empress Ophelia. No matter how much she hated the bitch it was necessary to bow. "Highness."

"That's Daska," Avery said. "Ophelia's body double— and Nicolai's security detail. It's a synth."

What felt like ice water trickled into McKee's veins. Avery's tone was light—but the warning was obvious. "I see,"

McKee said, as she eyed the robot. "It's a very good likeness. So, the empress is here as well?"

"No," Remy put in. "I wish she were. The *Victorious* crashed, and the Paguumis attacked. But the major, Daska, and Prince Nicolai were able to get away by entering one of the ship's escape pods and launching it. The pod landed a good distance away from the wreck, and it's my guess that the Hudathans found the unit and used it to bait the trap that killed Olson. They had to fend for themselves after that. Then, after spotting us, Major Avery chose an unusual way to announce their presence."

McKee looked at Avery, who grinned. "We were a long way off, and I was afraid the company would pass us by without noticing us. So I took a shot at a T-1."

"And hit him!" Remy exclaimed. "With a Paguumi muzzle loader at that . . . The slug hit Private Varco, and he was about to return fire when Major Avery raised a white flag."

"Nicolai had been wearing the shirt for days, so it wasn't very white," Avery said. "But it got the job done."

"I couldn't take a bath!" Nicolai said proudly. "We only had water to drink."

"That's right," Avery said as he tousled the boy's hair. "There's no way that Nicolai and I could pass inspection." As McKee watched them, she realized something important about the man she was in love with. Something that came as a surprise. Avery would make a good father.

Remy chuckled. "Well, it worked. Now it's time to do some planning. Daska? I know it's hot . . . But Prince Nicolai should get some rest. We'll be up all night."

It was nicely put. They couldn't discuss the effort to find Ophelia in front of Nicolai . . . And there was Daska to consider. Would the machine record everything it heard? Probably. And Remy knew that. Just as he knew it was important to control the narrative of whatever took place. His report, assuming he lived long enough to submit one, would be subjected to a great deal of scrutiny.

There was no way to know if Daska understood such subtleties. But even if it did, the robot was a robot and had to do what it was told so long as such actions were consistent with its basic programming. Daska extended a hand. "Come on, Nicolai . . . It's time for a nap."

For his part, Nicolai was used to being hustled out of rooms and offered no protest. "Good-bye, Major John. Good-bye, Sergeant McKee."

"It looks like she's a lieutenant now," Avery said.

Nicolai's eyes grew larger. "Do I outrank her?"

"Yes, you do."

"Good. I like to outrank people." And with that, he was led away.

"So," Remy began. "Let's talk about how to proceed. Based on the video that C-3 took, there's no way that we can use the Oboli Oasis or even go near it. That means we'll have to circle around. But which way? West or east?"

A map of the area was projected on a roll-up screen. Avery went over to point at it. "I think we should go east. That would take us up to the crash site."

Remy frowned. "Why would we want to go there?"

"According to your Jithi guides, hundreds of southerners are likely to be on the site collecting scrap metal."

Remy looked skeptical. "So?"

McKee found herself watching with interest as Avery sought to shape the situation without getting crosswise with Remy. Both men were majors, but Remy was in command, and the final decision would be his. "So," Avery said, "we're closing in on Ophelia's locator beacon, and judging from the signal strength, she's somewhere up north. That's where the *northern* Paguumis rule, and according to what Kambi tells me, the Hudathans have a base there. Ophelia could be in hiding. Or, one of the groups I mentioned could be holding her prisoner. If so, we could use some allies—and the southern Paguumis are available."

"Even though they killed a lot of our people?" Remy demanded.

"Yes," Avery answered. "It isn't pretty, but I think we need them."

McKee waited to see how Remy would respond. Avery had been invited to offer an opinion—so Remy couldn't complain about that. But it seemed safe to assume that Avery's suggestion had gone well beyond the level of advice Remy had been expecting. He would have to be careful. What was the nature of Avery's relationship with Nicolai? Had they been close prior to the crash? If so, that suggested a personal connection with Ophelia. Something Remy would be wise to consider.

After a short pause, Remy nodded. "There's a lot of risk associated with your proposal. If the southerners refuse to talk, and attack instead, we could take a lot of casualties. Even so, I think we should try it."

McKee knew that while it might have been Avery's idea, Remy was the one who would bear the responsibility for the decision. And her respect for the man went up a notch as a result.

The ensuing conversation focused on the next steps, and once it was over, Remy told McKee she could go but asked Avery to stay. That meant McKee wouldn't be able to speak with him, not right away, so it was time to get some sleep.

Thanks to Sergeant Jolo, a two-person shelter had been prepared for her in the shade of a tarp—and a bucket of water had been placed next to her sleeping pad. "Take the body armor off and pour water on your clothes," the noncom advised. "The evaporation will cool you down."

And it did. After the wet down, McKee fell asleep quickly and remained that way through the worst heat of the day. She woke shortly after 1400 hours feeling groggy. The bucket still had some water in it, so she took a sponge bath in the privacy of her shelter.

Then, for the first time since arriving on Savas, she eyed herself in the mirror that was part of her emergency kit. She was in dire need of a haircut. The scar was still there. And because of her visor, the skin on her face was shockingly white compared to her neck, arms, and hands. None of which was ideal. But what was, was.

It took five minutes to comb her hair, apply some lip gloss, and scrape the dirt out from under her fingernails. That was the best she could do.

As McKee left the shelter in search of an MRE, she was acutely conscious of the fact that she could run into Avery at any moment. But that didn't occur until evening as the camp was being torn down, and the sun was about to set.

With the exception of those assigned to guard the perimeter, the rest of the company was busy packing their gear and preparing to move out. After fixing a leak in Private Cole's cooling system, McKee was headed across the compound to get her pack. That was when she ran into Avery.

Both stopped, and their eyes met. People were all around, but none were close enough to hear. "When I heard you were here, it was like a dream come true," Avery said. "You look beautiful."

McKee smiled. "Yeah, there's nothing like a few weeks on Savas to make a girl look good. *Any* girl."

Avery laughed. "It isn't like that, and you know it. I want to talk to you."

"I'd like that," McKee said softly. "But we'll have to wait for the right opportunity. I hear you're going to travel on foot."

"I've got to stay with Nicolai," Avery replied. "It isn't his fault that his mother is a mass murderer."

"So you like him."

"Yes, for the moment anyway. But I'm worried about the

future. Ophelia downloaded a group of so-called advisors into his head, and they bicker all the time. Who knows what effect that will have."

"Yes," McKee said. "Who knows. We'd better get going."

"I like your six, so take good care of it."

McKee laughed, and they parted company.

Daska, who was watching from about a hundred feet away, made a mental note. The Humans appeared to know each other. That meant nothing in and of itself. But she would watch. Her job was to protect Nicolai and, according to her programming, *everyone* was a potential threat. That included Avery and McKee.

The company pulled out shortly after 1800 hours and set off in a northeasterly direction. Two of the drones led the way, with C-3 bringing up the rear. The cavalry platoon's second squad was on point, with the first guarding the company's left flank and the third on the right.

It would have been nice to place some T-1s in the drag position, but there weren't enough of them. That meant a squad of Remy's hats had been assigned to the six slot under Sergeant Major Hadley's command. Avery, Daska, and Nicolai were at the center of the column, with a squad of special-ops troops to protect them.

As usual, McKee was with her people on point. The moon was partially hidden behind a thin veil of clouds, but some of the light still found the ground. The result was a ghostly glow that frosted the top of the nearest rock formation and turned parts of the desert white. McKee knew it would be easy to get lost in the surreal landscape and ordered her troops to use their night-vision capabilities if they weren't already doing so.

Fortunately, the next four hours passed without running into any indigs. So by the time Remy called a halt, they had covered a very respectable ten miles. Half the legionnaires were allowed to take a break in place while the rest stood watch. They would switch twenty minutes later.

McKee checked to make sure that her squad leaders understood the drill before going off to find some privacy. Then, with an MRE in hand, she found a place to sit. She had just started to open the box when Avery materialized out of the gloom. He was carrying an AXE, and his helmet was tucked under one arm. "May I join you?"

"Of course," McKee replied as she eyed their surroundings. There was no one in sight; not that it mattered since it was common knowledge that they had served together on Orlo II. And what would be more natural than for the two of them to chat?

Avery sat on an adjacent rock. His voice was pitched low. "I missed you, Cat . . . I, well, I think of you all the time. But maybe I shouldn't. Things can change."

Avery's face was tanned but still looked pale in the moonlight. "They *have* changed," McKee said. "But not in the way you mean. Not a day has gone by that I haven't thought about you. About *us*."

Avery looked down and back up again. "Thank God for that."

McKee took another look around. "That will have to hold us for now. It's too dangerous to talk for very long."

"You're right," Avery agreed. Then he leaned in to kiss her lips. The contact was extremely brief but enough to remind McKee of precious moments on Orlo II. The MRE sat unopened as he vanished into the night.

Meanwhile, about two thousand feet away, Daska was reacting to the kiss as well. By that time, the robot had hacked into C-1's command and control system. That meant Daska could use the device for private surveillance missions when it wasn't under the direct control of a Human. And in this case, the robot had been monitoring the machine's video feed as it overflew the area.

After spotting two heat signatures which showed up as Avery and McKee on the company's electronic roster, Daska ordered the drone to hover above them. The machine was too high to listen in, but the synth was programmed to interpret nonverbal communications and knew what a kiss signified.

It appeared that the Humans had a sexual as well as professional relationship. Did that make either one of them a threat to Nicolai? No. But it meant they were worth watching. Daska broke contact with C-1 and went to prepare food for the boy. Just one of the many ways she was programmed to take care of him.

Once the break was over, the march resumed. The moon had set by then, and it would have been pitch-black without their night-vision equipment. Gradually, the ground began to level out, and they were able to travel more quickly as a result. Two drones led the way as they had before. And shortly after 0300, the one on the right flank detected two Paguumis and two zurnas camped within a half circle of boulders.

McKee expected Remy to circle around them and was surprised when he sent the platoon's third squad forward to capture the locals instead. The Paguumis were taken by surprise, forced to surrender their weapons, and brought in front of Remy. Then, with some help from Kambi, the officer was able to interrogate them.

McKee wasn't present for the interrogation so she had no way to know what was said. But shortly after the session,

Remy gave orders to change course. Not much—just a couple of degrees. McKee took note of the new heading and led the way. Dawn found the team near a pinnacle of rock and the hand-dug well located below it. A scattering of boulders provided some cover, and orders were given to create earthworks between them. Then, as her cyborgs went to work, McKee saw the prisoners leave the compound. C-1 was flying fifty feet above them. What was Remy up to?

The question went unanswered as the company set up camp around the well. And there was a lot of work to do since Remy insisted that the legionnaires take more precautions than usual. That made sense since McKee figured there was an excellent chance that the Paguumi warriors would return with a thousand of their friends.

Once the compound was secure, half the legionnaires were allowed to get some sleep while the rest stood watch. McKee was assigned to the first group. So she used some well water to wet herself down prior to crawling into the shade provided by her two-person shelter. She hadn't been asleep for more than a few minutes when the thunder woke her up.

Except that it wasn't thunder. Jolo appeared next to her shelter. "The major ordered everyone to stand to," he said. "The Hudathans are coming this way."

That brought McKee out of the shelter in a hurry, with her body armor halfway on and AXE in hand. "Hudathans? Where?"

"Look north," Private Ree said. "The ridgeheads are hunting for us."

McKee looked and saw that Ree was correct. The Hudathan ship was about the size of a Human destroyer escort and shaped like a wedge. It was *big*, but not so big that it couldn't operate inside the atmosphere. McKee guessed that it was at least five miles away but flying only a few hundred feet off the ground. She estimated that the ship's ground speed was no more than fifty miles per hour, which amounted to a crawl for such a vessel. That meant its repellers were working extremely hard to keep it aloft.

Thunder rolled as sticks of artificial lightning touched down all around the vessel. "They're trying to flush us out," Jolo said, and that made sense. Remy's voice was unnaturally loud in her ear. "Maintain radio silence. Do not acknowledge this transmission. All T-1s will stand by to repel enemy aircraft. Over."

McKee swore. The fifties wouldn't make much of an impression on the ship—and only two of her cyborgs were wearing cans. If the ship turned south, they were screwed. It would take twenty minutes minimum to remove additional launchers from the RAVs and mount them.

But the Hudathan vessel *didn't* turn south. And as it disappeared to the east, McKee exhaled. She was surprised to learn that she'd been holding her breath. Would the DE turn and come back? Maybe. But running would be a mistake. That's what the ridgeheads were counting on them to do.

During the next half hour, cans were loaded onto two additional cyborgs, who joined the others on the ad hoc AA network. Then, having lost a significant chunk of her rest period, McKee was able to lie down again. Sleep came quickly, and she was deep in a dream when her chrono began to vibrate.

The sun was still high in the sky as half the legionnaires returned to duty so the others could rest. McKee made a visit to the latrine followed by a trip to the well, where she filled her canteen. Then she stopped next to a RAV. A lot of MREs had been consumed by that time, and McKee was very conscious of that as she removed one from the dwindling supply.

So McKee ate some of her lunch and stashed the rest in various cargo pockets for use later on. After spending some time with the second squad, she was about to visit the first when one of the sentries shouted a warning. Her helmet was perched on top of her gear some hundred yards away, and it was necessary to climb up onto a rock to see what was taking place.

The sentries were looking north, so she did too. All she could see was a dust cloud at first. Then, after raising her binoculars, McKee spotted one of the company's drones. Streaming long behind it were a dozen Paguumi warriors, all waving rifles and riding hell-bent for leather. Because someone was chasing them? No. McKee was reminded of the Naa. This was for show, to intimidate potential enemies, and for the pure joy of it. The fact that no one was shooting at the digs was a clear indication that Remy had ordered them not to.

McKee had a pretty good idea of what had taken place at that point. By sending a drone with the freed prisoners, Remy had been able to impress their chief, communicate with him, and remain at a safe distance. And the plan had been at least partially successful since a band of warriors had been sent to do what? Time would tell.

The legionnaires watched as the warriors skidded to a showy stop just outside the compound. Gravel sprayed, animals squealed, and one of the Paguumis fired a navy-issue pistol into the air. A healthy reminder that primitive though they were, the locals had been able to close in on what remained of the *Victorious* and kill most of the survivors. It would be a mistake to underestimate them.

The sun rose high in the sky as Remy and Kambi went forward to welcome the visitors. McKee watched for a moment before turning away. There was work to do, and watching the Paguumis wouldn't get it done.

By 1730, McKee had her platoon ready for an evening departure and was stashing her belongings in a RAV when

Remy spoke to her over the command channel. That allowed him to dispense with the normal protocols. "McKee . . . Come see me. I've got a job for you."

McKee said, "Yes, sir," and wondered what sort of crap ball was rolling her way. A couple of legionnaires were busy taking the command shelter down when she arrived. Remy, Avery, and one of the digs were gathered off to one side. The Paguumi was wearing a necklace made out of #6 washers and was armed with a marine-issue shotgun. Remy waved her over.

"There you are . . . I'd like you to meet Subchief Huzz. He's going to introduce us to Chief Oppo. Let's take a drone, Kambi, a bio bod, and four T-1s . . . Including Bartov."

That would leave two of McKee's bio bods without cyborgs and they were certain to bitch. It couldn't be helped. "Yes, sir. When do we leave?"

"As soon as you're ready. The rest of the company will report to Major Avery while I'm gone. They should be able to catch up with us by midmorning, so we won't need to carry a lot of supplies."

McKee hoped that was true, and she could feel Avery's gaze as she saluted and did an about-face. It took thirty minutes to brief her squad leaders, choose which T-1s to take, and load them with extra ammo. Not because she was looking for trouble but in case it found her.

Then it was time to mount up and leave. Huzz and his warriors led the way. In contrast to their flashy arrival, the southerners rode slowly, as if expecting the T-1s to lumber along.

But once McKee was sure that Remy could handle it, McKee ordered Bartov to increase his speed, and it wasn't long before the borgs were pulling ahead. That forced the Paguumis to go faster in order to keep up. It was a childish demonstration of superiority, and McKee half expected

Remy to object, but he didn't. So they rode together, all enjoying the wild freedom of the moment as milky moonlight lit the way.

Later, rather than have the digs run their animals to death, McKee reduced speed. But the point had been made. Strange though the off-worlders were, they could ride.

The journey lasted a couple of hours, and McKee knew it was almost over when they topped a rise and saw thousands of twinkling lights in the valley ahead. Some of the southerners had come north to gather metal, while others remained behind to watch over the grazing katha.

That situation couldn't continue for very long, however, because the vast herd of katha would run out of grass before long. When that occurred, Chief Oppo would have to lead his people east along the grass path. And so it had been for more than a thousand years.

But that day hadn't arrived yet. For the moment, the southerners were still engaged in harvesting the sky metal. Groups of mounted warriors had been assigned to guard the encampment—so it wasn't surprising when a dozen of them came charging out of the gloom. Greetings were shouted, and Huzz spurred ahead to announce his presence and avoid bloodshed.

The legionnaires were surrounded by a mob of excited warriors as they thundered down a slope and into the vast encampment. Flaps were thrown aside as people came out to look at the strange apparitions who had appeared among them. McKee could feel their stares as she and her companions were escorted down the main street. There were lots of fires, and McKee could see an extra large hoga up ahead.

As the entire group came to a halt, Huzz slid down off his mount. Remy did likewise as McKee issued a series of orders. "I don't know what will happen next," she said over the squad freq. "But chances are that the major, Kambi, and I will be invited to enter that hab. Maintain a high level of situational awareness—and come a-running if I call for you. Copy? Over."

McKee heard a flurry of clicks as her boots hit the ground. C-1 was hovering over their heads and played the role of translator. So when Huzz spoke, there was some overlap between the Paguumi and standard versions of what he said. "Come . . . Chief Oppo is waiting."

The Humans followed as the Paguumi led them to the hoga. It was at least twice the circumference of those around it. Two guards stepped forward as if to block access. One of them spoke, and McKee heard him say something about "off-world freaks" and "weapons."

Huzz replied in rapid-fire Paguumi, and even though McKee couldn't hear the translation from where she was, the meaning was clear. Shut up and stand aside. They did.

A slender female was there to pull the katha-hide flap out of the way. Huzz entered first, followed by the drone, Remy, Kambi, and McKee. The dome had been blackened by years of cook smoke, but murals circled the lower walls, and McKee was impressed by how well executed they were.

The hoga's interior was taken up by a communal sleeping area, a kitchen, and what appeared to be a ceremonial space directly opposite the main entrance. A Paguumi was seated on a seat that had clearly been taken from the *Victorious*. There were at least a dozen notches in his head crest, a leather patch covered his left eye, and there were some holes where teeth should have been. "My name is Imeer Oppo," he proclaimed importantly. "And you are welcome here." Armed guards stood to either side of him and stared at the aliens with what McKee took to be open animosity.

"Thank you," Remy said, as he took several steps forward. "We are strangers here, but I was told that it is acceptable for visitors to give gifts, and I hope you will accept this pair of binoculars with my compliments. May you always see your enemies before they see you."

Oppo accepted the glasses, and after turning them every which way, brought them to his eyes. Then he uttered what McKee assumed to be a cackle of delight before lowering them in order to look at Remy. "I am very pleased with your gift and insist that you accept one in return."

With that, Oppo turned to signal one of two guards stationed at the hoga's back entrance. The Paguumi pulled a flap aside to admit a second warrior who had an animal on a leash. Or what *looked* like an animal on a leash. But as the creature came closer, McKee realized that she was looking at a Human who had been forced to crawl on hands and knees.

McKee dropped to one knee next to the man. His hair was a tangled mess and a foul smell surrounded him. As their eyes met, McKee saw a look of surprise on his face. "You're Human!" he croaked.

"Yes," McKee answered gently. "Who are you?"

A look of profound sadness appeared on the man's face. "I was captain of the *Victorious*. I am nothing now." And then he began to cry.

"Suzuki," Remy said. "The captain of the *Victorious* was named Suzuki."

"Shoot me," Suzuki begged. "Please kill me."

The chief thought that was funny and began to laugh. So his retainers laughed, too. And they were still laughing when Remy shot Oppo in the face.

CHAPTER: 12

Chiefs may plan—but the katha decide.

AUTHOR UNKNOWN
A Paguumi folk saying
Standard year unknown

PLANET SAVAS

Remy's pistol was equipped with a suppressor. So all McKee heard was a soft popping sound as the bullet punched a hole through Oppo's good eye and blew a hole through the back of his skull. The Paguumi jerked, wobbled, and slumped sideways in his seat. Blood dripped onto the katha hide under his feet.

McKee was still trying to absorb that when Remy turned and shot one of the chief's bodyguards. The body was still falling as Huzz clubbed another retainer with his shotgun. Three warriors remained. They were bringing their weapons to bear when the drone fired its energy weapon, swiveled, and fired again. The guards positioned next to the back door crumpled. That left the warrior on the other end of Suzuki's leash. McKee heard a pop and saw a third eye appear between the two the Paguumi already possessed. He went down as if poleaxed. Suzuki continued to rock back and forth and sob. "Well, don't just stand there," Remy said, as McKee turned to look at him. "Help drag the bodies into place."

With McKee's help, Remy repositioned bodyguards one and two so they were in front of Oppo's chair. One was armed with a navy pistol, which Remy placed next to his right hand.

In the meantime, Huzz was hard at work making it look as if guards three and four had been moving toward the improvised throne when they were killed. By that time, McKee realized that the whole thing had been planned in advance. With Kambi's help, Remy had been able to buy Huzz off. Or, more likely, the subchief had goals of his own. Not that it mattered. Oppo was dead either way.

"Okay," Remy said, as he surveyed the scene. "We're ready. McKee, tell your people to expect some gunfire and to mill around when they hear it. But they are not, repeat *not*, to shoot anyone. Got it?"

McKee nodded. "Yes, sir."

"Do it."

McKee did it. "Okay," Remy said, "when I give the signal, shoot the assassin in the face. Use your AXE. I want it to look messy."

McKee looked at him. "What about the warriors by the back door?"

"Chief Huzz will take care of that. Won't you, Chief?"

Huzz stood over a body. The shotgun produced a distinctive clacking sound as he worked the action.

"You've done this sort of thing before," McKee said accusingly.

Remy's expression was cold. "What? You thought it was all about wearing green berets? We're special forces, Lieutenant. We do hard things. The things other people can't or don't want to do. Now get ready . . . Fire on my command."

McKee placed her finger on the trigger, and when Remy

said, "Now!" she squeezed it. Half a dozen slugs smashed into the warrior's face. While that was taking place, Huzz fired his shotgun. The result was instant pandemonium.

More guards entered the hoga through both entrances. Their instincts were to attack the aliens—but Huzz was shouting at them in Paguumi. No, he insisted. The bodyguards were the ones who had attacked Oppo. But thanks to quick thinking on his part, and some help from the Humans, the plot failed.

McKee thought it was a very unlikely scenario and fully expected somebody to call the subchief on it, but no one did. Maybe some members of the tribe were tired of Oppo and wanted Huzz to take over. Or maybe they were truly taken in. In any case, there was a great deal of shouting and gesticulating as the dead bodyguards were towed outside. A crowd gathered, Huzz told the story again, and a cry of outrage went up. Moments later, half the mob ran off to find relatives of the murdered warriors and punish them.

As the hubbub started to die down, McKee heard a gunshot from inside the hoga. She rushed in with her AXE at the ready, but there was no need. A Legion handgun had been left on the ground as part of the staging. And having been left alone, Suzuki had been free to crawl over and make use of it. Now he lay near Oppo's lifeless body. McKee heard movement and turned to see Remy enter the hab. He looked down at Suzuki. "I feel sorry for him . . . But he made a lot of mistakes. Maybe this is for the best."

McKee had learned a great deal about her commanding officer during the last hour—and her previously positive opinion of him was beginning to slip. "So you installed a new chief. Now what?"

"Huzz says that Empress Ophelia was captured and given over to the Hudathans in exchange for a thousand-year peace treaty and unfettered access to the wreck. Huzz and most members of the tribe liked that. But when Oppo began to levy a 10-percent tax on the sky metal, his popularity took a dive."

"Which is why the Paguumis are willing to buy the ridiculous assassination-plot story," McKee observed.

"Exactly," Remy agreed. "So I agreed to help Huzz take over in return for his help in rescuing Ophelia from the Hudathans. The ridgeheads have a base north of here."

"So that's where we're headed?"

"Yes," Remy replied. "The rest of the team will arrive soon. We'll go after the empress right after we bury Captain Suzuki."

Remy made it sound so simple. But McKee knew better. She'd done battle with the Hudathans and barely survived. Now she and Avery would be forced to face them again.

SAVAS BASE 001

Admiral Nola-Ba was extremely happy. After weeks of waiting, the message had finally arrived. And it was everything he had hoped for. First, a battle group the size of his own had dropped hyper and was orbiting Savas. Second, new orders had arrived. He was to: "Convey Empress Ophelia Ordanus to Hudatha with all possible speed."

And then? No mention was made of what reception he would receive—but Nola-Ba felt sure that his previous rank would be restored and, depending upon the current state of clan politics, he might receive a medal or two. All of which would be welcome—but nothing compared to the full restoration of his honor.

So it was with a light heart that he made his way up onto the roof. The sun was high, which meant that his skin began to morph from gray to white moments after he stepped outside. The shuttle was waiting, and so was Empress Ordanus. She looked gaunt and wore little more than some filthy rags. But regardless of her appearance, Nola-Ba had to admit that the Human was courageous. Her head was held high, and her back was ramrod straight. "Where are you taking me?" It was said with all the self-assurance that one would expect from a monarch.

"To Hudatha," Nola-Ba replied. He saw the Human flinch and knew that she knew. Once on Hudatha, there would be no possibility of a rescue. At that point, all she could hope for was some sort of deal. A ransom that would cost her race dearly. "Put her on the shuttle," he ordered.

Chains rattled as troopers escorted the Human up the ramp. Nola-Ba took one last look at his surroundings. Savas was a shit hole, and it was good to know that he would never set foot on it again. The ramp gave slightly as Nola-Ba made his way up and into the cargo compartment. Ophelia was safely strapped into an oversized acceleration chair—and her eyes were closed as the shuttle's engines began to spool up. Then the ship was in the air and nosing out over the berm that surrounded the base.

That was the beginning of what would be a two-hour trip up to join the destroyer *Thunder Hand* in orbit. So Nola-Ba took the opportunity to activate his data pad and review the latest draft of his report. The goal was to highlight his accomplishments without being too obvious—and simultaneously minimize the role luck had played in capturing Ophelia.

Time passed, and Nola-Ba was in the process of rewriting paragraph sixty-seven for the umpteenth time, when the pilot's voice was heard over the intercom. "Sorry to disturb you, Admiral . . . But enemy ships dropped hyper a few minutes ago, and the *Thunder Hand* is breaking orbit to engage them. I was ordered to turn back and land."

The announcement came as an enormous shock, and Nola-Ba felt a momentary sense of despair. No! This couldn't be happening. Not now . . . Not when he was so close to leaving. He saw Ophelia's eyes pop open. Much to his surprise, she'd been able to pick up a smattering of Hudathan during her weeks of imprisonment, and judging from the expression on her face, understood what had been said. "It is a momentary reprieve only," Nola-Ba told her. "Your ships will be destroyed in short order—then our journey will resume."

"You'd better hope so," Ophelia said levelly. "Because if they aren't, you'll be the one wearing chains."

Nola-Ba would never allow himself to be taken alive—but there was no point in saying that. The shuttle was in a steep dive by that time—and Nola-Ba could feel himself coming up out of the seat. Only the harness held him down. "We have a fighter on our tail," the pilot said grimly. "Stand by for evasive maneuvers."

The shuttle rolled and began to corkscrew downwards. Nola-Ba had been a pilot in his youth and felt no discomfort. But the Human threw up. Her vomit disintegrated into individual globules that orbited her head like miniature planets. Then, as the planet's gravity started to take hold, the droplets were sucked down to the deck.

The stench was nauseating, and Nola-Ba struggled to ignore it as the aircraft jinked left and right. "We lost them!" the pilot said jubilantly.

"Good," Nola-Ba replied. "Return to base. Warn them that we're coming."

I will fight, Nola-Ba told himself. *And I will win.* It was a bold prediction—and he hoped it was true.

ABOARD THE HEAVY CRUISER *MARS*

Even though Admiral Hiram Nigata was seated on the bridge of the heavy cruiser *Mars*, he was, by virtue of his rank, a man alone. Because it was his responsibility to con-

sider the strategic situation rather than the fate of any one
vessel, including the one he was on. The *Mars* was the responsibility of Captain Somlyo and his crew. So Nigata sat
and watched the multicolored symbols battle each other in
the sphere-shaped holo tank in front of him.

Nigata had been hoping to find the enemy when his
squadron of ships entered the Savas system, and his wish
had been granted. Except that rather than the single battle
group that the diminutive admiral expected to face, there
were *two*. The ridgeheads had a combined force of two light
cruisers, four destroyers, eight destroyer escorts, and a non-
combatant supply ship.

But even though Nigata's squadron consisted of only one
cruiser, two destroyers, three gunboats, and a nearly defenseless transport—he had what might prove to be an
equalizer in the form of a seventy-two-year-old carrier
named the *Swarm*. Because, assuming that intelligence esti-
mates were correct, the Hudathan ships had only 124 fighters between them. And the *Swarm* was carrying a full
complement of 650 twin-engined Tachyon aerospace fighters. Each Tachyon was armed with twin energy cannons, six
missiles under each stubby wing, and a pair of "ship killer"
torpedoes nestled below their bellies. The heaviest load-out
of any ship-launched fighter in the Human or Hudathan
inventories.

Still, it was all Nigata could do to keep his face expres-
sionless as three enemy destroyer escorts (DEs) closed in on
the gunboat *Iapelus* and attacked her simultaneously. Nigata
saw a flash inside the holo sphere as the gunboat and her
eighty-six-person crew were reduced to their component
atoms. That produced a groan from the bridge crew and a
stern admonition from Somlyo.

But a flight of six Tachyons was closing on one of the
DEs, and it was only a matter of moments before it was
struck by three torpedoes and transformed into a miniature

sun. An eye for an eye. A cheer was heard this time, and the captain joined in.

The Hudathans understood the threat presented by the *Swarm's* fighters, however, and a destroyer was closing in on her. Nigata smiled grimly. The carrier's skipper was an officer named Constance Povy. And she knew better than to launch all of her fighters at once because if she did, they would run out of fuel at the same time.

So two-thirds of the Tachyons were still aboard the carrier, and minutes before the destroyer could close with the *Swarm*, a hundred fighters shot out to intercept it. They attacked en masse, and the destroyer's screens flashed incandescent as dozens of missiles and torpedoes exploded against them. The scale of the attack was irresistible, and it was only a matter of moments before the destroyer's shields failed. Explosions rippled the length of the hull, the ship broke in two, and pinpoints of light appeared as the wreck scattered dozens of escape pods in its wake.

But that was a distraction. The squadron's mission was to find and rescue Empress Ophelia, assuming she was alive and still on the planet's surface. To do that, Nigata had to put marines on the ground. Marines plus some armor. A battalion of leathernecks was already dropping down through the atmosphere. But their armor was still on the transport *Hercules*, which was under the protection of a destroyer, a gunboat, and two flights of Tachyons.

Sparks of light flared as an enemy destroyer, a DE, and a couple of dozen fighters zeroed in on the transport. And they had plenty to shoot at. The *Hercules* was far too large to land. That meant she had to send the marine corps' tanks down in assault boats and shuttles. So hundreds of small craft were swimming around the transport, and they made excellent targets.

Nigata felt his stomach muscles tighten as dozens of tiny lights went dark inside the holo tank. Each represented a ship that wouldn't reach the surface, supplies lost, and lives ended. Nigata gave an order that sent his second destroyer in to protect the transport, but she was still turning toward the *Hercules* when a bolt of energy struck her. That was followed by another, and *another*, which produced a momentary sun. "The moon!" an excited voice exclaimed. "The bastards have STS cannons on the moon!"

Nigata swore under his breath. The moon. Of course. The Hudathans had been there for a period of time and had the good sense to fortify the moon. His squadron had been fighting for its life from the moment it dropped hyper—so there had been no time in which to check on it. *Still,* Nigata thought to himself, *I should have thought of it . . . I should have . . . Focus,* he told himself. *Think.*

"Tell the *Hercules* to abort the drop and take up a position on the far side of the planet," Nigata instructed. "Once she arrives there, the landings can begin. And send some Tachyons to neutralize those guns while the rest of our ships pull out of range."

It was a good plan. The only possible plan. Because powerful though the STS cannons might be, they couldn't fire through the planet. There would be trouble though . . . since the marines were putting down in *two* widely separated locations. Maybe landing craft could be used to unite the marines, and maybe they couldn't. But that was what generals were for. In this case, a two-star named Hollister. Assuming the poor bastard was still alive.

"Uh-oh," the XO said, "it looks like one of their transports is laying eggs."

Rather than boats or shuttles, the Hudathans preferred to use egg-shaped landers to put their soldiers on the ground. Since the ridgeheads had no way to know that a Human battle group was on the way, it seemed safe to assume that they'd been planning to reinforce their ground troops from the beginning. And now, with marines landing on the surface, the need to do so was that much more urgent. The landers hadn't gone unnoticed by the Tachyon pilots, however, and Nigata could hear a mishmash of radio chatter by touching one of the buttons in his armrest. "Tally ho!" a female pilot said. "Watch my six. Over."

"Shit! They nailed Meyers . . ."

"Damn . . . Did you see that? My missile hit that egg square on, and it's still intact. Those things are tough."

"Give it a torpedo," another voice put in. "That should do the job."

Nigata switched his attention back to the holo tank in time to see one of his gunboats fall victim to a brace of DEs. His command was bleeding to death.

"Engaging," Somlyo said laconically, as the cruiser fired a broadside of ship killers at one of the enemy cruisers. It responded in kind and Nigata felt the *Mars* shudder as Hudathan missiles exploded against her shields.

What followed was a seemingly endless five-minute slugfest in which two powerful ships tried to batter each other to death. But the *Mars* was slightly larger, her shields were stronger, and she had more throw weight. So even with a Hudathan DE rushing in to help its sister ship, the *Mars* managed to win. There was no explosion. Just a flare as the other vessel's shields went down, its propulsion system dropped off-line, and it began to drift. "Let's finish it," Somlyo said grimly. "Prepare to fire energy cannons."

"Belay that," Nigata said. "Let them take her under tow."

The crew people sitting around Nigata looked at the admiral as if he was crazy, but the captain understood. "Aye, aye, sir. It will take most of what they have left if they want to save her."

That was Nigata's plan. To break the battle off while he still had some ships. Because *if* the empress was still alive, and *if* the jarheads managed to rescue her, it would be his responsibility to take the royal home. "They're going for it," the XO said happily. "Or trying to."

"Good," Nigata said. "Send the following message to all commanding officers. They are to withdraw to the side of the planet opposite the moon. Execute."

PLANET SAVAS

The fact that Huzz had not only helped to engineer Oppo's death but participated in the assassination, didn't prevent the newly elevated chief from staging a well-attended funeral for his predecessor. Thousands of tribal members came. And in keeping with Paguumi tradition, hundreds of the dead leader's katha were slain, butchered, and roasted over communal fires.

Then, in a transparent effort to buy the tribe's support, Huzz repealed the unpopular metal tax. It was a very popular decision and one that cemented his position as chief.

The rest of the team had arrived by this time and was camped a discreet distance away from the Paguumis, who were in the midst of the first of what promised to be a three-day mourning period. If carousing, feasting, and bride taking could be called "mourning."

That was a source of considerable frustration to Remy, who wanted to march north but couldn't do so without a sizable force of southerners to bolster his tiny command. For one thing, the legionnaires were sure to encounter the northern tribe and would have to do battle with the Hudathans as well.

But it was clear that the southerners were in no mood for war and wouldn't be until the wake was over, and their warriors were sober. That meant all the legionnaires could do was rest and catch up on deferred maintenance. The unit had been working the T-1s, RAVs, and drones hard, so there were plenty of issues that needed to be dealt with. It was also an opportunity for McKee to slip away and have a few minutes with Avery.

They left camp separately, made use of their knowledge of security to slip through the perimeter, and met half a mile from camp. It was a dangerous thing to do—but neither one was in a mood to be safe. Avery got there first. The meeting spot was on a low rise that would allow them to see anyone who might approach with their night-vision gear. The only problem was that it's impossible to kiss with a helmet on.

So the first thing McKee did was to remove her brain bucket before sitting down next to Avery. There were none of the romantic touches that he had arranged on Orlo II. No candles, no wine, and no bathtub. But there was the dim glow that emanated from the Paguumi camp, the moon, and the soft night air. No words were necessary as McKee entered the circle of Avery's arms and their lips made contact. It was a long, hungry kiss that left both of them wanting more. "We can't," McKee said as she pulled away. "Not here. Not now."

"I know," Avery agreed. "But we can talk. Tell me what happened after you left Orlo II. Tell me everything."

So McKee told him about the trip to Earth, about her run-in with Ross Royer, and the meeting with her uncle. That led to an account of the Mason assassination and her part in it. "Ophelia was there," she said. "I could have killed her. I *should* have killed her."

"You didn't know," Avery said sympathetically. "You did the best you could. No one could fault you for that."

"My uncle did," McKee said sadly, as tears trickled down her cheeks. "And now he's dead. I saw the news on Algeron. They sent troops down into the Deeps to find and kill him."

"But we're alive," Avery reminded her. "And we'll be together. All we need to do is survive this. Do you remember the plan we agreed on?"

McKee nodded. "I think about it every day. We'll leave the Legion, settle on a rim world, and begin new lives."

"That's right," Avery agreed. "So remember that. Focus on it. Ignore everything else."

"What about Ophelia?" McKee wanted to know. "The beacon is on. She's alive."

"It's impossible to know if she'll survive what's coming," Avery responded. "But let's say she does. Maybe we should back off. Who put us in charge?"

"That's easy for *you* to say," McKee objected. "Ophelia didn't murder your family. But it's more than that . . . She's evil. *Thousands* have died."

"I admire your sense of responsibility," Avery said. "Not to mention your courage. But I'm selfish. I want you for myself. And if you try to assassinate Ophelia, you'll get killed."

McKee stared at him through the gloom. "I'm sorry, John. I really am. I want you, too . . . But my uncle was right. I allowed Ophelia to live. And that means I'm responsible for every person she killed since then. I can't live with that."

Both of them stood. "I love you," Avery said simply.

"Don't say that, John," McKee said. "It hurts enough already." With that, she turned and ran away. The darkness took her in.

Daska had seen all of it via the drone that had been hovering above the lovers and felt nothing. No surprise, no sense of betrayal, and no anger. But the interchange did trigger a programmed "need" to report the conversation to Empress Ophelia. That was impossible, of course—and would remain so until Ophelia was rescued. The robot accepted that the same way it reacted to changes in the weather and the "pain" that stemmed from a worn coupler. What was, was.

It was just after dawn, and Remy was spooning some peaches into his mouth when the help he'd been waiting for arrived. He knew Human ships were present when contrails appeared high in the atmosphere. Not one or two, like they'd seen over the last couple of weeks, but *dozens* of criss-crossing claw marks. And as Remy came to his feet, people all around the camp began to cheer. "They're here!" someone shouted. "The squids are here."

But the celebration was cut short as a momentary flash was seen, followed by a tiny puff of white smoke. A fighter or a shuttle had been destroyed, but *whose*? Remy was still contemplating that when Lieutenant Ellis came running over. "I've got a Marine Corps colonel on the horn! He says they're trying to put some jarheads on the ground, but there's a whole shitload of ridgeheads up in space. He wants a sitrep."

So Remy jogged over to the "big horn" as the techs referred to the radio and identified himself. "This is Colonel Owens," a male voice said. "We're on the ground, but we've been forced to land in two different locations, neither one of which is anywhere near you. We'll regroup and make contact as soon as we can. In the meantime, your orders are the same. Find code name Gemstone and secure her. Over."

Remy said, "Yes, sir. We have recovered code name Cowboy. He's in good condition and ready for extraction."

That produced a brief moment of silence while Owens absorbed the news. "Well done, Major. That is a big relief. I'll pass the news along. We'll arrange for a pickup. Over."

"Roger that. We're getting short on supplies if you can spare any. Over."

"Upload a list," Owens replied. "We'll see what we can do. Over."

And that was that. Not too surprisingly, Huzz and a group of hungover warriors arrived an hour later. They had seen the battle in the sky and wanted to know what was going on. Remy had been careful to keep Huzz in the dark regarding the mission's *real* objective lest the local try to find Ophelia on his own. Insofar as Huzz knew, the legionnaires were there for the purpose of fighting the Hudathans. And that was sufficient.

"So," Remy said, in hopes of cutting the mourning period short. "My people are fighting the Hudathans in the sky. This is our opportunity to attack their base."

What Remy knew to be a sly look appeared on the Paguumi's face. "And what will we receive if the attack is successful?"

"All the metal in and around the base," Remy promised. "Along with weapons so powerful that you will rule the planet for many years to come."

"We will meet at Three Fingers as the sun goes down," Huzz said. "Then we will ride."

Chief Pudu was sitting atop his favorite zurna watching contrails etch themselves onto the heavens when the spy arrived. His name was Abu Mook, and he was a southerner by birth. But his wife was from the north and had been treated poorly while living among Mook's people. An offense that continued to anger him. That plus the money Pudu paid him explained why Mook was willing to betray his tribe. Eventually, the traitor hoped to make a life for his family in the north—but Pudu continued to stall the spy rather than lose such a valuable source of information.

Mook was small, too small to serve as a warrior, and

made most of his living buying plant materials from Jithi traders, which he and his family turned into various potions. And business was reasonably good because some of them actually worked. And, it was an occupation that allowed Mook to travel without raising suspicion.

Mook's zurna was hung with large panniers rather than the paraphernalia of war and, except for the Jithi-made pistols holstered to either side of the animal's neck, he was unarmed. Like the rest of his body, his features were small, and that made him appear younger than he actually was. Pudu's bodyguards knew the southerner and allowed him to pass. "Greetings," Mook said. "You grow younger with each passing day."

"And your lies grow more glaring with each rising of the sun," Pudu replied. Both of them laughed.

"So," Pudu said, as he looked up at the sky and down again. "What's going on?"

"The round heads are fighting the change skins in the sky," Mook replied.

"That much is obvious," Pudu replied dryly. "Tell me something I don't know."

There were times when Mook enjoyed his role as spy—and judging from his expression, this was one of them. "They say that Chief Oppo was murdered by his bodyguards. However Subchief Huzz and a delegation of round heads were in the hoga at the time."

Pudu was surprised. The Oppo he knew had been far too smart to surround himself with anything but the most loyal of warriors. Relatives for the most part who were honorbound to protect him. "What are you saying? That Huzz and the round heads killed Oppo?"

"It's a possibility," Mook replied cagily. "But only that. I have no proof. And Oppo *was* unpopular. The bodyguards could have been acting for others."

"I assume you are referring to the metal tax," Pudu said.

"Word of it spread via the Jithis. So Huzz took over without much opposition."

"None," Mook agreed. "Now he's coming north. A force of round heads and their fighting machines will accompany him."

"Why?" Pudu wanted to know. "To attack us?" That was an alarming possibility.

"No," Mook replied. "To attack the change skins. It's connected with the battle in the sky. All of the aliens want our planet."

"Yes," Pudu said thoughtfully. "So it would seem."

A white streak chased another across the sky until both disappeared into the distant haze. "So what will you do?" Mook inquired.

Pudu knew what he was going to do, or *not* do, as the case might be. If the southerners wanted to attack the change-skin base, then he would allow them to do so. Most would die just as many of his warriors had. If not eliminated during the fighting, the round heads would be severely weakened. *Then* he would strike and seize both the metal and a large number of alien weapons.

It was a good plan, too good to share with a spy, even one that he liked. "I don't know," Pudu lied. "I'll think about it. Come . . . You must be thirsty and hungry as well. We will feast, and you will tell me stories."

Pudu pulled the zurna's head around, sent an order through the neural connection that linked them together, and felt the beast take off. His knees hurt, but his mind was sharp, and it felt good to be alive.

What the Paguumis called Three Fingers was a rock formation comprised of three sandstone pillars. And when Team One-Five arrived, it was to discover that Huzz and approximately three thousand warriors were waiting. McKee could see few signs of organization as the locals rode in circles, raced each other, or brewed tea. But Kambi assured McKee that she was looking at a highly disciplined horde that consisted of three zin (battalions) and thirty gan (companies), all led by seasoned veterans. And having seen action on Algeron, McKee knew better than to underestimate native troops.

Remy assigned McKee to the point position as usual. Except now she had an additional force of eight Paguumis to act as scouts. They were led by a grizzled veteran named Imon Supatha. It was clear from the beginning that he didn't like riding with aliens, didn't approve of female warriors, and wasn't about to take orders from one. So, for reasons of pride, Supatha was careful to ride well out in front of McKee's T-1s at all times.

That didn't trouble McKee in the least since it meant that should an ambush be waiting, Supatha and his scouts were likely to trigger it—thereby giving her legionnaires more time in which to react. Besides, C-3 was aloft and providing a bird's-eye view of the area ahead. And with a thousand warriors on each flank, there was very little chance of a surprise from the east or west.

No, in McKee's estimation, the major threat was from the air, which was why every available set of rocket launchers had been mounted on her T-1s, thereby turning four of her bio bods into foot soldiers. An ignominious fate that they resented greatly.

In spite of Supatha's attitudes, McKee had to give the Paguumi scouts a great deal of credit. Even though the moon wasn't up yet, and the warriors weren't equipped with night-vision technology, they had an uncanny ability to find their way over, around, and through obstacles. And although they might veer right or left for a moment, they always came back on course. Did they have compasses? McKee didn't think so.

Knowing how much the Paguumis loved to ride their zurnas flat out, McKee expected the horde to surge forward and maintain a blistering pace. But the passage of three-thousand-plus bodies created enough friction to slow things down.

As the stars frosted the sky above, and an occasional streak of fire raced across the sky, the horde pushed north. Three uneventful hours passed, and it was almost time for a break when Remy's voice filled her helmet. "A marine assault boat and six escorts will arrive twenty from now. We're going to stop so they can take Cowboy aboard.

"Chief Huzz is passing the word to his people—but don't hesitate to double down on that. The last thing we want is to fire on the jarheads while they are trying to extract Cowboy. Over."

McKee took a twisted pleasure in delivering the news to Supatha via her drone. Just as she knew it would, C-3 scared the crap out of the Paguumi scout when it appeared out of the sky and spoke to him with her voice. But Supatha got the message and ordered his warriors to pull up. Thankfully, Remy and Huzz were able to bring the rest of the horde to a halt with a minimum of fuss.

The roar of repellers announced the boat's arrival a few minutes later, and Avery took Nicolai out to meet it. "The marines are going to take you up to one of our ships," Avery told the boy. "You'll be safe there."

"I don't want to be safe," Nicolai said stubbornly. "I want to stay with *you*."

Dust flew sideway as the boat put down, and Avery knelt next to Nicolai. He had to yell in order to be heard. "I'm sorry, son . . . But my place is here. With the Legion. Our job is to find your mother—and we need to keep looking."

Nicolai looked up into the light from Avery's helmet, and

tears ran down his cheeks. "I'm going to miss you, Major John."

Avery swallowed the lump in his throat. "And I'm going to miss you, Nicolai. Grow up, be strong, and be fair."

A couple of marines had arrived by then. One of them spoke. "The ridgeheads followed us down. We have escorts, but there's no telling how many of the bastards are coming this way. We need to lift, sir."

So Avery led Nicolai over to the shuttle. A pile of supplies had been off-loaded, along with three synths, all of whom wore Ophelia's livery. Bodyguards then . . . Sent to protect the empress should she be found. The sight of the machines made his blood run cold. Daska was present as well. And he could see that the robot was watching him. "Good-bye," Nicolai said, then he came to attention. The salute was textbook perfect, as was the about-face. Then the boy was gone.

Repellers flared, the assault boat took off, and veered away. Other engines screamed as Tachyon fighters passed over their heads and crossed a field of stars.

McKee was still on point and couldn't see the boat because the running lights were off. She could watch via her HUD, however, and was about to do so, when Bartov delivered a warning. "This is Charlie One-Three. There is an unidentified aircraft approaching at a high rate of speed from the northeast. I tried to contact it, but there was no response. Request permission to fire. Over."

The Hudathan fighter was dropping bombs by the time McKee yelled, "This is One . . . Track and fire!"

The cyborgs were widely dispersed but tied together via a shared targeting system. Their rockets sought heat, and most converged on a single target. The combined impacts were sufficient to blow a wing off a fighter. The fuselage hit the ground and cartwheeled two or three times before finally skidding to a stop. McKee had no way to know how many Paguumis were killed by pieces of flying wreckage but suspected that the casualty rate would be high.

"This is Six," Remy said. "That was some good shooting. Over."

Such praise was rare, and McKee felt a surge of pleasure. But when she looked at her HUD, she saw that the letters "KIA" had been posted next to three names. Varco, Perodi, and Hamu were dead. She soon learned that seventeen Paguumis had been killed as well. It was with a heavy heart that McKee went to examine the fallen T-1s. If parts could be salvaged from Varco and Hamu, it was her duty to do so even as their brain boxes were being buried. It was the only way that the dead could help the living.

SAVAS BASE 001

The base was blacked out. So there was only starlight to see by as Nola-Ba stood on the landing platform and stared up at the heavens. He was in a bad mood and for good reason. In spite of the fact that he was an admiral, the ships under his command were fighting a desperate battle without him.

Yes, he could order a shuttle to land where he was standing, but what then? The Humans had fewer ships but more fighters. Would the shuttle and its escorts be able to fight them off? Or would both he and Empress Ordanus be killed on their way up into space? Because under no circumstances would he leave without her.

Nola-Ba didn't want to die, but the thought of losing Ophelia was even worse. She was more valuable than an entire fleet of ships. Proof of which could be seen in the fact that the Humans had sent a ground team and a naval task force to find her.

Fortunately, there had been no attempt to attack his base, so she was momentarily safe. Or was she? Nola-Ba felt an unexpected emptiness in the pit of his stomach. There was only one Hudathan base on Savas, and it would be hard to miss from orbit. So why hadn't the animals attacked by air? Or from orbit for that matter? The answer was glaringly obvious. Because the clanless bastards *knew* Ophelia was there! And didn't want to harm her.

But *how*? How could they know? Then it came to him, and when it did, the thought was like a thunderbolt out of a clear blue sky. An implant. There was an implant in Ophelia's body. A way to find her should that become necessary. The device would be very small and powered by an even tinier battery or by her body heat. That was why none of his personnel had noticed it.

Nola-Ba was angry at his subordinates and himself as he opened a blastproof hatch and entered a lift. It took him down into the subsurface maze of rooms that had originally been part of the *Head Hunter*. A dagger commander named Oma-Da was in charge of security. He was asleep when Nola-Ba barged into the compartment that he shared with another junior officer. "On your feet!" Nola-Ba demanded as he slapped a light switch. "We have work to do."

Empress Ophelia Ordanus was sitting on the floor of her cell, leaning back into a corner. She was filthy, dressed in rags, and fighting depression. There had been jubilation at first. The navy had come to rescue her! And Nola-Ba couldn't take her to Hudatha. But that emotion had begun to fade as hours passed, and there was no attempt to save her. What were they waiting for? If she survived, she would order the Minister of Defense to launch an investigation.

No, that didn't make sense . . . It would be better to cast the officer in charge as a hero. Then, if he or she *wasn't* a hero, her synths could . . .

Ophelia's train of thought was interrupted by the sound of a muffled voice. Metal rattled. The door banged open. And there, standing backlit in the entryway, was the unmistakable figure of Admiral Nola-Ba. Ophelia felt a stab of fear. Had he come to take her away? Was this the beginning of the trip to Hudatha? "Take her to the interrogation room," Nola-Ba ordered. "Secure her to the rack and strip her clothes off."

The Hudathans were going to torture her! Just as others had been tortured. She had heard the screams. Were any of the crew still alive? She hadn't heard or seen another Human being for a long time.

Ophelia was terrified as two troopers entered the cell and took hold of her arms. Her feet walked on air as they carried her out into the corridor. Less than a minute later, Ophelia found herself in a low-ceilinged room being secured to a metal rack. It was slanted at an angle and positioned over a floor drain. What might have been bloodstains could be seen on the frame. Ophelia feared the worst.

Then came a moment of terrible indignity as the rags were ripped off her body, leaving Ophelia naked for all to see. *They're aliens,* she told herself. *They aren't interested in the way you look.* Even though the assertion was clearly true, it did nothing to make her feel better.

No translator was present, but Ophelia knew enough Hudathan to understand the order that Nola-Ba gave. "Scan her. The transmitter will be very small and hidden under the surface of her skin."

The beacon! They were looking for the beacon! That had been her hope, the central element in all of her rescue fantasies, and now they were going to take it away! Ophelia fought back the tears as a technician ran a hand scanner over the contours of her body.

The process didn't take long. An intermittent beeping sound was heard as the device passed over the vicinity of her neck. It grew louder as the technician maneuvered the scanner in behind her skull. "There it is," Nola-Ba said grimly. "Cut it out."

Metal screeched as one of the troopers turned the rack over. Ophelia found herself hanging from the straps and staring at the floor. Then she heard movement, felt something sharp penetrate her skin, and screamed. There was a pause followed by *more* pain and a grunt of satisfaction. She couldn't see Nola-Ba but could hear him. "Well done! Put a dressing on the Human's neck and flip her over."

There was a pause while a self-adhesive bandage was applied to the base of her neck. Then came the screech of unoiled metal as they turned her faceup. "Here it is," Nola-Ba said, as he held the tiny bb-sized globe between two sausage-like digits. "My technicians will hook it to a power source and place it on a zurna. Then we'll turn the animal loose and let your troops chase it!

"All right," Nola-Ba said as he turned away. "Take her back to the cell. And find a blanket. Humans are ugly enough with their clothes on."

CHAPTER: 13

Once more unto the breach, dear friends, once
    more;
Or close the wall up with our English dead.
In peace there's nothing so becomes a man
As modest stillness and humility;
But when the blast of war blows in our ears,
Then imitate the action of the tiger . . .

WILLIAM SHAKESPEARE
Henry V, act 3, scene 1, 1–6
Standard year circa 1599

THE HEAVY CRUISER *MARS*

In spite of a four-hour nap, Admiral Nigata felt tired as he made his way onto the ship's bridge. The lights were dim, people spoke in hushed tones, and the atmosphere was more akin to that of a library rather than a warship. Captain Somlyo looked up from the screen in front of him. The light gave his skin a greenish hue. "Good morning, sir. Or is it afternoon?"

"Beats me," Nigata said, as he dropped into his chair. "What kind of condition is our condition in?"

"The situation is stable," Somlyo replied. "We haven't been able to destroy the Hudathan moon base yet. So the ridgeheads own whatever portion of the planet's surface is available to them at any given moment. That means they can take potshots at the marines and prevent them from coming together. But we're using the bulk of the planet to prevent the STS cannons from firing on our ships."

"What about the landings?"

"Most of the jarheads are on the ground, but they're spread out and trying to get their shit together."

Nigata nodded. "And the Hudathans?"

"Their troops and armor are on the ground and maneuvering to engage the closest marines. We fire on them from space whenever we can, and our fighters are harassing them. They have some very effective antiaircraft batteries, however, so there's a limit to what the Tachyons can accomplish."

"So that's it?"

"No, sir. There are two new developments. First, the Legion was able to recover Prince Nicolai! He's on board, and the Doc says he's in good shape."

"That's wonderful," Nigata said. "Finally, something is breaking our way. And the empress?"

"That's the other development, sir. Ophelia's locator beacon began to behave in a very erratic fashion. It left the Hudathan base and began to wander around the desert."

Nigata frowned. "Is there a possibility that she escaped?"

Somlyo shook his head. "No, sir. We sent some fighters for a look-see. An animal called a zurna was running around free. Once they destroyed it, the beacon stopped moving."

"So the Hudathans found the beacon, removed it, and are giving us the finger."

"That's about the size of it, sir."

Nigata swore under his breath. "If they decide to move her, we won't know."

"That's true," Somlyo agreed. "Major Remy has been informed. He and his people are closing in on the base from the south. Unfortunately, they are one day out."

"Okay," Nigata said as he studied the holo map that occupied the center of the room. "We don't have enough throw weight to attack the moon base until we eliminate at least one enemy cruiser. What's the status of the ship they took under tow?"

"It looks as though the vessel's propulsion system is still down," Somlyo replied. "The ridgeheads took it out a way and left a DE to guard it. It seems reasonable to suppose that they're attempting to bring the drives online. That's what we'd do."

Nigata could pick out the red delta that represented the enemy ship now. It was floating well away from the planet, with a single red dot to keep it company. Was there another option? And if there wasn't, could he bring himself to make the necessary sacrifice? Or, to be more precise, to ask *other* people to make that sacrifice.

Part of what made the decision so difficult were his feelings regarding the empress. She wasn't worth saving. Not in his estimation. The unnecessary slaughter on Orlo II had been her doing. But what about the Human race? What about *Earth*? Who would take over in the event of her death? And would they be even worse than Ophelia was?

A full two minutes passed before Nigata spoke, and when he did, his voice was dull. "Which gunboat is in the worst shape?"

"That would be the *Leda*," Somlyo replied. "She took a lot of hits during the opening exchange."

"Okay. Take her crew off and ask for volunteers. Assuming you get some, put a skeleton crew aboard and order them to attack the damaged cruiser."

Somlyo looked alarmed. "She'll never make it, sir. The Hudathans will destroy the *Leda* before she even gets close."

"I know that," Nigata said irritably. "But the ridgeheads will be forced to respond by sending more assets to protect the drifter. And once they do, we'll go after whichever cruiser looks the weakest. With it out of the way, we'll have a better than fifty-fifty chance of destroying the moon base."

Somlyo had always been an ambitious man. But now,

based on the pain in Nigata's eyes, he no longer had an interest in making admiral. "Aye, aye, sir. I'll take care of it."

PLANET SAVAS

Now that the navy had arrived, and Ophelia's signal had been compromised, Team One-Five could no longer afford to rest during the day and travel at night. In order to reach the Hudathan base before the aliens took Ophelia off-planet, it would be necessary to march from sunset until noon the next day. And Remy would have pushed his people even harder had that been possible.

As a result, they were well inside the territory that the northern Paguumis considered to be theirs. So where were the locals? That's what McKee wanted to know as Bartov paused just short of a rise. By doing so, he allowed McKee to peer over the top without exposing more than her helmet. It was the sort of thing an experienced T-1 was expected to do without being told. And she made a mental note to mention it later on.

McKee's visor could provide some magnification. But if she wanted to look a long way out, there was no substitute for her binoculars. So she pushed the visor up in order to glass the area up ahead. The desert shimmered in the heat, and a distant hill appeared to float just off the ground. Supatha and his scouts were out in front of the legionnaires as usual—and she could see the wispy dust trails produced by their zurnas. But no northerners. Not that she *wanted* to see them. It would be wonderful if the team and its allies could attack the Hudathans without having to fight their way through a Paguumi army.

At their present rate of travel, Remy and Huzz planned to arrive at their destination just before dawn the next day. Then, assuming the navy could spare some fighters, the zoomies would prep the area immediately around the instal-lation. Unfortunately, they couldn't put any ordnance on the outpost itself without running the risk of killing Ophelia. The possibility didn't bother McKee in the least—but was unthinkable to the high command.

But with or without air support, the ground attack was going to take place, and McKee knew that fighting their way into a well-established Hudathan base was going to be very difficult. Avery was still acting as XO. Would he sur-vive? Would *she*?

McKee pushed such thoughts away to concentrate on the situation at hand. The immediate challenge was to find the one-thousand-gallon water bladder that had been dropped along their line of march. The water wouldn't be enough to meet the needs of three thousand Paguumis, but it would allow the legionnaires to remain independent and camp separately. The latter was made necessary by the fact that Remy had very little trust for Huzz, who, McKee suspected, had similar doubts about the Human.

Unfortunately, the water bladder wasn't where it was sup-posed to be, which was within a hundred yards of the spot where Bartov was standing. That meant the legionnaires would have to home in on the low-power beacon that was attached to it. A potentially dangerous task, what with Hu-dathans flying around over their heads. But, for the first time in her military career, McKee had real honest-to-God air cover. Three of the navy's aerospace fighters were flying lazy eights directly above her position. And when they ran low on fuel, more aircraft would replace them. Could they see the water bladder? No, they were too high, and had to be in case the ridgeheads sent fighters to intercept the company.

"Okay," McKee said. "Let's proceed in a line abreast. We'll maintain one-hundred-yard intervals. Maintain your situational awareness and monitor the nav channel. If you hear the beacon, let me know."

So the squad spaced out and began to sweep forward. Five minutes passed followed by ten more. Finally, just as McKee was about to break it off, Linda Mora spoke. "I've got it, Lieutenant . . . Or I think I do. The signal is faint and off to my left."

"Okay," McKee said. "Close in on it. We'll follow."

When they found it the bladder was resting about two hundred feet from the wreckage of a burned-out shuttle. What had taken place wasn't clear. Had a fighter been chasing the marines? And jumped them immediately after they dropped the water? There was no way to know. The only thing that McKee could be sure of was that the jarheads had died trying. Now there was more metal for the Paguumis to harvest and more next of kin to be notified.

McKee was forced to swallow the lump in her throat in order to make the call. "Charlie-One to Charlie-Six. The bladder has been located and secured. We will remain here until we're relieved. Over."

ABOARD THE HEAVY CRUISER MARS

Admiral Nigata didn't want to watch the men and women aboard the gunboat Leda die—but felt that it was his duty to do so. Especially since few if any of them understood their role as pawn in a much larger game. But he, too, was a pawn for others, all of whom would sacrifice him to protect their queen, and therefore themselves.

Having sentenced himself to do so, Nigata sat in the big chair and turned his attention to the holo tank. Shortly thereafter, a single spark of light left the relative safety of the Human fleet and accelerated out into space. Though currently immobile, the Hudathan warship might still be capable of defending itself, and if that was the case, the lives aboard the Leda would soon be snuffed out.

But regardless of that, the Hudathans couldn't let the gunboat get close enough to fire what could turn out to be a lucky shot. So the ridgeheads did what Nigata *wanted* them to do. They dispatched two DEs out to intercept the Human vessel—and in doing so stripped one of their cruisers of its escorts. That was an excellent beginning.

The sacrifice of the *Leda* wouldn't be enough, however. Nigata knew that. In order to destroy a ship with a throw weight nearly equivalent to what the *Mars* could produce, he'd have to do something unexpected. Something so crazy the Hudathans wouldn't understand his intentions. The problem was that his plan *was* crazy, and could quite possibly kill every person aboard the *Mars*, including Nigata himself. Because on his orders, Captain Somlyo and his crew were going to execute a maneuver known as a microjump. A term that referred to a hyperspace jump calculated to move the Mars a mere 250,000 miles. An inconsequential trip when compared to *six trillion* miles or a single light-year.

The difficulty was that hyperspace drives couldn't deliver such precise movements with any sort of certainty. That's why ships didn't enter or exit hyperspace until they were well clear of the celestial objects that might be nearby.

Some experiments with so-called microjumps had been successful, but most had not. So there was a very real possibility that the *Mars* would exit hyperspace outside the Altari system, leaving the rest of Nigata's ships vulnerable, or worse yet, wind up *inside* the planet Savas. An event that would kill the entire crew and might damage the planet as well.

Nonetheless, Nigata was determined to try it; more than that, he felt he *had* to try it in order to destroy the cruiser and open a path to the moon. So as the Hudathans fired on the *Leda*, Somlyo's voice was heard over the intercom. "This is the captain. All personnel will prepare for a hyperspace jump in ten, nine, eight . . ."

The crew hadn't been briefed about the jump, or the risks involved, since telling them wouldn't make them feel any better about it. Perhaps they thought the *Mars* was going home. But Nigata figured most of them were still thinking about the order when the countdown came to an end, and they felt the usual lurch, and some nausea. That was the moment when the cruiser entered another dimension.

But not for long. The downshift followed seconds later. Nigata's fingers dug into the armrests on his chair as he waited to die. But he *didn't* die. And as he felt the second bout of nausea, he was filled with a sense of joy. But where were they? Where they needed to be? Or five million miles out in space?

The answer came via a host of alarms as screens lit up with real-time video of another ship. The *Mars* was less than twenty miles from the Hudathan cruiser! And right where Nigata wanted her to be. Somlyo gave the order to fire. And the crew, all of whom were still at battle stations, complied. Most were just starting to understand what had taken place, but they knew how to follow orders and did what they were told. Torpedoes whispered out of tubes, missiles streaked across the narrow gap, and every energy cannon that could be brought to bear fired in unison.

Having been caught completely unawares, the cruiser's shields went down. Explosions rippled along the ship's hull, she shook as if palsied, and her drives fired as the Hudathans sought to escape the unexpected barrage of fire.

But it was too late. A torpedo sailed through an open hatch, entered the main launch bay, and detonated. The blast triggered more than a dozen secondary explosions as fighters blew up. Some were in the process of being refueled. So flames found fuel, followed the substance to its source, and set that off as well. The result was a miniature supernova that consumed all the available oxygen within a few brief seconds and blinked out of existence. All that remained was a debris field that would orbit Savas for a thousand years.

A cheer went up throughout the *Mars* as the heavy cruiser turned onto a course that would take her toward the moon. But Nigata wasn't cheering. He was searching the holo tank for a tiny green arrow and the name *Leda*. It was no longer there. A sacrifice had been made. And for *what*? A tyrant, a mass murderer, and a possible psychopath. Nigata felt sick to his stomach.

PLANET SAVAS

After catching up with McKee, the team made camp. And to the north of them, only five miles short of the Hudathan base, Huzz and his warriors did the same thing.

As McKee made the rounds, she could feel the tension in the air. None of the normal high jinks could be seen. And what talk there was had a subdued quality. As they cleaned their weapons, all of her fellow legionnaires were wondering the same thing. Would they survive? Or would they be buried on Savas? McKee knew how they felt.

That was why she went looking for Avery after finishing her dinner. Not to talk . . . Since opportunities to do that were few and far between. But to *see* him. To hear the sound of his voice. To take comfort from the knowledge that he existed and there was something to hope for, to survive for.

When McKee found Avery, he was sitting in a circle made up of legionnaires from different platoons. Hats mostly, but some of her people, too, all talking in low tones. Their eyes made contact, and a spark jumped the gap.

Sergeant Jolo offered McKee a mug of instant caf, and she accepted, so she would have an excuse to sit on an ammo crate and be near Avery. The legionnaires were telling stories, many of which were exaggerated, to keep their minds off what was to come. So hardly a word passed between McKee and Avery during the next fifteen minutes. But such was the bond between them, nothing had to be said. Both knew what they had—and what they stood to lose.

As the bullshit session began to wind down, Avery dumped a few drops of caf onto the bone-dry ground and stood. His eyes found hers, and he smiled. "Watch your six, McKee. Lieutenants are in short supply out here."

McKee nodded. "You, too, sir. There's no such thing as too many majors." That got a laugh—and McKee turned away. *Please God, don't let him die,* she prayed. But there had been other prayers, for other people, and most were dead.

Even though she hadn't been assigned to a watch, McKee didn't sleep well. Part of that was due to the noise from a navy shuttle as it made a delivery of personnel and supplies. But most of it was nerves.

That's why McKee was up a full hour before she had to be and busy checking on her platoon. Her helmet light projected a blob of white light on the ground in front of her as she crossed the encampment. There were rumors that the navy was about to clobber the Hudathan moon base, but that hadn't happened yet. That meant the marines were still taking STS fire and wouldn't be able to participate in the assault.

So without any armor, and without being able to attack the base with aircraft, the T-1s would constitute the heaviest weaponry the so-called joint force could bring to bear. That's why Major Remy had decided to join her platoon.

McKee reported to the CO at 0600. After ducking under some netting, she removed her helmet. Remy and Avery were standing over a video table looking at some images. Both men turned as she entered. Remy smiled. "Ah, the cavalry has arrived. I won't have to walk."

"No, sir. Private Kane is standing by."

"Excellent. Have you seen these? If not, you might want to take a look."

The sun wasn't visible yet. But, thanks to a hanging lantern and the illumination provided by the table itself, McKee could see the photos. Some had clearly been taken by navy fighters, while others were surface shots, courtesy of the company's hardworking drones. The outpost was located adjacent to the sand-drifted ribs of what had clearly been a large spaceship. A vessel too large to land and take off again.

The implication was obvious. Parts of the vessel had been used to create a fort similar to those once popular on Earth. The flat-topped mound was pierced with embrasures from which cannons could be fired. "What kind of artillery do they have?" McKee inquired.

"Naval energy cannons," Avery said ominously. "Powered by fusion reactors."

McKee winced. The cannons would be able to destroy anything short of shield-equipped tanks. That meant her T-1s wouldn't stand a chance if they took a direct hit. "So what's the plan?"

Remy pointed to a photo. "Because the fort is round, the weapons inside have a 360-degree field of fire. And that makes sense if you plan to defend it against mounted warriors. But the shape means that only two out of the six cannons can be brought to bear on any single quadrant."

"So," Avery said, as he picked up the narrative, "that's how we'll go at it. We'll attack one side of the fortification and ignore the rest."

"No offense," McKee said, "but two cannons are more than enough. They'll vaporize anything we send at them."

"True," Remy admitted. "But after they fire for one minute, they need a thirty-second cool down. So all we have to do is throw five hundred Paguumi warriors in after them, wait for the cannons to cool off, and off you go."

McKee couldn't believe what she had just heard. Remy intended to use five hundred sentient beings as cannon fodder. She looked at Avery and saw the caution in his eyes.

Remy was in command, their goal was one every officer should support, and the Paguumis could hardly be described as allies. They were in it for loot.

Still, the plan was so cold-blooded that McKee felt she had to say something. "That sounds like a good plan, sir. But is there some other way to force that cooling cycle?"

Remy frowned. "What would you prefer, Lieutenant? Would you like me to march the team into those guns? Compassion has its place, McKee, but this is war. Our job is rescue the empress—not mollycoddle a bunch of savages. Besides, you would do well to remember all of the people who were alive after the *Victorious* crashed. The Paguumis slaughtered most of them."

McKee opened her mouth to respond, but Avery cut her off. "That will be all, McKee . . . You have your orders. Carry them out. Dismissed."

McKee knew Avery was trying to protect her from herself—but felt a surge of resentment anyway. She came to attention. "Sir, yes, sir." Then, after a smart about-face, she marched outside.

SAVAS BASE 001

Paguumi scouts had been watching the base for days and occasionally taking potshots from the safety of a distant dune. Nola-Ba heard a clang, followed by a report. He decided to ignore it as he brought the glasses up to his eyes. The desert was empty for the most part, but that would soon change. In spite of the numerical advantage his ships had, they had been outmaneuvered and outfought. The loss of the cruiser *Ember* had been an especially devastating blow. A microjump! The Human admiral had taken a terrible chance and won.

Now, having received word that a nuclear torpedo had been used to obliterate the moon base, Nola-Ba knew that more Human troops would soon move against him. Fortunately, a battalion of Hudathan tanks were on the surface and ready to engage the animals.

Even so, a small but well-armed force of Humans was going to attack during the next few hours—and they would have thousands of Paguumi allies to help them. Not to mention air superiority. So what should he do? Remain where he was and try to fight them off, or take the empress and run?

In the end, the decision was no decision at all. It was imperative to put the empress aboard a ship and send her to Hudatha. The problem would be getting a shuttle down through a sky filled with Human fighters and back into space again. Still, what had to be done, *would* be done. Nola-Ba lowered the glasses, turned his back on the desert, and entered the fort.

By the time Remy, McKee, and her platoon arrived on the scene, the Hudathan base was surrounded by thousands of Paguumis. Most of the warriors raced each other, gathered in small groups, or sat in the shadows cast by their zurnas. The sun was up by then, and it was getting hot.

As Bartov came to a halt, McKee saw that most of the locals were well within range of the fort's guns but remained safe so long as they didn't charge the fortification. A scattering of bodies, all well short of the defensive berm, marked the path of a failed attack. Beyond the earthen barrier, steep slopes rose past a couple of gun ports to a flat area. For shuttles to land on? Yes, she thought so.

McKee's thoughts were interrupted as Huzz and his bodyguards came galloping out, banners flying and weapons gleaming in the sun. The Paguumi chief offered Remy something resembling a salute as he and his party skidded to a showy halt. "You grow more handsome with each rising sun," Huzz said grandly.

Remy, who had grown accustomed to over-the-top greetings, took the compliment in stride. "Thank you, Chief. And you look so fierce that the Hudathans will quake with fear."

Huzz nodded as if the statement was fact rather than outrageous flattery. "They are cowards. Why else would they hide under the dirt? You must drive the change skins out into the open, so we can slaughter them."

"That's one possibility," Remy agreed mildly. "But here's a plan that might work better. As you can see, the big guns can only fire at a single line of attack. And after they fire, they must rest before they fire again. So I suggest that you send a group to attack—and have another ready to follow up."

Huzz was no fool. He looked from Remy to McKee and back again. "All of the warriors in the first group will die."

McKee wasn't planning to speak—but did so anyway. "No," she said, "they won't. We will fire smoke bombs from a distance. Once they fall, the smoke will hide your warriors. Yes, the Hudathans will fire, but they won't be able to aim. So most of us will make it through." Remy looked at her, opened his mouth as if to speak, and closed it again.

Huzz produced the Paguumi equivalent of a frown. "*Us?* You will come?"

"Yes," McKee answered. "I will fight beside you."

Remy cleared his throat. "Well, then," he said. "The matter is settled."

SAVAS BASE 001

Empress Ophelia Ordanus was wearing clothes that smelled like the man who had died in them. And, judging from the odor, he'd been very dirty at the time. But baggy though the shirt and pants were, they were better than the blanket she'd been wrapped in earlier. Her thoughts were interrupted by a muffled thump. She felt something akin to a minor earthquake and saw dust trickle down from above. A bomb! The first explosion was followed by a second and a third.

Her mind raced. The navy couldn't drop bombs on the fortress itself without fear of killing her. But it could prepare the area around the stronghold for an infantry assault. Would the Hudathans kill her if they were about to lose? Possibly. But death would be better than a one-way trip to Hudatha.

Ophelia heard a rattling noise as the door to her cell swung open, and Admiral Nola-Ba appeared. He was dressed in full combat gear, including a sword that was strapped to his back. His voice was reminiscent of a rock crusher in low gear. "Come here."

There was no point in trying to resist. Ophelia's shoes were way too large but better than nothing. They made slapping sounds as she crossed the cell. "We're going up to level two," Nola-Ba informed her. "We will wait for the shuttle there."

"So you're going to take me off-planet." The words were in Hudathan.

"Your efforts to learn our language are going well," Nola-Ba said as he ushered her into the hall.

Ophelia shrugged. "I have nothing else to do."

"Still, it's a significant achievement," Nola-Ba observed. "Yes. A shuttle and six escorts are on their way down to the surface. Then, once we're on one of my ships, we will depart for Hudatha."

"I hope my forces shoot the shuttle down," Ophelia said flatly.

"They won't," Nola-Ba assured her. "We sent them a message . . . They know that you'll be on the shuttle."

Ophelia felt her spirits plummet. Nola-Ba was correct. If her forces believed she was on the shuttle, they would have no choice but to spare it. A bomb exploded outside, the fortress shook, and more dust fell as they followed the main corridor to the fort's core, where the elevators were located. The future of the Human race was at stake—but all the empress could do was hope.

A bomb tumbled to earth, bounced, and hit the berm, where it exploded. A column of mixed dirt and sand soared up into the air and came raining down. As McKee peered through her binoculars, she was pleased to see another gap in the defensive barrier. The entry points would be critical once the ground assault began.

"This is Condor-One calling Charlie-Six," a male voice said in her ear. "We're chasing a shuttle and six escorts, all of which are headed your way. Put some fire on the shuttle if you can. There's a strong possibility that the ridgeheads plan to put Gemstone aboard it. Over."

"Here they come," Bartov said over the platoon freq. "They're at four o'clock and coming fast."

"Charlie-One to all rocket-equipped T-1s," McKee said. "You heard Condor-One. Shoot that shuttle down."

As before, the T-1s were tied together via a shared targeting system. They fired their rockets in salvos of six. The results fell short of what McKee had been hoping for. The first fighter took a dozen hits and blew up. But the shuttle remained untouched, as did the other escorts all of which fired decoy flares. The second flight of missiles "spotted" the flares and went after them. The result was some harmless puffs of smoke and a lost opportunity as bio bods hurried to reload the empty "cans." McKee knew the shuttle would have time to land before the job was complete.

"Use your fifties!" McKee shouted, but the words were lost in a roar of incoming cannon fire as the Hudathan fighters broke formation and began a series of highly effective gun runs. Legionnaires and Paguumi warriors dived for cover as explosive rounds plowed furrows in the desert. The enemy ships were armed with rockets as well. One of them struck a zurna and blew up. That triggered a wild stampede as hundreds of zurnas ran in every direction.

"This is Six," Remy said sternly. "Do *not* fire on that shuttle . . . I repeat, do *not* fire on the shuttle. Over." And McKee understood. Now that the shuttle had landed, they had to assume that Ophelia was on board.

Meanwhile, Condor and two additional fighters had arrived and were fighting aerial duels. A Human ship took a hit and a chute appeared. Then the Tachyon rolled and burped fire. McKee didn't get to watch the plane corkscrew into the desert floor because Remy had arrived. He was mounted on Private Kane. "It won't get any better than this, McKee . . . Attack now."

McKee nodded. "Roger that, sir." Then she spoke to the platoon. "This is One. Stand by . . . We're going in. Over."

McKee stood, waved Bartov forward, and gave the order for the mortars to fire. Gray smoke billowed into the air as shells whistled over her head and exploded along the line of attack. McKee urged her people forward while Bartov carried her over to the point where Huzz and three hundred handpicked warriors were waiting. "Now!" McKee yelled into her translator. "We attack *now!*"

Huzz swung up onto his zurna and blew a note through his battle horn. His warriors surged around him. Then Huzz waved his rifle, and the combined force of Paguumis and legionnaires raced into the swirling smoke.

An order was given somewhere inside the fort, and the cannons began to fire. The Hudathan gunners couldn't see but didn't need to. The war cries and death cries were indistinguishable from each other. McKee shouted with all the rest and felt a strange joy as she led a mad dash through smoke and fire straight into the enemy cannons. Not because she believed in the cause but because she was riding with the Legion of the Damned, and they were charging the gates of hell.

Admiral Nola-Ba grabbed Ophelia's arm and pulled her onto the lift. The sounds of battle grew steadily louder as it rose. Once the platform came to a halt, troopers were there to open the hatch. Ophelia was forced to squint as she stepped out onto the roof. It was hot, and a cloud of acrid smoke prevented her from seeing much, but she could hear the steady rattle of gunfire. Her forces had arrived! They were trying to rescue her!

Ophelia tried to jerk free of Nola-Ba's steely grip at that point. He responded by letting go of her arm and grabbing her collar. Ophelia tried to hit the Hudathan as he plucked her off the deck and carried her over to a slab-sided ship. Bullets pinged all around as Paguumi sharpshooters went to work with their long-barreled trade rifles. But there was a lot of smoke, and they were a long way off.

A door gunner was firing over Ophelia's head, and hot casings bounced off her left shoulder as Nola-Ba grabbed the waistband of her baggy pants and threw her onto the ship. Then he and five of his troopers climbed aboard. Someone shouted an order, and the shuttle began to rise. It wobbled, steadied, and dived. That allowed the aircraft to pick up some additional airspeed but exposed it to ground fire. Bullets rattled against the ship's belly—and one of the door gunners took a slug under the chin.

As the trooper slumped forward, Ophelia saw what might be her last chance and kicked off her oversized shoes. Then, after two stutter steps, she dived for the open door. A huge hand caught hold of an ankle. Ophelia fell forward with her head out in the slipstream. Hot air tugged at her hair as Nola-Ba dragged her inside.

Pa Wuk and fifteen members of his extended family were standing on a rise surrounded by thousands of warriors, all of whom were waiting for the signal to attack the change-skin fortress. But before that could happen Chief Huzz and a force of handpicked warriors were to clear a path for the rest of them to follow. So all the Wuk clan could do was to yell insults at the change skins and watch the more fortunate warriors charge into the clouds of billowing smoke. It was frustrating, not to mention humiliating, to hear the sounds of battle but not be allowed to fight.

Still, there was plenty to see as a machine landed on the fort and took off again. Then, much to Wuk's surprise, it flew straight at him! That was an obvious provocation as well as the perfect excuse to use the Human boom tube on something more dangerous than a pile of rocks. Having found the launcher and three rockets in the wrecked starship Wuk had fired two of them while learning to use the weapon. Now, with one missile left, he wanted to kill something.

Wuk looked through the sight, heard a tone, and pulled the trigger. The launcher jerked, and a missile raced away. Thanks to the fact that the Hudathan shuttle was not only low, but headed straight at the warrior, the heat-seeking warhead had no difficulty identifying two potential targets. Both were air intakes for the ship's engines—but one was three degrees hotter than the other. And that was enough reason to choose it.

Wuk's relatives watched in amazement as the shoulder-fired missile entered the intake and exploded. The shuttle staggered, and black smoke poured out of the exhaust located on that side of the ship as the aircraft struggled to stay aloft. Wuk and his companions watched the machine pass over their heads. Then, as they turned to follow the aircraft, they saw it fly away. But the sky machine was trailing smoke as it disappeared over the horizon. "Well, that was a waste of time," Wuk's uncle said disgustedly. "You're an idiot." The boom tube was useless. Wuk threw it down and kicked it.

Bolts of coherent energy sizzled through the hot air as the Hudathan gunners fired blindly into the smoke and dust. McKee could see blobs of heat, thanks to the technology in her helmet, but little more than that as the cannon fire cut her people down. Private Harley Ross was killed, along with his T-1, as was Cory Dugan, and a cyborg named Linda Mora.

McKee didn't see them fall. But she heard a tone each time an icon disappeared off her HUD. And the deaths caused Bartov, who had a thing for Mora, to scream an incoherent war cry as he jumped over bodies to wreak revenge on the Hudathans. He fired upwards hoping to hit back and sparks flew from metal sheathing.

Paguumis were dying, too, and McKee was carried through a wild welter of blood as both warriors and their mounts were blown apart. And all the while the clock was running. How many lives could the gunners harvest before their cannons started to overheat? Fifty? A hundred? All McKee could do was hang on as blue bolts blipped past her helmet, and Bartov charged through the bloody rain.

Then, after what seemed like an eternity, the firing stopped. It was tempting to pause and enjoy the respite. But McKee knew that was the worst possible thing the survivors could do. Because in thirty seconds, the slaughter would start anew.

"Follow me!" McKee shouted, as she jumped to the ground in front of the berm. It would have been necessary to stop and blow a hole in the barrier had it not been for what the navy pilots had accomplished. But now, thanks to their efforts, the attackers had six gaps to choose from. And once inside, they would be able to get so close to the fort that the energy cannons couldn't be depressed far enough to fire on them.

McKee entered the nearest gap, with Huzz at her side. He shouted something in his own language, and his warriors took up the cry. Not to be outdone, McKee yelled, "Camerone!" and heard the closest legionnaires shout the name at the top of their lungs. Some of Remy's "hats" had arrived by that time and were mixed in with her people.

Moments later, they were through the gap and inside the perimeter. That was progress of a sort—but exposed the attackers to a withering fire from above. Not cannons this time but automatic weapons, held by Hudathans who were determined to keep the invaders at bay. "T-1s!" McKee shouted. "Kill those bastards! Use your fifties."

If the Hudathans were big—the cyborgs were even bigger. And as the groups collided halfway up the steeply slanted wall, the T-1s gave a good account of themselves. First with weapons fired at point-blank range—then via grasper-to-hand combat.

Though unusual, such fights were not unknown, and the legionnaires were trained to cope with them. Whenever possible, a cyborg would engage a Hudathan while his or her bio bod would circle around and attack the enemy soldier from behind. Some of the Hudathans chose to ignore the puny warriors but did so at their peril. Especially since there were weak points in their armor, like the spot right behind their knees, where a well-aimed stab could cut tendons.

Meanwhile, with Huzz still at her side, McKee led a phalanx of Paguumis and Humans up onto the landing pad. Others had reached the flat area first, and their bodies were mixed with those of the defenders they had killed. McKee had to step over Lieutenant Sokov on her way to the open hatch. His eyes were open, and he was staring up into the relentless sun.

Once inside, it became apparent that the fighting had been intense. The Paguumis were looting the place, and Huzz, who was waving a Hudathan sword, made no attempt to stop them. By working quickly and coordinating their movements via radio, the legionnaires were able to clear room after room and level after level before arriving on the lowest floor, where two gaunt-looking sailors were freed. They believed that the empress had been there but couldn't say how recently, or where she had been taken. McKee figured Ophelia was on a Hudathan ship bound for Hudatha. A fate that served her right.

Radio communications were sketchy deep inside the fortress—so McKee made her way up to the landing pad before reporting in. And as she looked down, she saw that thousands of Paguumis were streaming in through the gaps in the berm. There was no need for them to enter, but they were looking for loot. "Charlie-One to Six. Over." By looking at her HUD McKee could see that Remy was just inside the berm near one of the passages.

The response was immediate. "This is Six," Remy said. "Go. Over."

"I checked every room. Gemstone isn't here. Over."

"She was probably on the shuttle," Remy replied sourly. "But we have a more pressing problem to deal with. Over."

"Which is? Over."

Remy broke protocol by using her name. "Look at the horizon, McKee . . . Tell me what you see. Over."

McKee's binoculars were in the front pocket of her chest protector. She took them out and brought them up to her eyes. And there, as she swept the glasses from left to right, McKee saw the "problem" Remy had referred to. There was a dust cloud. And there, riding in front of it, was what looked like *thousands* of mounted warriors. Maybe tens of thousands. All closing on the fort. "I see Paguumis. Too damned many of them. Over."

"That's right," Remy agreed. "Now we know where the northern tribe is," he added dryly. "So get to work. Since we now own the fort we'll have to defend it."

THE GREAT PANDU DESERT

With only one engine to rely on, the heavily loaded shuttle had been losing altitude ever since it had been hit. The remaining power plant was cutting in and out as the ship skimmed the surface of the desert. Ophelia had been strapped into an oversized seat by then, but both of the side doors were open, and she caught a brief glimpse of a barren hillside as the shuttle whipped past it. "Get ready!" the pilot shouted over the intercom. "We're going in."

Ophelia thought she *was* ready, but soon discovered that she wasn't, as the aircraft hit the ground and bounced into the air. She felt the force of the landing all the way up through her spine and closed her eyes as metal shrieked, and all manner of loose items flew through the air. The fuselage bucked wildly as it slid over some sort of obstacle and pancaked in for a final slide. Finally, having spent all of its energy, the shuttle ground to a halt.

"Out!" the crew chief said. "This thing could explode."

So they released Ophelia and forced her out through the door. The sand felt hot under her bare feet, and the air was thick with smoke that continued to pour out of the badly damaged engine. In spite of the danger, troopers were hard at work trying to salvage what they could.

Ophelia's knees felt weak, so she sat down. Then, as Nola-Ba looked down at her, she began to giggle. Then the giggle turned to laughter. The Hudathan knew Humans well enough to understand what that meant. "What's so funny?"

"You are . . . You have me, but you'd be better off if you didn't! We own the sky, Admiral . . . That much is obvious. And the search is on."

Nola-Ba looked up. Contrails cut back and forth across the sky. The Human was right. If the search wasn't already under way, it would begin soon. It was time to hide.

CHAPTER: 14

Maneuvering with an army is advantageous; with an undisciplined multitude, most dangerous.

SUN TZU
The Art of War
Standard year circa 500 B.C.

PLANET SAVAS

McKee was standing on the fort's landing pad, looking out over the desert. The sun had set, and some early stars could be seen. But they were outnumbered by the glittering campfires that surrounded the fort. Most were fueled by dried katha droppings, and therefore small, but there were thousands of them. It was a disheartening sight. And that, she supposed, was the point. The northerners had spent the better part of the afternoon closing in. And now that they were in place, the very sight of them was enough to scare the crap out of anyone with half a brain. She heard the scrape of a boot and turned to find Avery standing next to her. "It's quite a sight, isn't it?" he asked rhetorically.

"Yes. They could take us right now if they wanted to."

"But they don't," Avery said quietly. His voice was pitched low. "Kambi says that their leader is a crafty old coot named Pudu. Rather than cut us off, he let us attack the Hudathans, knowing that the victor would be weakened and therefore vulnerable. And we won. Now he expects us to take one look at his warriors and give up."

"And will we?"

Avery looked around as if checking to make sure that no one else could hear before turning his gaze back to McKee. "We aren't here to defend Hudathan forts. We're here to find the empress. And she's gone."

"So?"

"So we promised Huzz and his people that they could have the fort if they helped us. And Remy plans to keep his word."

"Uh, oh . . . I think I see where this is headed."

"I'm sure you do," Avery said bleakly. "We're going to leave and let Huzz deal with Pudu. It's cold-blooded, but if we stay, we're going to die. And that includes everyone in your platoon. Yes, we can call in air strikes, and beat back an assault or two . . . But the northerners will win in the end. So Remy's cutting a deal."

McKee didn't like it but knew Avery was right. "How? Huzz won't let him go out and meet with Pudu."

"Kambi knows Pudu. So he slipped out of the fort at sundown. He took C-3 with him, and once he was able to make contact, Remy had a chance to talk with the old bastard. They cut a deal twenty minutes ago. There's a gap in the southern part of the berm. We're going to pass through it at 2200 hours. The northerners will provide cover fire if necessary."

"It *sounds* good," McKee replied. "But will the northerners keep their word? Or will they take the opportunity to crush us?"

Avery made a face. "I don't know . . . So we should be ready for every possibility. Brief your people over the platoon freq and order them to keep their mouths shut. If Huzz and his warriors get wind of what we're going to do, we'll be fighting for our lives *before* we leave the fort."

McKee looked down. Huzz and most of his warriors were camped between the fort and the berm. They were thick on the ground, and hundreds of fires could be seen. "How are we going to get through the southerners to the hole in the berm?"

"Chief Pudu will launch a feint against the *north* side of the berm," Avery replied. "As a result, most of the southerners will surge in that direction. We'll cut through those that remain. The hats are on foot, so they will depart first. Your platoon will guard the gap in the berm until the rest of the company is clear. I plan to stay with you."

McKee saw the look in his eyes. The message was clear. If they died, they would do so together. She nodded. "Yes, sir."

It had been a long, tense afternoon. Immediately after the crash landing, Nola-Ba, the pilots, five troopers, and Empress Ophelia put as much distance between themselves and the wreck as they could. But the group would be easy to spot from above. And it was too hot for the Human to travel very far. So the Hudathans had to hole up. A cluster of rocks offered scraps of shade and some cover should they have to defend themselves.

Nola-Ba had been tired to begin with, and the hot sun made him sleepy. So he ordered half his soldiers to keep a sharp lookout while the rest took a nap. That included him. He awoke an hour later, feeling thirsty and groggy. A swig of warm water solved the first problem—and the memory of the crash served to sharpen his senses.

The sun was lower in the sky by then—and that meant the party would be able to leave soon. The plan was to hike west and link up with the battalion of armor led by War

Commander Ru-Ba. Then, with tanks to keep the Humans and the Paguumis at bay, Nola-Ba would be able to wait for reinforcements.

Could things go wrong? Yes, of course. All he could do was try.

Ophelia felt better than she had in weeks. By some miracle, the shuttle had been damaged but not destroyed. And as long as she remained on Savas, there was a chance that friendly forces would find her. The locator beacon would have made that more likely, of course—but the odds of a rescue were still better than they had been. That's what Ophelia was thinking about as she rewrapped the rags around her right foot and secured them in place with a length of cord.

She heard movement and looked up to find Nola-Ba towering over her. "You are preparing to walk. That's good. We will leave in fifteen minutes."

Ophelia looked down. Her left foot was filthy and would have to remain that way until they found a dependable source of water. She started to wrap it. "Where are we going?"

"West. To join my ground forces."

"And then?"

"Then we will wait for an opportunity to board a ship."

"You won't get it," Ophelia predicted calmly as she stood and began to walk about. "The fact that we're hiding in some rocks says it all. You're losing assets every day."

"There's some truth to that," Nola-Ba admitted. "But I still have *you*."

SAVAS BASE 001

Stars glittered in the sky, and the light from many campfires lit the area inside the berm with a warm glow. In keeping with Major Remy's orders, the legionnaires gradually drifted to the south side of the fort until all of them were there. And they weren't alone. It seemed as if every square inch of the territory inside the berm was being used to cook on, camp on, or to stable animals. Because the southerners weren't about to leave their zurnas out in the desert where the northerners could steal them.

So as the Humans infiltrated the area, they made an already crowded situation that much worse. But as Bartov carried McKee into the seething crowd, she knew that the diversion was about to start. And once it did, the fighting would pull a lot of the Paguumis around to the north side of the perimeter. Yet, as the minutes ticked down to 1100 hours, nothing happened.

Was Chief Pudu playing some sort of trick on them? Or were the northerners running late? And did they know what time it was?

There was a sudden disturbance as a phalanx of bodyguards pushed their way through the crowd, cursing those who moved too slowly, and clubbing anyone who objected. Then Huzz appeared. He was in a bad mood. "Where is the Remy Human?" he bellowed through a translator. "I will speak with him."

Remy elbowed his way through the crowd and entered the open space created by the chief's bodyguards. That was when Huzz demanded to know why the Humans were all in one place—and Remy answered with some nonsense about the need for an inspection.

Finally, just as the conversation grew heated, the crackle of rifle fire was heard from the north. Huzz ordered Remy to send some of his forces to the other end of the compound before hurrying off to take command. Warriors, all eager to be in on whatever was taking place, streamed after him.

Remy's voice could be heard in every helmet. "This is Six. On my command, all special-operations troops will exit the fort. And remember . . . The northerners are supposed to let us through. If they don't, kill them. Over."

Warriors were still moving north, and Remy waited thirty seconds before he gave the order. "This is Six. Special-operations troops will follow me. Over."

Avery had appeared by then. He was mounted on a cyborg and could have assumed command but didn't. To do so would signal a lack of confidence in McKee's leadership abilities. That left her free to position the T-1s as she thought best. She kept two squads inside the berm, in case Huzz sent warriors to attack them, and sent the remaining legionnaires out to provide covering fire if the hats had to retreat.

Everything went fine for the first minute or two. Then McKee saw muzzle flashes out in the darkness and heard the rattle of gunfire. "This is Six," Remy said. "It's a trap. Fire at will. Watch your HUDs and close it up. Over."

McKee checked to make sure all of the hats had cleared the berm before speaking over the platoon freq. "This is Charlie-One. Split the first squad and send fire teams forward to protect both flanks. The second and third squads will form on me as we withdraw. Execute. Over."

Avery followed along behind as McKee led her people out through the gap. Once they were clear, she led the second squad up the company's left flank and sent the third to the right. At least a hundred mounted warriors thundered in, firing as they came. Something tugged at McKee's shoulder as she fired. A Paguumi fell, followed by a second, as Bartov triggered the fifty. The closest warriors and their mounts were torn to pieces as the heavy slugs tore through them. And the rest of the platoon was firing as well—creating a corridor of fire through which the company could pass.

But the effort to kill the Humans was only a minor and not very important element in Chief Pudu's overall plan. The *real* objectives were to eliminate Huzz, inflict heavy casualties on the enemy's best warriors, and capture a fortune in metal. Had it been otherwise, his vast horde of warriors would have closed in on the legionnaires and crushed them.

And as McKee glanced back over her shoulder, she could see rippling waves of gunfire as the southerners sought to defend their newfound riches and the northerners tried to take them. But there was no time for sightseeing, as warriors continued to attack the column from the east and west. It was a desperate moment because if the company was cut in two, and cut again, the legionnaires would die in clusters like the 7th Cavalry at the Battle of the Little Bighorn. Fortunately, Remy had something General Custer didn't, and that was air support. And it was on the way. "This is Hawk One, Two, and Three rolling in with HE, rockets, and guns," a female voice said. "Light those beacons. Over."

Each legionnaire had a locator beacon built into his or her helmet, or in the case of the cyborgs, into the com package located deep inside their torsos. Once "lit," the beacons would provide Hawk and her wingmen with an electronic map showing where the friendly forces were.

And that was good because as the navy fighters made passes down both sides of the column, the bombs and rockets were exploding extremely close to the legionnaires. As flashes of light strobed the darkness, McKee caught momentary glimpses of a neighboring hell in which warriors fired single-shot weapons at the invisible planes, animals pinwheeled through the air, and body parts rained down out of the sky.

But the battle was far from one-sided. The hats were running, and every now and then, one of them would fall. Most were rescued by companions, but a few were cut off, and quickly trampled to death. And McKee's platoon suffered casualties, too. Cocco Ree took a bullet in the face. It went straight through her visor into her brain and left her lifeless body flopping around on Alex Kosta's back. Then a couple of warriors managed to get ropes on the T-1 and jerked him off his feet. Once down, the combined efforts of two zurnas were sufficient to tow the cyborg away. He was never seen again.

Thanks to the fighters and the fact that Chief Pudu was primarily interested in the fort, Team One-Five managed to escape the area. And once they were clear, the legionnaires hurried to put ten miles between themselves and the battle before forting up on a rise. A scattering of rocks would provide some cover, but there was a need to dig a dozen fighting positions before the legionnaires could call it a day. McKee was looking forward to some sleep when a private tracked her down. "Major Remy wants to see you, ma'am."

McKee sighed. "Got it. Thanks."

McKee found Remy standing next to a RAV talking to Kambi. McKee was glad to see that the Jithi had been able to slip out of Chief Pudu's camp and follow C-3 to the team's current location. Both of them turned to greet McKee, and Remy was unexpectedly cheerful. "Sorry, McKee . . . I know you're tired—but the navy located the shuttle. It crashed not far from here. And they have some heat signatures all walking west. There's no way to be sure, but one of them is smaller than the rest and could be Human."

McKee felt a profound sense of disappointment. So much for her hope that Ophelia was on her way to Planet Huda-tha. "That's good news, sir."

Remy nodded. "This could be the opportunity we've been waiting for. Run those heat signatures down. And, if one of them belongs to Empress Ophelia, bring her back."

"Yes, sir. I'll pull a squad together. You'll need the rest of the T-1s for force protection."

Remy nodded. "I had hoped to have some help from the jarheads by now. But it sounds like they're ass deep in Hudathan tanks at the moment. So if you run into trouble, call on the zoomies. I'll tell them to stay close."

McKee tossed Remy a salute, which he returned. Then it was time to build a squad out of her badly mauled platoon. Four of her bio bods and five cyborgs had been killed. That was a third of her unit. Even if the mission was a success, the price would be high.

McKee chose bio bods Juli Amdon and Aatawa Singh, along with T-1s Greg Gallo, Nick Riley, and Peter Popov. The latter was left unencumbered so he could carry Empress Ophelia should they manage to free her. "We'll be wearing medals the day after we find the empress," Popov predicted.

"*And* digging latrines," Chow countered cynically. That produced a round of laughter because all of them knew it was true.

It took twenty minutes to rearm and prepare for what promised to be a wild ride. Then it was time for the cyborgs to carry their riders down onto the flat ground below. McKee saw Avery wave, and she waved back. What was he thinking? The same thing she was probably. It would be ironic if she was the one who rescued Ophelia.

Once free of the compound and flying through the night, McKee's darker thoughts were blown away by the cool night air and the sense of joy that often accompanied such moments. The speed with which the cyborgs could run, the freedom that gave her, and the power that went with it. Was that what Ophelia fed on? Writ large? Yes, McKee suspected that it was.

Bartov and the rest of the borgs were running at about forty miles per hour, which meant they would be able to close on the slow-moving Hudathans rather quickly. McKee hoped to get in among the bastards before they had a chance to fort up. Or, maybe the ridgeheads would kill Ophelia rather than let her escape. That would be just fine with McKee.

What McKee *couldn't* do was shoot the bitch herself because if she did Bartov, Amdon, Singh, Gallo, Riley, and Popov would be punished, too. That's what McKee was thinking about when Bartov spoke to her over the intercom. "I've got 'em," he said. "They broke radio silence."

"How far?"

"No more than three minutes."

McKee switched to IR. "This is One. We're coming up on them. Don't shoot any Humans. Over."

McKee received a series of clicks by way of a reply and spotted the enemy as Bartov topped a low rise. They were walking single file, and there was no mistaking the fact that the person halfway back from the head of the column was half the size of the rest. "You can see the prisoner," McKee said. "I want Bartov and Popov to pass on either side, grab an arm, and keep on going."

The Hudathans had spotted the danger by then and were in the process of turning toward the charging legionnaires. But they were still raising their weapons when Gallo and Riley fired their fifties. A Hudathan went down as if poleaxed, and a second fired a burst toward the stars as he toppled over backwards.

But McKee's attention was centered on the small figure who turned away from the charging T-1s and attempted to run. Except that the prisoner *couldn't* run. Not while wearing ankle chains. So the fugitive was hobbling south when Bartov reached down to grab one arm and Popov took hold of the other. Suddenly, the person was hoisted off the ground and held there as bolts of coherent energy stuttered past. But the attempt to kill the Human failed as Riley, Gallo, and their bio bods took the rest of the ridgeheads down.

"Circle around behind those boulders," McKee instructed. "Then you can put the prisoner down."

The cyborgs obeyed. Once behind the rocks, and there-fore sheltered from incoming fire, they lowered their burden to the ground. That was when McKee freed herself from the harness and dropped to the ground. The Human was down on one knee. And as McKee's helmet light speared her, she looked up. "A Human! Thank God."

McKee pushed her visor up out of the way before offering a hand. "You're safe, Majesty . . . Well, reasonably safe any-way."

Ophelia frowned as she accepted the proffered hand. "Sergeant McKee? Is it really *you*?"

"Yes, ma'am . . . It is. No offense, ma'am . . . But we need to get out of here. The Hudathans were talking to someone on the radio five minutes ago. Reinforcements could be on the way. Have you ridden a T-1 before?"

Ophelia was on her feet by then. "Once. For a photo op."

"Okay . . . You know what they're capable of then."

"I'm wearing ankle chains."

"Yes, ma'am. But we haven't got the time or the tools to cut them off. With your permission, Bartov here will lift you onto Popov's back. Then I'll strap you in, and we'll get out of here."

"Yes, of course," Ophelia answered. "My son . . . Can you tell me anything about Nicolai?"

McKee might have been impressed by a mother's concern if Ophelia hadn't murdered thousands of sons in order to take power and keep it. "Yes," she answered. "Nicolai is aboard the cruiser *Mars*. He'll be happy to see you. Bartov, please be so kind as to place the empress on Private Popov's back. Gently now."

It took about three minutes to get Ophelia properly po-sitioned and strapped in. Then, with her squad ready to fight if necessary, McKee made the call to Remy. "Charlie-One to Six. We have Gemstone. Over."

The response was immediate. "That's outstanding! Bring her in. Over."

McKee was back on Bartov by then—and ordered the cyborg to join the rest of the squad. They were standing a short distance from the dead Hudathans. "One of them got away," Singh said. "Should we chase him?"

"Hell no," McKee answered. "We got what we came for. Let's go home."

Nola-Ba was furious. The Human cyborgs had swept in, killed his troopers, and taken the prisoner with insulting ease. But it wasn't over yet. He could still redeem himself— and still return to Hudatha victorious. All he had to do was recapture Empress Ordanus. And the means to do so were on the way. A battle was raging about thirty miles to the west. Once the Humans had neutralized the weapons on the moon, their tanks had been able to mass and engage his armor. That clash was still under way.

But important though that battle was, it was meaning-less compared to the opportunity, no the *need*, to secure the empress, and thereby maintain the upper hand. And that was why Nola-Ba had given orders for a detachment of com-bat sleds to meet him. It was too late to use them for protection—but Nola-Ba could use the sleds to get Ophelia back.

Each highly maneuverable vehicle carried two troopers, a driver, and a gunner, and could achieve speeds of up to sixty miles per hour over flat desert terrain. Could they go one-on-one with the Human cyborgs? Nola-Ba was going to find out.

A voice spoke through the plug in his right ear. The sleds were two minutes out. Nola-Ba left the protection of the rock formation where he'd been hiding and made his way out to a point where he'd be easy to see.

Nola-Ba heard a growling sound and felt a sudden surge of hope as the first hovercraft appeared out of the gloom. In keeping with his earlier instructions, two gunners had been left behind in order to make room for him and his prisoner.

Nola-Ba waited for a sled to stop, climbed up onto the raised gunner's seat, and flipped a switch. The gauzy energy shield crackled and popped as it wrapped itself around him. The force field couldn't stop the big stuff but would vaporize smaller projectiles. Then it was time to release the safety that kept the gun barrel from swinging back and forth. There was a harness, too . . . But many troopers, Nola-Ba included, preferred to be thrown free should the sled take a hit.

Confident that everything was as it should be Nola-Ba leaned forward to slap the driver's shoulder. The hovercraft seemed to leap forward. He felt a sense of anticipation and renewed hope. The Humans thought they were safe from retribution. They would learn differently.

She was free! And it felt good. Better than anything else Ophelia had ever experienced. After being welcomed into a small compound by Avery, and introduced to Major Remy, Ophelia was shown into the largest shelter the soldiers had. Then came the reunion with Daska, who still looked the way *she* had prior to being captured.

But Ophelia knew there was a lot to do before she could afford to worry about her appearance. Nicolai was safe, Major Remy assured her of that, but what about the rest of it? "So," she inquired. "What's going on up in space?"

"The situation looks promising," Daska answered. "Arrangements are being made to take you up to the *Mars*. Once you board, the ship will enter hyperspace."

Ophelia winced as a synth began to peel the bloody rags off her feet. Small combat boots, courtesy of a female legionnaire, stood waiting. "We'll see about that," Ophelia said. "Tempting though your proposal is, the sudden departure of the *Mars* could hand a victory to the Hudathans."

"As you wish," the robot replied. "There is however a more pressing matter. One that could represent a more immediate threat."

"The Hudathans?"

"No. I refer to the relationship between Major Avery and Lieutenant McKee."

Ophelia had been happy to learn of McKee's promotion and fully intended to give her another one soon. "A relationship? What sort of relationship?"

"They're lovers," Daska replied matter-of-factly. "But that's the least of it. They plan to kill you."

The robot had Ophelia's full attention now, and she barely noticed as the rest of the rags came off her feet. "McKee? Kill me? I don't believe it."

Daska pointed a finger and a holo appeared in front of it. The video had been shot from above, and the lighting was so poor that the people below were unrecognizable, but there was no mistaking their voices. Ophelia listened with a growing sense of outrage as McKee described her role in the Mason assassination and her desire to kill the empress. By the time the recording came to an end, Ophelia was furious. "Kill them," she said. "Kill them now."

"That could be a mistake," Daska cautioned. "They are legionnaires, and we are surrounded by legionnaires, most of whom are ex-criminals. And they are loyal to each other rather than to you. So were we to attack their officers, they would probably shoot first and ask questions later. And effective though we are, the cyborgs, all of whom report to McKee, would destroy us and leave you vulnerable."

"So what would you suggest?"

"The traitors want to kill you *and* they want to survive," Daska replied. "Were it otherwise, you would be dead now. So I recommend that you wait for a shuttle to arrive. Once it does, and you're safely in orbit, it will be a simple matter to eradicate the entire company."

Ophelia frowned. *"The entire company? Why?"*

"The rest of the legionnaires have been exposed to a dangerous infection," Daska answered. "And protocol 478.12 specifies that '. . . all contaminated beings will be destroyed to ensure that antisocial ideas, philosophies, and values are not allowed to spread.' A Hudathan attack could be used to explain what happened."

Ophelia was pulling a boot on by then. It hurt, but she did it anyway. "I like it. But stay close . . . And keep the other synths close as well."

"All of the synths have been briefed," Daska assured her. "McKee and Avery will die. The only question is when."

The sun was about to clear the eastern horizon as Avery crossed the compound. The empress had taken up residence in what had been the operations tent, thereby forcing Remy and his staff into a smaller shelter. Once Avery entered, it became even more crowded. Remy looked up from a flat screen. His expression was grim. "The folks in orbit tell me there are a dozen combat sleds coming our way. Maybe they see us as a target of opportunity—or maybe they're after the empress. Either way, we're going to have a fight on our hands."

Avery shrugged. "The navy should be able to handle them."

"That's the problem," Remy replied. "In spite of the fact that the Hudathans lost most of their aerospace fighters in earlier battles, they're throwing what they have left at us. They're mixing it up with our people right now. So unless the swabbies put them away quickly, we'll have to fight the sleds by ourselves."

"So it sounds like they *are* after Ophelia," Avery concluded.

"Yeah, it's a very real possibility," Remy agreed. "She's

been warned. Make the rounds. Let our people know what to expect. Tell them we need one last effort from everyone on the team. Do you read me?"

Avery nodded soberly. "I read you. We'll be ready."

As Avery left the tent, he looked up into the morning sky, and sure enough, he could see a complex tracery of contrails. A sure sign that people were fighting and dying thousands of feet above. Gravel crunched beneath his boots as Avery made his way out to the perimeter. All of the company's remaining personnel were on duty, regardless of how tired they might be, and that included McKee, who was running on two hours' sleep.

She had a roll of tools spread out next to her and was working on Kane's knee actuator. Three bio bods were nearby. Avery addressed all of them at the same time. "A bunch of ridgeheads are coming our way . . . Take a pee if you need to and check your weapons. McKee . . . I suggest that you close that housing and give Kane a crutch. She can club the Hudathans with it."

The joke produced some chuckles but no laughter. The company was at 60 percent of its original strength, tired after days of fighting, and running on empty. But Avery had no choice except to ignore that as he circled the encampment.

The company was situated on a rise, but not much of one, which meant the enemy combat sleds could zip up and over the top if they managed to break through the perimeter. Making a bad situation worse was the fact that while about 30 percent of the encampment was protected by rocks, the rest was wide open. Fighting positions had been dug, and the dirt had been thrown forward to create a partial berm, but there were gaps that the enemy hovercraft might take advantage of.

It would be up to McKee and her cavalry to try to stop the incoming vehicles before they could penetrate the center of the encampment. The thought of losing her frightened Avery—and there was no way to escape it.

McKee had seven units left. Eight, counting Bartov and herself. The Hudathans were sure to attack the open gaps. And if they managed to break through, they'd be able to ride their sleds all the way to the ops center. Would the synths and the legionnaires posted around it be able to stop the invaders? McKee feared that they wouldn't.

So she positioned the first squad on one side of the gap and the second on the other. The plan was to put the ridge-heads in a cross fire. The danger was that the legionnaires might fire on each other. "Remember," McKee said over the squad frequency, "be careful who you shoot at. If you hit either Bartov or me, you'd better hope it's fatal."

That produced some laughs, but they were cut off as Remy's voice flooded the command channel. "This is Six. Here they come. Kill the bastards."

Engines roared as the sleds rounded a pinnacle of rock and came in fast. They were in a line abreast so as to divide the defenders' fire and bring their own weapons to bear as quickly as possible. Each vehicle had a driver with a gunner in back. They sat on elevated seats, and the shimmery force fields that protected them sparkled as small-caliber projectiles were vaporized. "Hit them," McKee ordered. "Hit them hard. Over."

The T-1s surged forward, firing as they ran—and what ensued was a whirling death dance. The cyborgs were extremely maneuverable, but so were the sleds. They could turn on a dime, slip sideways, and reverse direction. All while putting out heavy fire. Fixed weapons were mounted in the nose of each vehicle. That was bad enough. But, because the gunners could rotate their weapons through a complete circle, they were especially deadly. In fact, it was damned near impossible to get behind one of the sleds without taking fire from a pintle-mounted machine gun.

That was a lesson McKee and Bartov learned the hard way as they circled one in hopes of sneaking up on it. The gunner tracked them all the way, scored a dozen hits on Bartov, and nearly blew McKee's head off. She fired her AXE in return and swore as the Hudathan shield "ate" the 4.7 mm rounds.

Bartov had a solution though . . . And that was the underbarrel grenade launcher attached to his fifty. He fired it, scored a hit, and was close enough to take some of his own shrapnel as the projectile exploded. McKee heard metal rattle against the cyborg's armor while the Hudathan gunner was blown to rags and fell to the ground. The driver had survived, however, and as the sled slip-slid away, he continued to fire the hovercraft's nose guns.

Meanwhile Amdon and Gallo had gone down, Feng was flopping around in his harness as Chen continued to fight, and a T-1 named Cole was down on his knees. He was back-to-back with his bio bod at that point—and both continued to fire as the enemy sleds circled them like wolves. The end came quickly as Cole fell facedown in the sand and a hail of bullets ripped his partner apart.

Nola-Ba had kept his sled and two others back, firing at targets of opportunity, but avoiding the worst of the fighting. Not because he was afraid—but because he was waiting for the right opportunity. And when the cyborg fell facedown in the dirt, a path into the Human compound appeared. He leaned forward. "Now!" he shouted. "Take me straight in."

The driver opened the throttle, and the hovercraft surged forward. Other sleds were to his left and right. All of them fired their weapons as they ran at the gap between two machine-gun positions. Nola-Ba could see the automatic weapons winking at him, but none of the projectiles managed to penetrate the force field that protected him. That left Nola-Ba free to return fire, which wasn't easy from a moving sled. But by swinging the barrel back and forth, he was able to suppress the enemy fire.

One of the Human weapons fell silent, and the other could no longer be brought to bear as the hovercraft slid up the incline and entered the Human compound. Nola-Ba saw a sprawl of bodies and a single dirt-smeared face looking up at him as the sled bucked slightly and continued upslope. *They were in!* And the empress was waiting up ahead.

But the moment of jubilation was short-lived as a length of bar-taut wire sliced through the driver's neck, blood sprayed the air, and his head fell free. Nola-Ba barely had time to register the fact that the wire was anchored to a couple of innocent-looking posts when it made contact with the machine-gun mount. That caused the hovercraft to slew around.

With no hand on the throttle, the machine slowed, and Nola-Ba rolled off. As he came to his feet the *third* sled moved in to protect him. Together, they advanced toward the shelter on the very top of the rise. That was when three Humans exited the tent and began to shoot at him. Geysers of dirt shot up all around Nola-Ba as both the sled's driver and gunner fired in return. Bullets snatched two of the defenders off their feet right away. The third threw a grenade, which exploded well short of Nola-Ba.

He laughed, drew his sword, and continued to advance. That was when a shoulder-launched missile struck the remaining hovercraft and destroyed it. Nola-Ba managed to ignore the explosion as tiny bits of shrapnel peppered his leathery flesh. A Human was running straight at him now, arms spread wide as if in welcome, and that was a mistake.

The sword sang as it fell on a shoulder and nearly cut the man in half. This was when Nola-Ba realized his mistake. The alien *wasn't* unarmed. He was holding a grenade in each hand. And as Ka-Killer cut him down, the explosives fell free.

Surprisingly, there was some time to think. Not much, but enough in which to wonder why everything had gone wrong, why he was destined to die without honor, and why an animal would sacrifice himself in such a manner. For the empress? Yes, that must be it. Then there was a flash of light and a momentary sense of warmth. One journey was over, and another had begun.

Avery had seen the whole thing from the slit trench where he and Corporal Peters were prepping another missile. They had scored three kills so far, including two of the sleds that had broken through the outer perimeter, and were getting ready to fire again when a legionnaire threw a grenade. But it fell short, allowing a Hudathan to continue his advance.

Avery was bringing the tube to bear when Remy ran downslope with arms spread. It was a crazy, horrible thing to do. And Avery swore as the monstrous alien cut Remy down. Then he saw the grenades roll free. The explosions came in quick succession and blew the Hudathan's legs off.

It wasn't pretty and Avery shut his eyes for a moment before scanning for another target. The missiles he was using were heat seekers, but they were *smart* heat seekers, and could "read" the tags that each legionnaire wore. That allowed him to fire into the melee without fear of hitting a friendly. The pencil-shaped rocket flew straight and true. There was a loud bang as a sled disappeared in a flash of light. Remy's death had been avenged.

There were no sounds other than the crackle of flames produced by a burning sled, the occasional *pop, pop, pop* as rounds of unfired ammo cooked off, and the thump of her boots as McKee dropped to the ground. Her knees gave unexpectedly, and she landed on all fours. An act of will was required to stand.

Then, still wobbly from the intensity of what she had been fortunate enough to survive, McKee made her way over to where Carly Berg and Lisa Kane lay sprawled on the ground. They'd been lovers in the emotional if not the physical sense. And once Kane's knee actuator failed, the cyborg had been easy meat for the sleds. She told Berg to run, but the bio bod refused. So they died together. McKee knelt next to the cyborg and checked her readouts just to be sure. A servo whined as Bartov helped her stand. Then, walking side by side, they circled the rise, pausing to check each body.

There were some survivors but not very many. Those who could were giving first aid to the wounded. And that was nearly all of them. Only eight members of McKee's platoon were still alive, ten, including Bartov and herself. And only fifteen hats were still on their feet. Not enough people to repel a serious attack, but it was her duty to make such preparations as were possible.

Sleds littered the battlefield. Some were little more than charred wrecks. Others were hung up on rocks, had been flipped upside down, or sat seemingly untouched. There were bodies, too . . . Lots of them. Most of the aliens had been killed in combat. But some had been wounded and executed. It wasn't something McKee approved, but it was something she understood.

All of the legionnaires were aware that with the single exception of Ophelia and two sailors, the rest of the prisoners had been murdered after they fell into Hudathan hands. And, come to think of it, there was one more person who needed to die: the supreme bitch herself.

McKee went over to where Jolo was bandaging a leg.

"Take command of the platoon, Sergeant. I'm going to see Remy."

"He's dead," Jolo said bitterly. "Avery's in command."

McKee said, "Shit. Okay, move everyone inside the perimeter as soon as you can. Leave the ridgeheads where they are. We'll deal with them later."

"Got it," Jolo replied.

McKee turned to Bartov. "It looks like we have four T-1s left. Pull them together in a quick-reaction force and round up some bio bods to rearm them."

"Yes, ma'am," Bartov rumbled. "Look at the sky . . . I think we're on our own."

McKee looked up and was shocked to see two Hudathan DEs in the hazy distance, along with dozens of Human fighters, all duking it out. What might have been a Tachyon fighter exploded high above. Pieces of burning wreckage fell, but there was no sign of a chute. It appeared that the Hudathans were still determined to recapture the empress, and the navy was doing everything in its power to prevent it.

Well, McKee thought to herself as she trudged up the slope, *I have news for all of you. Ophelia is about to die.* What had been the ops center was riddled with bullet holes. Not because the Hudathans had been trying to hit it but because bullets were flying every which way. But if anyone could survive, the empress could. She might have lived a privileged life, but the bitch was tough as nails.

McKee paused to eject the magazine that was in her AXE and insert another. She planned to kill Ophelia first, then turn her attention to synths. With her weapon at the ready, McKee entered the shelter. But Ophelia was nowhere to be seen. Kambi was present, however, as was Avery, who turned to look at her. He nodded toward a legionnaire who was slumped over a com set. "It looks like Ophelia ordered the synths to kill Simms and destroy his com gear. Then she took the robots and ran."

McKee frowned. "Why would she do that?"

"Because she knows about us," Avery replied darkly. "I don't know how she figured it out—but I think Daska was involved somehow."

"Okay," McKee said. "But why kill Simms?"

"Ophelia was hoping that the Hudathans would kill us—so the last thing she wanted was air support for the unit. The entire company is expendable as far as she's concerned."

It made sense. For the first time, McKee noticed the pistol in Avery's hand. "You were going to kill her."

He nodded. "And so were you."

McKee looked at Kambi. The Jithi looked back. "How much of this do you understand?"

Kambi shrugged. "Enough . . . But remember, I have no love for your empress. Why would I? This is *our* planet."

"We should kill you."

"But you won't."

"No," McKee agreed. "We won't. So what now?"

"We go after her," Avery said flatly. "It's kill or be killed. Kambi will help us."

McKee looked at the Jithi, who nodded. "Like I said . . . This is *our* planet."

"Good," McKee said. "But no one else . . . It wouldn't be fair."

"What about the synths?" Avery wanted to know. "How can we neutralize them without a couple of T-1s?"

"Sleds," McKee answered. "I think one or two of them are still operable. They're fast, well armed, and will be identifiable from the air."

"So the Hudathans will think we're Hudathans."

"Exactly," McKee agreed. "Although our people will believe the same thing."

"Oh goody," Avery said sarcastically. "The navy is going to shoot at us. That'll be fun."

"It beats walking," McKee replied. "I hope it will, anyway. Come on . . . Let's grab some gear."

What with the need to find a couple of still-operable sleds, and provide Sergeant Major Hadley with orders, a full hour elapsed before McKee, Avery, and Kambi could leave. McKee could tell that Hadley didn't think that both of the surviving officers should go, but couldn't complain about an effort to find the empress, and didn't.

McKee and Avery quickly discovered that while the controls on the sleds were intuitive, the handlebars were too wide for comfort, and the seats were way too large. Kambi had located the tracks by then. Ophelia and her robots were headed toward the southwest. After meandering between wrecked sleds, the footprints took off at an angle and seemed headed for the mesa that could be seen to the south.

As McKee drove, the Jithi hung on to the gun mount with his left hand. That allowed him to lean out over the ground. "They're running," he shouted. "And look! One set of tracks is deeper than the rest. I think a robot is carrying the empress."

That was bad news insofar as McKee was concerned. It had been her hope that they would be able to catch up with Ophelia in an hour or so. But she'd seen Daska run and knew the robots were not only tireless but could carry heavy loads. It couldn't be helped, however. All they could do was follow the footprints and try to catch up as quickly as possible.

So as dozens of contrails chased each other across the sky, the sleds continued south. There were occasional pauses to check the trail, then they were off again. As the sun fell lower in the west, and the mesa grew higher in front of them, it was necessary to pass through a rocky defile. It led to an open area beyond, and they were halfway through it when a synth dropped from above. It landed on the back of Avery's hovercraft. The vehicle wobbled in response, and Avery had to let go of the controls to defend himself.

Steely fingers wrapped themselves around Avery's throat, and it became impossible to breathe as the sled ran up onto a ledge and flipped over. The motor screamed, then shut itself off as Avery rolled free. The synth landed on its feet, knees bent, ready to fight.

CHAPTER: 15

A synth cannot be bribed, blackmailed, or sub-
verted. If only Humans were so trustworthy.

EMPRESS OPHELIA ORDANUS
Standard year 2726

PLANET SAVAS

The synth was Humanoid in appearance but far from
Human. Its uniform had been spray-painted on, its broad
forehead was made of smooth metal, and its skull tapered
into a vertical ridge in back. All of which gave the android a
menacing appearance. The robots were typically armed with
machine pistols, but this one wasn't. Avery was reaching for
his pistol when the synth leaped into the air. He didn't have
time to dodge.

The machine hit hard, and the weight of it threw Avery
onto his back. Steely fingers sought his throat for the second
time—and Avery was trying to push the robot up and off of
him when a gun barrel appeared. He heard a loud *BOOM* as
the heavy slug entered through the synth's left temple—and
pushed a column of electronic brain tissue out through the
other side of its head. The result was instantaneous. The
robot went limp, and Avery rolled out from under it.

A harsh clacking sound was heard as McKee pumped another shell into the chamber and thumbed the safety on. "That's one," she said laconically.

Avery eyed the twelve-gauge. "Where's your AXE?"

"On my sled. But I knew what we'd be up against. Those 4.7 mm slugs don't have much stopping power. So I brought Big Bertha here."

"Good thinking. You saved my ass."

McKee grinned. "And a good thing, too . . . It's your best feature."

Avery made a face. "So, why leave a machine here?"

"To slow us down," McKee answered. "And to provide Ophelia with intel. All of the synths can communicate with each other. Now she knows there are three of us all riding Hudathan sleds."

"Shit."

"Yeah, that pretty well sums it up," McKee agreed. "Come on. Let's see if your sled will run."

With help from Kambi, they were able to turn the hovercraft right side up and start it. That was the good news. The bad news was that a blower blade was bent, and they couldn't run the vehicle at anything more than half power. "We'll leave it behind," McKee said. "All three of us can ride my machine."

"Maybe," Avery replied. "But, if Kambi's willing, there might be an alternative."

McKee looked skeptical. "Such as?"

"We send Kambi ahead on my machine, swing wide on yours, and swoop in when the synths come out to capture him."

McKee's eyes went to Kambi and flicked back again. "What makes you think they'll try to capture him? Won't they shoot him?"

"Yes," Kambi put in. "Won't they shoot me?"

"Because Ophelia will want to know where we are,"

Avery said patiently. "And the synths will have orders to intercept us if they can."

McKee nodded. "That makes sense. So, Kambi . . . What do you think? It's up to you."

There was a moment of silence while the Jithi gave the plan some thought. Then he nodded. "I will do it. This is *our* planet."

"Good," Avery said. "You can wear my helmet. Tell us the moment you see anything suspicious."

The next twenty minutes were spent showing Kambi how to operate the sled. The Jithi's driving skills were pretty limited, but with a patch of open desert up ahead, there wasn't much to run into.

So off he went, swerving wildly at times but mostly headed for the mesa that loomed ahead. The sun had set, but the moon was up. So McKee figured the Jithi would be hard to miss. As for the two of them, they planned to follow a dry watercourse that was headed in the right direction. The key was McKee's ability to track Kambi's position on her HUD.

But after a mere five minutes of travel, it quickly became apparent the constantly twisting-turning riverbed was going to make for some slow going. And instead of racing ahead of Kambi, McKee was hard-pressed to keep up. The fact that the watercourse was littered with boulders made a bad situation even worse. McKee managed to steer round most of them but had to leave the riverbed occasionally to bypass the largest obstacles. Would Ophelia's synths spot them during one of the detours? McKee feared that they would—but couldn't think of an alternative. The hard work of navigating a course through the dry riverbed continued for about thirty minutes. Then McKee saw Kambi slow down as his voice came over the radio. "I can hear them in the helmet," he said. "They told me to stop."

McKee couldn't reply. Not without allowing the robots

to listen in. So all she could do was look for a spot where she could steer the sled up onto the flat ground above. "Get ready!" she shouted. "They're in contact with Kambi."

Avery activated the force field and readied the machine gun. Avery wished he was strapped in as the sled bounced over an obstruction. Kambi was wearing his helmet, but Avery could see quite a bit thanks to the moonlight that glazed the countryside around him. The sled swerved right and left as McKee steered it through a maze of boulders.

Suddenly, they were out in the open, and Avery saw blips of blue light stutter away from the hovercraft as McKee fired the nose guns. Avery aimed the machine gun straight ahead and mashed the butterfly-shaped trigger. His tracers went wide, so he brought them back to merge with McKee's fire.

Then, as Avery strained to see his target, a shoulder-launched missile hit him. Or, more accurately, it hit the protective force field and exploded. The force of the blast took the shield down and caused damage to the machine gun. Avery felt a blow followed by a sharp pain as something entered his chest. Then he was sent flying through the air. The ground came up hard, and everything went black.

McKee wasn't sure what had taken place at first. One moment she was steering and firing the sled's nose cannons. Then there was an explosion, she felt pieces of something pepper the back of her helmet, and the hovercraft swerved and sideswiped a boulder. She managed to regain control and looked back over her shoulder. The gun was gone, and so was Avery. It was like a blow to the gut. McKee felt an overwhelming sense of sorrow followed by a surge of anger. A synth was running away from her, so she opened the throttle and gave chase. She fired, saw the blips miss, and made the necessary correction. That brought the fire on target, and McKee felt a sense of satisfaction as the robot went down.

But the robots were tough. McKee had learned that on Orlo II and wasn't about to take chances. So she circled the android, came to a stop, and felt the hovercraft wobble as she got off. The twelve-gauge shotgun produced a loud *BOOM* as she put a slug through its head. "That's *two*," McKee said grimly, as she pumped another shell into the chamber.

When she heard movement McKee whirled, weapon at the ready. But it was Kambi rather than a synth. She pulled the barrel up so that it was pointed at the sky. "Sorry . . . Did you see the other one?"

Kambi shook his head. "Only this one."

"It was a trap," McKee said. "I made the mistake of underestimating Ophelia. She's stalling in hopes that the navy will pick her up before we can find her. Come on . . . Avery's missing, and we need to find him."

Both of them got back on their sleds, and McKee steered back the way she and Avery had come. She kept her head on a swivel, but there was no sign of the second synth.

Minutes later she spotted a body lying on the ground and pulled up next to it. She took her helmet off as she stepped to the ground. "John! Can you hear me?"

There was no answer, and McKee feared the worst as she knelt at his side. There was blood. A lot of it and her hands shook as she felt for a pulse. It was there! Thready, to be sure . . . But a pulse nevertheless.

There was a bloodstain on the front of his chest protector, so she hurried to cut the straps that held it in place. Moments later she saw that the body armor had been holed and so had he. Each breath produced a spurt of blood.

McKee had seen sucking chest wounds before and knew they could result in a collapsed lung. But she could prevent that by applying a special dressing to the wound. A bandage that would prevent air from getting in and allow extra air to escape.

McKee fumbled with a pocket flap, found what she was

looking for, and pulled it out. The bandage began to wiggle as it sensed blood and practically jumped onto Avery's chest.

That was good but what about the piece of metal responsible for the wound? Kambi was kneeling next to her. "Turn your helmet light on," McKee ordered, knowing that it was a dangerous thing to do. But she had to see in order to treat Avery, and that had priority. "Here," she added, "help me turn him on his side."

Kambi obeyed and kept the helmet light focused on Avery's back as McKee cut the rest of the body armor away. And there it was—a small exit wound. The object had gone straight through! That was a blessing since she had no way to remove shrapnel from deep inside his body.

McKee put a self-sealing compress over the wound and turned to Kambi. "We'll place him on your sled. Find a place to hide. A spot where you can't be seen from above. Keep the helmet on. I'll use it to find you."

Kambi turned the light off and helped McKee drape Avery over the backseat. The retractable harness served to hold him in place. Kambi switched the light off. "You're going after them."

"I have to. I want to kill Ophelia . . . That's true. But now I *have* to kill her. She'll send an army to find us if I don't."

Kambi nodded. "There is a place south of here. A cave that only the Jithi use. I will take him there."

"Good. And, Kambi . . ."

"Yes?"

"Thank you." And with that, she left.

Ophelia was on the lowest level of the fort being held prisoner in a cell. The Hudathans had secured her to a metal rack, and she'd been there for what seemed like hours. Then the door swung open, and McKee entered. The legionnaire smiled evilly as she came over to stand only inches away.

Ophelia couldn't take her eyes off the scar. It made McKee look cruel. Like a person who, having suffered pain, looked forward to dispensing it.

But when McKee spoke, it was Alfred's voice that Ophelia heard. But that couldn't be since she'd been there when the synths threw her brother off the balcony into the abyss below. "That's right," Alfred said. "I'm waiting for you. Waiting to . . ."

Ophelia awoke with a start and found a face much like her own looking down at her. Daska! Thank God. Farther up, she could see a dusting of stars and the flight of a meteor as it flashed across the sky. Or was that a burning ship? One of the many that were fighting over her. "Yes?" Ophelia croaked. "What is it?"

"Fifteen hundred hours tomorrow," the synth answered. "That is when they will come for you."

The ground was hard, and Ophelia was lying on a shelter half. There hadn't been much time to gather supplies as she and her bodyguards fled the compound. Nor had she expected to need them with the navy so close. But in spite of everything Admiral Nigata had been able to accomplish, his ships were still outnumbered and worse yet, from her perspective, was the fact that the marines had been defeated on the ground. So help wouldn't be coming from that quarter.

By using Daska as an intermediary, Ophelia had been trying to arrange for an extraction. The task was made more difficult by the fact that the Hudathans were searching for her—and would respond in force if they thought a rescue attempt was under way. "How will it work?" Ophelia wanted to know.

"There will be *ten* landings," the synth replied. "At various locations. But only one will be real."

"Excellent," Ophelia exclaimed. "That should do the trick. What about the traitors who are chasing me?"

"Your plan was successful. Reez showed itself, they went

after it, and Steffa fired a rocket at the Humans. We believe one of them was killed."

"Which one?"

"Major Avery."

"Damn. McKee is the more dangerous of the two. What about Reez? Did they manage to kill it?"

"Yes," Daska said unemotionally.

"Okay," Ophelia said, as she stood. "All we have to do is make it to 1500 hours tomorrow. Tell Steffa to ambush McKee and kill her. Even if the effort fails, it will buy me more time."

"Steffa is on his way," Daska said two seconds later. "We are ready to depart."

Ophelia took a long drink of tepid water before handing the canteen to the robot. "All right . . . I will set the pace." And with that, she began to jog. Her boots were heavy but well broken in. But could she run far and fast enough? The answer, Ophelia decided, would have to be yes.

McKee knew what to look for by that time and had little difficulty following the synth's trail. It led west, then south, along the side of the looming mesa. Every now and then she checked her HUD to see where Kambi and Avery were. It appeared that the slower sled was headed for the north side of the mesa.

She was tired and had a hard time staying awake. It required an act of will to keep her eyes open and scan the area ahead. The sky was growing lighter, and visibility had improved. Suddenly, a hole appeared in the windshield, and a bullet buzzed past her helmet. A sniper!

The response was instinctual. McKee swerved and began a series of S turns. There! She could see a slight rise topped by a scattering of boulders. The perfect spot for a synth to lie in wait.

McKee heard a clang and knew that the robot had scored again. That meant the S turns were too predictable. So she began a series of what she hoped would be unexpected zigs and zags. The engine sputtered, quit, and caught again. Had the most recent hit caused some damage? Or was the sled running out of fuel?

Either way, it was imperative to reach the rise. If the vehicle stalled out in the open she'd be a sitting duck for the sharpshooting robot. The distance began to close, and as it did, the vehicle's course became increasingly predictable. McKee bent over and ducked low. She heard a report and felt the hovercraft jerk as it took a hit. Then it was time to grab the shotgun and roll free. The sled ran up the slope and slammed into a reddish boulder.

McKee assumed she was up against a single robot but knew assumptions could be fatal. So she was careful to stay low as she entered a maze of rocks. But as McKee passed between a couple of rocks, she heard the chatter of a machine pistol. She had to scuttle forward to escape a hail of bullets. Shit, shit, shit! How did the synth know where she was?

Then, as McKee rounded the side of a boulder, the answer came to her. It was the helmet! It was broadcasting her location on a frequency the synth could intercept. But could that work *for* her? Maybe.

McKee set the trap and ducked out of sight. Thirty seconds passed before the synth dropped from a ledge up above. It took the shock with bent knees before straightening up. The machine was reaching for the helmet when McKee pulled the trigger. That produced a loud *BOOM*. The robot was forced to take two steps backwards as the twelve-gauge slug struck its chest. The android looked down at the dent and back up again. The machine pistol was coming to bear when McKee pulled the trigger again. The slug blew a hole through the synth's head. There was a *thump* as it hit the ground. "That's three," she said, and felt suddenly dizzy.

There was a patch of shade, and McKee sat in it. She should collect the helmet, recover the synth's weapons, and check on the sled. But that would require standing up, and she couldn't summon the energy. Five minutes. That's all she needed. Then she'd be raring to go. McKee let her head rest on the rock, allowed her eyes to close, and sleep carried her away.

It was the heat that finally woke her. And when she looked at her chrono, McKee realized that more than two hours had passed. Two precious hours during which Ophelia had been on the run. She swore, got to her feet, and went over to the helmet, which she turned off. The locator beacon had betrayed her once. She didn't want that to happen again.

With that accomplished, it was time to collect the machine pistol, the ammo that went with it, and the rifle that had been left on top of the hill. McKee felt a sense of despair as she carried the arsenal down to the sled. The hovercraft had gone partway up the slope, slipped sideways, and flipped over. And it was too heavy to lift without help. All she could do was salvage the canteens, choose which weapons to take with her, and get going.

It was impossible to know what sort of situation might await her, and that made the choice of weapons difficult. But after giving the matter some thought, McKee settled on the sniper's rifle in addition to her pistol. Her logic was that it would be difficult to close with the fugitives, but she might be able to spot Ophelia from a distance.

Rather than leave the machine pistol and the shotgun for the next Paguumi who happened by, she hid both the weapons and eight pounds' worth of body armor in a crevice about two hundred feet away from the sled. Then she began to walk. The helmet was strapped to the pack, which contained extra ammo, two canteens of water, and a first-aid kit.

It took a while to find the synth's tracks and follow them back to the point where they parted company with the other footprints. Some had been made by standard-issue boots, while the rest belonged to a robot. And that robot had to be Daska since the rest of the synths had been eliminated.

That was the good news. The bad news was that the trail was hours old and degrading fast. Each gust of hot, dry wind blew sand over the impressions and made them more difficult to see. Still, even though the spoor was steadily disappearing, the line of march was constant and therefore predictable. Ophelia wasn't wandering around the desert. She was headed somewhere. To a pickup point? Probably. Daska could and would be in contact with the navy. That meant every hour was precious. McKee quickened her pace.

It was growing steadily warmer as the sun climbed higher in the sky, and McKee knew she wouldn't be able to catch up using a quick march. That forced her to adopt what the Legion called a double march—a speed roughly equivalent to a jog. Something any legionnaire should be able to maintain for hours at a time. Especially with a light load. Could Ophelia do the same? McKee didn't think so. Yes, Daska could carry the bitch, but that would slow both of them down.

Time passed, the sun beat down, and McKee wished she had a hat. But she didn't, so all she could do was watch the terrain ahead and choose the fastest routes.

An aircraft passed over her about thirty minutes later. It was very high, so there was no way to know who was flying it—or what the plane's mission might be. It did get McKee to thinking, however. By this time both she and Avery were listed as MIA. So the Legion would be searching for them. Still another threat.

Time and distance lost all meaning after a while. McKee felt as if she were floating along as the horizon swayed back and forth, and her boots hit the ground. And that was dangerous because if McKee wasn't careful, she could run into a trap.

So she forced herself to stop every now and then to take a drink of water and eyeball the terrain ahead. And it was during what might have been the eighth or ninth stop that she spotted a speck, no a pair of specks, off in the distance!

McKee brought the rifle around so she could peer through the scope. The images seemed to leap forward, and one of them was Ophelia! The empress was walking slowly, with Daska a pace or two behind.

McKee felt a sudden surge of energy. The bitch was within reach! With the rifle slung across her back, she began to run. The desert was flat for the most part, but there were dips. Each time she passed such a depression, the targets dropped out of sight. Then, as she topped the next rise, the figures were a tiny bit closer.

Meanwhile, McKee forced herself to think. What would the endgame be like? As soon as Ophelia realized that McKee was closing in on her, she would send Daska back to kill her pursuer. And that could work. So, what to do?

McKee ran halfway up a likely-looking slope and threw herself to the ground well short of the crest. Then, with the rifle across her arms, she low crawled to the top. Once in place, it took a moment to find the target and place the crosshairs on Ophelia's back. The logical thing to do was to shoot the empress right then. But, right or wrong, McKee wanted to confront the bitch—wanted to see the look in Ophelia's eyes just before she died.

So McKee swung the crosshairs over to Daska. The last synth had been able to survive a shotgun blast to the chest. So what impact would a .308 rifle bullet have on the robot? Especially at long range? Of course, McKee knew a great deal about robots, cyborgs, and their weak spots. One of which was the area right behind their knees. She could try for that.

That kind of shot would involve considerable risk, however. A miss could warn the targets and send them into hiding. That would force McKee to cross a lot of open ground before she could close with them. And the long gun would be a liability at short range. Yet what choice was there? She needed to stop them and to do so quickly.

McKee drew a lungful of air and let it go. The trigger broke, and the rifle butt kicked her shoulder. McKee saw the puff of dust slightly to the right of Daska and swore. The sight was off, the side breeze was stronger than she'd thought it was, or both.

The fugitives stopped and turned. That was when McKee realized that neither one of them had seen the bullet strike. It was the report they were reacting to. McKee had one last chance. She made the necessary adjustment and fired. The second shot was right where she wanted it. Daska's head jerked as the bullet struck the robot's right "eye."

It wasn't a killing shot, though. Not at that distance. There was something very Human about the way the synth brought a hand up to touch the shattered sensor. That was when McKee fired again and uttered a whoop of joy as her bullet pulped Daska's *second* eye. Blind now, Daska staggered in a circle, hands extended. And because the robot looked like Ophelia, it was like watching the empress. But Ophelia was untouched. She bent to retrieve Daska's machine pistol before turning to flee.

McKee stood and paused to reload the rifle before starting to run. It was no contest. McKee was in good shape, and Ophelia wasn't. McKee ran past the spot where Daska was walking in circles and kept on going. Ophelia was running full out by that time and turned to trigger a flurry of shots. The bullets went wide, as McKee continued to close in.

Desperate now, the empress stopped and turned with weapon raised. But McKee was ready. The pistol was up and rock steady. She fired, and the bullet hit Ophelia's left kneecap. The machine pistol went flying as the empress collapsed. "That was for my father," McKee said as she walked forward closer. "The next one is for my mother."

"No!" Ophelia said desperately. "You can have anything you want. Money, property, *anything*."

"Can you bring thousands of dead people back to life?" McKee demanded. "I don't think so." There was a loud report as she squeezed the trigger. There was a spray of blood as the bullet pulped Ophelia's right knee.

The empress wrapped her arms around what remained of her knees and produced a pitiful keening sound. McKee felt no sympathy for her. *"Who are you?"* Ophelia demanded as she looked up into the legionnaire's scarred face.

"My name is Lady Catherine Carletto," McKee answered coolly. "And this one is for Uncle Rex." There was a third report, and Ophelia's head snapped back as a third eye appeared between the other two. The body slumped to the ground.

McKee stood there for a moment. Her mind was reeling as she absorbed the full impact of what she'd done and what it would mean for her life. Then, hand shaking, she returned the pistol to its holster. What should she do next? The answer was obvious. Hide Ophelia's body. And do it quickly. Maybe, if she did a good job, it would never be found.

McKee heard the scuff of a foot and had already started to turn when Daska wrapped an arm around her throat. That was when McKee realized that although the robot was blind, it could still hear. And it had been able to follow the gunshots and the sound of her voice to the spot where she stood.

McKee brought both hands up in a futile effort to break the machine's grip. But the arm was like an iron bar. And as Daska tightened its hold it became impossible to breathe. McKee knew she had seconds in which to react. Her lungs were on fire, and she was about to lose consciousness. The fingers of her right hand felt for the pistol and found it. She thumbed the safety off as the weapon left its holster. Was there a bullet in the chamber? Yes, there should be.

Daska stood a head taller than McKee. That allowed the legionnaire to point the weapon up and back. She jerked the trigger and kept jerking it. The reports were deafening. But when the pistol clicked empty, the arm was still in place. McKee thought she had missed until the robot fell over backwards and took her with it.

They hit hard, McKee discovered that she could breathe again and fought to free herself. Once she was out from under the arm, McKee turned to see that the right side of Daska's face was gone, exposing part of its main processor. She rolled to her feet and gave the synth a kick. There was no response.

It was second nature to hit the release and slide a fresh magazine into the pistol. Then, with the weapon back in its holster, she went to work. Ophelia had been on her way to an extraction point—and it seemed safe to assume that it wasn't far away. So every minute was critical.

McKee ran a wide circle around the bodies and felt a sense of relief as she spotted the empty space below a wedge of upthrust rock. She didn't have the time or the tools required to dig conventional graves. But after pushing the bodies in under the rock formation, she could wall them in. Not perfect, perhaps, but it could work given a bit of luck. Savas was a big planet after all—most of which remained unsettled.

McKee grabbed Ophelia by the ankles and dragged her a hundred feet over to the rock. The empress wasn't all that heavy, but it was hot work nevertheless, and McKee was gasping for breath by the time the job was done.

Then it was time to go back for Daska. The robot weighed at least twenty pounds more than the Human had. It took every bit of McKee's strength to drag the machine over and push it into the shady crevice. Now both bodies were invisible from above. McKee allowed herself a swig of water before going out to kick dirt over Ophelia's blood and retrieve the machine pistol.

That was when she heard a distant roar and felt a stab of fear. An aircraft! Headed her way! McKee scooped the machine pistol off the ground and ran for the rock. As she dived under the overhang, McKee scrabbled forward so that her boots wouldn't be visible from above.

The boxy shuttle arrived thirty seconds later. It was low, *very* low, and riding its repellers. That would use a lot of fuel but allowed the aircraft to creep along. And it didn't take a genius to guess who the crew was looking for.

But they couldn't see Ophelia since she was only inches away from McKee. So close that McKee could see that the woman's left ear had been pierced twice.

The repellers stirred up a miniature dust storm as they jabbed the desert floor and erased the footprints that crisscrossed the area. A mercy for which McKee was extremely grateful. Sand continued to fly as two aerospace fighters roared overhead, and the shuttle continued on its way.

It was tempting to exit her hiding place, but McKee knew that would be a mistake. There were bound to be eyes in the sky. *Powerful* eyes looking down on that part of the planet's surface. No, difficult though it might be, the smart thing was to remain where she was until darkness fell.

So McKee lay next to the woman who had killed so many, wondered what would become of Nicolai and whether he would make a better ruler. Eventually, she fell asleep. And when she awoke, it was to a loud *boom!* A bomb? No. There was a flash of light and *another* clap of thunder. Then it began to rain.

McKee could hardly believe it. She wiggled out into the open and stood. Then, with head tilted back, she let the rain pelt her face, fill her mouth, and soak her filthy clothes. The feel of it was so good that she decided to strip down and take her first shower in weeks.

The rain helped to cleanse her body and clear her mind. Rain meant clouds, and clouds would prevent people from seeing her from above. So she freed the helmet from the pack and put it on. Could she risk using the light? Yes, she thought so, since it was separate from the rest of the electronics. And, thanks to the rain, the glow would be impossible to see from more than a hundred feet away.

So, dressed only in the helmet and her combat boots, McKee went about the laborious process of finding suitable rocks and carrying them over to what she thought of as the royal mausoleum. Stone by stone, she constructed a wall around Ophelia and Daska until the bodies were completely hidden. More than that, she tried to make the enclosure look natural—although it would take the passage of time to complete the task.

The rain had tapered off by the time she was done, and McKee could see stars through breaks in the clouds. McKee put her clothes back on, collected all of her belongings, and began the trek north.

All of the normally dry watercourses were running full, so it was slow going. And by the time the sun peeked over the eastern horizon, McKee still had something like fifteen miles to go. She couldn't travel during the day, though. Not without running the risk of being spotted by the people who were searching for Ophelia. So she filled her canteens, took shelter in a jumble of rocks, and ate a trail bar.

After that, it was a matter of napping through the heat of the day and worrying about Avery. Was he still alive? More than once she considered putting the helmet on her head and pushing the power button. But the longer she waited, the safer it would be. Because after days of searching, and with no clues to go by, the navy would be forced to conclude that Ophelia was dead. Killed by the Paguumis?

Executed by the Hudathans? Dead of exposure? All were believable possibilities, and if the navy was still fighting it out in space, they wouldn't have the resources to conduct an extensive ground search.

That was a comforting thought, and McKee clung to it as time passed and darkness fell. As soon as she thought it was safe to do so, she left her hiding place and began to walk. It would have been easy to miss the sled in the darkness, but thanks to occasional blips of light from her helmet, she managed to find the wreck without too much difficulty.

The vehicle looked the same, but something was missing. What was it? Then it came to her. Robot number four had been taken away. By the people who were searching for Ophelia? Yes. That made sense.

Eventually, someone would perform a forensic examination of the synth's injuries and conclude that the machine had been "killed" with a shotgun. Were some of its memories intact? That was possible. If so, they would be able to watch her shoot the robot. If not, they might conclude that the android had been killed by a Paguumi armed with a Human weapon. There was no way to know—so it was best to assume the worst.

Even though she'd been able to find the wreck with relative ease, it took McKee fifteen minutes to locate the crevice where the body armor and weapons were hidden. Then, with the machine pistol stowed in her pack and the long guns slung across her back, she continued north.

Eventually, once the mesa's bulk loomed to the right, she knew the time had finally arrived. There was a hollow feeling in the pit of her stomach as the helmet powered up. Would Kambi respond? The answer was no. Repeated calls went unanswered. And after sixty seconds of trying, she was forced to turn the helmet off without making contact.

McKee looked at her chrono. The time was 2236. Was Avery dead? Probably. But what if he wasn't? What if his helmet was off for the same reason hers had been? To avoid detection. He would know about her plan to contact him, however. Kambi would tell him. So, being a military officer, what would Avery do? He would check every hour on the hour . . . And trust her to think of that.

It wasn't much, but some hope was better than none. So McKee kept walking, checked her chrono more frequently than was necessary, and stopped when 2300 appeared on the dial. As soon as the helmet was up and running, she made the call. It seemed unlikely that anyone would be close enough to hear her—but she was careful to avoid using her call sign just in case. "Do you read me?"

There was no reply. Just static. She tried again. "Do you read me? Over."

Avery's voice was loud and clear. "I copy you . . . And we can *see* you. Power down and wait. Over."

Avery was alive! McKee felt a surge of joy. "Roger, that. Over."

She turned the helmet off and sat on a rock. Thanks to the map projected on Avery's HUD, he'd been able to get a fix on her position. Kambi would come out to get her. She looked at the stars. Could she find peace among them? It was too early to know.

More than twenty minutes passed before Kambi arrived. They embraced Human style. Then, as McKee took a step back, their eyes met. "How is he?"

"Better . . . *Much* better. He wanted to come. I said 'no.'"

McKee nodded. "Thank you."

"Come," Kambi said. "There have been drones. It is best to take cover."

McKee followed Kambi through broken ground toward the mesa. Eventually, when it towered above them, the Jithi led her down into a riverbed. Most of the water from the recent rainstorm had drained away, but pools remained.

They splashed through them. It seemed safe to turn the helmet light on, so she did.

As the main watercourse continued east, Kambi led McKee into a side channel. The ground sloped upwards before coming to an end in front of a large slab of water-smoothed rock. It had clearly been the site of a waterfall during the rainstorm because rivulets of water were still running down the front of it.

McKee was about to ask "What now," when Kambi put a shoulder against the right side of the rock and pushed it open. Upon closer examination McKee saw that a pair of iron pivots allowed the slab to open and close. "It's hundreds of years old," Kambi said proudly. "Jungle covered this area back then, and our ancestors were very clever."

"They certainly were," McKee said admiringly, as they entered a large antechamber. McKee examined her surroundings as Kambi pushed the door closed. A Hudathan sled was parked off to one side, and iron rings marked the places where animals might have been tethered a long time ago.

From there, McKee followed Kambi down a tunnel into a circular chamber, where oil-burning clay lanterns gave off a soft glow. A pool of water occupied the center of the room. "The level drops lower," Kambi said, "but the water never goes away."

McKee wasn't listening. Her eyes were on Avery. He was sitting on a stone bench and rose to greet her. "Cat . . . My precious Cat."

McKee entered the circle of his arms carefully, fearful that she might hurt him, and tipped her head back to accept his kiss. All of it was there. Everything she wanted and had hoped for. Then, conscious of the fact that Kambi was present, they parted, which was just as well, because Avery needed to sit down again. The next hour was spent catching up. McKee told Avery about the chase, the final confrontation with Ophelia, and the trip back. He told her about waking up in the cave—and how Kambi had cared for him.

That was followed by a celebratory meal consisting of three MREs, and McKee ate all of hers. Fortunately, their food, extra ammo, and other supplies had been aboard Kambi's sled. That meant they'd be okay for a while. But what then? Avery had given the matter some thought. "We need supplies," he said. "So, if Kambi is willing, we'll send him north to buy some."

"I am," the Jithi said solemnly. "The Paguumis know me."

"Yes, they do," McKee agreed. "And they know you were working for the Legion. You'll have to be very careful."

"I will be," Kambi assured her.

"He can buy Human ammo if any is available," Avery continued. "Plus food, Paguumi clothes, and a couple of pack animals."

McKee frowned. "Paguumi clothes? What for?"

"So we'll look like Paguumis from a distance," Avery answered. "It's a long way from here to Savas Prime. We won't be able to get there without being seen."

The mention of the only Human settlement on Savas caused McKee to frown. "And then?"

"And then we'll wait for a tramp freighter and go where it goes."

"That's it then? We're going AWOL?"

"Of course," Avery said, as if it were the most natural thing in the world. "How would we explain where we've been? And what we've been up to? Plus, who knows what Daska told the navy—or what synth number three might have recorded. But if we disappear, chances are the command types will conclude that we were killed. Especially since it would suit their purposes to do so."

McKee nodded. "Okay, I'm in. There's a problem though . . . How are we going to pay for the supplies?"

"That's easy," Avery assured her. "Just think what Kambi will be able to buy with a Hudathan sled!"

"But it's damaged, and it's going to run out of fuel."

Avery grinned. "They don't know that. Besides, the metal is valuable in and of itself. Trust me . . . Someone will go for it."

"Okay, but what about passage on a tramp freighter? How will we pay for *that*?"

Avery opened a pocket and produced a leather pouch. "With one or two of these. A group of Paguumi warriors gave them to me while Nicolai and I were hiding in an oasis."

McKee made a face. There was no way that a group of Paguumis were about to give Avery anything. She accepted the purse and was impressed by how much it weighed. It was filled with what looked like gemstones although none were cut or polished. She passed the pouch to Kambi. "How 'bout it?" she inquired. "Are they worth anything?"

Kambi's eyes grew wider. "Yes. These stones are worth a fortune!"

"You see?" Avery said proudly. "We can pay Kambi for his help—and go where we choose. You're rich again."

McKee *was* rich again . . . But in a more important way. One that the previous her would never have been able to understand. She went to sit by Avery's side. For the first time since that horrible day on Esparto, she was happy. And it felt very, very good.

EPILOGUE

If there is such a thing as a godforsaken place, Savas Prime would qualify.

REV. NATHANIEL JENKINS
A Thousand Days in the Wilderness
Standard year 2732

PLANET SAVAS

It took weeks for Avery to recover fully, and for Kambi to travel north, where he hoped to buy supplies. During his absence, McKee noticed that the contrails that had once been so common had all but disappeared. Had the battle in space been resolved somehow? There was no way to be sure.

But when Kambi returned, he brought news as well as two zurnas loaded with food, ammo, and camping gear. According to the Paguumis, the change skins had been forced to flee. And, for reasons the locals couldn't understand, most of the round heads had left as well.

Even though it might seem strange to the Paguumis the news made sense to McKee and Avery. Having rescued Nicolai and taken heavy casualties, the navy had every reason to pull out. Especially after the Hudathans left the system. Had a ship or two been left in orbit? Probably. Which meant the deserters would have to be careful lest they draw attention to themselves.

The trip from their hiding place to the town of Savas Prime took more than half a year to complete and was marked by three run-ins with bandits, a nearly disastrous river crossing, and a perilous journey through thick jungle. But it was a wonderful trip as well. A honeymoon of sorts, during which McKee and Avery fell in love all over again and made memories that would last a lifetime. So that by the time they arrived on the outskirts of Savas Prime, they were bonded in ways that most couples couldn't imagine.

McKee and Avery watched the community from the surrounding hills for three days, looking for any signs of military activity, but there were none. So they walked into town, entered the local bar, and ordered a celebratory meal. The owner was understandably curious about them, and clearly skeptical regarding their claim to have crash-landed their yacht a thousand miles away and walked to Savas Prime.

But he was friendly enough, and it didn't take much questioning to discover that once the Hudathans failed to return, robotic sentinels had been seeded into the Savas system. That allowed *all* of the Human ships to withdraw. The owner didn't know who was in charge on Earth, nor did he care. Like most of the locals, the only thing he wanted from the empire was to be left alone.

Two lazy months passed while McKee and Avery waited for a tramp freighter to arrive. Once it did, Avery reserved a tiny cabin and paid half the fare in advance. That was followed by an emotional parting with Kambi, who, having been paid with gemstones, was in the process of setting up an import-export business.

The ship carried McKee and Avery to Weller's World, and from there to Long Jump, a planet way out on the rim. A place where imperial law was more theoretical than real.

And it was there, fifty miles outside the frontier town of Fortuna, where they started a farm. Their solidly built house resembled a small fort, sat atop a hill, and possessed a sweeping view of the surrounding countryside. In the fields directly below the house, a crew of patched-together robots were hard at work harvesting a crop of nu-wheat.

McKee was standing on the veranda, looking down on them, when John arrived with a cup of caf. "It looks like the weather is going to hold," he observed.

"That's good," McKee replied. "We need two days to get the crop in."

"Yes," John answered. "And I love you."

McKee smiled. "Finish your caf. We have work to do."